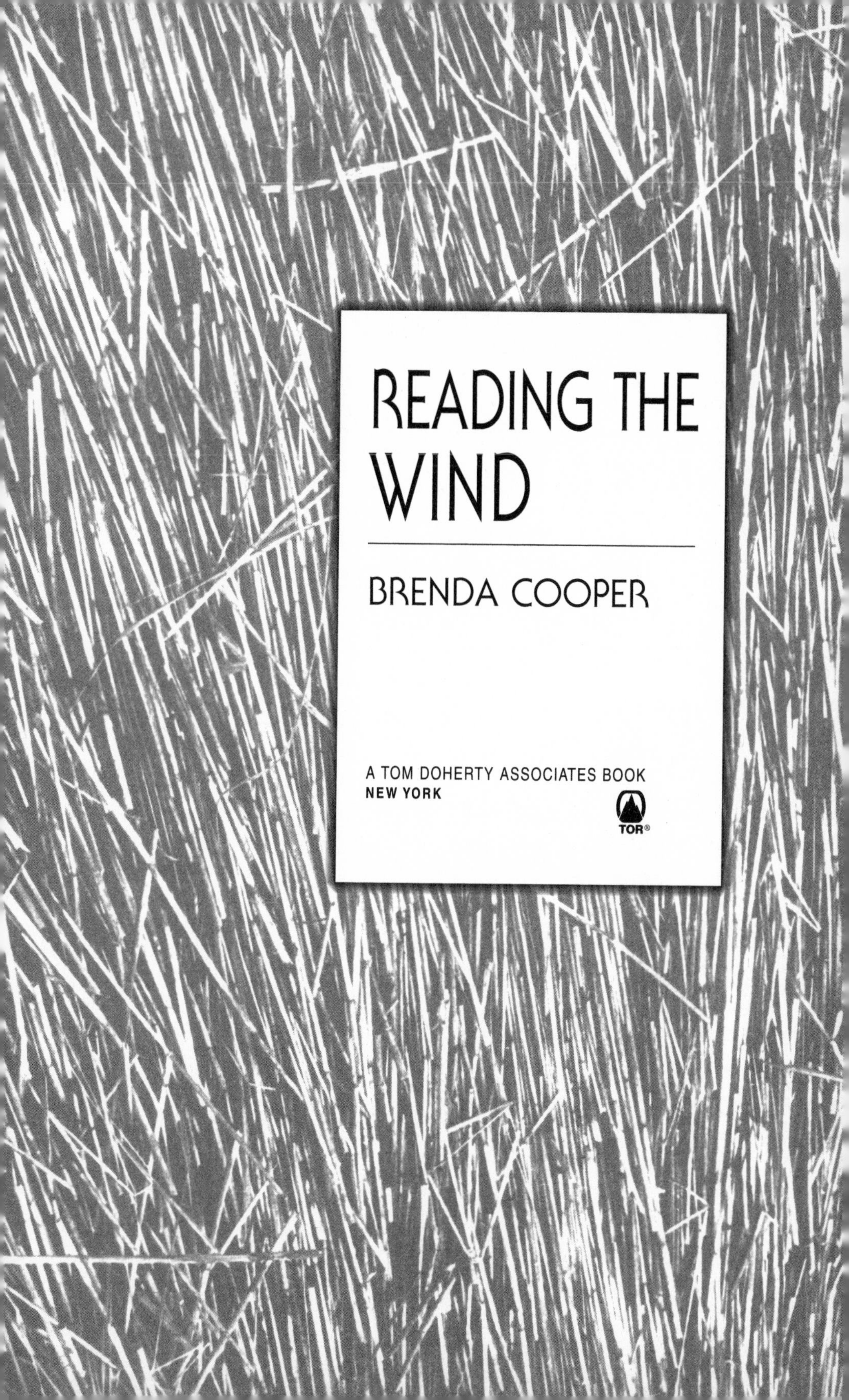

READING THE WIND

BRENDA COOPER

A TOM DOHERTY ASSOCIATES BOOK
NEW YORK
TOR®

This is a work of fiction. All of the characters, organizations, and events portrayed in this novel are either products of the author's imagination or are used fictitiously.

READING THE WIND

A Tor Book
Published by Tom Doherty Associates, LLC
175 Fifth Avenue
New York, NY 10010

www.tor-forge.com

Tor® is a registered trademark of Tom Doherty Associates, LLC.

Library of Congress Cataloging-in-Publication Data

Cooper, Brenda, 1960–
Reading the wind / Brenda Cooper.—1st ed.
p. cm.
"A Tom Doherty Associates Book"
ISBN-13: 978-0-7653-1598-4
ISBN-10: 0-7653-1598-X
I. Title
PS3603.O5825 R43 2008
813.'6—dc22

2008016956

First Edition: July 2008

Printed in the United States of America

0 9 8 7 6 5 4 3 2 1

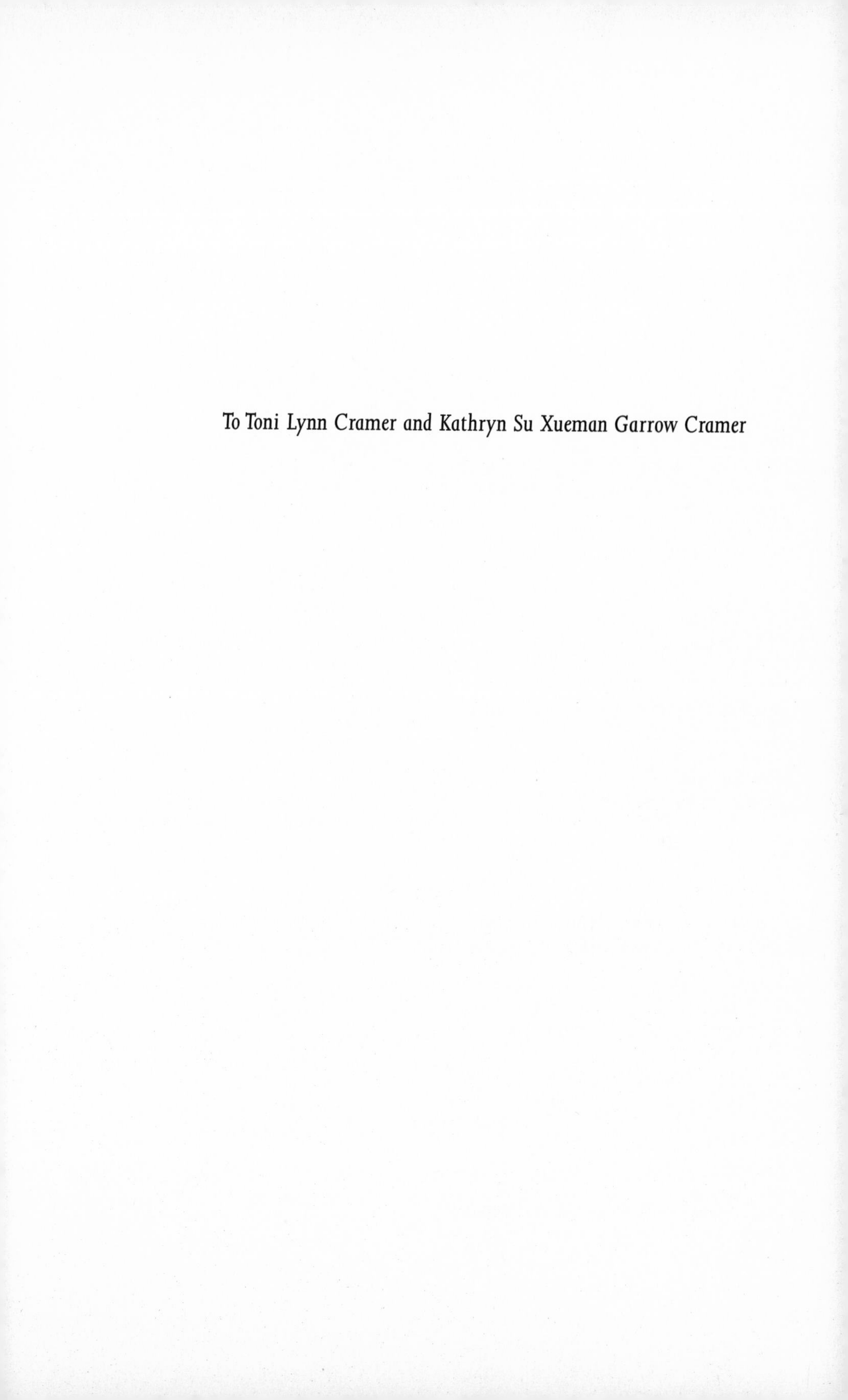

To Toni Lynn Cramer and Kathryn Su Xueman Garrow Cramer

ACKNOWLEDGMENTS

I appreciate my family. Toni and Katie have been patient with uncountable early morning and early and late evening writing sessions. Without their support, I couldn't do this and stay part of a family. Even the two dogs, Sasha and Nixie, suffered from lack of attention. Bless them all.

My father, David, read the entire draft of this novel and made excellent comments. My mother, Mary, and my son David, offered regular encouragement. My son reminded me to have a life every once in a while, including taking me skydiving for the first time.

My agent, Eleanor Wood, graciously read a complete draft, offered ideas, and pointed out mistakes. Tom Doherty, Bob Gleason, and Eric Raab from Tor supported this book.

Thanks to Tobias Buckell, Charles Coleman Finlay, and all of the other writers at the Blue Heaven writing workshop, for excellent critique and commentary. The Fairwood Writers worked through much of the first draft. Glen Hiemstra has been a constant support.

There are many other people who have offered support and help of one kind or another, and although there are too many to thank individually, I am grateful for all of the time and help that has flowed my way. I am truly lucky in the people I work and play with.

PROLOG

A CONTINUATION OF THE STORY OF CHELO LEE, DATED AUGUST 3, YEAR 222, FREMONT STANDARD, AS BROUGHT TO THE ACADEMY OF NEW WORLD HISTORIANS

The last story I told you was of our sundering. The long war for the wild planet Fremont ripped the seven of us apart: it sent away my brother Joseph, his sweetheart Alicia, our friend Bryan, and our best protector, damaged and broken, Jenna. The sundering sent them to the stars, aboard the silver ship, the *New Making*. It left three of us on Fremont: three genetically changed teens amongst a few thousand original humans.

I could have stayed with Kayleen in Artistos, where I grew up, but Artistos would have been full of Joseph's ghost: in our house, in the guild halls, in Commons Park, in the school.

Instead, I went with the West Band of field scientists, or roamers, to build a different life for myself. That choice was, in a way, a different and smaller sundering.

I no longer lived in my town with my friend Kayleen, but instead I roamed wild Fremont with the one other like us, Liam.

So the story I will tell you now begins after both the big sundering and the little sundering, after the ship flew away, and after I fled Artistos to become a roamer.

Two and a half years passed between the end of the last story and the beginning of this one. The first was my year of sharp pain from losing contact with Joseph. I spent the second year learning to be a roamer, and the rest becoming useful, maybe even needed, within the band. Becoming family.

By the end of these years, I was happy. I loved being a roamer, loved being able to hunt and run and be smart and be myself. The

West Band gave Liam and me respect in spite of our differences and we gave them more success than they had before.

Even though Liam and I didn't promise each other a future with words, our hands warmed when we touched, and we found each other in any crowd, across nearly any distance.

I had my own little wagon—no small thing.

And every year, we got to visit Jenna's cave twice. Our cave now. We named it the Cave of Power, and there we were learning who we were.

Perhaps, in spite of the gaping hole where my brother had been, I was happier than ever.

The only shadow falling on my life was the one I saw in Kayleen's eyes when we went to town.

PART ONE

CHELO ON FREMONT

WE SPEAK

Herb-scented smoke from the early evening fires lifted my heart while drumbeats lifted my feet. Cool spring air bathed my skin. My skirt swirled, slapping my calves as I danced behind Liam. A light sheen of sweat coated his back and thighs, shining nearly gold in the last full rays of the sun.

It was the end of our semiannual visit to town, a night reserved for the two bands of roamers to feast and compete together.

Twenty-five of us from the West Band had started this stick dance. Just an hour in, ten remained.

Our bandmates chanted with the drums, helping us dance the divide from dusk to night, holding bright torches. The pace increased yet again, the drums seeking to exhaust us, the chant to buoy us. Dark-haired slender Sasha fell away next, followed by red-blond blocky-and-strong Kiara. They rolled free of our feet and took torches, joining the chant, cheering for us, for the band. Every time I began to fade, Mayah's voice wormed into the part of me that could quit, blocking it, whispering, "shuffle, two, kick, three, turn, jump, jump . . ."

As the stars winked awake, my kicks grew higher, my dip and swirl lower and faster. The drummers increased the tempo until sweat poured from them like it poured from us.

The clacking of wood on wood warned us just before long, brightly painted sticks slid under our feet, horizontal, a foot above the ground. The swirling sticks demanded precision and height from our jumps. A crowd passed the sticks back and forth, hand to hand. The watchers were all roamers, most from our band, some from the East Band, friends and a few skeptics, two judges.

More dancers fell away, feet tangling, bodies rolling.

More sticks. The East Band had danced first. They'd managed five sticks—we already danced over ten. The joy of competition tore a grin from me. And it was the band's win—normal band members danced with us when we passed the East Band's mark. No one could blame our win on Liam and me. We were free to play; it didn't matter now that we were faster and stronger.

Contest had changed to exhibition.

A few of the East Band left the circle. Not all. Just the ones who hated our differences.

Three of us remained, then two. Me and Liam, jumping, kicking, close to each other then away, a dance between us more than for the others. Fifteen sticks, and still we didn't stumble. The stick-bearers grinned and raised them so high my skirt flew up past my knees. Drummers began to call for replacements. Chanters called our names: "Liam! Chelo! Liam! Chelo!"

Liam threw his head back and laughed, and I joined him, giggling, so short of breath the laugh tore pain from my belly. Pain or not, our laughter reflected joy in moving well, joy in success, joy in being with each other and surrounded by family.

I held out my hands, palms down and he shook his head, *not yet*.

Jump, twist.

He grinned at me, his dark eyes bright with exertion.

Swoop, turn.

Faces, grinning. Kiara and River and Sky and Abyl.

Hop, high, down, just the toes, then up again over two sticks. Cheers all around us. I reached a hand to steady Liam and we leapt together as one, holding hands. We side-hopped over the seated circle of watchers, just above their heads, landing hard, almost falling. After, we stood, slick with sweat and glowing in the firelight of twenty torches.

A cheer erupted, a celebration of our prowess and, perhaps, relief that we were done. The Last Night celebration of Spring Trading was now officially over, and the rest of the evening could be given to seeing friends.

I stopped by my wagon to change from my dancing skirt into pants and a shirt, and to slip light leather sandals onto my feet. My home was small, but it was mine—a tiny kitchen and an everything-else room just longer than I was tall and half as wide; light enough to be pulled by a single hebra. I'd painted the inside pale blue with clouds and birds and, here and there, the tip of a tree. A silver space ship arced across the ceiling, for my brother, who had gone into the sky.

Dressed for a trip into Artistos, I hesitated briefly in my doorway, centering. The wagon Liam shared with his parents, Akashi and Mayah, stood close to my smaller wagon, signifying we were all in the same family group. Maps decorated both, identifying us as geographers. Light poured from the window in Akashi's wagon, illuminating the designs. My fingers caressed the paint, running across the slight ridges where mountains and lakes dotted the terrain here on Jini, the largest of the two continents on Fremont. I had hand-painted them on the side of the wagon, not sure even at the time if I was painting myself into a profession or into Akashi's family. As usual, Akashi apparently knew my feelings, even the contradictory ones. He had simply smiled and helped me get tough parts, like Islandia's Teeth, painted right.

I shook my head, pushing aside the memory. Right now, I had to find Kayleen.

Liam emerged, dressed simply in a pale green hemp tunic and brown pants. Like me, he stood a head taller than most of the original humans on Fremont. A shock of blond hair hung over dark eyes, and a long braid twisted down his back nearly to his waist. He broke into a warm grin as soon as he spotted me. My grin answered his, and I immediately felt almost as much like we were one connected being as I had in the dance.

"We did great!" He reached for my arm, his voice tinged with pride and satisfaction. "Dad said he was watching from the hill. He thought we'd dance all night."

"Well, and I thought you'd never stop," I teased. "I thought we'd just go until one of us fell."

He laughed, not like in the dance, but soft and low. "We'd have worn out the drummers."

"Or ourselves." I stepped briefly into his arms, then pushed away, unwilling to be lost inside of his embrace. "Let's find Kayleen. I'm worried about her. She seemed so . . ." I searched for a good word. ". . . so listless yesterday. She didn't get excited about the maps we found in the cave on the way down and she barely ever looked at me."

He put a hand on my shoulder and looked past me, as if lost in thought. "She's trapped here. We're free."

For just a moment I was glad that she hadn't seen the dance. Then a flash of guilt at the thought ran through me, making me shiver. "Let's go." I squeezed his hand.

We jogged side by side, heading into town from our encampment in Little Lace Park. The Lace River ran down a short cliff to our right, full with rushing winter-melt water, singing into the gathering darkness. Here, we could walk freely, without sorting every sound for the dangers that roamed or grew in the wilds.

Twintrees and lace maples and redberry bushes lined the path, reaching new spring branches across, trying, as always, to reclaim any part of Fremont we humans struggled to tame. Night birds twittered and called to each other.

Kayleen still lived with Paloma in one of the four-houses a block away from Commons Park. When I knocked on their door, Paloma opened it, smelling of spring mint and redberry. "Chelo and Liam! Come in. How are you?"

"We're fine," Liam said.

Standing in her doorway, I remembered a hundred times I'd stood here before, starting when I could barely reach the knob. This close, streaks of gray showed in her blond hair and wrinkles blossomed like flowers around her blue eyes. "Is Kayleen here?"

She shook her head. "Almost never."

"Are you all right?" I asked.

She shook her head again, short and sharp, then smiled and said, "Sure. Will you come in for tea?"

I wanted to stay and talk to her. But finding Kayleen was more important. "Do you have any idea where she is?"

"She's probably down by the hebra barns—she has a young one she's taken a fancy to, and spends much of her time there." Paloma twisted her hands together. "She goes out after work every night, and only comes home to sleep. I don't even know what or when she eats any more."

I winced. "I'm sorry."

Paloma sighed and took my hand. "The nets work well right now. We've asked less and less of her. Even Nava leaves her alone some days. Kayleen's been helping Gianna with the satellite data, and she identified the tracks of the last three good-sized meteors almost perfectly. Gianna is almost the only one she talks to anymore." Her voice dropped lower. "I'm sure she misses you."

Even though there was nothing accusing in her tone, guilt tugged at me. I looked up at Liam. "Maybe we should stay in town next winter."

Liam turned to Paloma, his voice apologetic. "We *can't* stay now. The band needs us the most in summer."

"She would like to see you more." Paloma paused. "Me, too. You can stay here if you like. I . . . I'd like your opinion about Kayleen."

"We're leaving tomorrow. We have to go; surely you understand." I glanced down at my chrono. "We should get to the barn."

Paloma smiled. "I know. Look, I'll talk to Nava and see if Kayleen can come visit you for a while this summer. Is that okay with you?"

"Of course." I returned her smile and touched her hand. Small comfort, but all I could offer. "What about this baby hebra she's adopted?"

Paloma smiled again, as if she, too, were enamored of the little beast. "She has. A young one with the prettiest green highlights in her brown striping when the sun shines on it. Kayleen's training her. She already follows Kayleen around the pasture, and she'll be ready to ride by midsummer. She named her Windy."

I smiled, picturing Kayleen with the young hebra. "I hope I meet Windy."

Liam held Paloma for a moment, kissing the top of her head, and then I embraced her. Her head came to my shoulder, and for the first time ever it struck me that I could protect and help her more than she could protect and help me. "I hope everything works out all right," I murmured.

Part way down the street, I turned to look back. Paloma stood in the door, watching. She gave us a little wave.

I held my precious sun-fed flashlight, but left it off to protect my night vision as we jogged down to the barns. Even though warm night air tickled my skin, the winter had been harsh and long, and only about half of the fields had been planted so far. We passed a few people heading home from late-night chores, exchanging polite half-waves. Already, town life seemed small.

As we neared the barns, Stripes called out a greeting to me, and two or three other hebras whickered. Their tall graceful forms made black silhouettes outlined by the soft light from the barns. Their heads swiveled toward me. I went to Stripes and buried my face in her neck fur. She'd been in the common herd once, but Akashi had bought her for me the first spring after I joined the band. As he'd offered her lead to me, his eyes had twinkled with joy. "You need someone you know you can count on."

I'd cried.

I breathed in Stripes's dusty barn smell. "We'll leave tomorrow," I whispered into the long ear she swiveled down toward me.

As if in response, she dropped her big head over my shoulder, nearly an embrace. Her hot breath trickled along the back of my neck.

I pushed away gently and looked around. I didn't see Kayleen, or any other human movement. "I don't think she's here," I whispered.

Liam called out, "Kayleen!"

No response.

Low evening lights made circles on the rush floor in the long, tall barn. The hebras each came up to be greeted, turning their long ears toward us and asking silent questions with their wide, intelligent eyes. Two or three of the females had spindly-legged spring babies beside them, but I couldn't tell if one might be Windy. They were all beautiful.

Kayleen was not with any of them.

At the end of the aisle, I called again, "Kayleen, are you here?"

Still no answer.

We stepped out the back door into the big practice ring, and I called a third time. "Kayleen?"

Liam stepped out into the corral, and leaned against the metal bars of the big practice ring. "I don't see any sign of her."

A single light bolted high on the outside of the wooden barn illuminated his face and shone on his blond hair.

I walked over near him, and clambered up on the bars, sitting on the top one. It made me taller than him by almost a meter. "Do you remember last fall, when I told you Kayleen seemed so lost—somewhere—that I could barely get her attention?"

He reached a hand up and set it over mine where it clung to the bar. "Yes, I remember."

"I'm scared for her. Maybe, like Joseph, she's become too different."

"Have you talked to Gianna?" he asked.

"Not this trip, not enough to ask about Kayleen. Besides, Gianna is so much older. It's not the same as having *friends*." A brief shock of bitterness crossed my heart. "And you know who's here. Garmin and most of the other people our age haven't changed, so there's no reason to think they're kind to Kayleen."

"I know." Liam hopped up next to me on the bars. "But it's not like the East Band loves us. Surely some of how she's treated is up to her. If she's distant with us, imagine how she must be with everyone else."

I moved closer to him, brushing thighs. "I'd still like to help her if I can. I think . . . maybe she's living too much in the nets and not enough in the real world."

"Maybe."

His profile in the half light swelled my chest. Simply looking at him made me feel I could float from the bars and land on the barn roof. "Being with us in the wild, she wouldn't be in the nets so much. You have to pay attention out there."

Liam sighed. "Well, I wonder if she's focused enough for that? I wouldn't trust her to travel by herself. Someone would have to come back for her, and we'll be way out by Rage Mountain this summer. It would be too hard."

I nodded. "I should be able to help her. She and I used to be so close. . . ."

"She has to *let* you help her." He reached an arm over my shoulder and pulled me close, unbalancing us a little so I gripped the rail harder. "You can't solve every problem."

I never could. It had always taken us all. I missed Jenna's watchful eye and weird way of helping us learn, and I missed Bryan's silent strength. I even missed willful and lost Alicia with all of her pain and anger. Most of all, I missed Joseph. He'd be able to help Kayleen in ways I couldn't—he, too, rode the wind. And more. He flew space ships. Where was he, and how different from me had he yet become?

Liam must have felt my need, because he held me close and began to hum softly, a sweet song of summer fields. I looked up at a sky full of stars gathered around Faith and Summer. I searched for a third moon, which would have been a sign of good luck, but didn't find one.

The barn light switched off.

"Why did the light go off?" Liam asked.

"Because I couldn't stand to watch you two anymore," Kayleen said. "Because I'm crazy and I do crazy things. Because I live too much in the nets and not enough in the real world." A pause. Her voice, ripped with pain, floating down from the top of the barn. "I can't be trusted to travel by myself."

I sat up. How much had she heard? "Kayleen?"

She didn't answer.

I turned on my flashlight and shone it upward, looking for her. We called her name, and Liam took my light and scrambled up onto the roof. After a while, he called, "She's not here."

He climbed back down and stood a little distance from me, his arms by his sides, the closeness between us turned awkward by her sudden absent presence. She was fast—if she wanted to ditch us here in the dark, in her place, she could. I looked up at where the light had been, and spoke, hoping she was still close enough to hear me. "Kayleen. We're just worried about you. I miss you."

The hebras stamped quietly in their stalls and a cool wind blew softly through the rafters.

Liam added, "Come out. So we can talk."

We waited, still standing a little apart, listening carefully for any sound that might be our friend, our sister. Twenty minutes passed, in which we said nothing, afraid she would hear, or that she wouldn't hear.

We walked back, side by side, not touching, not saying anything.

KAYLEEN RESPONDS

The next day dawned clear and bright, with no sign of clouds. The clatter and calls of the East Band's departure made a chaotic background to the relative routine of readying my little home. I looked out the window every few minutes, hoping for a sign of Kayleen in the chaos of comings and goings. I watched for her as I fetched Stripes from the barn and rode her back to the wagons, as I tied her into her harness, and checked the long-rein I would use to guide her.

Stripes shifted in her traces, her head twisting sideways to watch me, her flanks quivering. She had been trained as a riding beast, and a slight sense of disapproval lingered in her eyes as I tightened her chest-band.

The wagons began to line up. I spotted Sasha, her younger brothers, and her mother and father in the lead. The single white streak in Sasha's long dark hair made a distinctive mark against the dark green lead wagon. I waited my turn, watching them start off, a ragged line neatening behind them as they headed for the High Road. Wagon wheels creaked and hebras called to each other. Goats bleated.

At least half of Artistos had turned out for our departure. Children clutched parents' hands or pointed at the various bright and noisy bits of the wagon train. Joseph and I used to do the same, clutching Steven and Therese while watching the long line of roamers snake away up the hill, wanting to go with them to find adventure. Some hot summer afternoons we pretended to be roamers running from paw-cats or climbing trees to catch new birds or animals.

A hand touched my elbow. "Chelo?"

I turned to find Paloma standing next to me. "Did you find her last night?" she asked.

I shook my head. "No. Not exactly." I didn't elaborate; I didn't want to worry Paloma more than necessary. "Did she come home?"

Paloma's eyes were filled with concern. "No. I hoped she'd be here—she's always come to see you off before."

Stripes stamped her feet and I reached a hand up to scratch her just behind her scraggly beard. "I know," I said. "I've been watching for her."

"I talked to Nava. She says Kayleen's too valuable to risk in the wild."

I didn't quite keep the anger out of my voice. "You mean it's possible Nava might lose control of her pet *altered* if she lets Kayleen spend time with us wild ones?"

Paloma grimaced. "Maybe."

I glanced at the line. It was almost my turn. "Doesn't Nava know Kayleen could escape if she wanted to?"

Paloma let out a short sharp laugh.

"Nava used fear to cage us, particularly Joseph. It didn't work, so now she's trying to make Kayleen too precious for her freedom. I rather expect this new tactic won't work either. You might explain that to Nava." I gave Stripes one last scratch and climbed up on the wide seat of my wagon.

Paloma shook her head. "Easier, maybe, to just convince her that the nets are working well enough to give Kayleen a vacation. Did you ask about staying next winter?"

I picked up the long-rein. "Akashi and Mayah were asleep when I got home." I swept a hand toward the wagons still waiting, like me, to leave. "I've hardly seen them this morning."

"But you will ask?"

"Of course." I glanced up to find Liam, who Akashi had assigned to be ride boss for this first leg, astride Star, beckoning me to start off. At Star's feet, a big-boned rangy red dog with white ears paced just out of kicking range: Ritzi, the lead camp-dog. She gave me an even sterner look than Liam's. I laughed at the dog, then looked back at Paloma. "Take care this summer. May your crops come in well."

"May you find new treasures." She reached a hand out to touch my thigh. "Thank you."

I smiled at her and clucked at Stripes, starting us off. The wagon moved more easily now than it had on the way down.

Lighter wagons or not, the ride up started with a long hot pull in bright sunshine. Sweat trickled down Stripes's flanks and dripped from my nose. The camp dogs followed us, running back and forth from the beginning of the line to the end. Ritzi led them, holding her white ears and white tail up as far as she could get them. Liam, too, rode up and down the line, checking on us all. The responsibility sat well on him, and he wore a serious smile whenever he reined Star up by my wagon and spoke to me.

After the first two hours, Liam called for a brief rest. He chose a spot known as View Bend, just below the rock fall remains we would soon thread through. He knew how hard the next part of the trail would be for me.

Tree-studded cliffs rose above and below us. Here, the trail was wide enough to take two or three wagons side by side. A thin strip of trees lined the stream near the cliff face, and the fresh scents of forest and new spring growth blew across the trail on a soft breeze. The older dogs flopped down to pant in the shade of the wagons, and the younger ones followed the midsized children as they ran off to fetch water from the stream for the hebras.

The cliff fell down away from us, yielding a long view. Artistos already seemed small from this height, the neat rows of houses and big oval of Commons Park looking like children's toy blocks, or a painting on a wagon side. The Lace River looked like a small winding snake, and smoke puffed from the industrial area on the far side of the river. I took a deep breath, happy to be away from the noxious smells of the town. I hadn't noticed them often when I lived there, but now that visits to Artistos were rare, its smelter and mill smell had become noticeably aromatic.

I closed my eyes and took another deep breath of forest and running water and sweaty hebra, of the oil used to lubricate the wagon wheels and of the goats and chickens we brought with us from Artistos. Only then did I look out over the grass plains, to the empty concrete pad, even smaller and further away than Artistos. The silver ship, the *New Making*, had sat on the pad until the year I was seventeen. When Joseph flew away.

Perhaps Akashi sensed my feelings. He climbed up on the wide seat next to me. "Still hard?"

The first year, he and Liam had stopped here with me. I had cried on their shoulders for hours at the loss of Joseph, of Bryan, and of Jenna. "Not as hard as it used to be." I swallowed and gave Akashi a soft smile. "He should be getting to Silver's Home any time."

"I'm glad you stayed. You've been a help."

Praise from him still made me warm, even though it was no longer rare. "Don't worry, Akashi. I'm happy." I sighed. "I know I did the right things—the best ones, anyway. It just doesn't stop me from wondering what it's like on the ship."

Akashi laughed. "Don't worry too much about the paths you don't go down." His expression turned serious. "Besides, you'll probably outlive us all, and it's hard to imagine any paths closed to you." He climbed down from the wagon and took my hand, briefly, squeezing it. "Call me if you need anything."

I smiled. "Sure. Thanks for stopping."

"Are you and Liam going to the cave tomorrow?"

I nodded. "Yes. Sasha promised to drive my wagon for the day we'll lose."

"That's good for her. She'll do well." Akashi walked off to check on the other wagons. Two boys, Justin and Amil, came over to Stripes and stood in front of her with a skin of water. She drank noisily, shaking her head up and down and splashing.

The boys, one tall, one short, laughed and wandered off, and a few moments later the long train of twenty-two wagons started back up the hill. New growth had covered the raw scars left by boulders and trees as they'd tumbled and fallen over the cliff face, and butterflies flitted through the bright yellows and whites of the spring flowers. I sang my way through the tumbled stones and the bones of the old rock fall. As I sang, I silently wished my adoptive parents, Therese and

Steven, good journeys. They had died here. I sang for them, to show them I was healthy and strong.

The next morning, just before dawn, I poured myself a cup of sun tea made the day before, now cool and tart, and pulled out a handful of small dried apples from last year's harvest. As I ate, light slowly faded the stars. This must have been the time of day Jenna most often snuck into the cave herself. She had shown it to us just a few days before she and Joseph left. It had once been a war base for our *altered* parents, and Kayleen used to joke that we were probably born there. During the years Jenna had spent living by herself on the outskirts of town, she had gathered many artifacts from the war, *altered* weapons and *altered* communication devices and *altered* tools and clothes. Our legacy. Much of it stashed in this cave.

Sasha's footsteps crunched across the road. Her dark eyes glittered with excitement. She greeted me warmly. "Good morning. How are you?"

Her excitement made me smile. "Great." I reached for a dried pongaberry, shrunk to half-size and flat. "Would you like to help me harness Stripes?"

She took the berry from me and went to get Stripes, her dark hair contrasting with Stripes's dun base coat and the yellow and light brown stripes that gave the hebra her name. Stripes bugled a soft greeting to her, and immediately nudged her for the treat. Greedy beast. Sasha fed her the berry delicately and then led her back. She had helped train Stripes to the wagon, and she and I had spent many days gathering pongaberries and twintree fruit and wild onion.

As we each picked up one end of the shoulder and chest strap to drop it over Stripes's head, she asked, "Where do you go? You always leave on this day and come back sometime the following morning. Is it so you and Liam can have quiet time together?" There was a hint of mischief in her voice. "I bet you two can run fast enough to get to a lake cabin in less than a day."

I laughed, saved from answering by Liam's enthusiastic, "Good morning!"

It took us a few more moments to extract ourselves. The morning shadows were still long when we started off, purposely heading in the wrong direction. After about ten minutes of easy loping, warming and stretching our bodies in the cool air, we turned up, still angling wrong, increasing our speed, racing each other. Redberry bushes and grasses slapped my legs. Spiky trip-vine and stinging ivy threatened to tangle our feet. Where the trees thinned to scrub, we turned almost back on ourselves, heading for the top of the ridge that separated the High Road from Little Lace Lake. We stopped at the high point, breathing hard from the long run and scramble.

He put an arm around me, holding me close, his breath only a little hard. "I love being out here, with just you and the wild."

I laughed at him, my face warm from more than just the run. "We're always in the wild."

He shook his head. "Maybe it's leaving Artistos. I've never liked town."

A pair of knotted twintrees—one taller than the other—twined around each other like lovers below us. Liam leaned down and kissed me, and I returned the kiss, fiery and hard. A tempting distraction.

But the cave called. I pulled away gently and gazed up at him. "Let's go."

We approached the cave from the top, dropping down, my feet stinging as I landed on the smooth floor. I reached up for the shelf we kept our flashlight on.

My hand came back empty.

"I have it."

Kayleen stood just inside the shadowed darkness of the cave's mouth, sunlight touching her face and darkness filling the void behind her. Her legs were spread wide and stiff, her dark hair combed neatly around her face. The dark blue of her eyes glowed nearly black, glittering and feral, a contrast to her unusually neat appearance. Her voice went with her hair rather than her eyes, too sweet for Kayleen, as if she were speaking a line she'd practiced over and over: "Hi. I knew you'd come here. I wanted time to talk to you. I'm sorry for being rude last night."

Liam sat cross-legged on the floor, like he sometimes did when talking to a misbehaving child. Kayleen responded the same way children responded to the gesture, sitting herself, fairly close to him but opposite. I sat, too, so we made an uneasy triangle on the cave floor.

I blinked at her, unsure what to say. I finally just said, "I'm sorry. I care about you, and I came looking because I hadn't seen you."

Only then did she look directly at me. "Do you really miss me?" she asked.

"Of course I do." How could she question that?

Her voice was even and sweet, cool. "I bet you don't. You didn't even look for me the first day you came down this time."

"I had to help set up for Trading Day. I watched for you all day."

"You're in love. I see it in your eyes." She glanced at Liam, the wildness in her eyes shaded with longing. For a moment she looked as vulnerable as a baby hebra before it stands the first time. I fought back a stab of hot jealousy.

This was Kayleen, and I loved her. But I would not give up my happiness for her.

Her eyes fell away from Liam and her gaze stuck itself to the smooth and nearly featureless cave floor. Her words spilled out low and fast. "I've been coming up here every few nights this spring. We can't take years to learn. I have to do whatever Hunter and Nava and the other Council want, and even Mom won't help me fight to change it. She says we have peace and we should keep it." She looked at me. "I'm sick of acting like Nava's slave."

Liam leaned forward, closing the gap between them, putting a hand on Kayleen's shoulder. "No one has seen you come up here?"

She snorted. "I can doctor the nets so anyone watching after the fact sees me in Artistos when I'm really here. I come here all the time."

I tried to keep from looking startled. Kayleen had always been compliant. "It's dangerous," I cautioned.

She shot me a disapproving look. "I'm *very* careful."

Liam dropped his hand, sat back, and turned the conversation. "What have you found?"

The feral look returned for a moment, raising the hair on the back of my neck. The cave held whole rooms of weapons, and generally we left them alone.

But Kayleen headed toward the room she had moved the skimmer into two winters ago, under cover of a storm. We followed her down a short, wide branch just to the right of the cave entrance, and entered an equally wide doorway.

Although Liam didn't say anything, I could feel him questioning the wisdom of following Kayleen. I had no answer; I didn't trust the Kayleen who walked in front of us, purposeful and sure of herself in this place where Liam and I always walked carefully.

A light flicked on, Kayleen's work. Her abilities felt like magic, even though I knew from working with Joseph that they reflected a connection between microscopic data readers that sang in Kayleen's blood and any *altered* technology tuned to her or others like her. A common genemod, but Liam and I did not have it, and there was no way to get it here, where everything *altered* was despised, and information about genetic engineering scrubbed from databases. Envy crossed my heart, followed by the memory of what those skills had cost Joseph.

I stood in the doorway, eyeing the skimmer, the *Burning Void*. Tiny sister to the *New Making*, the silver cylinder gleamed brightly even in the relative dark of the cave, twice as tall as me, twice as wide as tall, and so long I could have laid down in it ten times. It sat high on five wheels, two near the front, two near the back, and one just below the nose. We could walk under it and hardly bend.

As we approached, the silver passenger ramp unfolded and set down with a soft click on the cave floor.

Kayleen climbed up the ramp easily, as if she were intimately familiar with the machine. Liam followed her, and I followed him.

I drew in a startled breath at the young hebra with bright brown side-stripes who stood unsteadily between the door to the cargo bay and the last row of seats, blinking at us. She had been cross-tied to the last row of seats, with only a meter or so of room to move around. This must be the hebra Paloma talked about, but what on earth was she doing in the skimmer?

Kayleen sat relaxed, one leg thrown lazily on the seat in front of her. She smiled at me. "Sit down."

"Is that Windy?"

Her eyes widened. "How did you know about her?"

"Paloma told me about her. That's why we went to the barns to look for you."

Kayleen frowned. Relaxed body position or not, she felt like a snake about to strike. I glanced from the hebra to the open door, still standing.

"Hang on." She licked her lips and her fingers went to her hair as if to knot themselves in it, something she often did, but she put them back in her lap. "I'm closing the door so I can let Windy loose to meet you."

The soft whine of whatever mechanism controlled the ramp became background noise as the hebra bugled.

I glanced at Liam in time to see him to take two steps toward Kayleen. He stood over her, looking down, and I recognized the set of his stance from hunting, from the moment before he sprang into a chase. "Stop!" he commanded.

Kayleen smiled, looking up at Liam. The feral look in her eyes actually matched her expression this time, and as she raked her gaze across me I felt like prey. Me. Her best friend.

She flashed a map of Fremont from above—a satellite shot, on the wall screen in front. It rotated, the picture first showing Jini, where we were, and then sliding to hang above the only other land mass of any consequence, the continent Islandia, almost half a world away and closer to the equator.

The ramp clicked closed.

Liam stared down at her, stance frozen, his eyes wide and his jaw tight.

She looked up at him, apparently unconcerned. In a measured soft tone she said, "Too late."

A TRIP

As soon as Kayleen uttered the phrase "too late," I knew what she meant to do. Even knowing, disbelief closed my throat.

Liam's face transformed into one I had never seen, anger tightening his skin and lacing his muscles so they jumped. His dark eyes turned nearly black. He stepped toward Kayleen, leaning over her, strange and terrible and unlike himself. If Liam were anyone but Akashi's son, I'd have expected him to strike her, the anger poured from him so strongly.

Kayleen held her smile, her gaze on Liam, her body completely still, neither provoking nor backing down. They held that pose for three long breaths, not moving.

We killed animals when we hunted, but we protected each other. Always.

The baby hebra, Windy, bugled and struggled to back away, finding only smooth silver hull behind her, her cloven hooves slipping and scrambling. She shook her head back and forth like a rag on her long neck.

Liam took a step back.

Kayleen leapt up, vaulted one-armed over the last row of seats, and landed lightly next to the bleating hebra. She put a hand out, flat, in front of Windy's nose. Small soothing noises rose from Kayleen's throat. Her body language became the tough alpha of a trainer, tempered by a soft tone in her voice. Windy bugled again and then gathered her splaying legs under her, standing, shaking.

Another long beat of silence, all of us breathing, no one speaking.

The cabin felt small and close, the air thick with the mingled stink of fear and anger and upset hebra.

Windy lowered her head slowly and curled it against Kayleen's chest. Kayleen brought her right hand up and stroked the side of the hebra's face. Windy closed her eyes and moaned like a new foal at her mother's teats.

I glanced at Liam. The expression on his face was so incredulous that I nearly burst out laughing, regardless of the tense situation. Maybe because of it. But then Liam had almost no experience with Kayleen's mercurial nature.

I did. But did I know *this* Kayleen?

"Kayleen," I said softly, using the same tone she had used on the hebra.

She glanced at me, her eyes unreadable.

"Kayleen. You can't leave."

She raised an eyebrow at me.

Liam spoke. "The band needs us. They're going to Rage Mountain. It's dangerous there. They'll need us to hunt."

They were the wrong words, about us and not Kayleen.

She continued standing with Windy's head in her arms, continued the soft soothing movements and kept her voice soft. "Well, perhaps I need you. Perhaps I'll go crazy if I have to stay there another year. The nets give up their stories to me freely now, all the time, even into my dreams. I can see everything, hear everything. I watched you all last winter, and all the summer before." She searched my face for a reaction.

I struggled not to give her one, trying to look calm, to radiate calm. She'd watched us? Without telling us? Seen Liam and I kiss and hunt and watched me and Sasha train Stripes? Watched us train for the dances?

What did she make of what she saw?

She frowned when I failed to respond and kept going, her voice raised higher. "I tried living through you, imagining it was me laughing and dancing and running free. But it was too hard, what with everyone in Artistos treating me like dung. Everyone either looking down on me or afraid of me." She ran the long fingers of her free hand through her hair, bunching it, a contrast to the hand that stroked the hebra. "Rumors that I'd go crazy like Alicia and threaten the town. Jokes that I'd come get their babies in the night if the babies didn't behave. See, I let them see how strong I am. I didn't care anymore. I let them see how fast I can run and how far I can climb."

She buried her head in the soft striped fur of Windy's neck. I shifted on my feet, unsure whether to go to her or leave her alone. She raised her head again, and this time pain came through with her words. "They're scared of me. How can you have friends when everyone is scared of you?"

Liam cleared his throat. "So come with us to the band. Akashi will protect you."

It was a lie. Akashi would try, but he was one man. Kayleen knew it. She shook her head. "Nava would find me there, and make me go back. We're going farther away than that." She nodded toward the front of the cabin, sending our attention back to the vid screen.

There it was, what I knew she meant in the beginning: Islandia centered in the screen, a long thin strip of land dominated by the glowing red fires of the great volcano, Blaze. The southern edge of Islandia ran near the equator. There, hyperactive currents shredded the coast into a hundred bays and headlands where mountains, commonly referred to as Islandia's Teeth, plunged into the water. No one on Fremont had been there. The colonists didn't have skimmers, just shuttles that took them up to their ship, the *Traveler*, and back again every few years.

I stared at the image, fascinated at the idea of seeing Islandia up close, then shook my head to clear it of craziness. I couldn't leave Akashi and Mayah and Sasha and Stripes and . . .

Liam broke the silence before I did. "I'm not going."

Kayleen's answer was to speak a few more soothing words at Windy, and then to settle on the floor, near the hebra's wooden cage.

She closed her eyes.

Liam stepped over to her and lifted her chin.

She opened one eye and gazed at him. "Don't make me crash." The eye closed again, and her muscles slumped inside her skin. Windy nosed her gently, but apparently found Kayleen's boneless posture familiar. She raised her head and watched me and Liam calmly.

The *Burning Void* lifted smoothly, easily, rising under my feet. There were no windows. Dizzied, I took three steps to Liam's side and wrapped a hand around his upper arm. I might as well have clutched a rock. He stared unblinking at the screen.

Liam's band counted on him. He was heir apparent after Akashi. His long apprenticeship to his adoptive father had gained him so much respect that his orders were followed as unquestioningly as Akashi's or Mayah's. His first loyalty belonged to the band, not to Kayleen. To be powerless must have been a shock.

The image on the screen changed to the open mouth of the cave, then the low brush outside, and then blue sky as we climbed. A camera on the nose? Acceleration increased. I shifted and set my free hand on top of a seat for steadiness.

Liam pulled free of my light grasp. I nearly fell. He didn't turn, just went to a front seat, sitting stiffly and staring.

Kayleen stirred, blinking, as if she'd been asleep for a week. She groaned. "Sorry. I have to focus to get out of the cave."

Liam didn't turn around or respond.

She glanced at his back, her face a mix of longing and puzzlement.

The screen showed us passing up into clouds, flying a lazy circle. My stomach circled, too, and I sat. Were we really flying like birds? "Will people see us way up here?" I asked.

Kayleen grinned. "I hope so. I want the band to know what happened, that we left. I like them for liking you, and I don't want them to worry."

"They'll worry," Liam said dryly. Then, "Artistos might be able to see you."

Kayleen shrugged. "I don't care if they do. Besides, their nets are still off. I set them to go back automatically in an hour, in case I get out of range. I haven't been more than a half-hour's flight in this thing before."

"When you brought it up here?" Liam asked, probing, his voice carefully neutral.

"I've had it out every big storm this winter. At first I thought maybe lightning would hit it and I'd die and maybe that would be okay. But it always misses. Must be something in the ship's skin that keeps it safe. Artistos believes the nets go down because of the electrical energy of the storms." She grinned. "I taught them that. I don't think Gianna believes me, but almost all the science guild kids end up out with the roamers as soon as they get out of school."

"Why did you bring Windy?" I asked.

Kayleen looked directly at me for the first time since we'd taken off. "Because she's the only thing in Artistos that loves me unconditionally enough to go. Besides, we might need a pack-beast."

I glanced at Windy's unsteady young legs. Hebras grew fast, but she wouldn't be strong enough to pack anything useful for weeks, at best. "What about Paloma?"

"Paloma would not have come."

"Paloma loves you," I said. Surely Kayleen would come to her senses. She *had* to turn around.

Kayleen blinked, her eyes damp. Then she swallowed, her expression flat. "I left a note. She'll understand why I had to do this."

"Well I don't." Liam turned around in his chair, facing Kayleen directly. His face showed that he had come to some sort of conclusion—his eyes clear and intense, his expression neutral. "You have no right. You might as well be kidnapping us."

I refrained from pointing out that she *was* kidnapping us.

Kayleen simply looked at him and said, "Another year in Artistos and I'd have died or gone crazy. I talked to Tom and Nava and even Hunter, trying to make them see I had to be with you two, had to be with my own kind, and they ignored me. They like having a little compliant, captive *altered*."

"What about the colony and the nets?" I asked her.

She shrugged. "Gianna and Paloma can keep them up for a while. What did they do before, after all? We weren't always here."

My hands clutched the arms of my seat, knuckles white. With a conscious effort, I made them uncurl, blood flowing back to sting the tips of my fingers. "What if we come visit you more often? I don't know how, but we'll figure it out. Akashi and Mayah will understand."

She just looked at me, mouth open. "Chelo. I don't have a choice." Her voice caught in her throat. "I can't stay there. Maybe I can go back some day, but I can't stay now."

Something in her tone, her eyes, the set of her shoulders, finally convinced me. "I'm sorry, Kayleen." I cursed myself for being too self-absorbed to catch her need before it got critical. I glanced at Liam, at his beloved square jaw and bright-dark eyes and wide shoulders. This was worse for him. He only wanted to lead his band, to be home with his people. Kayleen was almost a stranger to him. He had never before been sundered from his family, not in a way he remembered. He was two years old when Akashi and Mayah adopted him, and they called him "son" from the first day.

Clouds and sky floated in the screen behind Liam's head. I sat beside him, leaving Kayleen in the back of the skimmer with Windy. He took my hand, squeezing it tightly. His fingers were cold. I laced my fingers through his, thinking of my little wagon making its way home, of Stripes and Sasha and Akashi. Of Kiara. Paloma. The faces of the band ran through my head, and I swore silently to myself that this would be a short trip. I would come home soon, home to my wagon and my hebra and my family.

ISLANDIA

The *Burning Void* took us over the ocean between Jini and Islandia. Kayleen remained silent, leaning against the bulkhead with one hand on the young splay-legged hebra's neck. Windy stamped her feet and shifted nervously. Her attention never left Kayleen.

I, too, watched Kayleen, looking for some sign that Artistos or the roamers tried to contact her. I saw none.

The nose camera showed blue-green water, a line of horizon, and above that, clear blue sky. The engines hummed softly and the image on the screen changed slowly. I spent an hour listening to the four of us breathe—the hebra's breath faster and louder than ours—the tiny movements of Liam shifting weight next to me, Kayleen changing her soft grip on the hebra, my own hands sliding on the seat, the hebra's feet shifting.

I couldn't stand the awkward silence anymore.

We were family! I stood and stretched, considering Liam's blank stare, wondering where his thoughts were. He hadn't offered a word since I gave up stopping Kayleen. It wasn't as if I'd given up forever.

I took two steps toward Kayleen, but she waved me away, either unwilling or unable to talk to me. I bet on unwilling; there didn't seem to be much to flying through the clear, empty sky. So I kept going, approaching slowly, keeping my voice soft. "Kayleen?"

She shook her head, a quick warning gesture. The skimmer lurched, dropping, my stomach falling with it. I gasped, grabbing the back of a seat for balance. Windy pasted her ears to the back of her head and her eyes rolled.

Kayleen's face screwed up and her eyes scrunched together.

Steady flight resumed. Kayleen patted Windy, and the hebra's ears inched back up.

I frowned. Had Kayleen told us the truth about how often she'd flown before?

I returned to my seat by Liam, alternating between staring at the empty sea in front of us and watching the silent play of anger, fear, and resolve across his features. We twined our fingers together, a soft caress. I had a thousand things to say to him, but nothing to say in Kayleen's hearing.

Time passed slowly.

At one point, Kayleen reached under the seat in front of her and extracted a bag which held bottles of water, bread, dried djuri jerky, and goat cheese. She set some of the food on the row of seats behind us. I realized my tongue felt as dry as the summer plains, and reached for the water, drinking greedily. Liam drank too, but neither of us ate.

Being Kayleen's prisoner seemed unreal. What could have twisted her heart and head so much? How could I have missed it? Already, I ached for Akashi and Mayah, for Sasha and Stripes. They must know we didn't want to leave. I imagined Sasha driving my wagon, clucking to Stripes, wondering where I had gone, cocking her head and listening for my return. How many band members might be in more danger because we weren't there to help them?

Surely we'd be home soon. I swallowed, angry tears stinging my eyes. I didn't know that.

Artistos had no way to follow the skimmer. It seemed to be powered by sun and air, like the rest of the *altered* technology, but the shuttles could only be re-filled from *Traveler*. When the stored fuel was gone, there would be no more. They would not waste a trip following us.

We had to make Kayleen take us home. Or not. I swallowed hard and struggled to feel positive. Wasn't I the one who had the gene-mods to see the best possible outcome in every situation?

Kayleen fed and watered Windy, who did exactly what any animal would eventually do, and eliminated right where she stood. The pungent odor filled the tiny space, the stink doing a fair job of representing my mood. It sparked something in the ship and an unseen fan turned on, increasing the flow of fresh air. It barely helped.

The first sign of Islandia was a dark smudge of smoke from Blaze turning a windblown wedge of the blue sky a dirty gray-brown. A hump of land rose on the line between sea and sky. It filled in, details resolving into a long, narrow continent painted with soft greens and golds, punctuated with violent reds of lava.

A jagged mountain range—Islandia's Teeth—marched the long length of the sea. At both ends—east and west—islands that looked like the tops of volcanoes poked from the water. Blaze spilled lava continually, cutting Islandia in two with the molten Fire River that came wide and bright from Blaze's mouth, narrowing to a thin brick-and-black trickle where it touched the far sea. The conversation between saltwater and molten rock threw a great gout of steam into the air.

The land around Blaze looked sere and empty. Jagged black stone gave way on both sides to dead, brown plains. Two or three peaks away, on either side, the continent greened into lush forests. Glaciers topped the highest peaks, and below them were lakes and the thin blue snakes of rivers running to the sea.

Liam also watched closely, leaning in, chewing on his fingernails. He twisted to look at Kayleen, who sat in the seat in front of Windy, idly scratching the hebra's ears. Kayleen's fingers had combed the neatness from her own hair so it stood out from her head in a hundred separate long dark curly strands. Her blue eyes focused inward, giving her a vacant look. Liam regarded her silently for a moment, then cleared his throat. "Where do you plan to land?"

Kayleen's eyes focused and she shook her head. She stood, walking unsteadily to the screen in front of us. She pointed to the long rounded tip of land farthest to the right from Blaze. "The mountains here are the oldest—Islandia was born from them. It's hotter than Artistos, and wetter, so there's plenty of water, and forest. There's probably game." The picture zoomed in, showing a wide valley with a river running through it, cupped by dense forest that marched to the top of mountains. "I decided this is our best bet."

"Can you reach Artistos through the nets?" I asked. "Do they know we're all right?"

She shook her head. "I can't communicate from here."

Liam's voice regained its edge. "Did you tell them you kidnapped us?"

Kayleen's chin went up. "Before we got too far away, I told them all three of us are all right."

"What did you tell them?" he pushed.

"That all three of us are together and that we're all right," she repeated, emphasizing her words as if Liam were a child.

"That's all?" I asked quietly.

She raised her eyebrows, then giggled. "That's right, isn't it? We're okay, and by the time we get back, we won't be fighting. We'll all get along just fine."

Right.

Liam leaned over and whispered in my ear. "She's crazy."

I ignored him. "Maybe, Kayleen. Maybe. But I wish Akashi and Mayah knew for sure that we didn't mean to leave. Can you tell them that after we land?"

She laughed. "I don't think so." The glaze fell over her eyes again and she mumbled, "I need to pay attention. I've only landed on the ground once, with Joseph, the night before he left. The cave has something that catches me when I come into it."

We flew over a dark peak whitened by ice near its top, with three waterfalls feeding a lake, which in turn fed the river below. It looked bigger than Little Lace Lake above Artistos, and *that* took three days to ride around. Beyond the lake, a small ridge stuck up just above the water line, and then the mountain fell steeply away again. It was hard to make out size from the sky, but the trees looked huge, and even though I spotted twintrees, I was sure most were trees we'd never seen.

The skimmer slowed as we crossed the lake, then circled over the valley. From this close, it didn't look as empty or as flat as it had from higher above. Small trees and bushes dotted the land below us. Rocks poked up and streams glittered in the sun, feeding into the river that ran down the center of the valley. I pointed at the screen, talking to Liam. "I don't see a good spot to land."

He squeezed my hand. "The skimmer doesn't need much—remember where Kayleen landed it before, in the trees above the plains?"

I nodded. Still, Joseph and Jenna had been with Kayleen then. She'd had help.

We circled a second time, lower. I closed my eyes and wished for us all to be safe.

We leveled out, lower again, heading for a long stretch of green. It looked flatter than the rest of the valley, although here and there rocks reared up in sharp jumbles. In two places, steam vented, white swirls misting the sky. The skimmer slowed, its engines whining.

Windy bugled, a high frightened noise that bounced around in the small cabin. I looked behind me. Kayleen had slumped down, her eyes closed, her arms tight across her belly.

I twisted back, needing to see, bracing my hands on the seat.

The nose wheel pounded the ground, bouncing up. Sky filled the camera for a moment then the view changed to a jolting jumble of greens and browns.

I slammed into Liam as the *Burning Void* slewed sideways. Grabbing the seat-arm, I dug my fingernails into the soft surface. Windy whined. Kayleen moaned, then screamed. The skimmer jerked again. Liam grabbed me around the waist, pulling me to him. He smelled of fear.

We tilted, then the machine jerked the other way and stopped, off-center, the floor canted sharply toward the nose.

Kayleen groaned and slumped forward. Windy nosed her, and she reached a single shaking hand up, touching the hebra's front leg.

Liam pushed himself to his feet, his face white. He extended a hand to help me up and pulled me close, murmuring, "Are you okay?"

I nodded. "You?"

Kayleen's voice, soft. "Sorry for the rough landing."

I turned. She stood, her face buried in Windy's neck. She was talking to the hebra, not us. Damn her. I shook my head, pulled away from Liam, and walked back toward Kayleen. He followed. Kayleen looked up at us, wiping the hair from her face with one hand while the other hand clutched Windy's halter.

"Are you all right?" I asked.

Her voice was a hoarse croak. "Thirsty."

A nearly full water bottle lay in the seat beside me. I handed it to her, watching her drink greedily. I searched for signs of the Kayleen I knew, but the girl in front of me had wild, cold eyes.

Liam cleared his throat. "We'd better go outside and see if the skimmer is okay."

A shiver ran up my spine. If it wasn't, we'd never get home.

Kayleen laughed, high and shaky. "I can feel the ship inside me." She laughed again. "It's in my bones, in my nervous system. When I fly, I am the *Burning Void*. I felt it when we landed hard, but most of her systems report fine."

Most of them?

Liam watched her warily, shaking his head. "Will the door open?"

She frowned. "I think the hold ramp will work." She unclipped one of the two leads attached to Windy's collar and took the other loosely in her hand. The hold door opened at her silent command, and the back ramp, the wider one used for cargo, began to hum and click as it extended.

I looked at Liam and shrugged, and we followed Kayleen and Windy, keeping a little distance from the hebra's baby-short white tail and sharp cloven hooves. We made our way down a walkway just big enough for Windy, threading between containers strapped to the walls.

Kayleen must have been gathering and storing for months. I recognized a few boxes: root vegetables like potatoes, dried meat, and fruit from Artistos. Even a small greenhouse, tucked neatly in sections behind a row of boxes. Five ships-skin-silver containers had clearly come from the Cave of Power. Unlabeled, they sat carefully stacked on the bottom row.

The hot breeze coming in from outside blew a slightly rotten smell into the hold. Liam, behind me, said, "It smells like Rage Mountain." He raised his voice, as if to make sure Kayleen would hear him. "Be careful. I'd leave the hebra in here until we can scout a little."

Of all of us, Liam was the only one who had been near an active volcano. The West Band was going there now, but we'd spent the past two years in the Ice Mountains.

The ramp stopped as soon as it hit ground, lengthened by our tilt. I blessed whoever built the *Burning Void* that it opened at all. The ramp bent slightly, so that the end was still essentially flat on the ground even though the upward tilt of the back of the skimmer meant it didn't start out straight.

Kayleen went first, leading Windy, pointedly ignoring Liam's advice. I followed behind her. Behind me, Liam bent down, looking over the edge of the ramp at the bottom of the skimmer, and groaned. I knelt close to him, my knee touching his. A small comfort.

The skimmer had come to rest with its front right wheel in a crevice and almost all of its weight on its nose wheel. Nothing looked broken, or even scratched, but we weren't going anywhere unless we figured out how to free the wheel and get the *Burning Void* onto flat ground. "How are we going to move it?" I asked.

He shook his head. "We have to find a way."

The ground was strewn with lumpy reddish and black rocks full of holes. Here and there, scraggly green and yellow grasses and tiny purple flowers poked up from the rocks. Some kind of evergreen tree, with a more twisted trunk and longer needles than I'd ever seen, grew in small patches, none over my height. Farther away, the ground must be less rocky; more varied forest surrounded us in three directions. The mountain we'd flown over loomed above us, blocking a good portion of sky. I could make out two other mountaintops clearly, one to the east and one to the west. Blaze was invisible from here, and its smoke had been going the other way. But I knew it was there, dominating Islandia.

Tiny white clouds hazed the late-afternoon sky above us. It would be dark in a few hours. A cool wind touched my cheek.

Liam grunted next to me. "Maybe we can right her if we build some kind of lever. But we'll need to make a path to take off from, too." He didn't sound too sure of himself.

Kayleen turned, grinning as if her dreams had come true. "We need to figure out where to live, first." She turned her head, surveying the area, as if trying to find just the right spot.

I wanted to go home. I wanted to take Kayleen and shake her, make her take us home.

Windy pranced on the ramp and butted Kayleen, nearly knocking her off. Kayleen laughed, a soft happy laugh this time. She took a few slow running steps and jumped, her feet crunching on the rocky ground.

Windy followed, without the jump. She stamped at the unfamiliar footing. She kept her head up, swiveling it around, her nostrils extended and her ears pricked. A rising wind blew the fine hairs on her neck and face backward and ruffled the tufts of white around her ears.

A high-pitched wail, then a full deep baying call, wafted eerily down the valley, followed by another one, and then another. A pack of something unfamiliar, calling back and forth to each other.

Liam stiffened next to me. "Don't go far from the skimmer," he called to Kayleen.

Kayleen looked up at us. "I brought a perimeter."

Liam sighed, but managed to keep his voice even. "Kayleen. It's late. Why bother setting up a perimeter now? We should sleep in the skimmer tonight, and try to right her tomorrow." More calls from the foothills added sense to his suggestion.

She looked at Windy. "I don't think she'll sleep inside. Besides, the floor's tilted. I brought tools to cut wood for a barn."

I shook my head, a sense of the surreal settling in my bones. Was she kidding? "We can't build a barn tonight." The idea of sleeping in the stinky, oddly slanted cabin didn't make me feel much better. Maybe we could clear the hold, but Windy would just stink that up, too. I grimaced. "All of the big wood is in the forest, and it's too far away. Let's set up the perimeter bells and camp at the foot of the ramp." I closed my eyes, briefly dizzy and powerless. "Windy will be safer if we can bring her in here if any predators come."

Kayleen apparently figured out we weren't going to go help her set up a house and barn at that exact moment. Her shoulders slumped. She buried her head in Windy's neck. When she looked back up she smiled at us. "Okay. If it will help keep Windy safe."

Liam leaned in close to me and muttered, "It'll keep you safe so you can fly us home."

Kayleen cocked her head, her voice slightly teasing now. "Still talking behind my back?"

I separated from Liam and walked down the ramp toward Kayleen. I held my hand out for Windy's lead. "I'll hold onto her. Liam can help you unpack the perimeter and get it set up." Only Kayleen could tune the perimeter, at least unless she had brought the type of tools Paloma and Gianna and the other members of the science guild used. I doubted it.

The two of them disappeared into the hold. I held my hand out flat and let Windy sniff it. She leaned her head down, acknowledging me, but only for a moment, going right back to testing the unfamiliar smells and keeping her ears pricked. Her skin rippled with unease and she danced lightly on her feet whenever a bird called or the beasts in the hills bayed. Windy was prey. I felt as vulnerable as she in this strange place full of unknown dangers.

I was alone for now except for the young, frightened hebra.

We'd find a way to get back. There wasn't any other choice.

Tears splashed down onto my hands, warm and wet. I let go, my losses spilling into Islandia's rough rocky soil with my tears.

By the time the sun danced on the horizon, we had a passable perimeter set up. Wireless devices hung on metal poles giving us a hundred square meters of warning space.

The *Burning Void*'s hold disgorged three cots, one large tent, and kitchen camp gear. The cots came from Artistos, the tent and shimmery silver lightweight sleeping blankets came from the cave. We might be using the same tools our genetic parents had camped with outside Artistos, both before and during the war. The idea offered little comfort.

Liam sunk a pole in the ground and tied Windy to it. She munched on some of last summer's harvest from the Grass Plains, still looking up regularly, but apparently feeling a bit better since we'd set up signs of civilization.

Kayleen pulled food from a large cooler. She sat on a stone, cutting up fresh djuri and some of last summer's root stock to make a stew. I squatted down next to her. "Can I help?"

She grunted, not looking at me. "No, this is my feast for you. I hoped you'd come of your own accord, and this would be a celebration." She continued slicing through long dried purple-roots and setting them in water to soften, still avoiding my eyes.

A celebration feast? I glanced over my shoulder at Liam, arching an eyebrow. "You never gave us a chance to come willingly."

"You wouldn't have taken it anyway."

I grimaced at the back of her head. "Liam and I need to talk. We're going to take a walk."

She shook her head, not exactly a yes or a no, but she reached for another root. I stood and walked off, Liam catching up in a few long strides. As we got far enough away to talk, he said, "She's crazy."

I took his hand, aware that Kayleen would see, and not really caring. "Maybe she has been for a while. But we left her, and what do we know about her experiences? We aren't Wind Readers, and we haven't been in Artistos. We don't know what it's been like for her."

He swallowed and looked out toward the mountains, painted brilliant gold on one side by the setting sun, dark and foreboding on the other side. "There is no excuse."

I watched the mountains with him, the high clouds above them now brilliant orange edged with bright gold. One of the small muscles in his neck jumped silently, repeatedly.

"What are we going to do?" he asked.

I chewed on my lip. I had become used to following his direction in the band; he knew the people and the routines, the dangers and the rituals. But only I knew both Kayleen and him well, if I really knew Kayleen anymore. I spoke softly, trying to reach past his anger. "I guess we're going to go back and eat her feast. The only way to get home is to try and reach her, to make her want to take us back." I squeezed his hand and leaned into him, looking sideways to where Kayleen sat, still huddled over her preparations. "Her mood has shifted a hundred times today. Remember when we were little, and she and I and Joseph always made sure we found you on Trading Day?" I turned my face up to his. "Maybe it's our turn to find her."

We stood face to face, hands still clasped, and he looked into my eyes. I looked back at him, feeling a wave of tenderness. We'd set out this morning hoping to find time to make love in the cave.

He spoke, his voice as soft as mine had been. "Are you saying you forgive her?"

I shook my head. "I'm saying I love her. I'm saying she's our family."

Water gleamed in the edges of his eyes. I'd had my cry, but he hadn't, and I knew he wouldn't do it yet. He cleared his throat. "My family is back on Jini." He held a hand out and brushed a stray lock of hair from my face. "And you. You're my family." He glanced toward Kayleen. "She's not. She's someone I see twice a year, and I don't understand her. I don't trust her. I don't see how you can."

"I spent almost every day of my life with her before I went with the band. I've always been the oldest, always been the one who had to keep us together, at least until the last few years. That matters to me."

He blew out a long, slow breath, looking away. "I'll eat her feast for you. But I can't do it for her. That will have to be enough."

I nodded.

"And tomorrow," he continued, "tomorrow, I'm going to make getting the skimmer ready to fly my highest priority."

I leaned into him, holding him, trying with all my being to tell him how much I loved him, needed him.

As we turned back to eat a feast we didn't want, the sun dropped below the low hills. I left my hand in his as we came into camp, unwilling to drop my connection to him just to make Kayleen feel good. She handed us our plates, her eyes shining with unexplained tears. We sat one on each side of her, awkward, each of the three of us alone. As the last light faded from the sky, the light from Kayleen's cooking fire danced brightly in the cold night.

5

DOG DAYS

Windy and I shared the last watch. She noticed the silence before I did. She lifted her long neck, sniffing the air, her nostrils extended, her stubby tail straight up. I stood, arms tucked close to ward off the night chill, the hair on my arms rising. Behind me, Kayleen and Liam slumbered in the darkened tent near the end of the ramp. In front of me, dark trees and rocks stood silent sentinel, washed lightly by starlight.

When Liam and I hunted djuri for the band, the world around us silenced. That same silence surrounded us now. Earlier, night birds and small animals had skittered from bush to rock to tiny tree, each sound slightly different from home. Now, no birds called and no little jumping animals moved. The light of two moons paled as it fell through clouds. The wind had even died. I stepped close to Windy's side, whispering, "What do you sense?"

Her skin quivered, but she didn't move or shift her attention to me. She smelled or saw something that I didn't. We stood, silent, straining to hear anything. I reached for her lead and untied it, holding it loosely in both hands.

Gravel crunched.

Something—not us—breathed out.

Windy exploded. She reared back, jerking me with her as I tightened my fists on her lead. Her eyes widened in fear as she yanked the lead line tight.

The perimeter bells peeled danger.

I screamed. "Liam!" and raced the few steps between me and

Windy, tugging on the line, trying to get close enough to grab her halter.

A single howl, close. I couldn't see anything. Low growls came from three directions.

Windy pulled her line taut, quivering, her back feet pointing at the danger. The whites of her eyes were clearly visible and her ears lay flat against her head.

Liam pulled on my arm. I jerked free. "No! Help me."

I'd lost a hebra to paw-cats once. I wasn't going to lose this one.

A low form rushed in from the dark, close. Half my height, brown and fast. Long—too big for a demon dog. It opened its jaws. Tongue and white teeth, the teeth gleaming in the faint starlight.

Liam whooped and it veered away. More ran past us, ten or twelve of them, a few body-lengths away, long and dark, sleek. Their white eyes and teeth glowed, their bodies visible as dark movement more than shape. They crouched low, circling. If they stood up they would be waist-high.

Kayleen grabbed Windy's line. She tugged, cursing. The terrified hebra knocked Kayleen to her knees and vaulted over her, bleating and disappearing up the ramp into the wide cargo door. Howls chased me and Liam as we leapt onto the ramp, stopping to grab Kayleen's shoulders and heave her up with us. The ramp jerked upward, closing fast as we tumbled into boxes and into each other in the suddenly small hold.

Something jumped at the ramp, missed, and fell back.

Windy bugled off to my right, back in the cabin. The hull rang as she kicked at it. Kayleen scrambled after her.

Muffled barks sounded outside, some close.

I pushed myself up in the darkness, testing.

One knee felt scraped. Not bad.

My voice shook. "You two okay?"

Liam, tense. "Fine. That was damned close."

The soft sounds of Kayleen comforting Windy competed with muted howls and ripping noises as the pack outside assaulted our gear.

Light slammed into the corridor. I thanked Kayleen for it under my breath, able to see the anger filling Liam's dark eyes. "Get Kayleen," he snapped. "You take Windy."

"Why Kayleen?" I asked. She and Windy were safe.

"Because she can find me a weapon." One look at Liam's face and I scrambled down the corridor, slowing as I went through the opening.

Windy had backed against the screen in the front of the cabin. Kayleen stood at her head, her back to me, talking softly to the shaking hebra. "It'll be okay. You're okay."

I took the lead from her. "Liam needs you."

Kayleen looked at me, her eyes wide. "Is he all right?"

"We're both okay. Just go see what he needs. I'll stay here."

"Don't leave her," she pleaded.

"Of course not." I reached a hand up to stroke Windy's long trembling neck. "Shhhhh . . . you're okay." I took over Kayleen's litany, focusing on the hebra, barely noticing as Kayleen left. "We didn't let them eat you. You were good, you gave me good warning." I couldn't help remembering Jinks again. Her death had bought me safety, probably bought my life. My hand shook on Windy's quivering neck, and I forced myself to take long deep breaths, struggling to slow my heartbeat. Hebras felt what we felt.

Part of my attention stayed focused on Windy, and I listened for Liam and Kayleen. I made out Liam's voice. ". . . I'll throw it. Tell me when."

What was he doing? The soft whine of the ramp opening back out was nearly obscured as the barks and howls intensified, surely now spilling through an opening. The ramp clicked closed and a muffled whump sounded outside, following by an animal scream and frightened yelps. Windy shivered, leaning into me, her skin rippling as the boundary bells pealed exit, barely audible through the ship's hull.

Kayleen and Liam came through the doorway, Liam's face quietly satisfied. "I think we drove them off."

"What did you use?" I asked, relinquishing my place next to Windy to Kayleen.

Kayleen answered. "Remember that crazy-ball? The one Alicia stole? I wanted to see what one would do."

I closed my eyes. The bones in my legs stopped holding me up as the adrenaline rush left me all at once. I sat. "Jenna said they explode and throw out hard objects."

Liam grinned. "Sounds like it worked."

"How do you know it didn't hurt the ship?" I asked.

"That's why we threw it just as the door closed," she said. "Jenna told me nothing hurts ship skin."

I hadn't seen any marks from our hard landing, and the *New Making* had sat on the grass plains for years with no sign of weathering. Still . . . "What about our stuff?"

Liam sat down next to me. "They were ripping it up anyway. They needed a message."

"They were bigger than demon dogs." I shivered. "Scarier."

"Yes." Liam sighed. "But they looked like cousins. Maybe we should call them big demons." He laughed, the sound marred by a nervous glitch.

Nonetheless it broke the tension and I smiled at him. We were all right. Even Windy. "Windy warned me. We'd have died if she hadn't sensed those things before the bells went off."

Kayleen crooned at Windy. "Good beast." Then she spoke to us. "Good thing I brought her."

I eyed the two of them. Kayleen leaned into Windy. The hebra butting her softly, her ears forward and soft. "You mean instead of leaving her safe in the hebra barn back home?"

Kayleen recoiled as my words struck her, and even Windy raised her head, looking at me accusingly.

"We'd all be safer somewhere else," I said, knowing it was the wrong thing to say, but not caring. It was truth.

"Like at home." Liam stood up. "I want to go outside and look around. Kayleen, are the boundary bells still working? Still showing clear?"

She nodded. "I'll go with you." She looked at me. "Chelo, will you stay with Windy?"

I frowned. I wanted to go with Liam.

Liam knew. "No, Kayleen. Windy will be happier with you. Besides, we need *you* safe. You're the only one who can get us home."

Kayleen looked torn. "Give her a minute to calm down, and I'll tie her back here. Then I can go stand in the doorway and watch."

We had to wait. Only Kayleen could open the door.

But that couldn't be right. Jenna had. Maybe I couldn't fly it, but this was my technology as much as Kayleen's. It belonged to all of us.

I thought of the reader Jenna had given me once in the cave, a pale way to read data buttons compared to Joseph and Kayleen's skills, but it had worked. Surely the skimmer had *some* manual controls. . . .

I stood, my legs still a little shaky. "Okay. I'm going to go back and clean up in the hold."

"Here," Liam said, "I'll help."

Kayleen had trapped herself into staying to comfort her hebra. For a moment, I saw her tense, realizing it, and thought she might try to keep us with her in the cabin. But she simply turned to Windy, her back to us, and began crooning again.

We hadn't really made much of a mess tumbling inside. Four or five boxes lay on the floor, some empty, so they must have held the camping gear. One of the silver boxes had been pulled out of its safe nest and opened. The crazy-ball had probably come from there. Ignoring that box for now, Liam and I stacked the others. As he finished setting the last one up high, I walked over by the hold door, really the ramp, now folded in so it looked like a square against the hull.

Most *altered* technology could be used by hand. Sure enough, I spotted three small symbols etched faintly onto the wall to the right of the door, about my shoulder height.

I studied them.

A circle, a triangle, and two lines next to each other. The circle for opening? I reached up and brushed my fingers lightly over the symbol. Cool air washed across my cheek as the door began to open. I gasped and felt Liam's hand on my shoulder. I touched the triangle. The lights began to fade slowly.

Damn.

I swallowed. The lines were to the right. I ran my hand over them, and the ramp stopped, partly open. I turned my attention back to the lights, trying to turn them back up, succeeding at plunging us into darkness.

"Good idea." Liam's voice in my ear, sounding pleased. "Not so good execution," he teased.

The lights bloomed back on and the door finished closing. Neither was my doing. Kayleen stood in the doorway, her mouth a tight, disapproving line. "I would have shown you how to do that."

Maybe. I bit my tongue and called back, "Thanks."

Kayleen came up beside us. "Windy's cross-tied. Before anyone goes out, we'll need weapons."

Ghosts of Jenna saying almost the same thing at the beginning of our fight with Artistos—the one that ended with Joseph leaving—flitted through my memory. I had kept a small light laser gun from that time, had even carried it everywhere with me the first year afterward. It didn't do any good today, resting in a spot I'd hollowed out for it in a cubby in my wagon.

What did Kayleen giving us weapons mean? That she'd rather die than fly us back under duress? After all, we could use the weapons on her. Or did whatever fantasy she'd built about our life here override her common sense completely?

Maybe she just knew I wouldn't shoot her.

I sighed audibly, resigned. "What did you bring?"

She gave each of us one of the hand-lasers like mine, small fast weapons that could be pocketed and wouldn't necessarily kill. They'd be enough to hold off something like the dogs in ones or twos, but not a pack of them. I already had a flashlight clipped to my belt, but she handed Liam one.

She pawed slowly through the box. I was pleased to see one of the little data-button readers meant for people like us who didn't bathe in information. There were a few more crazy-balls (wrapped carefully), some of the same thin stakes Jenna had laid out in the hangar on the Grass Plains, Kayleen's frizzer (which made us invisible to the Artistos data nets), and a multitude of things I didn't recognize.

Kayleen pointed at the long thin sticks. She said, "These are pretty traditional projectile weapons—aim, fire, if you hit the target you kill it. I practiced with them on djuri. They work, but they're hard to aim. Besides, I've only found one box of the projectiles." She set aside three small boxes that could probably be pocketed or strung on belts. "Good for disrupting data flows." She grimaced. "Not much use here."

She picked up an oddly shaped lump of ship-silver metal with buttons on it. "That's what I wanted. This thing sends out a range of sounds that we can't hear. When I played with it, some of the settings made almost everything, even the birds, get quiet. And some made them attack each other, and all the time I was just pushing a button. I've been trying to find information about them on the data buttons, but no luck." She shrugged. "If we see those dogs again, I want to try this. It might affect a whole pack."

Liam had that "she's crazy" look again. "Well, will it make them run away, or attack us, or lie down and lick our feet? I'll bet it's not the last one." He stood up. "Let's open the door. I want to see what we can salvage." He held up his right hand with the little laser gun in it. "Thanks for this."

She nodded, and Liam reached for the symbols by the door. I don't know whether his hand or her mind actually started it, but the ramp began to fold out. Chill air and the slightly acrid smell of the volcanic landscape spilled into the hold. Clouds now hid all the stars and moons, so the only light we had was the large rectangle pouring from the door.

Near the top of the rectangle, the bloody carcass of one of the big demons attested to the strength of the crazy-ball. Even dead, torn up by the shrapnel released in the explosion, the dog made me shiver: muscular, with long claws and longer teeth, short dark fur and a long nearly hairless tail. It was at least three times as big as the demon dogs back home. The ramp clicked down, fully extended. I swallowed and tore my eyes away from the dead dog.

A light wind blew across the land below us, rustling the grasses and something from camp, maybe our blankets. I listened more closely, making the sounds loud in my mind, focusing down. Finally, I heard what I was listening for: the sound of little feet as the small night mammals I'd heard at the beginning of my watch moved restlessly over the rough ground, scurrying for a last meal before morning.

I breathed out, whispering, "It's okay, they're gone."

As we walked down the ramp, shining our flashlights around, I still felt jumpy. Kayleen followed halfway, then stopped, a dark silhouette casting a long shadow in the light from the ship.

I knelt and traced a paw print the size of my hand in a patch of loose dirt. Standing up again, I looked around. The rustling turned out to be the remains of our tent. Whether by the dogs or the crazy-ball, the near walls had been rent into shreds which flapped softly against each other, eerie in the dusk-before-dawn.

Our cots lay in a jumble, overturned. Liam pointed out tooth marks on the metal, which had come from Artistos. I didn't see any marks on the *altered* metal, although some of it *had* been thrown around by the dogs.

We counted five more carcasses. All of the dead dogs had spilled blood from more than one wound. The blood smelled strong and rank, and buzzing insects gathered around. I remembered Akashi's description from the first time I'd seen a crazy-ball. *"If you throw that ball into a group of people, it will kill everyone close to it."* I hadn't been able to count the dogs, but there had been more than five. The bells had pealed exit and I'd heard them running away. Still, we wouldn't have been able to kill five with hand weapons and live.

One of the blankets had become a last resting place for the biggest of the dead demon dogs, a bitch with half of one leg ripped completely off. Gruesome. The blanket was covered in blood, a total loss. Liam wrinkled his nose. "We'll have to burn everything." He paused, staring at the dead dog. "How does she expect us to live here?"

"How did we learn to live on Jini? Paw cats are as bad." I glanced back at the skewed skimmer. "Maybe we should capture as much of this information as we can."

He laughed wryly. "That's what dad would do." He, too, looked over at the skimmer, shaking his head. "Maybe I'll draw one in the morning before we burn them. It would be good to learn about their habits so we can avoid them."

That sounded more like the Liam I knew, the roaming scientist. "Okay. I'll help." I had a good hand for recording details about animals and plants. "But I don't want to dissect one."

"Me either. Let's gather up what we can. I don't want to spend another night here."

6

BURNING THE DEAD

Two hours later, the three of us stood almost a hundred meters from the skimmer, watching flames lick up a pile of mutilated bodies ringed with deadwood. Sweat coated my scalp and back from piling up the carcasses and gathering fuel for the fire, and I shivered in the slightly cool breeze.

Liam picked up a stray piece of wood and tossed it on the fire, stepping backward quickly as smoke wafted toward him. Kayleen, too, stepped back. The pyre stank of burning flesh. Liam's voice carried a sharp undertone as he said, "So in less than one full day, we've gotten the skimmer stuck, nearly died in a beast attack, lost some of our stuff, and gathered up all the easily available fuel around us. What do you think we might do with the rest of our afternoon?"

The edge in his voice made me fidget. It wouldn't do to see it in that light. "We landed safely, survived a nasty surprise attack, and we have almost enough wood to help us stay safe tonight."

He laughed. "Always, always, you see the best thing possible."

I smiled back at him. "Well, now we have a drawing of a fantastic animal never before seen on Fremont. Think of the tall tales you can tell some Story Night back in Artistos."

"Great. A picture's sure to save our lives." He cocked his head at the skimmer. "I haven't come up with a good idea for levering it out of that hole."

Kayleen glanced at the skimmer, where poor Windy stood cross-tied inside again for safety. "When Windy gets bigger she can help pull it."

He glanced from the slender young hebra to the heavy skimmer. "If we can keep her alive long enough to get ten times her size."

Which she never would. I stifled a laugh.

He turned to Kayleen. "What's in the hold? Is there anything heavy and flat and at least three meters long?"

Kayleen screwed her face up. "The greenhouse pieces are long enough, but I don't think they're very strong."

I stared at the skimmer, thinking. "Kayleen, the ramp? Will it come off?"

Her eyes widened. "I don't know."

Liam started for the skimmer. I glanced at Kayleen. "Look, I'll watch the fire for a few minutes. You go see if you can help him figure that out."

She stared at me for a second, as if she didn't quite understand my words. "We have to know where to fly it before it will do us any good. We should figure out where we are going to live before we fix the skimmer. What if we get the ramp off and we can't get it back on? The hold will be open to everything. The demon dogs might get all of our food. Or anything else out here. Maybe the paw-cats are bigger here, too." She frowned. "But we *could* see if it looks possible. I mean, the ramp's heavy enough. We'd have to dig out the crevice the wheel's in—"

"Go," I interrupted her. She sounded almost like her old self, babbling through a problem out loud. Maybe she had needed to get out of Artistos.

She took my hand, squeezing it, looking more—sane—than she had in days. "I'm sorry Chelo. I'm sorry I got us stuck here. But I had to do it. I had to." Her eyes pleaded with me, and for a moment I felt my old friend by my side, saw her peering out of the crazy woman who had brought us here. "Do you understand?"

"No, I don't." I softened my voice. "Taking away our happiness won't make you happy."

She turned her gaze away, dropping my hand. I watched my friend—my kidnapper—as she walked away. Her shoulders slumped. Did she regret this? Right then, bathed in the stink of burning blood, I couldn't quite forgive her. I turned my attention back to the rank-smelling fire and picked up a long stick to poke at it with.

They came back half an hour later. "I think we can do it." Liam leaned in and grazed my temple with a soft kiss. "There's a bolting mechanism—it's pretty well hidden. We couldn't free it, but I'm sure we'll figure out a way." He stared down at Kayleen. "Surely you see that we can't live here. We can fly back tonight if we can get the skimmer out."

I glanced over at the machine. I didn't think it would be as easy to free it as he implied, but I held my tongue. The midmorning sun had pulled the chill out of the day, but interrupted sleep and hard work had left my back and arm muscles tight and twisted, and dried sweat clung to my skin.

The demon's pyre burned to embers, to the bones of dogs and the bones of the bigger wood, while Liam struggled to get the ramp off. Kayleen wandered between the two of us, silent, stopping to whisper in Windy's ear from time to time. When she stopped close to me, I looked for the Kayleen I knew to appear in her eyes again, but her gaze switched from unfocused to intent, never stopping on normal.

Free of fire tending in the now-punishing heat, I walked back to the skimmer to find Liam had given up on the ramp. He stood staring at a pile of *altered* metal he'd scavenged from boxes and the ruins of our camp last night. He shook his head at me. "Nothing looks big enough."

I put a hand on his shoulder. "We'll get it out."

By late afternoon, we hadn't figured out either what to put under the wheel to give the skimmer purchase, or how to pull it free. Liam stood staring at the sunken nose, sweat pouring down his arms. He kicked at a rock. "We're going to need her to agree to fly it anyway."

"She's not ready to do that yet."

"Damn her," he replied. "We'd best find someplace to camp tomorrow. Close by."

I moved next to him and held him, looking at the tilted skimmer. "Can we sleep in that thing?"

He shook his head. "It's too canted. Windy'll be on top of us. We'll do what we did last night, but I'll get Kayleen to set a bigger perimeter, and we'll gather more wood. If we can't sleep outside right next to the skimmer, how will we ever sleep in another camp? We can't make one here; there's not enough water. We're going to need to spend the rest of this afternoon just getting ready for another uneasy night." He fell silent for a long moment, looking up at the mountains. "But we can't let this place beat us yet, not if we're stuck for a while. We'll just have one hell of a fire and stay alert."

So he'd given up on the skimmer for now.

He squeezed me close to him, almost too tight. "Three isn't a big enough band to survive here easily. I just know it in my bones. This place is dangerous, and we don't have animals or wagons or anything."

We didn't. But we had each other. And Kayleen, who remained a wild card.

KAYLEEN'S STORY

That night we built our fire even closer to the ramp than we had the night before. The three of us stood wearily around the flames, holding our hands toward the heat. It smelled clean, like burning wood and bits of brush, with no taint of blood. Unable to shower, I had still cleaned up with water from the closest stream, a shallow thing sure to dry up soon. I used my dirty shirt for a washcloth, and put on a clean pair of work pants and a clean dark shirt from the pile Kayleen had brought. But washing the stink of blood and sweat and fear away only made me feel a little better.

I watched Kayleen's eyes. She had been all business through the afternoon, matter-of-fact and flat, showing no emotion. After dinner, she'd rolled up into a ball next to Windy, one arm over her face, maybe sleeping, maybe hiding. She'd just emerged a few moments ago.

Now, as she stared at the fire, not looking at either of us, her eyes bounced between the same flat deadness and periodic flashes of some emotion I couldn't quite name. Maybe not remorse, but at least uncertainty. I wasn't close enough to touch her, but I reached out a hand experimentally. She looked at me, then shook her head.

Liam was on my other side, closer to me than I was to Kayleen. He threw a small stick on the fire, then looked over at her. "Kayleen. If you really spied on us all year, you know that we matter to our families, to our band. They are safer when we're there." His hands twisted in his lap. "If we can fix the skimmer, I'm sure Akashi will let us keep you for the summer."

"And then what?" she asked. Her voice was bitter. "Akashi can't stand up to the whole Town Council. He can't risk the band for that, or at least he wouldn't."

I cleared my throat. "We could have died last night. If Windy hadn't warned me, we would never have made it inside the skimmer in time. If we all die, or if we get stuck here, one or all of us, we can't be any help to them. Three of us isn't enough to make a new town. Six wasn't. You were part of that conversation years ago, and you wanted to stay in Artistos with Paloma."

"And you were going to stay with me," she said. She stood, shuffling in place, her head down so it was hard to see her face. "You couldn't stand Nava either, or being there. And you left. You could leave. I couldn't."

I tried not to choke on the truth in her words. I'd gone willingly away to a loving environment, healing, barely thinking about my friend. Counting on Paloma to be enough. As if someone who wasn't one of us could actually understand. "You could have asked for help."

Kayleen didn't answer. Liam stepped forward like he was about to speak, so I put a hand out, signaling him to be still. He hadn't left her; I had. This was between us.

She stood for a long time, silent, staring out past the fire, into the darkness. Far off, demon dogs bayed, and Kayleen blinked, hard. "I want to be with you"—she looked over at Liam—"with you both." She swallowed, running her hands through her hair. "This is the only way I can do it. I feel better already. A little." She finally looked back at me. "Just being away from Artistos helps. I need you to want to be here."

"It's too late for that." I *couldn't* want to stay, no matter what guilt gnawed at me for leaving her at all, ever. "I *do* care about you," I said. "You aren't the only person in my life who counts, though."

She laughed. "But Liam's here."

Liam stepped around me to look directly at Kayleen. "I don't want to be here."

Her head came to his chin, and her slender body couldn't weigh much more than half of what his did, but she stood her ground, firm. "I know that." Her voice quivered a tiny bit. "I'm not going back now, not until I feel like myself. Do you know what I almost did? Do you know Klia?"

He shook his head. "I know who she is."

"She . . . Klia was the last straw. Last year, she refused to even talk to me, to acknowledge my presence. But I could hear her. I could hear what everyone there said, anytime they were near a node. So the data chattered in me, and the town chattered in me, and I couldn't turn any of it off." She stopped and stared at me, as if willing me to understand.

How could I? What would it be like to have so many conversations in your head? But I nodded.

She continued. "She told her father, who is in line for a Town Council position, that he should kill me. She said they don't need any holier-than-thou special people to help with anything, and insisted I'd go crazy just like Bryan and start beating people up. She said she'd seen me clench my fists around her, and that I was like a paw-cat living in town." Words tumbled quickly out of her mouth now. "He told Klia she had to wait, but he didn't tell her no. *He didn't tell her no*. And I wanted to kill her right then, to go down there and rip her throat out." She paused, breathing fast, looking at each of us for a moment.

The Kayleen I grew up with would never have wanted to kill anyone. Never. Maybe it had been shame that kept her from asking me for help.

Kayleen continued. "I've hunted, like you two. I never told anyone, but I've done it, run out of town as fast and far as I could and killed djuri. I even killed a baby paw-cat." She pushed up her sleeve, showing a long scar on her forearm. "See—it scratched me before I killed it. I could have killed Klia. If I'd stayed there long enough, I would have killed her or someone else." Her hands shook, and her eyes were bright with unshed tears.

Her pause stretched into a long silence. I shivered at the image of her hunting a paw-cat. What need drove her to put herself in so much danger? Finally, I stepped in close to her and put a hand on her shoulder. She didn't turn into it, didn't step away, just stood, quivering.

Liam watched us both, looking awkward and stiff. I pursed my lips. Couldn't he see her pain? I swallowed, willing him to unbend.

He didn't change his position or his gaze. He was close enough for me to hear his breath quickening as whatever inner thoughts that warred in him escalated.

And Kayleen watched him too, still standing with my hand on her, still not turning into it to let me hold her. Her shoulder felt like a rock. I spoke to her, keeping my voice soft and slow. "Did you tell your mom? Did you ask anyone for help?"

Her lower lip quivered and she unclenched her hands, leaving them hanging loosely at her side. "Paloma is one of *them*. She wouldn't hurt me, she loves me. But she doesn't understand. She can't. I don't even know if you can since you're not Wind Readers. For the first whole day that I can remember, there aren't a thousand thousand messages screaming at me through the air. I can only feel the perimeter and the ship, and they're like nothing."

We were all in the middle of tough choices. Some kind of hunting bird screeched off to our right, and something small gave a death cry, making me shiver. There had to be a compromise. "Liam?"

He didn't stop staring at her. "What?"

"We can't make her take us back. Until she does, we're stuck here. This is a hard place. Kayleen can't make us happy to be here, and we can't become happy to be here. Not easily." I swallowed. I didn't want to even try to be happy here. "But can we promise to stay for a few days, get some breathing room?"

He turned and looked at me, his eyes bright and hard in the firelight. "Do you expect me to be happy about that?"

"No." I said it softly, holding his eyes with my own.

Kayleen stood silent, waiting. Firelight played on half her face, touching her dark hair with gold. She licked her lips, then stepped back, giving him space.

I watched him, his jaw tight, his eyes still on me. I smiled, softly, willing him to see that giving her even a small concession in some way gave us more power. He turned to her. "We'll find a place to camp tomorrow night. But I'm not giving up on fixing the skimmer, and I want your help." He looked over at me. The price of backing down shone in his eyes, like a pool of loss that he couldn't quite cry out. "I don't want to winter here."

I nodded, thanking him silently, mouthing the words, "I love you," so that only he could see. A slight smile warmed his lips for just a second before he turned back to Kayleen.

She took a deep breath, blowing it out slowly. "Thank you."

At least she had it in her to see what he gave her. The demon dogs bayed again, still far away. Windy bugled, and Kayleen turned to look at her.

Liam looked over toward the foothills where the high calls of the dogs came from. "I'm serious. I don't want to winter here."

Kayleen nodded, then turned and walked to Windy, burying her face in the hebra's neck. I watched her go, wishing she had let me hold her instead of going by herself to Windy.

Liam enclosed me in his arms, leaning his chin on my head. "I don't know if I can do this," he whispered.

I glanced at Kayleen and Windy. "We'll do it together."

He squeezed me harder. "Might be the only way."

8

EXPLORATION

Kayleen's voice—singing just outside the open tent door—woke me from dreams of chasing Windy endlessly around the perimeter, never reaching her. Golden dawn light threaded its way in through the shredded tent windows. I pushed myself up, blinking sleepily. Across from me, Liam's covers lay tumbled into an untidy lump over his empty cot.

We'd made it through the night without losing a second round of gear. Maybe we had earned enough respect for one night's peace.

I crawled outside to a warming morning with clear blue sky directly above us and out toward the north ocean. South, piles of white clouds blanketed the mountaintops.

Liam walked toward me, lugging a bucket of water he'd filled from the closest stream. He set the bucket down in front of Windy, who plunged her long nose into it and drank noisily.

Kayleen squatted near the dying fire, cooking goat's-milk pancakes and singing one of the songs we had loved as children, about a djuri baby lost in the woods, having adventures. I shook my head uncertainly at the signs of fragile domesticity on both of their parts, and walked to the stream to wash. The shallow water ran down from the mountains through a small depression, singing lightly as it tumbled over pebbles. The cold water stung my fingers.

"Come on!" Kayleen called, setting out three plates of hot pancakes, cold djuri jerky, and some dried apples from Artistos' stores. As we sat down, she asked, "Which way shall we go?"

At least she was asking and not telling. I squinted at her face. She looked relaxed and happy; no sign of the crazy Kayleen who had kidnapped us showed. She didn't stare at us—either in mistrust or with naked need written all over her.

"Not in the direction of the demon dogs." Liam took a bite of pancakes, his brow furrowed. I'd heard the dogs again during my watch last night, far off, but either the fire or the previous night's explosion had kept them away. Their calls had all come from the low hills between us and the mountain, to the southwest. Liam set his fork down. "We'll go toward the forest, where there's likely to be more game." He pointed southeast, toward the mountains still, but about forty-five degrees away from where we'd heard the dogs.

I swallowed, wanting to go in the opposite direction entirely. "Wouldn't we be better off heading toward the north shore? On our way down, it looked like there were plains, and we'd be able to see anything coming our way better."

Liam continued as if I hadn't even spoken. "We should leave as soon as possible."

I cleared my throat, demanding his attention. "I don't want to go into the hills. It's safer in the open."

Liam looked at me as if I had two heads, and it suddenly dawned on me that it wasn't about the direction of our travel at all. He expected to make the decisions.

Kayleen appeared to share my observation. She stopped midbite, her fork poised in the air. "Wherever we go, we need access to wood. We'll need wood to build a house and corral. And we shouldn't go too far. If we can't get the skimmer unstuck we'll need to carry everything."

I grinned, pleased she understood about making decisions together. "But you also need to keep Windy safe from packs of those demon dogs," I countered. "And we can see them better if we're in the open."

Liam waved a hand back in the direction he'd first proposed. "We won't go more than a half-day's walk anyway, so we can come back here at night. I don't want to leave the skimmer unattended."

I frowned at him. "There aren't any people on Islandia. The *Burning Void* should be safe enough."

"I don't know yet if there is anyplace safer for us to be."

He still wasn't getting it. "We need to make decisions together."

Liam raised an eyebrow at me. "And that means?"

"That means you sound like you're telling us what to do."

He stared out over my head, his jaw tight. I spoke softly into his stubbornness. "You *are* the most experienced of us, being raised in the roamer band. I listened to you there, because you *are* Akashi's second. But Akashi doesn't lead by giving orders unless it's an emergency. We'll generally follow you, and we'll listen in an emergency, but we all get voices in major decisions." I'd be damned if I was going to train Liam to give me orders.

Liam swallowed, then looked down at me, his dark eyes softening. "All right. We should make a list of what we need. A place to land the skimmer. A sheltered place we can protect from demon dogs. Safe food storage. We need to be near water." He looked from me to Kayleen. "What else?"

Good.

Kayleen suggested, "Shelter from weather. I don't know what kind of storms there are here."

I nodded. The band's winter shelters were all near protected cliffs and one was in a shallow cave. Nothing like the multiple rooms in the Cave of Power, but enough to huddle inside during a cold wind. We survived by living lightly. Not cowardly, just . . . sliding through the balance of the wild as best as possible. Blending with it, leaving it unchanged unless we had to fight. That's how we always won the stick-dance, too. Blending with the movement, the rhythm. We would have to do that here.

Kayleen shrugged, looking over at me apologetically. "We do need to go toward wood. We've picked most of the perimeter clean of anything that will burn, and we'll need to bring back firewood."

We'd need more than one trip's worth of wood to keep a big fire going all night. But she was right. I sighed. "Okay, Liam, we'll brave the forest."

Liam used the last of the water from the bucket he'd given Windy to douse the fire, which spouted a gush of white smoke and steam. We shouldered our packs, Kayleen grabbed Windy's lead, and the three of us set off, shortly passing the perimeters. "Wait," I said. "Should we take the perimeter with us?"

Liam stopped, a thoughtful look on his face. "We'd just have to take the devices—we could find wood or stones to mount them on." Then he shook his head. "It's a lot to carry, and it's only a warning. Besides, I'd like to have the bells go off if anything comes here, whether we're here or not."

Kayleen looked thoughtful. "We know more now. I can tune them better, at least to the dogs. Maybe I can set the warning bells to dissuade them, like the ones around town."

I looked at her doubtfully. We'd taken portable perimeters around Little Lace Lake, and they hadn't done that. But who knew what her abilities were like now? "We don't have time to tune them today," I said. "We'd better leave them, in case we get back too late to set them tonight."

"We won't," Liam said.

Kayleen raised an eyebrow.

"Besides, we brought weapons." He grinned, a smile that didn't touch his eyes. "Let's go."

We started out with Liam walking in front, Kayleen and Windy between us, and me in the rear. I kept my silence, still not entirely happy with the direction we were going.

We crunched across a long stretch of rocky surface like we'd landed the skimmer on, walking slowly, since we had to pick our way through the rough footing.

After about half an hour, we started winding upward. The ground turned to dirt and sandy loam. Without an actual path, we made a few wrong starts as we pushed through vegetation, turning back when small cliffs or rock piles stopped us. I watched Windy's ears, hoping she'd warn us of anything we didn't want to encounter. She kept them up, swiveling them around, sometimes turning her head all the way back to look at me, as if to say, "Keep me safe."

The greenery grew steadily bigger as we gained altitude. Pairs of twintrees twisted their reddish bark together, rising taller than most of our twintrees back home. Tiny green circles hid in the long, thin pointed leaves. The fruit had yet to grow the spikes that protected it from birds once it began to ripen. Near the high tops of the twintrees, red and blue and yellow birds with long beaks watched us quietly, chattering to each other after we passed.

Twintrees seemed to be the only familiar big trees. I didn't see any tent trees, or lace-leaves. Here and there, unfamiliar tall evergreens with long spikes for needles towered above us. Denser underbrush than Jini's threatened our progress regularly. Big-leaved bushes grew as tall as our heads. Long ropy ground-huggers with nasty spines tried to trip us up, and twice we stopped to pull spines from the thick fur just above Windy's hooves. One of the thorns came away with blood dripping from its wicked, clear point

Liam wandered back and forth like the lead camp dog, Ritzi, sometimes putting up a hand for silence, bending his head, and listening to the forest.

He called a rest stop when we came across a clearing. A stream meandered through it, and a large pile of tumbled stones seemed to rise up out of the ground near the middle of the open space. After we watered Windy and found a way to lead her a little way into the rocks and still have a view, Liam pulled a notebook out of his pack and started taking notes.

Kayleen leaned over to me and asked, "What's he doing?"

He sat a little distance away, bent over the notebook in his lap, scratching furiously with his pencil, looking up from time to time and surveying the clearing. He'd taken time to catch his hair back in a braid this morning, and it fell down his back like a golden-white rope, gleaming in the midmorning sunshine. In spite of my frustrations, I smiled at the content, intense look on his face. "He's recording things he's noticed. Being a roamer is in his blood." I gave her my best evil grin. "Science will solve everything."

"Does that mean he feels better?" she asked.

I pulled out my water bottle and took a long, slow drink. "Better about what?"

"About . . . about being away from home."

"Being kidnapped?" I asked, keeping my voice neutral, trying for statement of fact rather than an accusation. "Probably not."

"Look at me," Kayleen said.

I did. She sat a meter away from me, long legs and long feet tucked under her, her dark hair loose and falling wildly around her shoulders. Her bright blue eyes contrasted with the yellow shirt she wore. Her mouth pursed, tight. Windy's lead rope lay loosely in her hands, and the hebra, below her, nibbled at blades of grass between the rocks.

Kayleen blinked, watching Windy. She kept her silence for a long moment before she said, "I'm sorry, Chelo. I'm sorry I had to kidnap you, sorry you wish you were home."

She spoke softly enough that Liam probably couldn't hear her, although I wasn't sure. He didn't look at us or give us any sign, just kept jotting notes.

Kayleen looked over at me and continued. "I'd do it again, because . . . because I had to. I've explained that. I had to leave, and I need you two. I really do. But I'm still sorry I had to." She glanced over at Liam. "Will he ever forgive me?"

Before I could answer, he closed the notebook and stood up. "Let's go," he said. "We've only got a few hours before we have to turn around if we don't find anything."

Kayleen looked at me, pleading for an answer, and I spread my hands, indicating I didn't know what he would decide. She hesitated, then asked very softly, "Do *you* forgive me?"

In answer, I reached a hand out to help steady her, squeezing her hand softly. She squeezed back, then dropped my hand and jumped lightly down next to Windy. It was the best I could do—I couldn't really say yes, but I could show her I had come to understand. At least partly.

She stayed silent for the next hour as we threaded slowly up to a ridge that offered a good view. Down to our right, sunlight glinted off the *Burning Void*'s silver hull. South, trees obscured a clear view of Islandia's Teeth, but to the north the ocean made a thin blue-green line on the horizon. From here, it was even possible to see the white steam clouds where the Fire River dumped its molten rock into the ocean. Down the opposite side, another valley had a single wide river running through it, and here and there, puffs of smoke hung above the trees on the way down. "What are those?" I asked.

Liam squinted at the smoke. "I'm not sure. Near Rage Mountain, we found a lot of places with warm water, and a few places where warm water came up to intersect cold water, and those spots steamed. Maybe it's the same here."

"Can we go look?" Kayleen asked.

I glanced up at the sun, which was almost directly above our heads, then looked back down at the peaceful valley. There was water and wood, and *warm* water would be a treasure. Especially if we wintered here. I swallowed. But surely we wouldn't. The valley opened up wider at the far end. "I'll bet we can make a big circle instead of backtracking, and then we might have time."

Liam seemed to follow my logic. "I think we can. But more importantly, why haven't we seen anything bigger than birds?"

I looked around, realizing that it was a good question. "Maybe we're scaring them off?"

He frowned. "Maybe. There must be prey—we've met at least one predator."

I nodded. "Maybe we'll see something in the valley."

His lips thinned. "I just hope we can handle whatever we see. Let's move." He struck out along the gentle downward slope that made up the ridge's spine. Twice, he led us around piles of boulders stacked at the ridge's center, and once we had to avoid a tangle of downed trees.

Finally, Liam angled downward, threading his way through tree trunks that appeared to lean into the ground against the steep sides of the hill. The footing was soft forest loam, dried spiky needles, and here and there, the bones of large leaves. Our feet slid down a half-meter for each step, and it felt like we fell down the steep mountain as much as walked. We emerged from the trees about halfway down the valley's length. The sun shone into our eyes, part way through its downward curve. Liam held out his arms, signaling us to stop. "Shhhh," he said. "There's almost no wind. I want to watch the valley floor for a few minutes."

"We don't have time," I whispered.

"Stopping and really seeing may save our lives." He fell silent, watching. Windy nuzzled Kayleen. I stood alone, watching like Liam, trying to see what he saw, to look through the eyes of a born roamer.

A carpet of low light green spring grass covered the valley. Here and there, animal trails were visible. Small bushes and trees hugged the riverbank, about twenty meters from us. Forest rose up behind us and opposite us, on the far end of the valley. A slight wind had come up, singing through the tops of the evergreens. Between the river's trees and the forest, almost nothing except sunshine and low grass and the occasional rock. One plume of the whitish steam we'd spotted from atop the ridge rose up a few hundred meters downriver from where we stood.

Next to me, Liam and Windy went completely still. Liam pointed. I followed his gaze to spot movement on the far side of the river. Big animals, gathered together. I squinted, trying for details. They looked a little like hebras, but with much longer legs and slightly shorter bodies. They had longer necks, more than half as tall as their legs, and they were solid colors rather than the various stripes and spots of hebra coloring. I made out two duns, a black, a golden, and a deep chestnut color. They walked with a slightly lurching gait, but something about their movement convinced me they could run.

"Can we get closer to them?" I whispered, no longer caring about how we spent time.

Liam furrowed his brow and looked at each of us, his gaze lingering longest on Windy. She would draw attention for sure. "You go," he said. "Go quickly and come right back. And be careful—prey animals that big imply predators that big."

No kidding. Big or in packs. Everything here seemed bigger than life. "I don't want to see paw-cats twice my size. The ones at home are plenty big enough, thank you very much." I took a deep breath, pleased that he trusted me to go, and suddenly nervous. "Are you sure we should separate?"

His eyes showed uncertainty, but he put a hand on my shoulder and squeezed gently. "It's midafternoon. Demon dogs hunt dusk to dawn, at least at home. So do most predators. Just don't cross the river. Don't go where I can't see you. Get a better look and come back quickly. I'll keep Kayleen and Windy safe."

I nodded and left, crouching low and moving slowly and as evenly as I could, trying to appear like a normal part of the field. The grass only came to my ankles, providing no cover. At least there was no cover for anything else either. Lizards and small mammals scurried out of my path every few steps, but nothing large appeared to be in the valley except the herd across the river.

I slowed down even more, conscious of passing time but not wanting to spook the beasts until I got closer. I neared the trees by the river, rising up to a full stand once I reached their meager cover. The air remained still. The river ran about seven meters across near me, but quickly darkening and running deeper. Here and there, tiny fish flashed near the surface. The trees closest to the edge had thrown long ropy roots into the water. Thin green grasses grew from the roots and floated in the current. Trees across from me obscured my view, so I edged north, trying to find the herd.

A clear spot rewarded me with a great view. The animals had neared the river, perhaps to drink. They were much taller than hebras. Now that they were near the trees, it was clear they could browse the treetops if they wished, and they wouldn't have to reach very far to do it. I held my breath, watching the apparent herd leader, a great golden animal, come down the break in the trees to stand on the far riverbank, head up, nostrils extended. Its body was sleek, the fur shorter than a hebra's and its feet more like a bird's, except wider and sturdier. At least, instead of cloven hooves, I saw three thick toes on the ground for each foot. Halfway between their toes and their knees, sharp claws stuck out to the side on each front leg.

I breathed out slowly, completely entranced by the animal. It was beautiful, majestic. Big enough for its size alone to demand respect; the top of my head might not reach its chest. I swallowed, holding my breath, doing my best to blend into the trees.

Three other animals, a dun, the black, and a deep chestnut, bunched at the top of the path, watching the golden leader, waiting. Its gaze swept around, and for just a moment, its dark eyes landed on me. Curiosity flashed in them, and then fear.

I nearly jumped out of my skin as the golden animal let out a high scream, and the herd wheeled and ran, the leader following. They bounced up and down as they ran, looking awkward, but they *were* as fast as they were tall. I soon lost sight of them, my view obscured by the trees. They were more beautiful than anything I'd seen on Jini, and it took me long moments to tear my eyes from the place they had been.

The riverbanks were muddy and well-tracked. The tall beasts had captivated me so much I hadn't even noticed. Liam would have noticed the tracks earlier.

I bent down, studying. Small tracks, birds and mammals. I crept back south along the river toward where I'd entered the trees. In one spot, a half-meter path boasted bigger tracks, with four toes and a big pad.

Canine or feline? I set my hand down—confirming what my eyes told me. The tracks were nearly as wide as my palm. Reflexively, my hand returned to my side and pulled the small laser gun from my pocket. It was the only thing I carried, not enough against anything big.

The large tracks went down to the river and disappeared, not returning. So something that could swim? On Jini, paw-cats didn't swim, although they did cross rivers and streams at fords low enough for them to walk across.

I glanced again at the sun, wishing Liam were here to look with me. I could just go get them. But we had to start back soon. I jogged up the river further, watching my footing, stepping carefully over roots and stones. I passed where my own tracks ended and kept going, more slowly, breathing hard.

Something splashed in the water near me.

I turned my head toward the sound. Ripples spread out from a point. I watched for a moment, but nothing else happened.

"Chelo!" Kayleen's scream split the air, off to my left, behind me. I turned and ran toward the sound, clearing the trees in moments. I stopped, looking around. What trouble were they in? My breath and heartbeat pounded in my ears. I couldn't see them. Liam's voice, demanding. "To your right!"

I twisted my head right. How had I missed it? A cat. Not a paw-cat—longer and shorter both—crouching ten meters away and looking at me. It would be fast, but the moment I looked at it, it froze. Golden, like the herd leader, with black feet and ears and a black tip to its tail, which twitched. Back and forth. Back and forth.

It did not seem to know what to make of me, but surely if it chose to, it could catch me. Neither claws nor teeth showed, but they must be there.

The little laser gun felt cold and hard in my right hand. The lasers didn't kill fast—the most it would probably do was scare it. I could jump and yell, and try to scare it that way. I could ignore it and walk slowly away, a tactic proven occasionally successful against a single paw-cat if it was already well fed. But I had no idea if this animal was by itself, or if it would act like a paw-cat. I didn't dare break my gaze away to look, because then it would decide, and perhaps run for me. Not many of its steps separated us.

There was still no wind; it couldn't smell my fear.

It decided, lunging at me. Claws and a mouth and long teeth.

I jerked my hand up, firing the laser at its face. Every pore of my being wanted to run, but I stood. The cat twisted its face away and the bright color of the laser gun slid down its face to the side. It screamed, an angry, wounded scream, but ducked its head and kept coming.

Three meters. The cat was as long as I was tall. It crouched. Too far, I thought.

Then it leaped and I kept the gun on it, ducking at the last second. Not too far.

Claws raked my scalp. I screamed at the hot sharp pain.

Far off, Liam and Kayleen both yelled my name. The cat rolled over me. Past me. I lifted my head, blood dripping down my face, obscuring the vision in one eye.

It gathered itself and ran. Away. The black tip of its tail bobbed unevenly. It stumbled.

Heart in my throat, adrenaline pounding, I raced behind, aiming the laser at its back, at the great squared head as it turned to look at me. It stood unsteady, then leaped, running again, unevenly. Still fast. I raced after it, breath sharp and hard, feet digging into the low grass.

It stopped. Stood. Swayed. A small cry escaped its lips, almost a whimper. Close enough now, I saw blood pouring from one eye. I raised the gun again, aiming at its face. The light played across its other eye and it mewled again and dropped.

Liam called, "Chelo!" Fear edged his voice. Close, so close. I sank to my knees, watching the cat. Liam stopped a few meters away and approached carefully. It lay stretched out, one leg at an odd angle, its golden, bloody face marked with dark scars where the laser had burned fur, and in a few cases, raw flesh. Its tail still twitched and its sides heaved.

Carefully watching the dying animal, Liam stepped slowly to my side. "Are you okay?" he whispered, touching my cheek.

My breath was still fast and my hands shook. "I . . . I think so. Thanks for the warning." I reached up to sweep the blood from my forehead with my free hand. My palm fell back coated in red, blood dripping from my fingers into the green grass. "I don't—don't look so good, do I?"

He shook his head, looking around, his eyes narrowed.

"Are there more of them?"

"I don't see any more." He grimaced. "You were right. I should never have separated us." He stepped in toward the dying cat, pulling his knife out.

I held out my hand. "Let me."

He stopped, then grinned. "Sure." He held out the knife. "Be careful—it's not dead yet."

"It will be." The knife felt heavy and solid in my hand. The cat struggled, pushing up feebly with its front legs, and I grabbed it under the chin and cut its throat with the knife. Blood gushed out over the blade, warm on my hand, and pooled red in the grass. My own blood dripped from my forehead and mixed with the dead cat's blood.

As I let go of the great head, slick fur slid through my fingers until the head lolled back, staring from empty eyes. I stayed straddled over the carcass, staring down at the dead cat. Its jaws could have severed my throat or backbone. I put a hand up to my savaged head, feeling the deepest rent, smiling a bit at the idea I'd won. I'd brought down djuri with my bare hands, but I'd never directly taken on any kind of predator. My smile broadened.

Liam came up next to me, his words echoing my thoughts. "It could have killed you."

I wiped his blade clean on the grass and handed it back to him. I stepped away from the carcass, standing unsteadily, wiping another handful of blood from my scalp. "Can you look at my head?"

He shook himself. "Of course." He stepped to my side, still looking around. "Kayleen!" he called, loudly. "Come here."

I glanced across the valley toward where she and Windy must be waiting in the trees. I couldn't see them.

Windy bolted from the tree cover, running free. She angled away from us, toward the narrow end of the valley closest to the mountains.

WINDY

As soon as I saw Windy burst from cover, I screamed Kayleen's name. She would never have let the hebra free like that. Liam took my hand and we raced toward the spot Windy had bolted from. My head swam, but fear gave me enough strength to hold onto him, to keep my footing as he pulled me along.

Liam slowed down ten meters from the forest, putting a hand up to warn me not to race directly into possible danger. He called her name. "Kayleen?"

Silence.

Still no movement.

He held his knife in one hand and pulled the laser gun out of his pocket with the other. When he glanced at me, his eyes were wide and frightened.

Bushes rustled. "Kayleen—are you there?" I asked.

Her voice came from up above us, quivering and soft. "I'm here."

I looked up, scanning the trees for her, my knees suddenly weak with relief. She was alive.

"Are you okay?" Liam asked. "What happened?"

Her voice tumbled through the leaves, and a single twintree branch quivered hard, as if she were shaking it to tell us where she was. "I heard something up above us, coming down, following our tracks. Windy spooked and pulled me off my feet and I lost her lead and she ran. I heard whatever it was keep coming. So I climbed up here." I looked up, unable to spot her, watching for the twitch of branches.

Two pair of twintrees shared the light with a few evergreens and two taller trees with broad trunks and wide yellow-green leaves.

"Is it still there?" Liam asked.

"No." A pause. "I don't think so. I threw branches at it, and I used the disruptor button. It headed back up the hill. A big thing, as big as the dogs, I'm sure." Another pause. "But I think there was just one."

"Can you climb down and come out here?" Liam asked levelly.

Tree limbs rustled against each other. Kayleen's feet thumped into the soft ground and she exhaled loudly. "I'm coming." She emerged, sap staining her clothes and two large scratches across her face. One hand bled. She ran into my arms, holding me tightly.

In that moment, I forgave her everything.

Liam stepped close to us, laying a hand gingerly on each of us, his brow furrowed with worry.

"Did you see where Windy went? Is she okay?" Kayleen pushed gently from us and looked around. We did the same. There was no sign of the panicked hebra.

"We saw her run off." Liam pointed in the general direction of Windy's escape. "I have no idea where she went. We were running toward you." He put a hand on Kayleen's shoulder and looked at her quizzically. "We'll look after I know how you and Chelo are." He looked back at Kayleen's bloody face and hands. "Are you sure you're okay?"

Kayleen squinted at my face. "Better than Chelo," she said. "What happened to you? The last I saw, that cat had almost landed on you. Are *you* okay?"

"I . . . I don't know. We didn't take time to look. It scared us when Windy ran out and you weren't with her."

Kayleen stepped over and reached a hand up toward my head. "Bend down. Let me see. People came to Paloma a lot with injuries. I helped her."

I took a deep breath, steadying myself. My footing felt strange and the valley wanted to whirl around me.

"There's no color in your face except the blood," Kayleen said. "Sit down before you fall down." Then to Liam, "Get my pack. I brought medical supplies."

I knelt rather than sat, wanting to be able to get to my feet easily.

Liam disappeared and reappeared quickly, all three of our packs in his right hand. He set them down and stood a bit away, still keeping watch.

Kayleen pulled a shirt out of her pack, doused it with water from her water bottle, and carefully wiped the blood away from the top of my head. "Does that hurt?"

I grit my teeth. "Not much. What do you see?"

"It scratched you. Not very deep, except one place I can see bone. Scalp wounds bleed a lot—it's probably not as bad as it looks."

She folded the bloody shirt up and set it across my head. "Here, hold that down. Stop the bleeding."

I clamped the damp rag to my head while Liam quickly helped Kayleen wash her own wounds. He pulled two big spiky evergreen needles from her palm. They came out slowly, Kayleen's face screwed up in pain as the long needles inched outward. "They have barbs on them," she grunted through clenched teeth. "Try not to leave anything behind." Lastly, at Kayleen's direction, he pulled out a container of Paloma's all-purpose antibiotic salve and applied it liberally to Kayleen's hand and face.

As soon as he was finished he looked over at me. "Should I put some on your head?"

Kayleen plucked the jar from his hands. "Not yet. I want her to keep the pressure on for a little more, and then I think we need to dig up the medi-tape to close the worst cut."

"What?" I made a face at her. "Did you bring a whole apothecary with you?"

She laughed. "I'm my mother's daughter." Pain flashed across her face. "In some ways." She squinted down at me. "You're probably going to have a little bit of a scar down your right temple." Then she turned her gaze outward, in the direction Windy had gone.

"Will she come if you call her?" I asked.

Kayleen chewed her lower lip. "She might. If she can hear me." Her voice trembled. "If she's okay."

Liam frowned, glancing toward the carcass of the cat. "Let's go out to the middle of the field. Halfway to the cat—she won't come near that easily. But I don't want to draw attention here, where there's cover for whatever scared you."

We picked up our packs and headed wearily away from the forest. Thirty paces out, Liam turned and looked back. He kept going, another twenty paces or so, and then stopped for a few moments and watched. We saw little movement—none of the big beautiful grazers, no scary golden cats except the dead one, nothing unknown and clawed leaping from the forest. Three birds wheeled above the cat carcass, but apparently we were too close for them to land and investigate.

"Okay," Liam said. "Call her."

"Windy! Windy!" Kayleen's voice belled out across the field, loud and clear. She shaded her eyes from the late-afternoon sun, watching the field.

I turned to Liam. "We'll never get back before dark, now."

He looked down at me, his face gentle but his eyes far away, lost in thought. "I know. I think we should stay out here in the open." He looked up at the sky. "There's already one moon. I expect two more. If it stays clear, we'll be able to see well enough, and there's plenty of wood."

I eyed the forest. "Probably."

He glanced over at Kayleen, his brows furrowed. "I hope we find that darned hebra soon. I hope she comes by herself."

We didn't, and she didn't.

After about ten minutes, Kayleen gave up calling and turned to us, her eyes pleading. "We need to go find her. She doesn't know anything about dangerous animals."

Liam pointed up at the sun, canted way too close to the horizon. "We'll have to camp here. We have to get set first. Then we can look."

Tears sprang to Kayleen's eyes, but neither she nor I argued. We gathered wood from near the riverbank, making three trips. Then, while Liam stacked the wood, I knelt on the grass while Kayleen painted my scalp with Paloma's salve and glued together the worst bits with medi-tape, muttering. "I think you should just shave your head until this heals. But I don't have anything to do it with."

"That's good."

"You really are lucky. I hope Windy comes back. I was so mad at myself when she pulled away." Proudly: "She is getting bigger. She's much stronger. A few weeks ago she wouldn't have been able to pull free. I hope we do get moons tonight. You're going to look like quite a sight. We should call you the-woman-who-tangles-with-cats. You still have scars from the last paw-cat, the one that killed Jinks. You're going to look as bad as Jenna if you keep this up."

She sounded so much like herself, I just let her go on, not interrupting her monologue. Maybe now we had the Kayleen we were first worried about, the one who couldn't focus well enough to survive in the wild, but wasn't crazy either.

I let her ramble the whole time she finished working on me, not even listening to the words she said after a while, but just to the rise and fall of her voice.

Liam dug a shallow pit to protect the grass, lining the edges with rocks. He stacked some of the wood inside the pit, and the rest in two small, neat piles. Then he dragged the cat carcass over, sat down on a thick log, and pulled out his notebook. "What should we call it?"

"Do we have to do that now?" Kayleen asked. "I want to go find Windy." The luminous rays of the sun's last full stand in the sky poured down on her face, painting her dark hair with reddish highlights.

I wanted to find Windy, too. "Let's all go. Just a little ways—we need to be back before dark. But I don't want to be separated."

Liam sighed. "No, that didn't work out too well." He stood up, looking down at the cat. "I don't want to go far enough for this to draw scavengers. It's *our* dinner." He glanced back up at the sky. "I need to record this, and skin it, too. Why don't you two walk up the middle of the valley, just a little ways, and call her again? We can look in earnest tomorrow if she doesn't come back."

Kayleen sighed. "Come on, Chelo. I can't stand the idea of Windy spending the night alone."

"Liam, please? I don't want to be separated," I repeated.

"All right. But not far."

The trip was in vain. We didn't see or hear Windy, or much of anything else before the tips of the western hills made inroads into the sun's disk, and the forest shadows reached across the field for us. As the light failed, it sucked the heat from the air. The three of us walked back closely, Kayleen and I arm in arm, Liam on my other side. "She'll be okay," I whispered.

Kayleen's voice sounded small. "She has to be."

I held her closer, not knowing what else to do.

Back at camp, Liam lit the fire, and the three of us stood around it for a moment, warming our hands. "Did anyone bring a pan?" he asked. He'd warned us about not carrying too much, and been completely sure we'd get back. Surely, he didn't have one. Me either. Kayleen smiled a secretive little smile. "Of course I did. I have a pan, and an extra knife."

And we were the roamers.

Liam and I looked at each other balefully as Kayleen rummaged in the bottom of her pack and produced a pan, a cup, a full set of silverware, and a long metal knife. She looked up at me and grinned. "We might have to eat one by one."

I laughed. "That's fine." I took the knife from her and turned to help Liam skin the cat. He shook his head, returned to his stone and pulled his notebook back out, settling in immediately with a focused look on his face to draw an outline of the beast. I smiled at the way the firelight played along his face even though some daylight remained. "I think we should just call it a golden cat," I said. "It's rather pretty."

He raised an eyebrow. "It's probably not directly related to a paw-cat." He pointed to its nearly ruined face. "Its head is shaped completely different, and it has shorter teeth. Shorter claws, too. The body style is much lower, and the tail longer."

"So is 'golden cat' okay?"

"Sure. Your kill. You can have naming rights."

I liked that idea. I hadn't named anything on Fremont, and Liam had named three new species of birds just in the last year.

As I turned back to the fire, Kayleen screamed, "Windy!" and raced past me, toward the river. I squinted and made out Windy's head poking through the brush, and then her body, a silhouette with a tall shadow. We had decided to camp away from any cover, but the river was close enough that I heard Windy's high welcoming bugle as she trotted out to meet her person.

Kayleen slowed, walking carefully up to the hebra. I smiled as she and Kayleen touched noses. Kayleen picked up Windy's lead, which somehow hadn't gotten her tangled in anything, and the two of them walked back, heads together, like two old women friends.

I turned back to Liam. "Perhaps this will all work out, after all."

He grunted. "Right, and the sun will rise twice tomorrow." But I caught a small smile playing across his lips as the last of the daylight faded. I looked up. It was a three-moon night, a good-luck night, clear and cool. A small shower of meteors streaked across the sky from right to left. Even though I wore the scars of my day on my lightly throbbing head, hope touched my heart as I looked up to find Destiny, Faith, and Dreamcatcher all visible in the night sky.

We'd need the luck to survive the night in the open with no perimeter.

10

A TEMPORARY HOME

I took first watch, sitting with the fire at my back. Kayleen lay close to me, curled in a ball with her head on her pack and one hand clutching Windy's lead. Liam stretched out on my other side, periodically moving restlessly.

Grass rustled in front of me.

Something large, given away by the silence that surrounded it. My laser was in my left hand, and I curled my right hand around a rock nearly the size of my fist.

The grass rustled again, about five meters in front of me, a shivering in the moonlight. Windy's head went up and Kayleen pushed herself to a seated position, watching me. She, too, seemed to hear whatever was out there. As she turned toward it, I burst into a stand and threw the rock. Something large raced away. Just one, so more likely a cat than dogs, or something new.

Kayleen gave me a thumbs up, and stayed seated. She held up a rock in her fist, the firelight glinting on a vein of something bright and metallic in the rock. I gestured her toward me, and she came and sat near by, pulling Windy as close to the fire as the hebra was willing to come.

We sat in silence, listening carefully to the night noises of the valley: the rustle of small birds gathered in the trees near the river, the screech of big hunting birds over the grasses, the skitter of small mammal feet, and, twice, high nervous calls that may have been the normal sounds of the beautiful, big animals I'd seen in the valley.

The sky clouded over, and before it was time to wake Liam great drops of rain splattered and hissed on the fire.

Dawn found all of us awake, dripping wet, standing together near a firepit soaked in rainwater. The sky had cleared again, and mist rose from the damp grass as the heat of the day kissed it awake. I rubbed at tired, stinging eyes and said, "I guess the three-moon promise was luck if you count not being eaten."

Liam grunted. "Every day of being alive here is luck." He handed out meat we'd cooked the night before. "We might as well find out more about this valley before we head back to the skimmer." He pointed down toward the sea, a blue line an hour's walk or so away, with nothing but grass, river, and rocks between us and it. "There's probably no shelter that way. We'd best go up-valley and see if we get lucky and find a cave or something."

We shouldered our wet packs and chose a faint animal path near the tree-lined river and followed that up, watching for a good ford. Liam and I stopped regularly and recorded information about the various tracks we saw, while Kayleen stuck close to Windy and kept watch.

We rounded a long slow corner of the path by a bend in the river, coming upon a gush of white steam-clouds pouring up from a crevice between two rocks. The sour-egg sulphur smell became so strong as we neared the steam that I started breathing through my mouth, which was only slightly better. It left an aftertaste. As we neared the steam, heat turned our faces red, and Windy pranced and threw her head up and down. We stopped a few meters from the source, unwilling to get closer. "What is that?" I asked.

Liam looked at it. "Akashi told me it probably means there's magma—hot, liquid rock like the fire river, down there. And water. The molten rock and water fight—hence the steam."

I looked down at my feet, shifting uneasily. The rock I stood on felt firm, but how far down was the hot rock? I'd seen the Fire River, at least from the air. Could I slip and fall into a fire stream?

Liam caught my look and elaborated. "This whole continent was made from active volcanoes. I guess they both were, but Islandia is geologically younger. We've found hot springs—warm water pools—and steam vents like this all along one of Rage's flanks." He eyed the hole in the rocks, his lower lip twitching. "Akashi worries about them and doesn't let us camp near them, although I've never seen any noticeable changes, and we haven't recorded any as far as I know."

Kayleen asked, "What does Akashi mean by 'near?' "

We'd noticed a few of these from the top of the ridge, so the valley must be pockmarked with them. "We won't be able to stay far away if we decide to live here," I said.

"There might not be anyplace here that doesn't have any," Liam mused.

The idea of standing on something like the Fire River made me nervous. "We don't have to camp right by one."

Liam laughed. "We won't."

We worked our way around the hole in the ground and kept going north.

Near the head of the valley, the ground became rockier. The river narrowed and deepened, rushing through a shallow gorge. The trees clustering around the river towered over our heads. The brush grew longer thorns, so we had to pick our way more slowly.

"Should we turn back yet?" I asked.

Liam, just ahead of me, stopped and turned around. "No. Hear that?"

I listened. A low rush of sound spilled from the trees above and in front of us. "Waterfall," I said.

Liam grinned. "I bet that's worth seeing."

The sound called me, too, and I picked up speed. We clambered up a slender trail between several large boulders, Liam ahead, then Kayleen and Windy, then me. The waterfall filled the air with sound, so I lost track of the tap of Windy's feet and even my own breathing. The air felt damp, and tiny sun-sparkled water droplets gathered on the ends of my hair. At the top of the biggest boulder, Liam turned and grinned. We scrambled up, all four of us standing on a slightly damp, slightly slippery, but thankfully flattish gray rock. Ahead and above us, the river thundered off the top of a cliff and fell a hundred meters in a long, slightly curved arc to land in a pool of water at our feet. Across from us, the same herd of tall herbivores I'd seen the day before grazed in a clearing.

I breathed out slowly, soaking in the beauty of the waterfall and the beasts. Vines covered with red flowers plunged down the cliff opposite us, like a second fall of flowers rather than water. The lush green of early spring growth screamed from every corner. It was a pocket valley of its own, a few hundred meters long and almost as wide.

Liam looked at Kayleen, his eyes sparkling. He pointed at the wide clearing the herd grazed in. "They think it's relatively safe."

Kayleen's face shone. "Then perhaps we've found a home."

Liam looked down at her, his lips pursed. "A temporary home. You're taking us back. In time for the roamers' fall visit to town."

She blinked up at him. "If we get the skimmer free."

"When we get the skimmer free." He looked back at the waterfall and the secret little valley, his eyes, too, alight. "It sure is beautiful."

Maybe this was what the three moons had promised us. But I still shivered inside, remembering the golden cat, the demon dogs, the sleepless night in the rain. The three of us were small and fragile compared to those, or even to the powerful waterfall in front of us.

PART TWO

JOSEPH GOES HOME

11

THE DEAD, WAKING

Metallic air seared my nostrils. Pain, bringing me back from someplace very far away, someplace past memory. I tried to say my name—Joseph—but my mouth wouldn't move. I couldn't even feel it, much less control it. I felt my right little toe. Just my right little toe, tingling. I reached out with it, struggling to touch something. It moved, but found only empty space. My heel touched the hard bed below me. Dampness filled my toe, the top of my foot, my ankle, a slow pulsing wave of blessed water anointing me with life from inside. I gasped. My chest jerked involuntarily.

I was . . . this was . . . the *New Making*. My reawakening.

Water crept into my fingers and the pads of my palms, filling them. Dry eyes and nose and mouth told me how much freezing had parched my cells. Grit glued my eyelids shut. I struggled to open them and failed.

Memories returned. I'd tricked Jenna before I slept, dipping into the ship's systems, changing when the *New Making*'s med-bots would wake me. I should have three days alone.

There were things I needed to know. My parents had been on this ship; traces of them lived in its databanks. But Jenna had refused all my questions, driving us through getting the ship in order after we took off, and then insisting on cold sleep. I couldn't risk having no time before we landed.

I gave up on my eyelids after one more struggle and settled for moving both of my index fingers.

Had I been caught? Was Jenna awake? If so, was she angry?

I sensed the deep thrum of ship's data just outside my skin, hovering separate from my consciousness. I felt so dry. If I had enough water, would data surge inside my skin and fill me?

Chelo would disapprove of me tricking Jenna. I could see Chelo's face now, her dark hair pulled back tightly so her dark eyes looked bigger than normal, glaring at me, her stare a combination of anger and big-sister concern. Chelo's lips would be tight against each other, and she'd have one hand on her hip. And yet there'd be a smile trying to get out. Knowing how Chelo would hate it, tricking Jenna didn't feel good.

But Chelo wasn't here. I closed away the missing part of me she represented. She'd made her choice. I understood, but understanding and accepting weren't the same.

I wiped my eyes, clearing away junk, ripping eyelashes, blinking at the small, spare room. A groan escaped me as I reached my right arm out, grabbing my pilot's coat from the chair nearby, draping it across my chest. What I needed, direct contact. My fingers found a strip of threaded conductor. Finally, data filled my blood, as good as water. Better. Data raced through my being, spoke to my heart.

Something scraped on the floor near me; adrenaline surged. I turned my head. Leo. My pet maintenance bot, adopted at Jenna's insistence to keep me safe on the ship. Waiting where I'd told it to, ripping a small smile from my cracked lips.

My eyes slid closed again. I descended into the shipsong, riding it, building it back into my body. Bots reporting. Mostly well: enough well. A miracle, given we had no human roboticist. Food enough in the tiny garden, freezers still working, air breathable everywhere. Engines clean and silent, still running fast: three weeks from landing on Silver's Home.

Where was Jenna?

Asleep in her frozen bed. Maybe far away, like I had been.

I experimented with a long stretch. My toes touched cool metal, my back arched into the stretch, my torso rose. Everything slow, a half-beat behind the time I thought the commands to move.

Alicia. Sweet, dark, dangerous Alicia. I licked my lips. Her frozen signature showed proper, complete stasis. I imagined Alicia's dark eyelashes framing her violet eyes. Maybe I should wake her? I wanted her with me, but it was doubtful that I could control her. Best not wake her yet; Jenna would already be mad.

The vast emptiness of the ship surrounded me, and I sent my senses into the lullaby of the shipsong, the test:report, test:report, test:report of sliding successfully through space.

Some time later I blinked easily and felt normal, except for a driving urge to stretch every muscle in my body at once. I did my best to manage the feat, ending up seated cross-legged with my coat across my lap.

Thirst drove me to the tiny sink in the corner. I downed three glasses of water, shaking fingers splashing it onto my shirt. Each glass made me feel freshly alive, more able to move. Water like oil for my joints.

I let the data flows fall to a soft cadence, something I would hear only when trouble or change happened. Jenna had taught me that trick in the three months we spent awake, alone. She was as deaf to data as Chelo, but also like Chelo, she knew how to get me started, how to steady me. Jenna also knew what tools to provide. She encouraged me to learn the ship's computer, which she called Starteller, even though she told me it wasn't a true autonomous intelligence. But she talked to it all the time through her voice and her fingers, or with a far tinier and more elegant earset than the simple ones used by Fremont's colonists.

I spoke to it in gulps, in ideas, in floods of information.

Starteller was smarter than anything on Fremont. Heck, the ship's galley was smarter than anything on Fremont. I laughed, my lips cracking. Maybe smarter than *anyone*. What a strange waking thought.

I rested, checking on the other three again: not breathing, maybe not being. Leo sat next to me as if it were a dog instead of a robot. In fact, Leo was the same size as some of the roamers' smaller dogs, except round and silver with six spidery legs. From time to time I reached a hand out and ran it over Leo's slick surface. It felt like oil more than metal, except hard. I told it, "Good Leo. I'm glad you're here." It had no visible ears, but it heard me.

Leo read data much like me, pulling it from the air, and so it followed my silent commands and knew to step aside when a person or another robot moved in its path, as if it were omniscient. But really,

Leo was fairly stupid, with a small set of a few thousand commands it could perform on its own in response to its original job as a simple maintenance and patrol bot.

I was glad for its company, even if it was stupid.

Even though a map of the *New Making* lived inside me, I asked Leo to lead the way to my parents' quarters. With six appendages, it walked upright along the corridors on four, using two to balance on the handholds. When it got ahead of me, it stopped and waited for me. It never chided; like all robots it simply waited, emotionless. Nevertheless, I took each stop as encouragement to move faster.

My body grew less clumsy the more I made it move. It felt different on the ship than at home—lighter—but Jenna maintained what she called "living gravity" everywhere except in the ship's nose, so I climbed easily up or down levels, and walked through horizontal corridors.

In my head, *New Making* lived like ten buildings stacked on top of each other. The bottom two were engines and workrooms, the next one a storage hold full both of things to colonize Fremont but never used, and of the scientific fruit of Fremont, gathered mostly before the war. Rocks, minerals, seeds, and some of the glass, weavings, and jewelry made on long winter nights in town. Things my people had brought, things my people had made; I had ties to both people, to both sides of the war I am too young to remember.

Above the hold, the garden level also had room for labs and experiments and a ship's hospital half as big as ours back in Artistos—three rooms and a storeroom. Just above, in the level of the frozen, Jenna and Alicia and Bryan waited.

The first level of crew's quarters sat above the frozen. After that, the common level, which included the Command Room, then another set of crew's quarters, and everything above served as labs and storage, except the very nose of the ship, which was weightless and could become an escape pod.

I commanded Leo to take me to the higher of the two crew quarter levels. It led me up to the doorway to the living quarters, then slid through, stopping just beyond so that I could still see one long arm trailing in the open door, as if it were saying, "I'm waiting for you."

Red and green and yellow pipes and dark blue handholds covered the walls, a chaos of physical plant designed to support the fifty people who could live here. *New Making* could support up to two hundred people, fifty on each living level, as long as half were always frozen.

I pushed past Leo and went through a door on the right, following directions gleaned from Starteller's records. Each set of rooms could serve twelve or thirteen people. Shared bathrooms and galley space clustered near the ship's center. The outer walls were lined with rooms big enough for one or two, for sleeping and storing personal effects.

The common seating between the galleys and the sleeping spaces stood empty. Chairs clustered as if waiting for conversations. I passed through them to the sleeping rooms. My parents had shared the one at the end.

Their bed filled the wall opposite me. A gold coverlet embellished with a planet and seven moons had been laid neatly across it. A picture of Fremont. Had my mother made it to display her dreams of her new home?

Closed cupboards lined one wall, tempting me. But first, I lay across the bed. Inhaling deeply, I struggled to find some human smell, something left of their energies. But the room did not smell of people, just of the sterile ship's air touched with garden smells, metals, and oils.

I swung my feet from the bed and reached for the cupboard and pulled open the doors. There were four squared shelves. The bottom two held clothes. I left them for now, looking in the others. The top two were smaller. The left one must have belonged to my mother. A metal necklace of bright silver set with shimmering beads lay next to matching earrings, delicate and simple, pinned to a soft deep blue cloth. Beside them lay a tray with a mirror, a hairbrush, and a blue painted box strapped to it.

I carefully loosed and lifted out the box and opened its lid to find it stuffed full of papers and pens. I took out the papers. Drawings. Drawings of people, and of plants. Some people in her drawings had obvious genemods—a woman with wings, an over-muscled strongman, a man with four arms. I found one drawing from Fremont, a picture of a hebra, quite well done, with the long neck and beard, the head swiveled as it looked behind itself.

Half the drawings were delicately rendered pictures of a handsome man with long dark hair, blue eyes, and a broad smile. He looked as normal as I did, with no obvious mods. The hand that rendered the portraits had been tender, showing intimate moments such as the man looking up at the stars or sitting on a couch, relaxed, watching the artist.

Surely this was my father. Who else would she have drawn so often? I spread the drawings out on the bed, looking from one to the other. His eyes were set wider than mine, but I had his chin, his easy smile. An ache spread in my throat. "Leo? What do you think? Am I like him?" I thought for a moment that my words had fallen on deaf ears, but Leo did leave its post at the door and come sit by the foot of the bed.

The right-hand cubby wasn't as neat. It held a brush, a headband full of data threads like the one of his Jenna had given me on Fremont. I took it out and ran it through my fingers. The threads woven into the band were bright purple and blue and gold, and the leather had become stiff from disuse. I worked it between my hands until it became slightly more pliable, then pocketed it.

Near the back, I saw a little carved wooden box. I lifted the lid and found a data button nestled in soft velvety-red material. I took it out, palming it, and sat back down on the bed.

The first data thread I followed proved to be sets of still pictures, clearly labeled with names and places and times. The years were high: 568, 571. We were on Fremont year 224 when we left. We counted ours from the settling of Fremont—perhaps they counted from the settling of Silver's Home?

I recognized some of the same people my mother had drawn. The seventh picture showed my mother and father when they were about twenty-five, around ten years older than I was now, or at least had been when we left Fremont. They stood against a railing, both smiling, my father's arm around my mother's shoulder. In the picture, he seemed sparer than in the drawings, maybe younger?

My father stood tall and slight, with legs that looked built for running. His physical genemods might have simply been to build a perfect athlete's body. My mother appeared to be a taller and just slightly older version of Chelo. Thin and strong, with a squared jaw, an intense look, and small breasts and hips. She, too, could be a runner, or maybe a climber. Her biceps and the muscles of her forearms made ridges under her dark brown skin. Her hair was long and straight, braided to fall on one side. Chelo sometimes braided her hair like that, and I wondered if it was from a memory of our mother. The photo was labeled David and Marissa Lee.

Marissa.

I hadn't known her name. I said it three times to myself. "Marissa, Marissa, Marissa." My voice was swallowed in the emptiness of the tiny room, the larger crew quarters, the great ship, itself tiny amongst the stars.

A tear splashed onto my hand, startling me. I had cried before, at the foot of the *New Making* on the Grass Plains, and in the dark of the night, bawling because they abandoned us. Maybe it was being in their space, actually knowing what they looked like, that they'd had lives of their own, but these tears felt different, tears for *them* instead of tears for me. What had they experienced on Fremont, what had it cost them to leave us?

In the picture, my mother looked up at my father's face, as if admiring his nose or the turn of his jaw.

There was more, but for now, this bittersweet picture left me full.

I nestled the data button in my captain's coat pocket next to the headband, took my mother's hairbrush, and closed the cubbies. I gave a silent call to Leo, and it clambered up to me, settling on four arms, leaving the other two in front of it. I patted it for being obedient, as if it would notice, and told it, "Good night." These words, like the others, reverberated in the emptiness. I curled up and fell deeply asleep on my parents' bed.

When I woke, I took Leo, ate, and went to the ship's nose. I'd only been here once, with Jenna, in freefall. It felt entirely different from anything on Fremont and it took a good head for math to move with economy.

Even here, *New Making*'s skin was windowless and smooth. I could call up data via Starteller, but there was no projection wall so any video was inside my head, fighting my normal vision, making me feel off balance. I anchored myself by hooking my feet in some of the webbing festooning the walls, and took the data button back out. It helped to feel its shiny silvered surface hard as a pebble in my palm, to caress it with one finger of my other hand. Some level of physicality helped me stay grounded, present in both the webs of data and in my body. I no longer had Chelo by my side to be my link to the physical.

I followed different threads, ignoring the pictures for now. Stored data about the ship. Links to financial records. Probably useful, but I had no context to understand any of it.

Then, finally, something truly personal. I found my father's journal.

They realized the planet was inhabited a few days before they landed. He described how they'd spotted *Traveler*, the colonists' stranded ship, in silent orbit around Fremont. And then, on landing day:

> *Disaster. Jenna led an expedition to meet them, and she says they have a claim from long before ours. It is valid in their minds. They remain simple and weak, calling themselves original humans, attempting to preserve primal human genetics. Or at least, what is left of them. Jenna told Marissa they hate us being here.*

I pictured them landing, Jenna still whole. She might have been pretty, and perhaps stood taller, before her arm was ripped from her socket and one eye torn from her face in the last battle of the war. She might have laughed often.

I read forward. He didn't keep detailed notes for the next few weeks, just short entries about when visits happened. Apparently he and Mom stayed on the ship at first. Then the lack of progress frustrated him, as did the leader's choice to humor the illegal settlers, to try and convince them with words. I slid hastily forward, looking for the entries nearer the war, looking for information about us.

In one entry, he proclaimed:

> *This is our home, our dream. We sacrificed for it, and we earned it. They have no right, except that they exist. We cannot kill them simply for existing, but they must honor our right to be here. Marissa is beside herself—one of their leaders, Hunter, said we could stay as long as we give up genemods. As if we could give up being ourselves. If we're ever going to send enough goods back to settle our claim, we need to*

start now. We have fifteen years to get one ship home, and we are wasting the first of them talking to slow humans unwilling to reach their own potential.

That was close to the last entry. Ship's records suggested he and Mom left the *New Making* shortly after that. Apparently, he didn't take the journal with him. Three weeks later, the war started. I knew they had come back, but clearly he had not chosen to add to his journal on their return trips. There was not even an entry for Chelo's birth, or mine.

But he had given me a clue, and an odd hope. If it took the *Journey* as long as it took her sister-ship, the *New Making*, to go home, then the *Journey* may not have left in defeat. She may have left to secure our claim.

I unhooked from the netting, and let myself float free, connecting more fully to the *New Making*'s data trove. It felt as if I myself flew between the stars, ship and self indistinguishable one from the other.

Starteller informed me Jenna's waking sequence had begun. There was no way to hide from her that I had been awake, so I didn't bother. I toyed with meeting her in her waking room.

Jenna was a fighter, a predator with quick reflexes. Surprising her didn't seem like a good idea. So I took the path of least resistance and left her a note that I waited for her in the Command Room. I set out a glass of water for her, sat in one of the side chairs, and watched a picture of Silver's Home on the wall screen.

She came in, opening the door with her one arm. Her short hair hung in gray wisps around her ravaged face, highlighting her missing eye and the devastation of folds and wrinkles surrounding it. She had grown even thinner on the ship than when she ran wild on the outskirts of Artistos, hunting and living from the land. As if being someplace with no immediate danger had drained her of vitality. Her one steely-gray eye fixed on me, and I waited to see what she would do.

Her voice was as cool as her eye. "I presume this is no accident?"

I shook my head, offering no defense.

She took the glass of water I'd set out for her and drank it. Her voice was sharp as she asked, "What did you do with the time?"

Her question and the look in her eyes made me feel as if I'd betrayed her. I swallowed hard and sat up straight. I told her what I had done, trying to make the story sound noble but hiding nothing, including my visit to my parents' room and what I had read in my father's journal.

When I finished, she said, "Yes, they may have made it back in time." She sighed, and held her silence for a long moment. "But it would have been close." She waited again, watching me. "I suppose you had to begin to drive your own destiny eventually, and I knew you were curious about your parents." She stared at me, evenly, so still I felt her anger in her silence. "I don't expect any further choices that you don't consult me about."

"Why not? I'm an adult now, and I know how to handle the ship."

She laughed, her laughter stinging and a little scary. "Flying a simple ship with a preprogrammed course is nothing like maneuvering on a planet full of sophisticated people and complex politics. You *must not* act on your own when we arrive. The first few days on Silver's Home may be dangerous."

"Why?"

She turned her back to me and went to the galley and poured herself another glass of water, drinking it quickly and pouring yet another, which she held in her one hand while she looked me up and down as if trying to read my soul. All she said was, "Silver's Home will appear safer than Fremont. But it is far more dangerous, especially to you."

"Why me?"

"Because no one with your strength can afford to be so headstrong."

She walked out of the room, as if she couldn't bear to talk to me right then.

DECISIONS

Images of the *New Making* crashing into the ground raked my nerves.

The special pillowed chair in the command room held me securely, my head fixed in place by a rigid but padded rest. I stared up at the piteously glowing blue ceiling. Jenna stood behind me, silent and still, her brow furrowed as she looked down at me. The light from the control displays gleamed across the ridges of scar tissue on her face: red, orange, white, and blue; like sunrise over a distant mountain ridge.

The soft hums, clicks, and beeps of the controls blended into a continuous background noise that by now was familiar, almost soothing. I stroked my captain's coat, running my fingers along the bumps of the data buttons, the plush, velvety fabric interwoven with tiny, slick data threads. Even though I no longer needed it for daily status checks, I wanted to be sure I had the best possible communications with *New Making* when I started braking. I took a deep breath of the cool, recirculated air I'd probably breathed a thousand times before, and let it out slowly, willing myself to relax, to open to the data flow. Braking. Nothing to it.

Starteller displayed the maneuver for me, and Jenna had already told me everything she knew. She made it sound easy. But for Jenna, killing paw-cats was easy.

"Relax, Joseph."

I glanced up and caught her deepening frown. "You've worked through the simulation with Starteller," she said, her voice as stern as her expression. "You have performed equally complex tasks before. If you don't relax, you won't be able to maintain optimal contact with *New Making*."

"I'm okay." She was right. I could do this. I had to control my nerves. Had to prove to her I could do it.

Had to prove it to myself.

I took another breath, closed my eyes, and started counting down slowly from ten to one as I let it out. *Ten . . . nine . . . eight. . . .* My heartbeat slowed. The pillows and Jenna and even the coat slowly faded to background. . . . *seven . . . six. . . .* Time shifted. The friendly background noises slowed, deepening with my breath. . . . *three . . . two . . . one.*

Like water through an open flood gate, data from *New Making*'s main engines poured into me, filling me, seeping into my mind, my blood, my muscles, my bones. My body became larger, heavier; I was the ship, my skin proof against the icy vacuum of the empty space I sped through, a flash of light and heat. I was the engines, thrusting against my own speed; my muscles bunched as I dug in, braced against it to slow my own headlong momentum.

The part of me that hummed and sang with the big ship fought hard to stay on course. I locked my shoulders, holding my vast, metal body along my trajectory. I was the ship, turning, and I was the small, surging engines fighting myself.

This was piloting. Managing the feel and balance, searching for anything going wrong. Like knowing by the feel of the reins when a hebra smells a predator. The fear that overcorrecting will drive you spinning into a trap.

My human body sweated, water pouring down the sides of my face. I felt Jenna bathing my forehead and chest in cool water.

Dissonance.

Dissonance. The ship fighting itself and me the balance, tiny adjustments one way and then the next. Breath and water and Jenna stretching my arms, massaging my shoulders. Dissonance dropping away, gradual silencing of the roaring engines. A long, slow last turn through space.

Sweat pouring down the sides of my face, sticky and salty. Momentum and math taking over, running the consequences, everything falling together, just right.

Jenna's calloused palm on my forehead.

Turned, back in a good trajectory, the growling main engines themselves fighting our forward momentum like a goat butting us, legs splayed, stubborn. Winning, slowing us. Our trajectory felt fine and fragile; I stayed immersed in the delicate sweetness of balance and direction, checking and adjusting and re-checking.

"That's enough, Joseph. We're stable. Come out of it."

Jenna's words tumbled into my ears, tangling in a jumble of noise before clattering into place and acquiring meaning. Time to let go, to be just Joseph again. The ship receded from my body, my mind. Gleaming blue swam in my vision as I pried my eyelids up.

Jenna's face wavered into focus above me. "Four hours is long enough, Joseph. You've done it. Now, get some rest."

I grunted and sank back, my body an unwelcome place, full of aches and twinges that kept me hovering at the edge of sleep. The clicks and chirps of the computers and readers, Jenna's muted footfalls, the whoosh of the air circulation—all of it unnaturally loud. I tossed fretfully for a time before finally passing into deep dreams of the ship and the open space we flew through. Starlight kissed my skin, my fingers tingling with the cold.

Four days passed, then five, then six. Flight had been easy, but now we felt the thrust of slowing. Moving around the ship was harder. It crossed my mind that Jenna knew enough about the ship and however its gravity and cabin were set up to free us from feeling the steady pressure of the engines, now in front of us. I asked, and she looked at me as if I were a puppy or toddler. "It reminds us we're in the hardest part. Ships rarely come to harm on long steady runs. It's the stress of slowing and landing that costs lives. You need to feel the ship without insulation." Her look softened, but only a little. "There is nothing to do unless something fails, but if it does, there will be seconds to react. Maybe."

Jenna sent messages saying we were coming home.

While we waited through the long, slow braking, Jenna forced herself through hours of endless running and weight-work sessions, building her one arm and her long, slender legs. At night, in the half-hour before the ship's lights dimmed, she sat in our common room and squeezed a metal spring to strengthen her fingers. I got off easier, running an hour or so every day and doing pull-ups in the hard-framed doorways. During free time, always connected to the ship, feeling it as if it were my own subconscious, I wandered the corridors or the remaining threads of the data buttons. I re-read my father's words, chose alternate formats, listened to the sound of his voice over and over. I searched the button, but my mother apparently never spoke to it directly.

Restlessness drove me back to Jenna regularly, checking for any word from the planet. None.

We turned again, easier and slower, on target for the spaceport on Li, the largest of the twelve continents. This time, Jenna shifted and fidgeted at my head. Nerves, or more trust in me? The closer we came to Silver's Home, the more distracted Jenna seemed. She muttered at the air.

The turn finished. An hour later, Jenna drove us back to weights and running. Although she didn't say anything, she often stared forward between sets, toward Silver's Home, her mouth set in an increasingly tight line. Her speech became shorter and more clipped. She failed to reset a bicep machine correctly and a weight cylinder rolled off and hit the floor with a huge bang.

"What could be wrong?" I asked. "Why hasn't anyone answered us?"

Jenna didn't look at me, but bent to pick up the weight. She wore a thin, sleeveless shirt and the muscles in her back stood out like ranges of mountain ridges and valleys. Sweat formed rivers in the valleys. Scars crossed it all: a diagonal web from the twisted shoulder of her missing arm almost to her hip. She didn't answer.

"We'll hear soon," I said.

She looked over her shoulder at me as if it wasn't my place to reassure her, but instead of rebuking me she simply said, "We'd better."

An hour later, Starteller dinged. I reached for the data, but the message was scrambled to Jenna. That left me watching in silence from across the room as she sat on a bench and communed with Starteller. Her back was to me, so I couldn't see her face, but she slumped a bit as she listened. Just as she turned to talk to me, a second ping indicated another response.

There was nothing to do but watch mutely as she heard the second message and spoke a subliminal response to at least one of them. She would have spoken up if she wanted me to hear her.

I waited, foot tapping, struggling not to show my impatience.

When she turned, her eye was so wide and her mouth so tight she might have been slapped. Her voice flat, she said, "The Port Authority is demanding that we dock outside the system, at Koni V station, and turn the ship over to them."

I blinked at her. It took a moment to find my voice. "Does that mean we're in trouble?"

"It means the Family of Exploration is in trouble."

"Isn't that us?"

She stepped closer to me and sat down on a bench. Her fingers swept through her hair, a gesture of futility. "Good answer. Yes, that's us."

She'd only told me a little about the Port Authority, but I knew they managed all interstellar travel, most of which was between Silver's Home and four other planets that were close to it—less than a year's flight for the furthest away. Which was *much* closer than Fremont, which was three years away, but with room for faster flight. "Do we have to obey them?"

"A good answer, and now a good question." The corner of her mouth quirked up, turning her scars into a fan. "We have much in the hold of value, maybe enough to help the Family. I haven't answered the Port Authority yet."

"So who did you answer?"

"My sister, Tiala."

I had never imagined Jenna with family. Except us. Was the call good, or not? Her expression remained blank, almost too blank.

"What did she say?" It would've been nice if Jenna offered information without making me dig it out of her.

"She says there is only money trouble, and that the Port Authority is making too much of the problem." She paused, her finger rubbing the twisted edge of her mouth. "I trust my sister's heart. Defying the Port Authority may be a dangerous choice, though, so we will wake up Alicia and Bryan. And then we will decide together.

"We had better hurry.

"In the meantime, I will ignore the Port Authority until we are too far along to easily turn for Koni station." She arched her single eyebrow. "If we get stranded there without resources it could take a year to work our way planetside."

It didn't surprise me that Jenna didn't accept orders.

"We should wake both Alicia and Bryan at once to save time," she said. "You might wait for Bryan in his waking room."

"I'd rather wait for Alicia."

She laughed, a rare expression from her, but more common on the ship than it had ever been on Fremont. "I know. But she knows me, and he does not."

She had a point. Jenna had interacted with Bryan very little on Fremont. During the weeks she showed us the cave and helped me understand how to heal the channels that had burned closed with my adoptive parents' death screams, he had been Town Council's captive. One look at his injuries and Jenna had ordered him frozen before we even left Fremont. "All right. How will he feel?"

"Cold sleep doesn't heal or harm. He'll still feel like someone beat him up."

"Great."

She hesitated, as if reconsidering her decision. Then she said, "After Bryan wakes, take him down to the hospital. I'll work on him. If he can't walk, let me know and I'll come for him. After I chat with Alicia, we'll meet you at the hospital. And don't forget Bryan won't have any context for landing on Silver's Home." Her voice took on a note of irony. "At least Alicia stayed awake until after we took off."

Jenna had fought us both to get Alicia to accept being frozen two weeks after we left. "You might have to be more careful than me," I said.

She laughed, her second laugh in a short period of time. Maybe she enjoyed ignoring the Port Authority.

Two hours later, I paced quietly beside Bryan's warming body. He breathed, softly and shallowly. His usually bronze skin looked pale against his dark brown hair. Unlike mine, Bryan's body clearly displayed his core genemods—he was wider and taller and stronger than the rest of us. Always the strongest person in Artistos, he had been the victim of Artistos' prejudices. A gang of young men our age in Artistos, led by Garmin, had shown him their fists.

The skin around one eye and all down the cheek below had lost its swelling to the cold, but purple and yellow bruises made a strange map across his features. Medi-tape from the Artistos hospital closed slashes in his skull and along one arm. A taped tear decorated one bicep, bruises blushed his hands, and cracks highlighted his knuckles. A dirty gray cast enclosed his right leg, and a long jagged cut, barely scabbed, snaked up from somewhere inside the cast, rode across the top of his knee, and ended halfway up the inside of his thigh.

He had always been the strong one who protected us in Artistos.

Now, he lay pale and inert, vulnerable.

I fidgeted, waiting for him to move and speak and become himself.

His skin slowly took on color. It warmed his cheeks, crept up his chest, and seeped into the hollows of his neck and face. Twenty minutes passed before he finally groaned and licked his lips.

"Bryan?" I whispered.

At first, nothing. Then he sat bolt upright, surely an act of will more than strength at this point in the process, and looked around. "Joseph." His voice was hoarse, nearly a croak. He rubbed his eyes and groaned, then shook his head. He must've been thinking clearly, since he immediately asked, "When and where are we?"

I couldn't remember what he knew. We'd learned so much while he was imprisoned, then hospitalized, then beaten again. "We're going to Silver's Home, where our first parents came from. We'll land in about two weeks. We left Fremont three years ago."

"Chelo?" His voice trembled. "Did Chelo come with us? Is she here?"

"No." I reached a hand out to steady him, then dropped it, uncertain.

He sighed at the unwelcome news. I handed him a glass of water I'd set by the bed, and stood silently as he sucked it down like a breath of air. He blinked. "Do we know she's all right?"

I shook my head as I refilled the glass. "Jenna says there are no facilities left on Fremont for that kind of communication, not without the *New Making*. She thinks they *can't* send us a message. I bet they wouldn't even if they could." I handed him the second glass. He drank slowly and carefully as I continued. "We probably won't know anything until we return."

His eyes lit up. "When are we going back?"

"I don't know." I reached out and put a hand gently on his cast, noting that it felt mushy now, maybe a side effect of freezing. "But we are. How do you feel?"

He laughed softly. "I wish you hadn't asked." He touched his face, wincing. "If I think about it, everything hurts."

"I'm supposed to take you to Medical when you're ready to walk."

He slowly stretched his least-injured leg. As he lifted the other leg a few inches and set it back down, pain flashed across his face. "Not yet, I think. I'll have to lean on you."

He'd come in to the *New Making* leaning on Alicia, her slight form twisting under his weight.

He licked his lips. "Kayleen and Liam stayed behind with Chelo?"

I refilled his glass and watched him take this one more slowly. He knew Liam and Chelo had become close. "Yes."

"I miss her. I miss them both already. Kayleen chattering like a bird at everything and Chelo—steady and always there." He handed me the glass and clutched his damaged hands together in his lap. "I hugged her the last night before you all left me. I wish I'd never let her go."

Waking must've been making him muzzy; Bryan almost never talked about his feelings. I filled another glass and watched him drink it.

I introduced him to Leo, who had been sitting still and silent in a corner, and he laughed and said, "You always did like to have pets."

I bristled. "It's more than a pet. Leo can call for help. Maybe Jenna will give you a bot of your own."

He laughed for the first time since waking. "All right. Calm down, I like it." His voice strengthened, and finally he stood up to walk. He almost fell the first time, but ten minutes later we headed for the door, Leo leading us. Bryan's weight bore down on my shoulder and hips, at once both astoundingly heavy and like warmth from home.

By the time we reached Medical, sweat shone on his forehead and upper lip, and his dark eyes were again filled with pain. As we came in the door, Jenna stepped forward. She took his weight from me without speaking.

Alicia stood a few feet from me. I leaned back against the door frame, feasting my eyes on her. She watched me warily, not coming close. Her dark hair framed her face and spilled down her small breasts, hanging loose nearly to her slender hips. She wore the same outfit she'd left Fremont in: tight green work pants and a shirt so white it made her hair seem as dark as the void we traveled through.

I walked to her, holding out my arms, wanting to feel her fill them. She let me hold her, but didn't curl an arm around to touch my back for long moments. Eventually, she rested her head on my shoulder, smelling faintly of ship's oil and the chemicals that woke us.

I let her go and stepped back for a second. Jenna was still fussing over Bryan, laying him down and straightening his limbs. She looked over at us and said, "Go on. . . . I can manage him."

Needing no more encouragement than that, I took Alicia's long slender hand in mine, and Leo and I led her to one of the common galleys. We sat in the small, nearly featureless room. She ignored Leo, who settled back into wait mode, silent. I handed her a cup of water. "How do you feel?"

"Angry." She held the glass loosely and scowled at the floor. "Why didn't you demand that she wake me up? What have I missed?"

I shrugged, wanting to calm her. "I was frozen, too. Jenna and I just came out of it."

"What will happen to us when we get to Silver's Home?"

"I don't know." I poured my own glass of water. "I'm glad you're awake." I sat down across from her, watching for her reaction.

She looked away. "What will people think of us? We won't know anything about how to live on Silver's Home! And getting information out of Jenna's impossible." She took a long sip from her glass. "I think she's still mad at me."

Well, I was still mad at her, too. But just a little. Alicia was our risk taker, and now I knew how risk twisted a situation and widened the possible outcomes. Looking at her—her dark curls, her white skin, her slender frame and long fingers, her violet eyes—my own anger was hard to feel anymore, drained away in the raw fear and joy of flight. I sighed. "You did steal a weapon she told you to stay away from."

A flash of the defiant Alicia surfaced. "If I hadn't, we'd still be on that god-forsaken plain, dithering." She sat back and wiped her hair from her face. "And Bryan would still be captive."

And Chelo, at least, might be with us. I blinked back tears, feeling my sister's absence in Alicia's presence. I didn't know exactly what happened back in the Commons Park Amphitheater, but Alicia started it and Chelo finished it, and no one died. I think Alicia, at least, would have died if Chelo hadn't gone.

I tried for a light tone. "Besides, Jenna's mad at me, too. I reprogrammed the ship to wake me a few days before her."

She grinned. "Good for you. Did you get in trouble?"

"It was worth it." I commanded the white wall to project an image from the ship's forward cameras. Silver's Home now took up half the wall, big enough to see the ships and habitats and space docks ringing it. "That's our people, Alicia. *Altered*, like us." An image of Bryan's damaged face flashed through my mind. "Maybe we have to learn to fit in, but surely they won't beat us up for being different."

She leaned forward, peering at the planet on the wall. "I want to know enough so that we aren't different when we get there."

It finally dawned on me that Alicia the Brave felt lost and frightened. I went to her and rubbed her shoulders and told her everything I knew, which didn't feel like much at all. I included the messages, and that Jenna would want decisions from us, but I didn't ask for her answer. I showed her the pictures from the data button, pointing out my parents and the tall elegant buildings in the background, but I couldn't even say where on the planet the pictures were taken.

She twisted gently under my hands. "That feels good."

When I leaned down to kiss her, she kissed me back, but pulled away after only a moment. "What else have you learned?"

Disappointed, I tried zooming in on the camera image dancing on the wall in front of us. It fuzzed out before there was enough detail to do any more than make out cities, which covered at least half the land, and see that transportation buzzed regularly between and in the cities.

Strings of continents and islands butted up against each other like a necklace near the equator, thinning a bit partway up, and filled in again at both poles, which were white and less populated, but still more settled than anyplace at home. I walked to the image, pulling data from Starteller as I went. I pointed at the continents: "There is Li, where we're going, and next to it is Juh, and just past that string of islands—the Silver Eyes—that one's called Black's Mountains. . . ."

I glanced back at the expression on her face. Alicia, afraid? I looked at the display again, trying to see it through her eyes. The busy landscape, the many continents and islands—it contrasted so with Fremont. Jini and Islandia would fit together on Li, and leave room for more. All together, we would not fill a single city.

On Silver's Home, all the land appeared tamed. Even the seas were full of cities, floating or maybe rising on platforms. A human place, and sitting there beside Alicia, my blood pounded in nervous anticipation. Alicia was our adventurer, our risk-taker, and Silver's Home had apparently cowed even her, at least for the moment.

We were heading someplace where I wouldn't be a freak, and that *had* to be better than Artistos. Besides, Alicia would bounce back—she'd wanted to leave the most of all of us.

I leaned into her, kissing her fully on the mouth. She returned my kiss, greedy for touch. When we separated, I whispered, "Jenna will be busy for a while. Follow me?"

She opened her mouth wide as if to protest, then her eyes sparkled and she said, "Go."

Jenna and Bryan woke us up after what felt like the best sleep I'd had since we left Fremont. Jenna clattered noisily in the kitchen when I knew from experience that she could make breakfast so quietly I wouldn't hear her at all. I opened my eyes and pushed up on one arm. A new white cast gleamed on Bryan's ankle. The old meditape had all been pulled off and replaced with something clear, showing the neat seams of his cuts. Even his bruises had faded some.

I climbed out of bed and sat in one of the soft chairs scattered throughout the common space between the galley and the sleeping areas and grinned at him. "You look better."

He nodded. "As long as I don't die of starvation."

Suddenly hungry as well, I said, "Me, too."

Jenna glared at me, but said nothing about Alicia and I sharing space.

"Alicia! Time to get up," Jenna called out as she poured juice made from garden berries, and brought it over, one purplish-red glass at a time. "We have choices to discuss."

I helped Jenna lay places and cut up tomatoes and carrots. I opened up packages of what Jenna called "spaceman's waybread," a hard, nutty wafer kept in dry stores, probably ever since the *New Making* left Silver's Home. I liked its crunchiness and the way it gave me a lot of energy for just a few bites.

Alicia emerged just as all of the food was ready. She hugged Bryan, sat beside me and took my hand, and ignored Jenna entirely.

"Did you hear back from your sister?" I asked Jenna.

Jenna glanced up at me. "Did you fill Alicia in?"

I nodded.

"Good. We got a second notice from the Port Authority that said the same as the first."

"Can they make us do anything?" Alicia asked.

"Sure—they can make us die. But they won't." Jenna shook her head. "They want credit, and we can't give them that if they kill us on the way in."

Bryan leaned forward. "Do they ever shoot ships out of the sky?"

For the second time, Jenna shook her head. "But they certainly could. You four should know that. Because it's dangerous, I want your approval for what I plan to do." She looked at us, fixing us each with her single eye, making sure we knew she wanted our attention. Unsettlingly, her gaze rested longest on me. "Defying the Port Authority could get us all in trouble. I'm going to refuse to follow their landing instructions. Joseph will have to make his first-ever landing under duress and possible danger. And we won't be met very nicely."

Bryan looked at her evenly, his taut emotions once again almost palpable. In his kind, even voice, he said, "If I understand the options right, the other choice is to leave the *New Making* somewhere we can't get to it, risk having her cargo stolen, and be far from all of our—what do you call it? Affinity group?"

"That's about right," Jenna said.

"But why would they expect us to do that?" Alicia asked.

"I don't know."

"Well, count me in." Alicia's eyes almost glittered with excitement.

"Me, too," Bryan said. "I'm tired of being told what to do."

We all were. I raised my glass. "To a safe landing on Li continent."

All four of us drank together, turning our lips red with the juice.

LANDING

The ping of an incoming message caught me with a spoonful of hot cereal halfway to my mouth. The message was from the Port Authority, but again, it was coded to Jenna. I looked up to see the content of the message reflected in the tight set of her jaw, in the way her hand fisted on the table beside her empty plate. My appetite vanished.

Alicia noticed I'd stopped eating and paused, following my gaze to Jenna. Her spoon sank to her bowl and she sat straighter. Bryan, too, stopped eating and sat up. We watched Jenna, like three djuri alerted by a sudden movement in the tall grass. When she refocused and looked at us, her smile balanced between cunning and anticipation.

I fingered the data threads in my captain's coat, reaching deeper into the ship's data stream for the reason behind her smile. The message's trail was closed, but a sudden insight crossed my mind. "Hey, Jenna," I asked, "the Port Authority didn't like you before you left, either, did they?"

Her only answer was a twisted smile that disappeared as soon as I noticed it.

She stood, taking her plate. I followed with my bowl and spoon. Nothing short of a life-threatening emergency excuses leaving anything loose in a spaceship. As she washed her plate, her voice was quiet and controlled. "They figured out we're not on course for Koni station. They claim the spaceport on Li is closed; Tiala told me yesterday that she would try to meet us there, so it wasn't listed as closed in the nets then."

We were half a day from the point where we'd be so caught in Silver's

Home's gravity well we couldn't turn away easily. "Who's right?" Alicia asked.

Jenna laughed. "Maybe both of them. But if we try to land, my bet is they'll let us." She finished stuffing her clean plate in a drawer, grabbed my bowl and spoon, did the same. She started for the door. "I'll meet you all in the Command Room."

Bryan looked up. "Where's that?"

I was two steps toward the door, following on Jenna's heels, and turned at his question. Alicia answered before I could. "I know where it is. We'll be right behind."

That was all I needed. I nearly beat Jenna there. "What should we do?"

"I'm going to ignore the Authority for a few more minutes."

"And then?"

"I need you as connected to the ship as you can get—go deep. You may not need to do anything. But be ready to react." She walked over toward the pilot's chair, taking her usual place at the head of the chair, giving me an intense, warning glance. "*And* stay focused enough on us to hear what happens."

Right. Easy for her to say. I settled into the chair, leaning back a little for comfort. Alicia and Bryan tumbled through the door, taking seats, looking at each other and then at us.

Jenna put her hand on my shoulder. "Relax."

I closed my eyes, reaching for the meld of data and body.

Alicia's voice, a little strident. "But what can *we* do?"

The ship fed me reports, one by one, the data dancing through my consciousness in a set pattern. Every single sensor reported as completely normal. Jenna's reply to Alicia floated over my head, patient and calm. "There is nothing to do yet but be ready."

"Which means?" Alicia demanded.

Jenna's short, sharp response was, "Be here where I can see you."

Alicia held her silence, the muscles in her neck taut and her eyes snapping frustration.

I didn't have time to worry about her. My thoughts raced across a flood of ship's statistics, half-focused on each reality, the firm weight of Jenna's hand on my shoulder keeping me balanced between the two. Anticipation licked along my nerves.

I opened my eyes to see that Jenna had asked Starteller to display data on the two vid walls. Silver's Home, bright and clear, on one wall. The other wall displayed a map of our trajectory over a washed-out version of the same picture. The red line that represented *New Making* arced in toward a yellow fuzz symbolizing the planet's atmosphere. A blue light blinked near the dot at the end of the red line that showed where we now flew. Alicia and Bryan leaned forward, watching closely.

Jenna said, "The blue dot represents Koni station. Even though it's physically closer to us than Silver's Home, it's really farther away because we would have to turn and slow to dock." She stopped, making sure Alicia and Bryan understood, waiting for each of them to nod in turn. "The blinking green light on the planet is Li Spaceport."

I knew the map; our trajectory danced more clearly inside me than the one on the wall. Bryan sat still and quiet, watching thoughtfully, and Alicia's expression flickered through amazement, curiosity, and a touch of resentment. She stared at the wall, one hand drumming softly on the table, her black hair loose and falling down her back.

A pink line showed up: a circle all the way around Silver's Home, touching the atmosphere a quarter-turn of the planet away from the spaceport. As it hit the yellow of the atmosphere, the line fuzzed out a little, a flash of purple. And on the other side, it came down neatly in the middle of the green light representing the spaceport.

Jenna continued, "There is no easy way to talk real time with anyone except the Port Authority until we get into the atmosphere. Tiala is trying to reach members of our affinity group, and I hope to talk to them as soon as I can." Finally, she was giving up information freely. "In the meantime, I need to give the Port Authority an answer soon. I'll let you all hear what I tell them." She sat, still next to me but not touching for the moment, watching the screen pensively.

I dove deeper into the data, my eyes still open but my focus inward so that I *saw* the data streams first and foremost. I tested my reach into every reporting device and sensor I knew of, calling in reports, checking. What if the port was closed? What if we had to maneuver really fast? Could I give the ship commands quickly enough?

Preparing to land felt as new and scary as the first time *New Making* rose under me, thundering and surging toward the open sky as we fled Fremont.

No matter what happened, this was the end of that beginning. Let it be good.

Jenna's jaw moved in that slight way I'd learned meant she spoke to her earset subliminally. Words flashed on one screen. On the other screen, the red of our path extended a bit closer to the planet. I read Jenna's message:

"*New Making* to Port Authority. Previous communication acknowledged. We are pleased to be coming home. Regret to inform you we need to land at Li Spaceport for medical and cargo reasons. Will discuss on landing. Please provide landing instructions."

Bryan smiled at Jenna's polite message, but Alicia's eyes narrowed. "Why are you being so *nice*?"

"Because they can still shoot us out of the sky." She looked almost sorry for Alicia. "If we can talk or bluff our way home, we will. Besides, any communication may show up in court later." She ran her fingers through her short gray hair. "Like coming before the Town Council. We cannot be the aggressor. And I'm betting they cannot afford to."

Alicia grimaced. "You sound like Chelo."

"Good." Jenna turned back to look at the screen. "We should hear back soon. We're close enough there's just about zero communication delay. I've left everything open; you'll all be able to see any messages."

Bryan stared intently at her, as if measuring her. "And the conversation has already started. So why wait, now?"

Having nothing useful to say, I stayed deep in the data. If they weren't going to shoot at us, what could they do? I reviewed our trajectory. We had entered the right coordinates days ago, during the long wait for a response from Silver's Home. Now, I just needed to tell the ship when to use the commands already embedded in its myriad systems. As long as Jenna or I gave it the go-ahead in time, we'd be fine.

Apparently Jenna thought the same. She turned to address Alicia and Bryan. "When we land, I expect all of you to stay near me. Don't answer any questions unless I tell you to. Don't let them separate us. Pretend you need me."

Bryan laughed, slightly edgy. "That should be easy. We do."

Jenna looked long and hard at Alicia, her voice as steely as her gaze. "You, too. You will need me when we get there."

Alicia blinked up at her, unafraid. "For a while."

Jenna narrowed her gaze in anger, but turned away. "That will have to do." She took a few steps toward the screen, where a return message glowed.

I nearly jumped out of the chair as a deep masculine voice began to speak. "*New Making*. Li Spaceport is closed. Jenna, you are not a trained pilot. Turn and dock at Koni Station." The message was repeated verbally, and left glowing on the screen, taunting me.

Jenna frowned.

Did they think she was the only one aboard? Had the *Journey* returned with a full manifest of who was alive and who was dead? Was that why they took so long to answer? Was everyone, even Jenna, listed as dead?

She composed a return message, the frown sticking to her face and the small muscles in her neck tight. "Pilot Joseph Lee is aboard. We are in good shape to land at Li."

A break in the steady flow of the ship's data drew my attention; one by one, each sensor reported out. I hadn't commanded that. My breath came faster. I reached down to push myself up a little. "Jenna. Someone is querying the ship, making it report status. Is that normal?"

In moments she was at my side. "You're sure?"

"All systems have reported out to something I don't recognize. Not to me, nor to Starteller."

"They can't do that," she whispered. "There's no Wind Reader strong enough to query our data from way out here." She put her hand on my shoulder and looked at the screen.

I dove deeper. All was quiet. "I don't see any trace right now."

"It wasn't Starteller? You're sure?"

"I'm sure."

"It can't be a person. It must be something automated. Something new."

Bryan and Alicia sat still, watching us.

Another tug. I closed my eyes, feeling the hum and movement of the ship, focusing on the low growling engines, on the interface to Starteller. Swimming in a stream of data, facts and figures brushing my consciousness. There: a presence. Working with Kayleen, I had sometimes felt her in the data streams. This felt like her, but not. Someone else. Stealthy, but strong. Stronger than Kayleen. I sank into the interface, struggling to find the intruder. There. I felt it. Probed.

It didn't give, didn't let me read it. It felt like a mirror, reflecting my queries, visible more by its absence and its location, its disturbance of the normal.

I pushed harder, trying to force it open like I had the colony's computers. It stuttered, the sequence out of balance to my awkward bashing at it. Then it—*turned*—querying me. Not words. Curiosity. Surprise. It wanted to read me. I heard my physical voice screech as I clamped down, closed myself off, and surged back to the surface.

"What happened?" Jenna asked.

I'd lost it, gone too far. I'd cut myself off from everything. I shouldn't have done that. "It's in the interface."

"Where?"

"To Starteller. But it's not Starteller."

Jenna must have seen the desperation on my face. Her voice was firm, supportive. A gentle command. "Go back down. No physical harm can come to you. Stay open, stay friendly. Stay like the messages I've sent. We have nothing to hide."

Fear arced up my spine as I opened myself back up. This was not Fremont; Jenna was not Nava. I couldn't refuse—the others depended on me. Closing my fear away, I breathed deeply and whispered my old chant, the one I'd made up when I was five and first learned that data sang in me. "Blood, bone, and brain."

Fluids and fuel began to feed into the thrusting engines ahead of the command we had not even given. Whatever, whoever, was trying to steer the ship.

My ship.

"Blood, bone, and brain." I dove, opening the conduits between myself and the ship's systems, myself and Starteller and the hydraulics and the robots. I fed the engines a command to wait, to stay until Starteller gave them a set of instructions from *me*.

The engines waited.

So deep, the ship was my body and I existed inside its nervous system.

Had Starteller been compromised?

I'd surprised whatever was here. Data moved so fast—what had happened while I was out? I probed. Our instruction set looked untouched, ready to execute. I didn't see anything else. Where were we in time? Could we tell the ship to follow our commands now, take control? Did I dare run up and ask Jenna?

I wove a warning bot into the interface, forcing myself to slow enough to be sure it was strong, telling Starteller to let me know about any commands, even commands that came from me. I bounced a query command against my warning and it pinged inside me. Perfect.

Clenching my fists and wiggling my toes, I pulled myself up into my body, feeling the flow of breath and blood again, and then not, past that to a more normal physical space. I didn't lose all access this time, but floated along the top layer of the data streams, attuned for messages from Starteller.

My eyes opened. Jenna leaned over me, close. My voice babbled in my ears, into the air of the room. "It's there. They want to turn the ship. Tell them . . . tell them not to." The edge of the headrest near my cheek felt cool, a contrast to the heat pouring through my body. I checked for activity and heard Starteller's silence and the engines' silence. Good.

Jenna's voice, firm, polite. Barely polite. "*New Making* to Port Authority. Don't force us."

It came again, strength I couldn't control. I dove deep, surrounded it. "Who are you?" I asked.

Surprise. Wonder. Human emotions. A voice, information resolving into a query. "Marcus. How do you know I'm here?"

I was right: a person. "I hear you."

Still surprise. Starteller sent me Marcus's knock at the interface door.

Did it/he hear me? "You're trying to turn us. I can't let you do that."

"Who are you?"

What to say? "Joseph Lee. Why are you trying to stop us?"

"It's a task the Port Authority gave me." The foreign data stream opened, and I felt a presence stronger than me, scary. Human, but more. Beyond it, through it and then beyond, an ocean of data full of waves in languages I didn't understand, fast, terrifying. Everything on the planet below us as data. All of it connected to Marcus. I wanted to fall into it, to ride the connections and see what lay at the ends of them. They felt so full and deep I could go into them forever, lose myself.

Was so much data real, or was it a trick?

I couldn't follow that path right now; I needed to focus on the ship. Who was this Marcus to stop me, to tempt me? My own anger danced around the edges of my consciousness, and I pulled hard on it, using it for a focus point, drawing myself back fully into *New Making*.

Stronger or not, it was separated from the ship in a way I wasn't. Whoever it was had a time delay built in. Nanoseconds, but I was faster.

I bounced through the interface to Starteller, starting our command sequence. Early, but I calculated and added the right delays.

This was *my* ship.

I turned my attention back to the presence, bristling against its strength. It flashed up, big, melding suddenly with *New Making*'s data streams. Too big, nanosecond delay or not. Marcus could wrest control from me with a flick of thought.

Marcus laughed. At first I thought he was mocking me, but his laughter was warm, touched with true humor.

He let the first set of our commands reach the thrusters.

More information, no voice to it, just raw information turning to words. "Joseph Lee. Perhaps you are as good a pilot as your father."

I stopped, jerked inside myself. "You knew my father? Is he alive? Is he down there?"

"Later."

I wanted to know *now*. But I needed to fly, and whoever Marcus was, I couldn't win against him.

He let me win.

I hated that.

The others needed to know what I had discovered. As I opened my eyes, sweat dripped from my forehead and the heat of data ran through me like a small fire. I moaned and blinked. "It's okay," I whispered.

The Port Authority voice spoke again. "Cleared to land. You will be met."

What and who had I felt and talked to?

Jenna's voice, confused. "What happened?"

My vision cleared. Alicia and Bryan, seated and still, watching; Bryan's face worried, Alicia's curious. It'd be nice if *she* was worried, too. Straying. I was straying. I couldn't afford it. "I . . . talked to something or someone. Marcus. It said it would help us land. At Li, I think. I don't know why."

Jenna frowned and pursed her lips. She glanced at the message on the screen, and when she looked back, her gaze was a little lighter, and the frown gone. "Marcus. Has he grown so strong?" She paused. Long moments stretched before she said, "I know why he might help. An old debt. And your strength. That would . . . impress him. He will have seen your value."

I smiled, feeling stronger and a little proud, if still shivery and quaking. But I didn't have time for fear. "I gave the sequence to the ship."

She handed me a glass of water, watching as I drank it. "Are you okay?"

"Sure." I handed her back the glass, sinking into the chair, the ship still singing in my bones.

"Good." She gestured and I straightened out, fitting myself into the chair. She attached the straps, pulling them tight across my legs and torso and forehead, turning the command chair into a re-entry couch. There was time, but I understood from her actions that I might not come up fully again until we were inside the envelope of the atmosphere. She leaned down and whispered in my ear. "Fly, Joseph. Bring me home. Bring us home."

"Home." The word tasted scary.

I wanted to ask her more about Marcus, but a soft shift in the ship pulled me back down. Marcus was still there, silent, watching. Was he testing me?

He didn't invite attention, just hovered in the data stream.

Fine. If he wasn't going to help directly, I had work to do.

I willed relaxation, willed openness, picked up the threads of data, riding them, querying them. They felt right. Ship's robots tucking themselves into safe positions, thrusters opening for the slight turn down, the ship's gentle response, less dissonant than braking. Smooth.

Time passed, a readying, a waiting. Through it all Marcus was there beside me, doing nothing. Not approaching, not falling away. Just watching. Perhaps he knew he frightened me?

I checked and rechecked. Aware always of the strange presence that didn't belong there with me, but made no new moves. The joy of flying took me, and I rode down deep in the ship's embrace, offering myself to it totally. It seemed like days, but time immersed in data is tricky, and I knew we approached the atmosphere in a lazy slow circle around the planet that really only took hours.

Other ships flew through the space, keeping distance, going about their business.

I watched our trajectory, marking time by our movement. I had left Fremont's atmosphere in this ship; I knew what to expect. Braced. The *New Making* shivered as we touched the shell of air around Silver's Home, slowed, shivered harder, but she didn't buck, didn't alter course. Her skin heated and tiny coolers in the smooth surface absorbed the heat and fell away, skin shedding, their sensors ripping from me as they separated, new ones awakening. The *New Making* fought free, and then we were through the atmosphere, and on a long, slow course for our landing.

Thirst and heat pulled at me, demanding to be slaked and damped. The ship was past the point of no return; she would land. For now, a few long moments of simple flight inside the atmosphere. I set alarms to tell me if Marcus did anything, unsure if I knew how to really tell.

Irrationally, I wanted him to tell me how well I'd done. As if I should trust him. Not yet!

At the surface of the data, I twisted my head. "Straps. Take it off."

No response. Oh, right, they were strapped in, too. "Jenna?"

Then she was at my side, loosening the brow strap. I reached for her. She handed me a glass of water, and as soon as I drank it, she bathed me in more water so it dripped down my face on either side, making small puddles in the chair, cooling my heated skin. "You've done well so far."

I licked the water from my lips, smelling my own sweat and exhaustion.

"Are you ready to take us down?"

I'd never landed. Just taken off. I took a deep, steadying breath. "Sure, ready as I'll ever be." Marcus wouldn't let me make a fatal mistake. The thought startled me. Was it right? "Marcus knew my father."

She blinked at me. "Yes." Her hand stroked my forehead, soothing. "Don't ask now. Finish this."

"Did you call your sister?"

"Not yet. It's time for you to go back down."

I went.

Landing was poetry of machinery and data, of the physical and of light. Flight: the big engines off now, the little thrusters adjusting, the ship's surfaces adjusting, interacting with air and gravity and wind, slowing us. A dance—force and balance and weight, the pull of gravity and the strength of the engines.

A stop, far above, seconds or less, our nose pointed up at the sky we'd just powered through. Silent engines. The beauty and sheer terror of being so big and resting against only sky, if just for the space of a quick breath.

The engines flaring to sudden life, a pillow of exhaust under us.

The long, slow settling of the ship as it lowered itself laboriously, carefully, to the surface. Marcus watching, a distant presence as we touched down.

And then it was just me, testing and checking one last time. All of the systems that controlled flight and movement quieted, each winking into rest. Even my companion Leo, gone to storage for the landing.

14

SILVER'S HOME

I had landed the *New Making*. I was a spaceship pilot for sure now. I opened my eyes. Jenna leaned over me with a worried look, as she worked the straps free from the chair. "Come on. We need to hurry." I was glad of her help; my arms felt too heavy to move.

Alicia and Bryan, already loose and standing, gathered around me. Alicia handed me a glass of water, her whole face shining with excitement. She leaned over and kissed me, right in front of Jenna and Bryan, then blushed and stepped back. My cheeks grew hot, too, and I smiled.

Bryan handed me a chunk of waybread. They watched closely as I sipped the water and bit into the dry, nutty bread. Jenna mopped the sweat from my forehead with a cool, damp towel.

"Marcus?" she asked. "Is he still here?"

"I can't feel him anymore. He stayed until we landed."

She pursed her lips. "I wish I knew why he was here at all. No matter now—we have work to do." She glanced at Bryan and Alicia, both sweaty and in rumpled clothes. "You two—find some clean clothes. Brush your hair. Bryan, get the shirt I found for you yesterday." She made a go-on gesture with her right hand. "Get ready. Try to look your best."

Neither of them complained; they just moved off to their appointed tasks, Bryan limping but holding his own weight better than he had that morning.

Jenna reached her hand out, helping me stand.

My knees buckled, and I collapsed to sit on the edge of the chair, breathing hard, my vision swimming. We must be feeling the planet's natural gravity. I felt heavier than exhaustion alone could account for.

Jenna frowned. "We'll give you a few minutes." She glanced up at the wall screens, now both blank. "Stay here. Alicia and Bryan can take you to clean up when they get back. Wear your captain's coat when we leave. They'll need to know who landed us." She started toward the door and turned back. "Are you okay?"

I nodded. "Just . . . tired." With the bone-deep tiredness, elation. "But we did it."

A smile broke through her frown, but just for a moment. "We did. Hurry. We've got a half-hour or so before the pad finishes cooling and gets prepared for us to disembark. I don't want to be boarded—I told them we'd be outside soon." She glanced down at her own clothes. "I have to change. Are you sure you're okay until we get back?"

"Yes." My voice sounded small and tired. I tried again. "I'm okay." Better.

She left, and welcome silence surrounded me. My head filled the quiet with questions. What was out there? How much trouble could the Port Authority get us into? Me into? Heck, we'd landed well, we'd been safe. How much did they dislike Jenna? What about Marcus, who'd gone against their orders when he let us land? I stood again, my legs still shaky, and walked slowly to the sink, splashing cold water on my face to stop the questions I had no answers for.

Alicia and Bryan showed up shortly, scrubbed and clean, Alicia's hair a dark velvet halo around her face, her strange, violet eyes almost glittering with excitement. I wanted to watch her forever, to have her kiss me again.

Surely there was no one so beautiful.

She bounced on her feet, taking my hand, standing close enough for me to smell soap on her skin, faint but pleasant. She did kiss me again, a soft brush of her lips against my cheek. I leaned down to kiss her properly, surprising her so she made a soft "oh" sound before returning the kiss. I tore my eyes from her to look at Bryan, who had turned his face away from us. The dark blue shirt Jenna had found for him hung loosely on him, not hiding his size, but covering some of his injuries.

The three of us went down to our quarters, where I pulled on a pair of my own pants and a shirt that had belonged to my father: deep blue and silky soft. My fingers shook as I did up the buttons. Alicia helped me roll up the slightly too-long sleeves, then stood back, a quirky smile on her face. "You look quite handsome."

Maybe. I didn't feel handsome; I felt exhausted. I smiled back at her, pleased with her comment and glad she didn't see how weak I felt. Bryan did. Even injured, his face still bruised and one leg still stiff when he moved, he reached a hand out to steady me. "Let's go."

When would I get back? Jenna hadn't said not to take anything, and I wanted my father's journal. I stuck the data button in my pants pocket, and reached for my mother's jewelry, tucking it safely away in a big pocket inside the captain's coat before I shrugged the coat on. I could give the jewelry to Chelo someday.

Back in the Command Room, we found Jenna pacing, dressed in bright green pants, black boots, and a loose gold shirt, the empty sleeve tucked inside. The outfit softened her, hiding both her scars and her strength. There was nothing to be done about her face, of course, but she'd trimmed up her hair and combed it in such a way that I saw more of the good side of her face than the bad. A bright blue beaded necklace hung down over her chest and matching earrings glittered below the short silver-streaked hair on either side of her face. She put a hand on the necklace. "My data access." She shifted restlessly. "Let's go."

Wait. What had I missed? "Did you hear from Tiala? Did the Port Authority say anything else?"

"The Port Authority refused to let Tiala in. We'll have to go to her. And no, no more messages from them. But there will be a greeting party." As if we hadn't heard it the first time, she cautioned us again. "Now remember, no one say anything unless I tell you to. Don't let them separate us."

We followed her into the elevator. She'd never let us use it before, but maybe it was meant for when the ship was on the ground? Or maybe she didn't want to muss her clothes? I choked down a sputtering laugh.

We emerged from the elevator at the bottom level, standing close together just outside the closed door. Jenna turned and caught my eye. "No matter what anyone says, you did well." She swept her gaze across us all. "And for now at least, you are all members of the Family of Exploration. No matter what condition the group is in, that keeps you with me. Do you understand?"

We all nodded. Alicia took my hand and squeezed it, her fingers cool and dry. Bryan squared his shoulders, looking apprehensive. "Let's get it over with," he said.

Jenna raised an eyebrow at me and turned to look at the door. I opened myself again to the data flows and commanded the *New Making* to open the door and extend the ramp.

Silver's Home hit me.

Noisy, unfamiliar information poured into me, scraping along already-exhausted nerves, setting muscles twitching. The data demanded attention. A thousand—no, a million, or a million million conversations, an inescapable babble even stronger than I'd sensed connected to Marcus. What scared me then had clearly been filtered. Now, chaos threatened my ability to focus, to think; swirling connections between threads forming, falling, and reforming; status of a thousand things I didn't recognize; information structures so complex they rose and fell like living things. I stumbled into Bryan, who grunted in pain and grabbed for me, unable to stop my fall. I clamped down, shutting out the noise, my head throbbing. As the pain began to recede, I found myself in a ball on the floor, my hands over my head.

Time for ten breaths passed.

I looked up. Through blurry vision, I made out Jenna staring down at me. She said, "I'm sorry. Are you okay? I should have known how this place would affect you." She reached down for my hand, and Alicia took the other, one rough hand, one soft.

I breathed, focusing on my roiling belly. No wonder their Wind Readers went crazy. "I'm okay. Just give me a minute." My knees felt shakier than when I'd first stood up from my captain's couch. Another deep breath. Wouldn't it just be great to throw up all over Silver's Home?

Nice first impression.

The ramp outside clicked down. I swallowed hard and straightened my shoulders.

If I could land the ship, I could walk out of her in one piece.

I kept myself closed off to data, empty, focused only on the here and now, on my breath, on standing firmly, shaking with the effort of such small things. I wished my voice sounded firmer as I asked, "Are we ready?"

"Stay near him, you two," Jenna said to Bryan and Alicia. "We'll walk slowly."

We descended the ramp in small, slow steps, our heads high. A warm breeze dried the sweat from my face. I felt slightly heavier here than at home. Thankfully, not much.

My eyes swept Li Spaceport. Tall gleaming buildings with rounded edges dominated the view. A few short squat windowless buildings sat closer to the ships. Two of the spaceships loomed nearly the size of the taller buildings, their hulls bristling with protuberances that could be for scientific studies or could be weapons. Something about the way they looked made me guess weapons.

Most of the other ships were bigger than *New Making*.

Between the landing pads, red flowers lined gently curving walkways. Beyond the spaceport, empty spaces, then more buildings in almost every direction, each one bigger than anything we had on Fremont. Bright blue skies dotted with pure white clouds. A larger sun than ours, gleaming on ships and on the city, highlighting bright metallic colors around the spaceport and softer lavender and blue and gold on the buildings in the distance.

Air vehicles, mostly smaller than the *Burning Void*, traversed the sky in neat patterns. A bright bridge arched through the city in the distance, the glittering light making it seem to dance from building-top to building-top. Alicia gasped and Bryan's hand went to my shoulder, gripping me tightly.

Fremont's tiny spaceport smelled like oil and heat and dust, but this smelled of flowers and fresh air. Clean.

Such brightness everywhere felt almost as overwhelming as the flood of data. I focused on Jenna's back, on my steps, on my balance and keeping the bread and water in my stomach where it belonged.

Beyond the neat crisp lines of Jenna's gold shirt, I spotted four people standing at the bottom, watching our descent. Two women. Two men. All four wore dazzling white shirts emblazoned on the front right sides with a silver rocket, fatter and squatter than *New Making*. Even with different hair colors, the four looked similar: high cheekbones, carefully swept hair cut so it fell loosely just above their shoulders, and tall slender builds.

Maybe like Jenna would look if she were whole.

To a one, they looked like Town Council in a formal meeting. Severe, watching us closely, particularly focusing on Jenna. The shortest female, a blonde, brought a hand to her mouth, pity flashing in her eyes. I disliked her instantly; Jenna didn't need her pity, or anyone else's.

As we neared them, the tallest one, a red-haired man with white streaks running through his hair near each temple, put up a hand to signal us to stop. "Jenna King?" he questioned, his voice unsure.

I'd never thought of Jenna with two names. She laughed, an undercurrent of nerves in her voice. "Yes. Returned from the planet Fremont with three members of our group left stranded." She gestured at Bryan and Alicia. "Bryan Armstrong and Alicia Gupta."

After a moment of silence, she gestured at me. "And Pilot Joseph Lee." I nodded as she said my name, following her lead and keeping my face neutral.

He looked me up and down, as if stripping my captain's coat from my body. His icy gaze made me want to squirm away, but I planted my feet and met his eyes until he broke contact and nodded at us. "Lukas Poul, Port Authority." He inclined his head. "It appears Fremont did not treat you well, Jenna." There was a slight emphasis on her name, and I wished I could see her face. "There is much the Port Authority wishes to talk to you about."

Jenna's voice was cool and controlled. "It's good to be home. We will be happy to follow you." She looked at me and fingered the necklace. The ramp behind us rose. She shifted her gaze to Lukas. "We will, of course, allow the Authority to board after our cargo manifests have been reviewed, and I have been able to explain what we carry." She gestured at Bryan's cast. "There are other priorities. We need to get Bryan medical care soon."

Lukas glared at her. He didn't introduce the other three, but said, "Follow me." As he turned and we started after him, they followed us in a loose semicircle. Lukas Poul walked fast. I struggled to keep up, not wanting to find out what our three herders might do if I lagged.

It was hard not to stop and gawk at the gleaming ships we passed.

Lukas led us and our herders to a tall building near the center of the spaceport. We followed him into an elevator which went up to the fifty-sixth floor. He didn't seem to give the elevator any specific commands, but it obeyed his will. But then, Jenna hadn't done anything obvious to close the ship's door, either.

Lukas led us from the elevator to a large room with views of the bright ships and flower-lined paths spread below, so high we looked down on the smaller ships, including *New Making*. I squinted until I found it, standing still and silent and closed just like she had been on Fremont. People moved about below, so tiny they might have been children's toys.

The room's layout echoed *New Making*'s Command Room, with walls for vid and for writing on, and a large silvery table. Except this room would barely fit inside the ship. Lukas stood at the head of the shiny table and gestured for us all to sit. He sat after we did, and the other man remained standing by the door. The dark-haired woman stood behind Lukas, hands clasped behind her back, pretending not to watch us. The blonde leaned casually against a wall, making no pretense.

Jenna sat at Lukas's right hand, and I sat next to her. Alicia and Bryan sat opposite us, far away across the big table.

Jenna kept her eye on Lukas, so I did the same. He watched us both, his bright blue eyes neutral. His red hair looked even more striking in the artificial lighting, a flame where it touched the white shoulders of his shirt. His features were set neatly in the angular lines of his face, his skin perfect, his fingernails neatly trimmed. He appeared used to control. In contrast, Jenna's bright outfit, which had appeared so full of authority and power on the ship, now looked too soft and highlighted her ravaged face. But *her* eye looked like it did when she hunted.

Did Lukas even see her cool assessment of him?

He broke the tense silence. "Jenna. If you would like to talk alone, there is a private room next door."

She leaned forward. "Anything the Authority has to say to me can be heard by any members of my affinity group."

Impatience sharpened the lines of his face, as it had when she closed the ship's door behind us. But he plowed on. Perhaps with no choice? What power did Jenna have? "How did you come into possession of the *New Making?*" he asked.

Jenna answered him calmly. "*New Making* is the property of the Family of Exploration; I am a senior board member. Our other ship, the *Journey*, should have returned already."

Lukas nodded. "*Journey* no longer belongs to the Family of Exploration." He swallowed, hesitating for a fraction of a second. "And neither does *New Making*."

Alicia gasped, but Jenna held up her hand, her voice a notch lower than it had been. "Why?"

As he leaned toward Jenna, the woman behind him stepped closer to his back. His voice sounded full in the big room. "Your group chose to forfeit her for debts incurred."

Jenna spoke quickly. "I need verification."

A stream of data floated in front of us all, numbers and words I couldn't read. I didn't dare reach for it; I didn't want to pass out on the table. Jenna stared at the glowing figures for a long time, finally nodding. "Not forfeit; but held as collateral. Very well. We claim her contents, a combination of goods we brought with us to Fremont and did not use and scientific data from the planet."

I bit the inside of my mouth to keep myself from speaking. We *needed* the ship to get back to Fremont and get Chelo and Kayleen and Liam. *New Making* was *my* ship. I'd flown her here. If I hadn't been able to do that, she wouldn't belong to anybody; she'd be sitting silent and lonely on the Grass Plains of Fremont.

Lukas looked sour. His jaw moved: a conversation with someone else not nearby. So he wasn't a Wind Reader. After he finished, he cleared his throat and stood, some of the formality falling from him, but his voice, if anything, colder as he said, "I have been a lousy host. Would you like something to drink?"

Jenna glanced at us, then sat back in her chair. "We are already troubling you too much. Bryan needs care. I have been away from home a long time, and would like to see my family. I will return soon to begin unloading the ship."

Lukas smiled, a fake smile that didn't touch his eyes. "I will trade you the ship and its contents for the right to bond your pilot to us for five years."

I stiffened, my hands turning to fists. Alicia shot out of her chair, leaning over the table toward Jenna. "No!"

Jenna's gaze flicked to Alicia just long enough to gesture at her to sit down, then returned to Lukas. "The contents are not yours to trade." Her voice stayed even, almost imperious.

"You will consider my offer?"

All thoughts of being tired fled. I was not trade goods! I forced a deep belly breath, made my hands relax the fists his words had encouraged. Wiggled my fingers. Jenna wouldn't trade me. Not for anything. She hadn't protected us on Fremont to lose us now.

Jenna shook her head. "I need to discuss this with the Family of Exploration. Surely you cannot expect me to make such a decision now?"

Lukas inclined his head slightly.

Jenna nodded back. "I'll return as soon as I have enough information. I expect it will not be more than a few days."

Bless her. But she hadn't exactly told him no. I did my best to glare at him; she'd given me no commands not to glare, just not to speak. Besides, she was looking at him and she couldn't see my expression. Alicia looked like she was about to explode in nervous giggles and even Bryan raised an eyebrow at me.

Lukas noticed. He laughed, his laughter puncturing my anger. "Jenna, your pilot has much to learn about our world."

She cast a disapproving look at me. "I intend to teach him." She stood. "And now, we should go."

Lukas nodded coldly. "Ming will lead you out."

I stood, keeping my gaze straight in front of me, as cool as possible. Sweat trickled between my shoulder blades and ran slowly down my back.

Ming, the dark-haired herder, turned and led us out. She didn't speak until we were outside of the building. Then she spoke to *me*, her voice quiet and a touch amazed. "Pilot Joseph, you are lucky he is allowing you to leave. Thank Marcus."

Why would she say such a thing? What influence did the mysterious Marcus have on these people? Was she implying Marcus was on our side, or even that she was? I nodded at her. "I'll thank him if I ever see him."

A silver skimmer waited near the edge of the spaceport, sleeker than the *Burning Void*, almost as long, but lower to the ground. "I called you some transport," Ming said, smiling sweetly and unconvincingly. "I added the bill to the total debt of your group." She glanced at Jenna. "Let me show you how to fly it."

Jenna nodded, silent, listening as Ming explained the skimmer's interfaces. Unlike the one I'd flown at home, it had hand controls and a clear display that showed the long flat stretch of hard surface in front of it. Ming glanced at Jenna's missing arm, pursing her lips. "Can you fly it?"

Jenna snorted. "Of course."

There were four seats under a bubble of something clear that looked like glass but felt softer as I touched it. Jenna opened the bubble and climbed into the pilot's seat, gesturing to me to take the other front seat. Alicia helped Bryan ease into the wide backseat behind me and sat next to him. Ming stood silently, watching, a tiny smile brushing the edges of her lips.

The bubble top closed over us, shutting out the sounds and smells of the spaceport. Jenna followed Ming's instructions, pushing buttons and pulling a lever. The skimmer jerked twice, getting about two meters away from Ming, then stopping. Jenna cursed and touched her necklace. The skimmer started slowly down the hard path, gathering speed, and then rose smoothly. "Why didn't the Authority witch tell me I didn't need the hand controls?" Jenna said to no one in particular.

What did it mean for us that even Jenna was having trouble navigating here?

15

JENNA'S SISTER

I stared through the bubble as we rose above Li Spaceport and turned toward the glittering city. The sun rode lower in the sky, almost directly behind us, its light bouncing from bright smooth surfaces.

Alicia spoke from behind me. "Jenna—why can you fly this? You couldn't fly the other skimmer at home."

"Very few of our own data nets ever came up on Fremont—just simple nodes to communicate with the ship from our bases, and a strong local set in the caves. That made us dependent on Wind Readers, but it couldn't be helped. Here, the ship has a support net. I just give it directions." She touched her blue necklace. "And we all have plenty of interfaces." She glanced at me briefly before turning her attention back to the stunning view. "If we'd gotten a really good set of our own nets up, we would have won the war. But the Artistos data net kept our data out of Artistos, for the most part."

"So what do you need Wind Readers for here?" Bryan asked.

She laughed. "All the hard stuff. We have smart communication and smart nets and smart machines, but we limit the ability of machine intelligence to create."

I watched the city grow in the window, bright and light and airy. It seemed to me that a machine could do more than I could. "Why?"

"On worlds where machines were encouraged to create, only the machines lived."

That brought silence to all of us for a few moments. "So how do you stop the machines?" I asked. "Don't you have AIs here on the planet?"

Jenna didn't answer at once. "It's never built into them to create.

Just to obey, and sometimes to be creative about the right answer to a difficult problem. But the machines here have no desire to create art or life."

Alicia changed the subject. "You won't trade Joseph will you? What did you think of the Port Authority? How come they were so mean?"

Jenna grunted. "Of course I won't trade Joseph. The meeting? We don't seem to be in as much trouble as I expected."

"Ming suggested Marcus had something to do with it," I said.

"Maybe." She glanced over at me. "I'd like to know why."

So would I.

"Who's Marcus?" Alicia asked. "Are we going to see him? Why does he want to meet Joseph?"

Jenna didn't answer. She banked the small skimmer left in a big lazy circle. A river snaked below us, its banks lined with tall buildings and its surface full of movement and color. Artistos had a few small fishing boats, only good when the river ran slow. Below me, boats of every imaginable shape and hue danced on the water like insects. There were so many they should have hit each other, but they didn't. Jenna finally answered. "Marcus is a lone creator; he belongs to no visible affinity group. Or at least, he didn't." She touched the blue necklace, probably giving some silent command. "He was not so powerful when we left." She shook her head. "I can't say I know who or what Marcus has become. We should look him up, but not now. We're meeting my sister."

Surely with the power I'd sensed on board the *New Making*, he could find us if he wanted to. I shivered. He had been so *strong*.

Jenna pointed at the river. "That's new. There used to be hundreds of lakes, and now it looks like a river surrounds the whole city."

"Did they *make* the river?" Bryan asked.

Jenna swept her arm in front of her. "That's what drives the economy here. Change. Parts of the city change daily in some ways; the cumulative effect is a lot of change."

Alicia leaned forward, one hand on my shoulder. "Are we taking Bryan to a hospital? How will you find your sister?"

Jenna laughed. "Yes, we'll get Bryan some better care. All of us. But first, we'll see Tiala. I know where she lives—she hasn't moved and I doubt she's changed much at all. Tiala is—not a risk-taker. She is a researcher for the University of Creation, and has been since she was twenty."

"So how old is she now?" Alicia asked.

"She's two years younger than me, so that makes her about . . ." Jenna hesitated a moment, as if adding it up in her head ". . . one hundred twelve."

Silence. Nava had once told Chelo we would outlive the unaltered colonists, but I hadn't realized by how much. Jenna's gray hair was the only clear sign of age that touched her. Even with her severe injuries, she was the strongest and fastest person I'd ever seen.

Jenna kept the tall buildings at the city-center to our right and the wide sparkling river between us and the city. To our left, the buildings were lower, except for a huge misty-looking dome. Bryan pointed at the dome. "What's that?"

"Flyspace."

I remembered my mother's drawings of winged people. "Is that where the people with the wings go to fly?"

"They live there," Jenna said. "Most of them. Domes hold the kind of microclimates that are too sophisticated to maintain in the city."

So they managed microclimates inside the city? Temperature and what else? Could I see one? Activity surrounded the tall buildings: planes flying, boats moving, all of it too far away to really make out details. "How long *do* people live here?" I asked, squinting at an arching bridge.

Jenna shrugged. "Life extension is a process, and some people might live forever. Some were born before Silver's Home was settled over five hundred years ago. But people die here as well. We haven't engineered away every disease, or every accident." She laughed softly. "We haven't engineered away stupidity, either." She touched her gray hair. "We did get rid of old age."

"So what about the people back home?" Alicia asked. "Why don't they live longer?"

"What do you think?" Jenna returned.

Alicia leaned forward, chewing on her bottom lip, frustration showing in her narrowed eyes. I was more used to the way Jenna had always taught us on Fremont. "Because they think it's noble not to change?" I asked.

Bryan said, "They're more scared of changing than they are of dying."

Jenna asked, "Alicia?"

"Because they think they're better than us," she said. Her fingernails dug into my shoulder. "They think we're not as pure. That's what my old band used to say. Ruth called me a monster, and most of the band thought we're all monsters. That our parents were monsters."

Jenna laughed softly, agreement rather than contradiction. "All of your answers have some truth," she said. "Remember that many people are convinced they have the one true way to live. Even here. Try not to be like that yourselves."

The craft began to fall slowly through the sky, nudging down on a strip of hard surface beside a long green rectangle of grass. Jenna rolled the craft to a stop near two similar skimmers at the end of the hard surface.

Structures the size of our buildings on Fremont lined two sides of the park, with ample room between, and a walkway connecting them all. In front of us, a ball the size of a house floated in a flower garden. To my right, a clear square that might've been a house let me look right through it to tall trees filled with yellow and orange flowers behind the clear square. Each building appeared fantastic and different from all the others. We had nothing like this on Fremont, nothing even close. And these were small, maybe the least of the wonders here.

Jenna opened her door, and the scent of grass and various unfamiliar flowers drew a smile from Alicia. The air felt warm, like late spring on Fremont, but this grass didn't smell dusty like our plains. There was no bitter redberry touching the air, and no clanging metal or acrid burning scent like those of our smelter and mill. Even exhausted as I was, the joy of being on a new planet sang inside me, and I scrambled out of the ship as fast as I could, Alicia and then Bryan on my heels.

We grinned at each other. Whatever this place might become to us, we were here. We'd flown between stars. The first time I had laid eyes on the *New Making*, a gleaming silver bullet standing silently on the Grass Plains below Artistos, it had called to me.

If only Chelo had come, too.

Alicia stepped back from our circle of three. "Where's Jenna?"

Bryan pointed. Jenna raced across the grass, away from us, toward a dark-haired woman who ran toward her. Something gold and orange and red fluttered behind the woman. A bird? They stopped and looked at each other, circling like cats before a fight. Then the other woman enclosed Jenna in a tight embrace.

Surely this was Tiala.

The bird—I could tell now that it was bird, but unlike anything I'd seen—fluttered over her head in small, tight circles, making a high-pitched call.

Eventually, we walked near them, and I heard crying above the sounds of the bird. The two women sobbed, their raw voices blending, full of joy and sorrow and longing. I had never heard Jenna cry, not when chased by people trying to kill her, not hunting, not when we began the short fight for our freedom on Fremont. Never. Her shoulders shook, one strong, one half destroyed. The tiny sliver of her cheek that peeked out from under Tiala's hand glistened with tears. Her breath came in tight short gasps. Her one arm snaked around Tiala's back, a strong, stout arm with skin turned white under the sterile lighting in the *New Making*.

The bird fluttered above them, its circles wider now. Alicia stared up at it, her mouth open in awe. She took Bryan's and my hands, standing between us, whispering, "It's beautiful. So pretty."

I pulled her close. "Not as pretty as you." Its voice alone sang out that it existed for its beauty—rising and falling, pleasant even as it flew, watching as if in some consternation over Jenna's return. It sounded like bright feathered bells flying above us.

Tiala and Jenna were the same height, but Tiala looked little older than Alicia, dark hair caught behind her back in a shimmering silver clip. She wore a simple grass-green tunic accented with tiny yellow and orange leaves. Even with eyes red from tears, she was breathtaking. More beautiful by far than any of the women on Fremont, her skin was smooth and clear, her hair nearly perfect. She held Jenna so tightly I would have expected anyone else to break.

As we neared the two women, Tiala murmured, "Poor baby, poor baby," over and over. There was no pity in the words, just acceptance. It took a long time for them to even notice that we stood watching them and the bird, openmouthed.

When they finally separated, Tiala wiped her hands across her damp eyes, looked at Jenna, and laughed through her tears. "I'm so glad you're home."

I breathed out, happy to have some of their shared tears turn to laughter.

Tiala must have seen our amazement at the bird. "Bell," she called, a soft command. "Come."

The bird settled on her shoulder, its tail feathers trailing nearly to her waist.

Jenna used the sleeve of her silky golden shirt to wipe her eye and cheeks. She turned, as if to introduce us, then stopped, squinting toward the late-day sun—back in the direction we had come from.

Then I heard what Jenna had clearly heard first—the soft whine of a skimmer. Jenna glanced at Tiala, who shrugged.

Jenna's stance changed subtly, her feet a little wider, her knees bent, the same way she stood watching a clearing for signs of djuri to hunt. Following her cues, I watched carefully. Was it the Port Authority coming back to get us?

Alicia's hand found mine and I squeezed tightly, seeking grounding, then opened a little of my ability to read the data flowing by us in the air. Surely it would not be so strong out here where so much more open space surrounded us.

Wrong.

Data poured into the small crack I'd made for it as if a thousand snakes hovered in the air outside my skin and turned inward all at once. I quested briefly toward the skimmer, looking for identification, suddenly dizzy. As I slammed my senses closed, I tasted a familiar energy amongst the raw wild data of Silver's Home.

I stiffened.

Marcus.

16

MARCUS

As soon as I recognized Marcus in the dataflood, I slammed every internal barrier I had down again. My stomach dizzied and my hands shook as I watched his skimmer land neatly next to ours. Fancier than what Ming had called for Jenna. A big, silver bug with five legs and a bubble-head.

Alicia clutched my hand. Bryan stood on my other side, our silent, stoic observer. Jenna and Tiala were just in front of us, Tiala's bird, Bell, on her shoulder. For the first time since I saw her, Bell was silent, her head cocked to one side, her nearest round black eye fixed on the skimmer.

A tall, slender man slid onto the grass and started toward us. Sunlight spangled his dark brown hair with reddish tints. He wore simple loose brown pants and a belted white tunic. Except for some indefinable fluidity in his movements, he looked normal. At least until he came close enough to make eye contact. His deep green eyes had the same intensity I'd felt when I met him inside the *New Making*. Flecks of gold floated in spring-grass-colored pupils that radiated Jenna's wildness, Lukas's power, and Nava's single-minded drive all wrapped up inside one person. Like Akashi, only doubled or tripled.

I still wore the captain's coat, a clue.

He smiled at me. "Joseph. Nice job flying in, especially for a rookie." His words were silky, laced with warmth. Mothers might give up their babies to that voice.

"Thank you." I struggled to keep my voice from shaking. He had power. It rolled from him even now, and I had felt the truth of it deep in the ship's data flows. "It's good to meet you."

He looked at Jenna, his eyes narrowed in concern. "Jenna. Damn. What happened to you?"

She ran her gaze up and down his body. She stopped for a moment, looking into his eyes, testing him in some way I didn't understand. After a moment, the tightness left her jaw and her shoulders relaxed. "A war, Marcus. A stupid war, fought stupidly." She smiled. "I ended up near the business end of a missile, in the last battle. I got left for dead."

Tiala watched her closely, her eyes wide. Perhaps this was new information for her?

Jenna gestured toward the three of us. "You've met Joseph. Alicia and Bryan were also born on Fremont. I brought them home."

Marcus raised an eyebrow as he took in Bryan's cast. "Did the wrong end of a missile hit you, too?"

Bryan responded with a wry laugh. "Just the business end of some stupid people's fists."

Jenna added, "But it took a lot of them to bring him down." I hoped Bryan heard the pride in her voice.

Bryan shifted uneasily under Marcus gaze, then stuck his hand out. "Pleased to meet you."

Marcus returned the handshake. "I hope Silver's Home is a little easier on you." He didn't say he expected it to be.

Bryan took a step back, watchful as always. "I hope so, too."

Marcus glanced at me. He might as well have read my thoughts. "No, I don't know where your father is. I saw him once after he got back. He insisted the people on Fremont are backward and neurotic."

My father was alive! I put my hand in my pocket and touched the data button that held his journal. Excitement flooded me. He'd made it back—he'd probably flown the *Journey* back, just as I thought.

I felt lighter, as if I could raise my hands and fly.

Before I could get a question out, Marcus said, "He's a pilot. He could be on any one of the five worlds right now."

"What about my mother?" I asked.

He shook his head. "I don't think I've ever met her."

Surely she was a Wind Reader, too. I realized with a shock that I didn't know that. Bitter disappointment laced my elation. After looking at her drawings, I had felt linked to her.

"Will you tell me about my father?"

He laughed. "Not now. We don't have time." He turned to Jenna. "He has to go with me."

I blinked, stunned. Jenna stiffened. Alicia dug her nails into my forearm and blurted out, "He's not! We just got here."

Marcus shook his head. "The Port Authority may have let you go, but they tracked you. I came for you."

Came for me? To go with him? Leave everyone? I swallowed hard, afraid, and entirely unwilling to show it.

Alicia stepped between me and Marcus. "No! Everyone wants him, but we need him."

Marcus looked down at her. "I heard Lukas asked for him." He took Jenna's hand. Surprisingly, she gave it to him. "The Port Authority would ruin him. He's unformed, but he has more raw strength than ten other Wind Readers combined." He turned to me. "You are dangerous to yourself and to this place. You need protection while you learn what you are."

Protection from what?

Alicia balled her fists at her side, looking up at Marcus with a fiercely protective gaze that unnerved even me. "If you take him, then I'm going, too."

I swallowed and squeezed her hand, tried to stand as strong as she did. "I don't want to be separated from Alicia."

The look he turned on Alicia was kind, but completely firm. "I am not the right teacher for you, Alicia. And Joseph will need to focus."

"I can help him!" She hesitated. "Besides, I'm smart. I can learn from anyone. I can even learn from you."

"But you are not a Wind Reader." He laughed. "Besides, it appears you need to learn patience. Tiala will be better at teaching you that than I will be."

Alicia glanced at Jenna, who held up her hand, signaling Alicia to be still.

Alicia drew her lips into a tight line, and tears glistened in the corner of her eyes. She didn't say anything more, but she didn't have to. She hated to lose.

We couldn't fight both Jenna and Marcus in this strange place.

Jenna stood completely still, as if she'd gone inside herself to assess the idea. I held my breath, waiting for some sign from her.

When it came, it somehow didn't surprise me. "I've taught you all I can, for now. I knew they'd notice you when you flew in, but I didn't know how badly they'd want you, even untrained." She looked past Marcus, scanning the sky. Her voice sounded lost, and not much like herself at all. "I don't know if I can keep you safe."

What kind of place was this that *Jenna* couldn't protect me?

She looked at Marcus. "When I last saw you, you worked alone. Are you affiliated now?"

He shook his head, smiling softly, apparently amused at the question.

"I appreciate your offer, but I don't know if we can take it. I . . ." She hesitated, glancing at Tiala for a second. "I don't know what kind of resources I have yet. It will take days or more to sell the ship's contents, and I can't yet tell how much the Port Authority will try to block me. How much do you need?"

Alicia gasped.

How much? Did Marcus want credit to train me? I hadn't expected that, but maybe that was the root of Jenna's questions about affiliation. What was he offering anyway? It had sounded like a command.

Marcus stepped back and shook his head, still looking bemused. "Well, I suspect I could get the Port Authority to pay me a pretty penny to train him for *them*. The newer ships the navy flies need strength like his, or mine." He arched an eyebrow and cocked his head, reminding me for a moment of Akashi, playing to an audience onstage during story night. "And there may be war here soon. There's tension between the Five Worlds. Islas is building up its fleet, and signaling some nasty intentions toward us. Lopali is with us, but Paradise and Joy Heaven haven't signaled their preferences." He grimaced. "Or at least they haven't told us."

Jenna grimaced. "How much do you want?" I asked.

He looked at me. "You could earn your own way."

It felt like a test. "What do you mean?"

"It may take months, or more, to teach you about this place. Jenna could teach you a little, but I'm one of the only people who can teach *you* how to ride data. You should never have seen me inside the *New Making*. I should have been able to turn that ship like an unseen hand." He pursed his lips and shook his head, a chiding humor in his voice. "But your control is really pretty poor."

I bit back a sharp protest and waited. He hadn't answered my question yet.

"I work for hire. That's what I was doing today—and I won't be getting paid for that job, now, I suspect." He grinned. "You'll be able to help in a few months. You can work off your training."

I bit my lip. Working it off sounded better, more noble. But that was exactly what Jenna had chosen to avoid when she refused the command to land at the space station. Without taking my eyes from Marcus, I said, "Jenna, isn't some of the cargo mine?"

"Yes." Approval. I had said the right thing.

"Then we'll pay, Marcus." I tried to radiate strength. "If I go. But first, I want to know why you're doing this. Why did you come for me at all?"

"Because I don't want you working for the wrong people."

When I looked at Jenna, she was smiling at Marcus's answer. So I looked back at him and said, "Very well." I hadn't been to Trading Days twice a year for nothing. I didn't understand value here. Not yet. "You can work out the price with Jenna."

Alicia spoke up. "What about me?"

Marcus looked at her. "Ask Jenna."

Alicia recoiled slightly, but pressed on. "Surely you're not taking him off by himself?"

He ignored her, turning toward Jenna. "Four hundred credits for the first month, then three hundred a month after that."

Tiala gasped. "That's the price of a small ship!"

I blinked, surprised, but held my tongue yet again. I didn't want to leave Alicia, but I needed a way to understand this place—its data, its people, and what I could be here.

Marcus kept his gaze on Jenna. "It's a high price, but I keep my freedom by having enough credit to buy it. Jenna, you know what you've brought here." He nodded at me. "I won't have time to do much of anything else for the next few months."

Jenna put her hand on Tiala's free shoulder. Bell leaned around and twittered at her until Tiala raised a hand and said, "Okay, Bell." The bird quieted immediately.

"Tiala," Jenna said, "there's plenty. Even though I can already tell I'll need resources for other things, Joseph may be our future. I'll pay."

Tiala shook her head. "That's a lot of credit." She watched me silently, but not unkindly. I had the sense she was trying to decide if I was worth a small ship.

Alicia stepped back near me, taking my hand. "What happens to us, Jenna?" She sounded betrayed. "You said you'd teach us what we need to know. And now you're sending Joseph away. What happens to us?"

Jenna looked pained. "You'll stay with me until I find out more. Then, you two will need teachers. But no one is about to chase *you* down."

Bryan cleared his throat. "Is someone about to chase Joseph down?"

Marcus answered. "We aren't going to wait around to find out."

I blinked at him. "Do I have to go now?"

Alicia's fingers tightened around my arm, and she stepped close to me, watching Marcus's face.

"Yes." He smiled warmly then. "I will not be easy on you."

But . . . I looked from Alicia to Bryan to Jenna. I hated feeling weak enough to ask the next question. "By myself?"

He frowned at me. "Perhaps I haven't been clear. Drop your shields."

"My what?"

"Go on. Tell me what you can learn about this ordinary little park here. Open yourself up to its data."

I swallowed hard, my pulse racing.

I had to try.

I opened. Silver's Home screamed at me. Numbers. Coordinates. Lists of credits. Names and words I didn't know. So much more than we had on Fremont, so much faster. Data threads plunging into me and pulling me out of my body. Shattering my core. I crumpled to the grass, landing on my knees, then all fours.

"Stop," Marcus commanded.

I couldn't. There wasn't enough strength, enough cohesion. Too much data filled me. Pieces of my very being seemed to float away in the data.

He bent down next to me, his face serious and still. Silence bathed me until I stopped shaking. "You need to come now," he said.

Alicia knelt by my side. I didn't remember that she'd touched me, but her palm caressed my cheek.

I smiled up at her, drinking her in, suddenly wanting to take her in my arms so badly it was a physical need like thirst. I settled for taking her hand. "He's right. I have to go."

She nodded, her tears still caught in her eyes, her back straight. Her lower lip trembled, just slightly. "I know."

"You'll stay in touch?" I asked.

She stared up at Marcus, and if looks could hurt, he'd need meditape. Her voice came out small and fierce. "I'll make sure. Somehow."

"There must be some way to communicate here." Bryan sounded angry and looked lost. He'd been beaten, then shoved onto the ship without really knowing what had happened, stayed asleep for most of the journey, then woke up to land in this strange place soon after. He'd lost Chelo, his best friend, and now he was losing me.

I wanted to ask Alicia to take care of him, but I knew Bryan too well. I tightened my grip on Alicia's hand. "You two take care of each other."

"We will," Alicia said.

She extended a hand, and I took it and stood up, my legs shaking.

Marcus said, "Time to go."

Bell flew circles around our heads, her feathers gleaming in the late afternoon brightness as if she were, herself, a tiny sunset. I'd never seen such behavior in a bird. In dogs, but never in a bird.

Jenna leaned in and hugged me, Bryan pulled me close for a second, his large arm enfolding me, and Alicia clung, only stepping back when I pushed myself gently away. I looked at Tiala, struck again by the differences between the sisters. Tiala could have been Jenna's child, or grandchild. We had actually never quite been introduced. "Pleased to meet you, Tiala."

She inclined her head. "Good luck."

I turned to Jenna. "When will I see you again?"

Marcus answered for her. "Not for at least a few months."

That felt like a lifetime. I looked once more at all of them, drinking in their shapes, the angles of their faces. I swallowed hard, and said, "I'm ready."

17

LEARNING

The smell of baking bread woke me. I rolled over, stretching out on smooth, soft sheets scented with something like outdoor garden air, rich and complex. The bread! It called to the empty hollow where my stomach used to be. The last thing I'd eaten was the waybread in the Command Room.

I struggled to sit up, every muscle sore. Vague memories of landing somewhere in the dark. We'd flown here through the dark, and I had given into exhaustion almost immediately.

I was alone.

Except for Marcus. Who was he, really?

When we arrived, Marcus's arm had steadied me and led me up dimly lit stairs. I recalled deciding he was putting me into a bed and that the right thing to do was close my eyes.

He'd left me clothed, but my shoes lay neatly at the side of the bed, and the captain's coat hung on the corner of an ornately carved wooden box that cupped the bed. I pushed a light green coverlet away and padded to the bathroom attached to the room. In the mirror, I looked exhausted and shell-shocked. I splashed cold water on my face, struggling to wake, driven by hunger.

I did not feel like myself at all, but like some character in the made-up stories Akashi used to tell at community fires.

A fresh set of clothes had been set out—simple blue pants and a green shirt, soft to the touch. The seams were sewn with data threads like my father's old headband, and the belt-line of the pants had a subtle blue-on-blue design shot through with gold data thread. By now, I knew the thread was merely an amplifier, and that, in fact, it did me little good. And why would I want to amplify the data here? I so wanted to reach for it, to have it steady me, extend me. Like at home. Like on *New Making*. I stayed closed up, changed, and went in search of the source of the bread smell.

Downstairs, I found an empty kitchen the size of the common kitchen in Artistos that fed whole guilds. The alluring smell issued from an oven set into the wall. Surfaces gleamed: silver metal and natural-looking brown and gray and black stone. A cook-surface that could have fed half the community filled the middle of the large room, with wood and stone countertops surrounding it. Tools and dried herbs I didn't recognize hung from walls, and a wide, low stone shelf with three sinks spaced far apart lined half a windowed wall, light spilling onto the stone.

On the other side of the window, flashes of bright color and movement drew my eye to a garden. Red and gold flowers vined up trellises, trees with maroon and green leaves twisted into geometric shapes that couldn't be natural, but looked somehow exactly right. The walled garden dwarfed the huge kitchen, as wide as the long window, at least fifteen meters, and twice as long. Paths and benches and large stones, tiny lawns, and a small stream filled the open places. Huge purple flowers on long stalks, a golden bird with a silver beak that looked as artificial and perfect as Tiala's Bell. I walked to the sink, leaning close to the window, inundated by perfect details.

"Do you like it?"

I jumped at the sound of Marcus's voice, as if pulled from a trance.

"This is part of what I can teach you. We are all creators on Silver's Home, and Wind Readers make the best creators. You have the ability to create spaces of beauty if you want to. For me, it is a way to practice my skills and hone my sense of balance all at once."

"But how?" I whispered. "How does reading data translate to creating something like this?"

Marcus wore clothes much like mine, loose blue pants and a simple off-white shirt. He was a few inches taller than me, and slightly thinner, although strong and wiry rather than gawky. I recalled his green eyes from the day before, and now they seemed full of all the greens in his garden. He cleared his throat. "All living things are driven by genetic data. Reading the Wind of data is the first step to weaving that data into changed patterns. We have a better track record than machines for creating life, as if the life inside us speaks to the life we are making." He grinned at me. "Oddly enough, machines can design a better spaceship."

I laughed at that, somehow not surprised. "This must have taken forever."

His laugh sounded warm and silky. "It's not done. To get this far took fifteen years."

I still couldn't tear myself away from the window. "Do people who aren't Wind Readers create biological things?"

"They could make up the pieces of this—a flower, a tree, and some can even design birds or other pets. Often the best possible choice is to team a Wind Reader with someone good at strategy or with a strong artistic bent. Only a powerful Wind Reader can see the interrelationships necessary to make a whole ecosystem. A team without a Wind Reader cannot do it."

A pair of red and blue birds twice the size of my hand flew in playful circles across the garden, alighting in a tree with blue-green leaves nearly a meter across. "How do you keep the birds in?"

"I designed it so they'd want to stay here. It's a microclimate, and the shifts in heat and humidity from the garden to the rest of the property discourage migration." He paused. "But sometimes they leave. If they do, I wish them luck."

"So if I leave you will wish me luck?"

"*When* you leave I will wish you luck." He took my arm, gently, peeling me away from the window, and led me to a small table set with plates of bread and fruit, glasses of water, and two steaming mugs of something black that smelled bitter. "Sit. You need food."

No kidding. Now that the garden's trance-hold on me was broken, my stomach screamed in my ears. I reached for a slice of bread. "What's in the cup?"

"It's col, a mild stimulant. It's pretty much our traditional morning drink on Silver's Home—the flavoring ingredients can be changed to match individual taste. It will tune your nervous system and help you think more clearly. I gave you the taste I like—luko nut and butter—but you can start experimenting tomorrow."

I wrinkled my nose at the bitter smell, but took a sip anyway. The col tasted sweeter than it smelled, and unlike anything I'd ever tried. Almost immediately, colors looked slightly brighter, and sounds seemed crisper. I tore open a warm roll and bit into it, feeling it dissolve in my mouth. Was everything here better than anything I'd ever experienced? I took another bite, then another, finishing the bread. I reached for the strange fruits, trying something yellow and round. Sweetness filled my mouth, and a bit of juice dribbled down my chin.

He watched me, his eyebrows slowly climbing toward his hairline. "Slow down. Your body is starved, but you should never overfill it." He sipped his drink, and I noticed he had taken only a bite of bread. Disciplined. My cheeks burned lightly.

Marcus sipped his own col, a satisfied expression on his face. He seemed both strong and completely at peace.

Would I ever have that sense of coiled calm? I ached for Alicia, for Bryan, for Jenna. For Chelo. I wanted freedom, but surely I was more trapped now than the birds in Marcus's garden. "So where do we start?" I asked.

He held up a hand. "I know you have questions to ask me. First, I need to learn enough about you to design your first few days of training. Tell me about yourself and about Fremont. Start with your oldest memories." He settled back in his chair, watching me closely.

So I told him about growing up a spoil of war, about losing Steven and Therese, about being taunted and threatened, and Bryan's beating.

At that, Marcus fell silent. After a few moments, he prodded. "Tell me more about the other children like you."

Should I tell him about all of us? I glanced at his face, his eyes. They didn't hold anything mean. Secrets, surely. Secrets I wanted to learn. And Jenna trusted him. I chewed my lip, unsure how much to reveal.

He took one of the yellow fruits, biting into it slowly. Waiting.

"I already told you about Bryan. Alicia had it worst, though. She was adopted by a band who hated us, with a leader who had lost her family in the war. Her *parents* locked her up like an animal once." My hand shook, showing my anger, spilling a little of the hot drink on the table.

I wiped it up, refocusing, then looked at Marcus. "Some people were fair to us, some our friends, but we scared most of them. Some people hated us because of the war—because of family members they'd lost. But it wasn't our fault. We were just babies then."

Anger flashed in his eyes. He masked it, his cool stare returning. At least he cared. He took a deep breath. "Tell me more about the colony."

"It's small, a few thousand people. There's only one city, Artistos. Most people live there. There are two roamer bands—scientists, really—that come and go. They're each over a hundred strong. One had Alicia and hated her, and one had Liam and loved him."

Marcus drew me out with questions, asking about the bands and how people lived day to day, little things like where we got our water from (the river) and what we built houses out of (wood and metal) and about what we wore (woven hemp, djuri and goat hide, goat's wool).

"Where was Jenna?" he asked.

"People tried to kill her for years, but they weren't strong enough or fast enough, even a lot of them together. She lived outside town, and she finally made a truce by killing the paw-cats and demon dogs and yellow snakes that got inside the boundaries. She dumped their bodies in the park. She was too strong and too smart for them to kill, and she taught people to need her." I remembered how she'd looked the few times she came into town, her hair a long uneven braid from having to catch it back with one hand, clad in paw-cat hide, wild and damaged and free. "All that with one arm and one eye missing. When I was very little—around seven or eight—I wanted to live by her side in the wild more than I wanted anything except to fly the ship."

He raised an eyebrow at that and almost laughed, pleasure touching his eyes. "So, Jenna learned to be innovative. That might be good for her—she used to stick to rules and tradition as if her life depended on it."

"She's not like that, now. People have to watch out for her."

Marcus just laughed. "Why do you think Jenna stayed around town?"

"To help us. She taught us a lot, mostly by making us learn things. She saved a skimmer and a bunch of other technology, and eventually she gave me one of my father's old headbands full of data threads and enough clues to figure out how to use it. She saved up a bunch of—our—technology."

He pursed his lips, and turned his questions back to more general ones about Fremont and Artistos. After an hour or so, he suggested a short break and we cleaned up from breakfast. He led me to a bench in the garden.

A palm-sized butterfly with a rainbow pattern on its wings flitted over and landed on my arm. Marcus glanced at it. "That's one of my first creations that bred true—I call them light link butterflies. I was about your age when I designed those." The butterfly took off, hovering for a moment in the air. Together, we watched it fly to a bush twice my height and disappear into bright blue and green flowers. Marcus turned back to me.

He settled himself comfortably, one long leg crossed over the other. "Now, tell me about your relationship with data. How did you first learn you could feel it differently than other people?"

Chelo had told me the story so many times I had no idea if I remembered the actual events or her side of them. "I was young, maybe five, and Chelo seven. We were in Commons Park, in the middle of town, playing catch. I remember knowing something was wrong, feeling off balance and suddenly scared. And then I knew what it was—and I said the word. 'Demons.' Chelo knew I was scared—she can always tell what I feel—and she knelt down next to me, and then the bells pealed for demon dog entry and people ran by us to find the pack and get it out of town."

"What do you do to access data on purpose?"

"At first, I had to go almost into a trance. Chelo helped me by being near. She isn't a Wind Reader herself, but she took care of me." I closed my eyes, breathing in the smell of foreign dirt and different plants, momentarily homesick.

"Chelo is a full sister? Where is she now?"

I nodded. "She's back on Fremont." Years distant. If I left now, it would take three years to get back.

"It was easier for you with her nearby?"

I rose to stretch, turning away from him, not wanting Marcus to see how lost I felt without her.

Apparently he didn't need to see. His voice, which had been all business, softened. "You must miss her. Sometimes family is designed to support each other, and that must have been how your parents designed you and Chelo."

Jenna had told us a little back at Fremont's spaceport, and told me more on the ship. "We were designed to be a team. Liam and Chelo to lead and support, both capable of either, me and Kayleen as Wind Readers, Bryan to be physically strong and thoughtful, and Alicia to keep us on our toes, to take risks. There were more, but they died in the war." I remembered a story Paloma and Tom told us once, in the tent. "One of them died in Jenna's arms when she got blown up. I only know about the others because Jenna told us." I sat back down next to him. "I do miss Chelo. I want to go back for her." I shifted, looking at him. "Jenna could help some, but she never fit as well as Chelo. But I don't really *need* either of them to access data anymore—just for other things. The data threads that Jenna gave me made me stronger. When I wore the headband, I could do things when I was awake that I couldn't even do from a trance before that—I could feel the whole network—everything." I had felt so powerful then. Lord of a tiny trickle of data, compared to the relentless flow here. "After a while, I didn't even need the physical data threads anymore."

He blinked at me, looking surprised, but didn't say anything.

"I could manipulate their nets, turn them on and off, hear almost everything they said. And they couldn't sense me doing it, couldn't prove it was me."

He rolled his eyes. "Is that why you had to leave?" he asked.

"No." My cheeks grew hot again. "Well, maybe partly. But mostly we left because Alicia picked a fight with Town Council, and Jenna wanted to come home. But I wanted to go, too. I wanted to fly the ship. It had been sitting there all that time. And when Jenna told me I could fly it, I knew I had to."

He laughed. "It's probably in your blood. And I mean more than just the nanocytes. What did flying the ship feel like?"

I blushed. "It's even better than sex."

He threw his head back and laughed even harder. "Did you ever tell your girlfriend that?"

"Of course not!"

He was still laughing, not at me, but kindly. It felt like laughing with a friend, like something man to man passing between us. The warmth stayed in his voice as he asked, "So, now I know it felt like the best thing ever, but what was it like to fly? What did the data feel like?"

I sat back down next to him. "It wasn't as easy as the nets on Fremont. I had to stay close to trance on the ship, because there was so much more there—more data than in all of Artistos. The coat helped."

He nodded. "You're lucky that nothing unexpected happened when you landed. That's why I waited until you came down in one piece."

I bristled a little at that. "I wasn't fully stretched. I could have done more."

"Pride," he said dryly, "might be your best friend or your worst enemy. You can't handle our nets yet."

That stopped me. I couldn't bear the nets here. Yet. But I'd do something to be proud of here; I just knew it. All I said was, "I know. Your nets feel different."

"They aren't. Not much." He leaned forward, his hands on his knees. "I know where to start now. The difference you feel is the size of the conversation. On Fremont, you had a single interconnected network—maybe a few if you count the satellite data, etc. But a handful, at most. The ship is a single network. A big one, and you did well. But here . . ." he waved his hand around in the air, taking in the garden and the house and maybe the whole planet ". . . here there are a million conversations all running at once. Even though a single blade of grass doesn't send out data about itself, every single blade of grass has data collected about it."

I looked around, counting up the blades of grass in my head. Millions.

He continued. "Data threads weave into many webs, some open to everybody, some secured." He stood, too, and spread his arms wide. "The big webs include a finance web—the credit balances of everyone and every affinity group and every government here. An affinity web that tracks affiliations. A law web. Webs for each art form. A geo web that describes the places here in detail. Constructs really, so that people can understand related data through a single interface. Everywhere, local webs interact with bigger webs."

He fell silent for a moment, and I tried to remember what I'd felt when I stepped off the ship, and then again when I tested his skimmer. It fit—a million million bits of data and even more connections between them. "How does anyone keep track of it all? How do you keep track?"

"No one can, or needs to. The trick is getting at what you want. You have to understand the linkages. For example, this garden has its own web that connects to the house web that connects to a web over the whole property that connects to the city, then the continent, then the planet, then to our space web. The geo web connects to other webs—for example, to the law web. If the rules are different for Li Spaceport than they are in the flyspace, the geo web can tell you that."

I blinked at him, trying to understand so much complexity. A sudden thought crossed my mind. "Is everything here tamed?"

He laughed. "We have no wandering predators here. Like your—what did you call them? Demon dogs and paw-cats. But we have predators. Perhaps you would consider them tame, compared to wild Fremont. Here, there are designed predators, big game that suicidal idiots hunt over on Water Lily continent." He snorted. "Some people die that way every year." He fell silent for a moment, then said, "But we have people that are predators, too."

"I've met people who are predators."

"It sounds like you have also met governments that are predators. Some of ours are the same. But it would be risky to think you understand the dangers here for a very long time."

He'd said people might be looking for me. "Am I safe here?"

He turned, a feral grin touching his face and satisfaction shining from his green eyes. "Not only are we standing inside a secure web, broadcasting only what we want, but some people here consider me a predator."

I recoiled a bit; it was easy to forget there must be more to Marcus than the teasing teacher.

But there was more to me, too. I had hunted, brought down fast nearly man-sized djuri with my bare hands. "Are you a predator?" I asked.

His eyes widened, and he looked like he was about to choke on his tongue. He took a deep breath, either trying to stop some outraged comment or trying not to laugh. After he calmed down, his voice grew serious. "Yes, but only to people who want too much power. See, Joseph, I believe in the balance and beauty of creation more than the beauty of power alone. I believe that people need to be able to choose what mods they want, to design themselves." His green eyes almost glowed with energy, and he fixed them directly on me, demanding my attention. "There is a lot of beauty here." He swept his arm in a wide arc, taking in the entire garden. "But we force some things on people before they're born, things they can't change. Like wings, or extra arms. We play god too hard, and too fast, and we may design our own doom if we aren't careful. Other societies on other planets have done that, and we seem to have forgotten the lessons they left for us. There are powerful groups here willing to sacrifice long term good for immediate gain—some for power, some for attention, some for reasons I don't understand."

It sounded complex. On Fremont, they forced things to be the same, and hated us for being different. Here, they made people different on purpose. Either way, it was about control. I shivered, even though the temperature was perfect.

He watched me closely. "Sometimes I do things to disturb the status quo." He paused, apparently realizing how intense he sounded. He shook himself, as if shaking off strong feelings. His voice lost some of its fire, turning into a calmer lecturer's voice. "The most fun people to shake up are the government—they can do the most ill, or the most good. They need people to keep them on their toes."

I remembered how I met him. "But sometimes you work for the government."

"There are some things only I can do. And some of those things, I don't mind doing."

"So tell me again why you are training me."

"You should not have been able to do what you did—learn to read the wind on your own, fly a ship. Not and stayed sane. But you did. That implies much balance inside of you. You intrigue me." And then, laughing. "Besides, I'm getting paid."

"I haven't forgotten this is a job for you," I blurted out. Silence fell between us, and I thought about the other things he'd said. "I'm off balance," I said, more softly. "I can't even open to the data here—it almost kills me."

He put his hands on my shoulders and looked me in the eye. "If you work hard, I'll teach you the beauty of creation."

"I want to learn."

He dropped his arms. "Sit down." After I sat on the cool stone bench, he said, "Lean back, close your eyes, and feel the garden."

I took a deep breath and opened. Data poured in, temperature, air mix, pressure, bits from every plant. In no more than two breaths it was too much. My stomach roiled while pain slammed into my forehead. I opened my eyes, searching for Marcus.

He seemed to be trying not to laugh. "Listen more carefully next time. I did not suggest you ride the garden's data, but that you feel the garden itself. Close your eyes again."

"But if this is a single system, why can't I handle it?" I protested.

"Who said this is a single system? There are webs here for plants, for animals, and traces of the geo web and affiliation web. My security web, letting some things in and keeping others out. And more. Linkages between them all. Now, close your eyes."

I wanted to ask more questions, but his commanding tone of voice didn't encourage questioning. I closed my eyes.

"Good. Now, feel the temperature. Tell me about it."

"Warm, not too hot."

"Is there a wind?"

"No."

"Smell the grass."

"Okay."

"Can you smell just the grass?"

"No."

"Try."

And so we worked.

He pushed me to separate and then synthesize my senses, focusing down on one thing, one thing, one thing, then another. It felt like work for a schoolchild.

We drank water, but didn't eat.

I grew incredibly sick of isolating one sense at a time, one individual thread within one sense at a time. My stomach and head hurt, but there was no way I'd admit it to Marcus.

He pushed me until the mid-afternoon sun turned the light a deeper gold. Finally, he said, "Stop."

My stomach cried out for food, but I didn't want to look weak and ask. "Did I do well?"

"What do you think?"

I had only used my simple senses for information. "How will this help?"

He cocked his head and gave me a half-smile. "Sit back down and try again to read the garden's data."

I did. Again, data poured in, filling me, jolting my body. At once I was overfull and light as air. The two feelings together seemed twisted, as if my body was falling, even though the stone bench was hard and cool under my back.

"Focus on the temperature."

Threads of data pulsed around me and through me. They bunched, separated, knotted, and stretched. Paying attention to one thread at a time felt easier now, and one by one, they became knowable. Some clearly originated nearby; queries produced the history of plants or the composition of dirt. Unchanging threads were from temperature sensors or other mechanical devices. Data about butterflies and birds swarmed chaotically against data about and from trees, and everything linked to information about place. I sampled, fighting a sense of falling, of losing myself. The temperature thread had to be from nearby, had to be steady. I focused on steady straight threads, checking one by one. Location. Air pressure. Humidity. Finally, I could whisper, "Twenty-three degrees."

"How many square meters of land are inside the garden fence?"

I dove back down, querying. Pain lanced through my stomach, and the data threads seemed to bunch and knot more than they had the first time. Surely that wasn't the data itself, but me. I forced three deep breaths, and on the last one I came fully into physical presence, coughing and spluttering.

Marcus looked like he was hiding a laugh again. "Did you progress?"

"Sure, now I can go catatonic and get sick as a dog just to find out what my skin will pretty much tell me."

He threw back his head and laughed loudly. "Exactly. Good thing. A sense of humor."

Alicia always teased me for being too damned serious. I watched him as he reached into his pocket and tossed me a handkerchief. "Wipe your face. We'll break for lunch and then work on something physical."

I groaned, thinking of Jenna's endless physical sessions on the ship. She'd taught me and Chelo and Kayleen this way—making us work for knowledge. Maybe it was a habit on Silver's Home.

But food? If it tasted like breakfast had, it would be worth all the work. I grinned, wiped my face, and followed Marcus into the house.

I sat at the table while he bustled about the kitchen. After a few minutes he looked over at me. "You could help."

Of course I could. Chagrined, I got up and stood near him. He handed me a knife and some tomatoes. "Cut these up into small cubes." As soon as I'd started in on them, I drew up my courage. This morning he'd told me not to ask questions, but surely now I could? "Tell me about my father."

Marcus frowned. "I never knew him well. He's strong, but I don't think he's as strong as you are. Before they left, he was very intense, always focused on making money to finance the journey. He did that by flying ships between planets."

"Like taking stuff from place to place?"

Marcus shook his head, reaching for some small round green vegetables I didn't recognize. "People. It's not much use taking stuff—almost anything can be made anywhere. That, by the way, is why whatever you brought with you from Fremont will fetch you a lot of credit. It's unique."

"We brought some art, but most of it is just scientific samples and stuff."

"Newness has value. Whatever you brought here, people will eventually copy it, and change it. If you brought paw-cat DNA, there will be paw-cats on Water Lily by next summer."

Akashi would hate that. The West Band always returned captured animals to the wild once they'd studied them. "Isn't it wrong to sell things just so they can be copied?"

Marcus pushed his pile of cut vegetables to one side and turned to watch me finish cubing the tomatoes. "Does that mean you think it's wrong to create things?" He waved a hand at the garden window. "Almost every idea and every thing starts as something we improve on. But there is always a beginning, even if it's hard to see."

Akashi would probably hate everything about this place. But I liked it; I felt I belonged here more than on Fremont. I thought about how to answer Marcus. "I guess that—here—it doesn't feel wrong. I want to make flowers for the garden—I'm already thinking about what they look like. But Fremont isn't made, and mixing the two feels strange."

"If your parents had succeeded, Fremont would be closer to this place by now. They went there to start with new things. To explore, but also to create. They thought a fresh start would let them create a fantastic world." He grimaced. "Maybe the paw-cats would be as big as houses."

The idea confused me, so I returned to my original questions. "You saw my father after he came back. And I know the Family of Exploration is in trouble of some kind. What did he look like after he got back? How was my father?"

Marcus held out two cupped hands for the tomatoes and dumped them into the bowl he had been filling with cheese and vegetables. "He looked bitter. His eyes were years older than when he left. I guess, maybe sad, too." He shook his head. "I'm sorry; I didn't really notice much more. We aren't friends—we just know each other."

Maybe it would make him happier if he knew I was alive. "Can we find him?"

"When you can post a find-me query to the webs, you should do that."

"But you could post one now!" I protested.

"How do you know I haven't?" he asked, and then he started for the table with the bowl of vegetables. I stared at his back, trying to bore holes into it. I did want to learn from him—I needed to. But why couldn't he be more straightforward? He was just like Jenna!

As we sat down, I kept pressing. "You said he looked sad. Was he with anyone?"

"No, I had a drink in a bar with him. Look, he's likable enough, at least he was, just a little intense. Jenna will probably find him."

"When can I see Jenna and the others?"

He grinned, holding up a hand flat in front of me, signaling a stop. "Maybe that's where you get your intensity. Maybe it's inherited. Don't worry. You haven't lost them forever."

"I promised Alicia I'd stay in touch."

"That little slip of hellfire who came with you? I don't blame you."

I nodded, feeling pleased he saw how beautiful she was.

"Hmmm. First love? Don't answer. It must be. Jenna will keep her busy. But you and she will both change while you're here."

Duh. "I want to talk to her."

He shook his head. "You're safe with me, but there's no reason to make this place a target."

"A target for what?"

"Attention. For people who want the power you may eventually have."

"Won't your geo web tell anyone who asks where I am?"

He looked pleased with himself. "No. I blocked queries about your whereabouts."

Meaning the webs didn't report out that I was here automatically? "So not all data can be relied on?" I asked.

He looked at me as if I was asking whether the moons were made of water. He shook his head. "Only a stronger, wiser Wind Reader could get in here."

And of course, there weren't any. Maybe pride was his biggest weakness, too. It didn't seem like the right thing for me to say, so I dug into my salad, wondering if it was prison food or school food.

PART THREE

SETTLING ISLANDIA

18

SEED STEALERS

Dirt coated my fingertips as I twisted tiny weeds into my palm, yanking them from under the bushy tops of young carrots. A red bird landed on the top crossbar of our small greenhouse. The bird pecked at the clear plastic, leaving whitish marks where its long black beak nearly punctured the roof. Liam had named it a "black-throated red seed-stealer" in a fit of pique. The many bright, long-beaked, wild birds were a plague, stealing seedlings and anything bright and shiny we left out. At this rate, if we did winter here, we'd be living on forage.

Maybe we could eat the birds.

I threw the weeds aside and stood outside, blinking in the bright sunshine. The steady thwack . . . scrape . . . clunk . . . thwack of Liam cutting wood was nearly obscured by the waterfall. I sighed, already exhausted after a morning's work. Our now-strong perimeter had screamed at the ever-hopeful demon dogs three times last night. Good for us; bad for our sleep.

The perimeters kept large predators at bay, but I watched my footing for snakes and trap-spiders as I walked past the waterfall, stopping only when I reached the top of the rocky path that led to our little encampment, which we'd dubbed West Home in honor of the band we might never see again.

We'd made no progress freeing the skimmer.

At the path's summit, I looked down over Golden Cat Valley. Kayleen raced along a path she and Windy had worn to dirt across the center of the valley. The hebra followed her, keeping up easily. They ran through white, purple, and blue flowers peppering the knee-high grass, Kayleen's black hair streaming behind her. She began twisting away from the path, keeping Windy right behind her with voice command, training her to follow. It was only in this daily race and play that Kayleen ever looked truly happy.

Liam came up next to me, his bare torso clothed in sweat from chopping wood. My belly warmed and my cheeks flushed at his nearness. He pursed his lips, ready, I was sure, to tell me what we needed to do next. We'd been here nearly seven weeks, and every day had its long list of tasks. We'd set and re-set the perimeter, hauled piles of goods from the skimmer, built a one-room house and small corral, set up the greenhouse, and explored the valley. Still, it was nowhere near enough. I expected to be building food or wood storage next, so I looked up in surprise when Liam said, "I think we should go west. I want to pack today and head for the Fire River tomorrow."

Much more fun than endless woodcutting. "Your roaming blood is telling," I teased, reaching up to stroke his cheek. "You haven't complained about missing home for a whole day."

He narrowed his eyes at Kayleen and Windy below us. "We'll get home if I have to build a boat."

"Right. A day's flight is a month's sail, even if we had the materials." I lifted my face for a kiss. He leaned down and took my offer, but only for a brief brushing of the lips.

"I miss being alone with you." I said it softly, but loud enough that he heard me.

He kissed me again, just as briefly, then looked down at the valley, the girl, and the hebra. I took his chin in my hand and turned his face back toward me. "She's not here to see us right now. Kiss me."

He did, periodically glancing at the valley. Intimacy had become tough.

"I hate it that you're watching for her," I said.

He pulled me in close. "I'm sorry. It's just . . . so awkward. When we're close, she looks so hungry."

"She chose this," I whispered. But I'd given in, too, letting a combination of exhaustion and unease keep me from doing more than just curling next to him in a tangle of limbs at night. Our tiny house offered no privacy except during Kayleen's watch, and of course, she was awake then. "We should start the second house soon," I said.

"I wish."

I took his hand. There were a million other things that mattered more. We sat quietly, watching Kayleen race. She'd placed six long-range warning perimeter nodes along the sides of the valley, so it had become a reasonably safe place as long as Kayleen was around to read them. Unlike the more sophisticated equipment we'd used protecting West Home, these didn't deliver audible warnings.

He glanced at me. "Are you up for it? The river? It will be at least a two-day trip. Probably more."

"All of us?" I knew the answer. We never left the perimeter unless we were all together.

"We can use Windy to pack. She's strong enough now; I've seen Kayleen on her back a few times, although standing still." He winked. "After all, Kayleen told us she brought Windy for a pack animal."

"Right. Damned hebra's almost her dog." The friendly green-striped beast remained her closest confidante. If I didn't like her too, I'd have been jealous instead of just concerned. "Sure, I'll go. We've got to learn more about this place sometime."

His eyes twinkled. "Now who sounds like the roamer?"

A few moments later, Kayleen and Windy made their way up to us, sweat glistening on Kayleen's bare shoulders and soaking Windy's chest and withers. "Good morning," Kayleen said cheerfully as she neared us, her eyes shining with exercise adrenaline. "I saw some of the tall-beasts near the end of the valley."

"Did you get close?" Liam asked.

She shook her head. Our perimeter kept them out of West Home, and the herd had shrunk by two after one night when the demons bayed hunt for hours. They kept a polite distance from us, no matter how small and insignificant we tried to appear.

"Are you up for a trip?" Liam asked carefully.

Kayleen's eyes widened. "There's too much to do."

We started down the path toward home, Windy picking her way carefully between the rocks just ahead of us. Kayleen added, "I don't want to take her out there yet. She's not completely trained."

"She follows you pretty well now," I pointed out.

Kayleen looked back at me. "I'm not risking her past the valley."

"We have to explore sometime," Liam said. "Best when we can count on the weather. We'll hunt the valley out if we never leave."

Kayleen kept slightly ahead of us, hiding her face. Her shoulders had stiffened. "It's not safe out there."

Liam caught up to her and pulled her around gently to face him. "I know you're used to living in a town. Artistos has enough resources inside the perimeters, but we don't. We haven't got enough crop started to feed a child, much less all three of us."

She pulled away from him and searched our faces. But at least, not crazy. The crazy look almost never touched her anymore. She dropped her head and looked away. "Can we wait a while? We need to build some place to store grass for Windy."

Liam's voice sounded soft, almost as if he talked to a child. "We'll help you do that today. And tonight, we should pack up. We'll only be gone a few days."

She didn't answer. Group decision-making had evolved into two against one when we disagreed, and Kayleen surely knew she'd lost this battle.

"Come on," I said. "We have a big enough pile of logs to at least start a storage bin."

She grimaced, then shrugged, as if pretending it didn't matter to her. She took my hand and said, "All right." As if by an act of sheer will, she moved quickly in front of us, ready to start work in the frenetic, focused attitude that drove her all day. She only seemed to feel safe when she worked so hard that sweat poured from her.

Late that afternoon, the shelter over half built, she and I took a short break. We perched on the rocks rimming the pool, sitting close to each other, the waterfall's spray coating our hair with tiny jewels. She turned to look at me, droplets like freckles on her face, her legs dangling so one extra-long toe skimmed the water. Her arms lay crossed in her lap, still. Kayleen moved all the time—stillness telegraphed control and fear for her.

Her blue eyes gazed steadily at me and she spoke loudly to fight the waterfall's tendency to whip sound into its own rush. "Chelo. You and Liam, you shut me out. There's three of us. You can't always shut me out. There's no one for me but you two, no mate except Liam." Her words rushed out as fast as the waterfall. "And you're in the same boat. You know neither of us could stand to be with someone unaltered." She uncrossed her arms and her trailing foot twitched, making cross-wakes in the waterfall's ripples.

I pulled my knees in tight to my chest and made myself small.

She didn't wait for me to answer. "You know this. You're our leader. Or maybe you and Liam, together. You're supposed to see the future, see that we need to stay family." She reached a hand out toward me, but let it fall back into her lap, turning her gaze out to the waterfall. She mouthed the word "please," or perhaps she said it out loud and the waterfall took it, since she no longer faced me.

I felt as if I tottered at the top of the waterfall, ready to plunge, only I couldn't tell which way to jump to miss the worst of the rocks in the bottom of the pool. Really, I hadn't had a clue how to answer, except that I knew Liam wouldn't choose to be with her, not now, anyway. He was still too mad at her for stealing his summer. So I cleared my throat. "It's not my choice to make, not entirely. I think you need to talk to Liam and me about it together."

I couldn't tell if the fresh water on her cheeks was from her eyes or the waterfall. She shook her head. "Not yet. I can't talk to him yet. I can barely talk to him at all. I hoped you would talk to him."

It took three long breaths to find words to answer her. "I don't know how, and you're right, it's not time." I stood and leapt out over the rocks into a deep part of the pool, cleaving the water cleanly and shallowly, swimming toward the spot where the waterfall plunged into the pool. I fought toward the falling water until I was completely exhausted, kicking, managing at best to stay in one place, struggling, going nowhere. The roar of the waterfall and the gritty smell of the sharp, wet rocks filled me.

I forgot Kayleen and her request, and Liam, and that Joseph was gone. I gave myself to the fall and the pool so completely that when I crawled back onto the rocks I lay, panting, unable to move.

When I sat up, Kayleen was gone.

19

THE RIVER

Early the next afternoon, we left our safe haven and struck up the opposite ridge along a path Liam had found a week after we landed. The long climb took us nearly two hours. We stopped for a moment at the top of the ridge. Looking behind us, I couldn't see our valley at all. Golden Cat Valley, of course, but the waterfall—West Home—all of that was well hidden. The Fire River wasn't yet visible—at least three ridges separated us. Probably more. We'd decided to cut through the next valley, exploring, and then go along the north coast.

The cave was halfway down the ridge, overlooking a valley much like Golden Cat Valley, except twice as wide, and home to a much larger river. Herds of grazers moved slowly down the valley. Not djuri. Taller and rounder and slower. Apparently they made up what they lost in speed with an aggressive breeding program. Kayleen had spotted them first, making their way across the wide end of Golden Cat Valley in a long, fat line. She had named them "blazes grazers."

We stopped in front of the cave, looking around. Ten meters wide and five deep, the cave was flooded with light from the late afternoon sun. "We'll sleep here," Liam said. "At least I know it's safe."

Kayleen drew her brows together. "We have two more of the long-range nodes like I have in the valley. I think I'll set them up here. This would be a good place to hide if we ever need to."

"Hide from what?" I asked.

She shook her head. "The dogs. The golden cats. Anything. What if our perimeter breaks somehow?"

Liam looked up and down the wide path to the cave. "Something hoofed and heavy made this path. I'm not sure how safe it really is, since there'll be predators around any path that prey takes. Still . . . we might as well use the nodes."

I peered in. A pile of wood sat pre-stacked against one wall. The floor was rocky, fairly flat, and dry. Toward the back, the cave ended in a jumble of rocks.

I turned to Kayleen, who held Windy's halter tightly. Windy's head was up, her eyes big enough to show the whites surrounding her huge green-brown pupils. "She smells something she doesn't like," Kayleen said, stroking the hebra's neck.

"There's some kind of small animal that lives in here, or at least visits. I spotted some tracks in the dust last time I was here." He started picking up wood and moving it to the ledge in front of the cave. "We should keep a fire going all night."

Kayleen started into the cave, leading Windy. A tiny low-slung animal with a bushy black tail darted from the woodpile and fled out the door. Windy backed away, snorting, pulling Kayleen back. She and Kayleen disappeared from sight around the corner. Liam and I laughed, and after a minute, we heard Kayleen's laughter joining ours. So they hadn't gone far. "Is that all?" Kayleen called.

Liam poked at the woodpile with a sharp stick until he dislodged two more of the little beasts, one of them hissing and snapping as it ran. At the bottom of the woodpile, he found a nest with three perfectly formed little brown eggs in it. He frowned. "Odd for a mammal to lay eggs." He looked around. "Well, they won't come back, now, anyway." He carried the little nest carefully out the door. "Maybe they'll find their eggs," he said doubtfully, then called, "All clear," to Kayleen.

This time, Windy came in easily enough, although she remained nervous and kept her ears pricked.

Liam started the fire while Kayleen stripped Windy's packs and settled her into the corner farthest from the woodpile. I set up bedding for the three of us, carefully putting us all about the same distance from each other. Kayleen looked over at me, a pained look in her eyes. "You don't have to do that. You can sleep with Liam." She turned her face away. "It's okay with me." Her tone of voice belied her words.

Liam, overhearing, glanced back at us both. "Kayleen." He said it as if she were a child, and I sensed both concern and frustration. "This is fine for tonight. You don't want to be alone. Well, you don't have to be, at least not any more than we do."

Her lower lip quivered. "Well, why do we all have to be alone?"

He blinked at her. "I'm not entirely sure what you're asking," he said, although I think he knew.

I knew.

As he looked at her, Liam's gaze softened. I couldn't read the emotions behind his eyes. Maybe affection, maybe pity. Maybe some of both. He'd point-blank asked her to be clear, and he watched her intently, patiently.

Of course the problem would have occurred to him as well. But he was going back to lead his band. Even though most relationships in the bands were one man and one woman, some were two people of the same gender. But always two. The three of us being together made sense, and some of the things the townspeople had said about the *altered* they hated and fought implied more complexity in relationships. But we had never seen it.

I, too, watched Kayleen.

Her gaze flicked back and forth between the two of us. The longer she stayed away from town, the more like herself she became. The young woman standing here now, clutching her bedding to her chest, was my friend again, someone I knew. In spite of our awkward conversation last night.

What she said was, "I love you both." She paused, and the words sank in, sharp in their simplicity. Her eyes looked damp, but her chin was high. "I don't want to be alone my whole life, and I don't want to make Chelo alone her whole life. The other men, Bryan and Joseph, they're gone. We don't know if they're ever coming back. So why do either Chelo or I need to be alone?"

Liam looked over at me, searching for my reaction. I bit my lip, waffling again between the two choices that haunted me. Looking at her, at them both, I was pretty sure that the key lay between me and her.

So instead of answering Liam's unspoken question, I spoke to Kayleen. "You're right. This is untenable, at least for long. But we haven't given up on the skimmer, or getting home."

I waited, letting her absorb that much. She watched me, her gaze guarded and hopeful.

I added, "How can we three all live together in Artistos or in one of the bands? We need to think about that." Inside, I cursed myself for being a coward, for putting the choice off. But the risks! What if we tried this, and failed? What if we destroyed our friendships reaching for something more?

Liam sat cross-legged, his chin on one fist, his braid falling down his shoulder. I had seen Akashi in the same pose more than once. Liam even sounded a little like his dad. "I've thought about it, too. I'm sure we all have." He looked at each of us and we both nodded. He continued. "Three of us becoming a family, more than we are now"—his face reddened, and I felt my cheeks grow hot, too—"well, it's an intriguing idea, and maybe someday it will work."

Kayleen's eyes brightened, as if the answer gave her hope.

Liam must have seen it, too. He shook his head. "Kayleen." He waited for her to focus completely on him. "Kayleen, I can't do this, not now. Not until . . . until we get home or decide we can't."

She flinched, glancing quickly at me, pain flashing across her features, then she looked back at him. I understood his answer, but did she?

His gaze softened some as she waited for his next words. "I . . . I didn't know you before this. And I started out mad at you."

She nodded.

"Now, you and I can at least be friends. Maybe we are, except we can't be equal until you no longer hold us hostage."

Kayleen frowned.

If we couldn't get the skimmer to work, she had no way to change that. He didn't quite say so though. He did add, "Until you're healed."

Kayleen's voice trembled. "I'm much better now."

Liam looked at me. "Let time work. I'm not ready." So now he and I were poised together at the top of the waterfall, looking to see how to jump.

But we didn't have to jump today.

Windy shuffled and the fire crackled and we split apart, tending to the small chores necessary to sustain ourselves. As the sun lowered, shadows crept up the wall until they filled the entire cave. We sat by the fire, mostly quiet. Liam worked on a new fishing spear he was carving, Kayleen worked on a bigger halter for Windy, and I stared out over the dark valley below us, my back to the fire and to the other two, thinking about all the possible branches of our future. I did not want to die here.

Mid-morning found us swimming across a wide river. Soaked, we swore we'd find a better ford the next day.

About noon, we came to the north edge of Islandia, the sea side opposite the jagged teeth, for the first time. Red-rock cliffs banded with black and gray plunged hard and sharp into the water, and great blue-green waves crashed up the cliffs. Liam squatted on the edge of a bluff above a shallow inlet, looking at a cliff face opposite us. "See the bands?" he asked.

Kayleen said, "Yes. Eruptions. Layers of eruptions."

I ran my eyes up and down the cliff. There must have been at least a hundred eruptions. I swallowed, looking back at the mountains, at the puffs of white steam that were the mountain's hot breath.

We walked along the cliffs, keeping a bit back, the crash of the waves giving rhythm to our movement. Ahead of us, still far away, the steam from the Fire River's meeting with real water rose from the sea, white against the blue sky. The plume changed shape moment by moment, writhing and twisting, sometimes thickening, rising in a column, stretching at the top if it hit a wind current, other times separating into two or three wispy ropes.

As the light began to shift to dusk, we still didn't seem to be much closer. Kayleen pointed to a headland which jutted out farther than any we'd seen yet. "Let's camp there. I'll bet we can see the river at night."

Liam eyed the open ground uncertainly. "It's pretty exposed."

Kayleen shrugged. "That's good. Nothing will sneak up on us."

So we set up camp, finishing a quiet dinner as the sun fell behind the steam from the Fire River, shimmering in the mist and painting it gold. As the sky darkened, thin red streams of molten rock seemed to emerge from nowhere, dropping from the top of the cliffs down into the sea. Sullen orange, hot golds, sometimes reds, they brightened as the sky darkened. We watched the delta of the Fire River, far away, so brilliant and beautiful that it struck us silent. We scooted close to each other, with me in the middle. I held Liam's hand, and Kayleen's, and we sat that way for close to an hour. The night was warm enough that we had no need for the fire except protection, but eventually we grew sleepy enough to light it and choose watches.

There was no more direct discussion that night about transforming our relationship. Instead we each seemed determined to talk of the wind against our skin, the differences between these valleys and the great Grass Plains of home, of the Fire River, of how our greenhouse might be faring against the birds without us, of whether or not the fire needed another log.

Awkward as our words were, there was heat and uncertainty and hope underneath them. My skin burned when I looked at either of them, and my stomach grew light and feathery. Islandia's hot blood seemed to run inside us, changing us the way it changed the land.

Islandia itself seemed aware of our silent dilemma. Meteors streaked by overhead in three great clumps, and I imagined Gianna back in Artistos, tracking them. A small earthquake rumbled under us in the middle of the night, passing quickly, but warning that such things lived around volcanoes.

I fell asleep slowly, my nerves on fire, aware of every movement Kayleen made on first watch, of every time Liam turned in his sleep. I drifted near the surface of consciousness, twisting, cold and then hot, until Liam woke me to take the last watch. The fire, the Fire River, a carpet of stars, and three of our small moons kept me company. And wafting down from the hills nearer the mountains, the eerie calls of demon dogs.

I woke the other two to break camp, and we kept going toward the Fire River. In just a few hours we found ourselves picking our footing carefully through a desolate landscape of sun-heated lava flows only occasionally punctuated with scraps of green as tiny plants struggled to survive. Long cracks required that we puzzle out the ground like a maze.

The sun heated the rocks so it hurt to touch them.

By noon, Liam called a halt. "We're not going to get much closer." Disappointment filled his eyes, but he was too much the roamer band leader to put us in the middle of danger he didn't understand if it could be helped. We'd flown over this, and knew it was barely the edge of a huge empty charred place.

"Well, at least we learned the next valley is like ours, and that there are plenty of grazers around," I said. "And we saw the river."

Liam smiled.

Kayleen simply looked relieved and turned Windy around and started right back, not stopping until we reached normal ground again.

That night, we camped in the same spot, again watching the light of the river play with the dark sky. Rain soaked us, and we started back the next morning wet and tired. We chose to head up the valley to find a better ford through the deep river.

We found a wide spot where the water wound slowly through banks lined with trees and big rocks, and waded in, the water cool around our ankles and then our knees. Liam led, with me behind him, and Kayleen and Windy trailing us. In the center, the water came up to my waist. I had to lean into the current to keep my balance. Ahead of me, Liam had already reached a shallower spot, and stopped to turn and watch us.

The large shape of a hunting bird left a shadow on the sun-sparkled river. It dove, and I turned just in time to see Windy leap up in the air, balancing on the slick rocks with her back feet, screaming in fear. The bird came almost close enough to touch her before swooping back up. Kayleen fell, twisting sideways. Windy leapt past us, splashing me and Liam as she headed for the far bank.

Kayleen called after Windy, her feet going out from under her as she struggled for purchase against the current. I reached out to her, but she slipped away downriver.

Overbalanced, I gasped as the slippery river bottom gave way beneath me. I floated meters behind Kayleen, picking up speed as the deepening river tugged me mercilessly away from our ford.

Liam yelled, "The bank! Head for the bank!"

In front of me, Kayleen's head bobbed and her hands flew up and down as she fought to stand.

The current gripped me, forcing me near the center of the water. I floated with it, feet downriver, watching for rocks, hoping for a tree branch I could grab, trying to keep Kayleen in sight.

The river narrowed and sped up, splashing over jagged rocks.

Liam's voice had gone faint, calling our names.

My right foot slammed into a rock, twisting me, ducking my head under. Water filled my nose and mouth and I hit something hard with my left wrist while my right hand grabbed the slippery surface of a protruding rock. I clutched at it, fingernails scraping slippery moss, managing to spit out a mouthful of river water and look around wildly.

No Kayleen.

The center of the river frothed against rocks. The current took me again. I angled away from the center a little bit, and finally the current spit me into calmer water.

Liam found me pulling my way onto the bank through long slippery roots. He helped me climb up and held me close. "Kayleen?" he whispered.

I shook my head. "She's below us."

We followed faint animal trails downriver, sometimes barely able to see the water, calling her name.

It took twenty long minutes to find her floating faceup by the bank on our side, her torso caught in a long twisty root. Water streamed past her, spreading her hair out like a curtain. Blood seeped from a cut on her cheek and mixed with her hair.

We clambered down into the water near her and Liam leaned down over her face. "She's breathing."

She wasn't moving.

We lifted her gently from the water. Liam carried her to a small clearing, her head lolling against his arm.

She didn't wake as Liam set her down. "What if we lose her?" he whispered.

There wasn't an answer. My fingers touched the cut on her face and slid down around her head. They came back bloody from a scrape on her scalp. "I think she hit a rock."

Liam looked up from her feet, which he'd been straightening out. "She has some other bruises starting already, but I don't think anything's broken."

"We need the first aid."

"I know," he said. "It's in the packs." On Windy's back.

"Did you see where she went?" I asked.

He shook his head. "I don't want to leave you to find her."

I looked around. It was midday, the time when most predators slept. But there was plenty of cover nearby to hide dangers. I stripped off my soaking-wet shirt and held it to Kayleen's head. "I don't think there's any help for it. We can't carry her all the way back. Not like this." We were on the right side of the river, but there remained either a trip up the twisty path to the cave or a longer, slightly easier hike back to the sea and then up Golden Cat Valley. "Maybe Windy will be looking for us. She doesn't like being separated from Kayleen any more than Kayleen can stand to leave her."

"I won't go far." He leaned in and kissed me, then bent down over Kayleen and kissed her cool, white forehead, his brow furrowed. A few moments later, I heard him calling for Windy.

I bathed the blood from Kayleen's cheek with a strip of my shirt while I held the rest tight against her damaged scalp. Her eyelids fluttered once but didn't open.

Liam's voice seemed far away. Birds began to talk in the trees near us. A flock of the red seed-stealers landed on a branch, chattering and watching, curiosity all over their thieving faces. I waved my free hand at them and they flew up and away, a crimson flock of flowers disappearing toward the river.

I wished them back, worried as the sound of birdsong in the nearest trees stilled. What was out there?

Kayleen groaned, and I called her name, softly. "Kayleen. Kayleen. Wake up."

She groaned again, twisting her head in my hands. Her eyes opened and she put a hand to her cheek. "Stings." Then her eyes widened. "Windy! Where's Windy?" She pushed herself up to sit. "And Liam? Are they okay?"

At that moment, we heard Liam's voice calling out, "Chelo?"

He emerged, leading Windy. The packs were canted slightly on her back and runnels of blood covered one ankle. He glanced at us, making sure we were okay, and said, "I found her caught in a pile of tripvine."

Only then did I notice that his hands were bloody, probably from freeing the hebra.

My right ankle throbbed, but I had already proven I could stand on it. So I did, righting the packs and pulling out enough medical supplies for three people and a hebra.

An hour later, we began a limping slow walk through the late afternoon, heading for the cave. Evening clouds bunched above us, blocking the light from the moons, threatening rain before we found shelter.

That was three close calls. Four, if you counted landing at all. Our luck couldn't hold forever.

PART FOUR

A COMPLEX PLANET

20

A TEST

Morning sun streamed over me as I struggled to empty my being of everything except awareness of the potted rainbow-flower shoot in front of me. Marcus wanted me to be the plant.

As in to notice nothing else.

Data from the garden flowed all around me, not coming in, not touching me. I could relax in its presence, reach for it if I wanted, but it could no longer reach for me. I knew the compound well now. I'd run the seven-kilometer perimeter, tasted the data inside until I could read everything but the security system, at least as long as I didn't go too deep or too far away. When I tried, I still felt nauseous, which made Marcus raise his eyebrows and tease me.

Marcus had told me this morning that since I could shield easily, I could go out with him. I supposed he meant an accidental brush with the public data stream wouldn't double me over.

We hadn't left Marcus's compound, and I'd been here almost seven weeks. The prospect of going someplace new kept dragging my attention away from the tiny plant.

I focused again. The plant's five silvery green leaves each ended in a wicked, tiny tip. It smelled faintly sweet, tough to distinguish from the stronger scent of the soil. It did not give off its own data, but nanomolecules mixed into the dirt and water sang to each other constantly, faintly, a melody of dirt and root and leaf and air and water.

I closed my eyes, watching the data structures the nano made, the elegant play of reporting. I knew, now, that it was all nanotechnology married to biology—even in me, the receptor. The stories in the garden data were told between invisible nano in the dirt and water and air and invisible nano in my blood, which married biological structures in my brain. Wind Readers read the wind of nanotransmitters.

I read the stories the plant told me.

Looked at one way, I saw the plant as a whole—the shape and the vector of its growth. Turned again, data structures illuminated water flowing up tiny threaded roots to feed the leaves. Strange that such a small thing—something I would never have noticed on Fremont—had such complexity, such beauty to its tender life.

Alicia would love it. In my imagination, her eyes lit and her fingers reached out to caress the small, light-green leaves. Then they touched me.

"Well, you had it for a moment." Marcus's voice came from just above me. I blinked, shuttering away my connection to the data. I hadn't heard him open the kitchen door. He bounced on his feet, all coiled energy. Perhaps he felt as cooped up as I did. "Maybe, if you're really good today, I'll give you a pot with two plants tomorrow morning," he teased.

I smiled up at him. "I was thinking something bigger, like a bird."

"You'd be so overwhelmed it would peck your eyes out." His eyes glittered with good humor.

"Try me," I suggested.

"Not yet. Even Wind Readers sometimes find visual acuity handy."

I sighed, handed him the pot, and stood up. "Well, then, let's go while I can still see."

He set the pot on an ornate black-iron workbench by the garden. I followed him along the stone path skirting the outside of the house to the skimmer pad, a narrow, flat surface of smoothed stone grown in place using the same kind of technology that hummed in my veins. Too small to see, but big enough to change the world.

As we climbed into the skimmer, he looked over at me. "Stay shielded until I tell you not to."

I frowned. I wanted to try roaming free in the vast nets here, to see if I could do it yet. "What are you worried about?"

"Rumors of you got out. Most people are ignoring them, but not everybody." The skimmer's engines began to hum their waking song.

"Rumors?"

The skimmer rose, smoothly. He grinned, a fairly evil, silly grin. "All about the otherworldly boy who flew a starship. This place is sometimes given to gossip. At least the Wind Reader's web is."

"Well, I did fly a starship!"

"You did." Marcus smiled. "But somehow you've become bigger than life. The flight has become harder, the *New Making* crippled, and depending on which version you hear, the Port Authority either has you hidden away, or you escaped from them and went into hiding. The Authority, of course, is completely silent on the subject. Which feeds the gossipers."

"So what about the Port Authority? You said they followed me. But we haven't seen them."

"I'm pretty sure they know you're with me. They'll find you when they're ready to. The trick will be getting you ready for them."

"Are they the government?" I asked.

He pursed his lips. "Part of it. There's some power in the lawkeepers here—Port Authority and Planetary Police. But they have to follow rules, and that can keep you free. There's more dangerous power in whatever affinity groups are ascendant at any one time."

I sat silent, uneasy. On Fremont, of course, everyone knew everyone. The six of us *altered* stuck out from the crowd like paw-cats in a herd of djuri. But why the hell wasn't I invisible here?

This was the first time I'd been aloft here since the day I landed the *New Making*. A fence surrounded Marcus's compound on three sides, and the bright blue-green of the calm sea made the fourth border. Two maroon kayaks rested by the shore. The kitchen garden, itself fenced, small beside the large square of the main house roof and the round cones where turrets rose on two sides. Large lawns and artful trees, the neat squares of the big warehouse full of equipment we worked out in, the two garden sheds, and last, the guest house. The house stood roughly in the middle, with no roads or paths in or out, just a spot to land the skimmer.

After a lazy turn, we headed away from the water.

I dragged my attention from the view, which hadn't erased the queasy feeling in my stomach. So people here were talking about me. I frowned. "Artistos's gossips made up stuff about us all the time. But why so many rumors on a planet full of free data?" There were interfaces everywhere. Not just objects like Jenna's necklace, but in clothes, in skimmers, in chronos. Marcus had shown me how to use some of them, even though they were flat and slow compared to the song of data in my blood.

Marcus grimaced. "Current information about you is not exactly accessible. The absence of information on a planet full of data calls attention all by itself."

"Point," I said, chewing on my lower lip.

After a few moments, a cluster of tall buildings became visible in the distance.

I squinted at them. "That's smaller than the city by the spaceport."

"Yes. We're on Foral, a big island just north of Li. I like Foral because people here pretty much leave each other alone. Besides, there's more room for gardens."

I looked down. No roads cut up the green expanses below me, although houses dotted the low hills. Yet it wasn't wild. Humans clearly controlled all the space. This was so different than Fremont, where we struggled to tame one scrap of land for a single city. "Where are we going?"

"To the university."

A school. Everything here outstripped and outdid everything on Fremont. How would a school here be like learning in a Guild Hall? I watched for the open land to give way to city. "How fast will this go?" I asked.

He answered with a burst of speed. Our shadow fled across the ground. The skimmer stayed remarkably stable, and Marcus sat back, touching nothing.

Below us, roads appeared. Ground vehicles hummed between buildings that were not houses like Marcus's, but seemed likely to hold many families like our four-houses, only maybe these were twenty-houses or thirty-houses. The skimmer slowed. The city gleamed in front of us, at least fifty tall buildings, most slender, all different. If the buildings below me were thirty-houses, then before me were hundred-houses and more, webbed together with walkways and floating gardens. Skimmers flitted between buildings, and people filled the walkways and lawns in seemingly random patterns. The predominant color was green, all shades of green, punctuated by purple flowers and yellow trees and tan buildings and blue lakes. I didn't need to open myself to the city's data to feel overwhelmed.

We circled over a huge iron-red and deep green complex of buildings, nearly the tallest in the city. Round orbs of buildings, tall spires of buildings, blocky buildings with no windows. We angled down toward a landing strip already cluttered with skimmers, most small.

"Why here?"

In a dry voice, he said, "This is Foral University. They train Wind Readers. Your clumsiness will be lost in a sea of students who often lose touch with reality. People call them wind-burned."

"Great." I made an extremely unhappy face. "I get to hang out with a bunch of people who are likely to turn crazy any moment."

"Easy boy." Marcus landed us nicely between two smaller skimmers. "I used to teach here."

"Can I fly the skimmer back?" I asked.

The bubble opened, flooding the cabin with the scent of freshly mown grass. He opened the door, hopping out. "Only if you're very, very good." He put a hand up in warning. "Stay shielded."

"Right, right. I know." I followed him across the grounds toward a big, windowless building. "What are we going to do here?"

"We?" he shot back over his shoulder. "*We're* not going to do anything. But you are going to hang out in an isolation room and try very, very hard to follow its instructions."

"An isolation room?"

He stopped at a door and waited, apparently having a conversation with someone I couldn't see or hear. The door opened, and we went in.

I gaped at the walls, floor, and ceiling of the long corridor, which flashed nano-paint pictures of wildly different scenes I had no reference for. Underwater shots of a domed city lit from within so it glowed yellow-gold against dark water, a desolate rocky landscape, winged people flying an intricate dance in the air inside a different kind of dome. He waved a hand at the walls. "The five worlds. We used to train people from all of them here."

"Used to?" I asked.

"Now it's just Silver's Home and Lopali. Sometimes a few from Joy

Heaven." His voice had a hint of sadness in it. Before I had time to ask more, he opened a door, and I followed him into a small dark room, my eyes adjusting from the brightness of the corridor and its alluring pictures. I blinked, trying to see what was in the room.

Nothing. Really, really nothing.

Black walls, black floor, black ceiling, and a rectangle of light from the open door.

Marcus sat on the floor, and gestured for me to sit near him. He sat in the dark, the sharp angled light from the door cutting across one foot, so that for a moment it looked like a lone foot, bereft of its owner. While I couldn't see his face, his voice now sounded serious. "You've pretty much learned in a few weeks everything they spend five years teaching young Wind Readers. Except, of course, you don't have the cultural context. You didn't grow up here. We'll work on that over the next two weeks."

"Okay." My voice sounded big in the darkness.

"Teachers use these rooms to help students jump to the next level. If the students succeed, they get to go on with their training. Otherwise, they go out into the world and make do with what they have, which is still quite a lot. I want to see how you do." He shifted, and his foot disappeared outside of the line of light. "Here, the intel webs expect behavior out of the norm, and you won't be noticed unless someone is looking awfully hard. Besides, these rooms are tightly shielded on purpose. It's the safest place I could think of to get an independent test of your skills."

"Safe?"

"You have enough power for people to want to use you. We already know the Port Authority finds you interesting. Commercial affinity groups might want you to help them make new products or entertainments. You're untutored still, and vulnerable. People who need more power to push through their own agendas could find someone as naïve and biddable as you are a tempting target."

"Naïve and biddable?" I used my most unhappy voice, trying to cover dismay with humor.

"Sure. You'd be just as excited about the new things you're learning if the Port Authority was teaching you, or someone designing flyers or flyspaces, or doing genetic engineering for one of the other planets. It will take time for you to develop a sense of the morality of creation. Like I said, you will eventually have to choose a side in the coming war. You're too powerful not to."

I swallowed, dissatisfied with his answer but allowing that it had a kernel of truth. "What do you want me to do?"

"Do what the room says, and learn, but don't push the boundaries too far. That's all. Don't show off. I suspect you can't yet tell friend from foe."

Still stung at the idea of being naïve, I asked, "And which are you?"

His answer was quick, his jaw briefly tightening with anger. "Don't joke here. This is serious." He regained his control, calming. "I'm slipping an old friend some credit to cover this time."

I shut up. Marcus remained a puzzle to me. I liked him. He made me work, and the work made me happy. As far as friend or foe, well, I would bet on friend, but he clearly had plans for me that I didn't understand. Yet.

Marcus stood up, tall in the small, black room. "I'm going to close the door—the room won't work with more than one person in it. Besides, I need to go see someone. I'll monitor you from her office. I'll be back for you in an hour. Don't leave. The room will give you verbal instructions."

I nodded, uneasy.

He stepped out of the room, closed the door, and the rectangle of light disappeared completely, plunging the room into darkness more complete than I had ever experienced. My senses seemed cut off—I felt the floor where I touched it, but my eyes might as well have been closed, and the only scent was my own familiar odor. I scratched at the floor in order to have sound, then stopped, realizing how silly it was. What was I supposed to do? Did I have to start something?

A voice spoke into the darkness, feminine, vaguely electronic, a little bit seductive. "Lie back, close your eyes, and listen inside yourself." The voice reminded me of Alicia.

The room had given a generic instruction, probably keyed to anyone who used it. I complied.

A single light burst inside me. A stream of yellow-gold data. The voice asked, "Do you see the data thread?"

"Yes."

"Focus on it. See where it takes you." No further instructions. The room remained silent.

It was easier here than in Marcus's garden. No other data competed for attention, nor any physical sensations except the ones inside my own body, which I had long ago learned to ignore.

Throughout the thread, I read simple concepts that I now knew enough to relate to individual webs. I accessed them one by one. A new thread burst into visibility with each concept, each thread linked to the main one. The first concept was *physical space*. A map spread out—one I felt as much as I saw, a thick layer of information covering the outline of the university. The data sharpened only where my attention focused, in the room, in the building, in the university. The thread only went to the boundaries of the school. Nothing living, nothing inside the space—just the space itself. I dropped that thread and reached for the next one.

I couldn't access it.

I pulled the sense of physical space back into my consciousness, and the next concept, *temperature*, became accessible. It lay on top of the spaces, showing me warmth and cold. So it was a test? I experimented. If I dropped any thread, I lost the others. I kept picking up data. My own body temperature. The speed of my heartbeat. The heat of another student in a nearby room. Ten other people in the building. A room at the far end where a meeting was being held. The identities of the people in the meeting—meaningless to me, but names I held in my head.

The room didn't care what order I picked up threads in. It didn't let me ask general questions, but I watched for anything that might lead to my father, to Alicia, or to Fremont.

Nothing.

I spiraled out, picking up threads one by one. The construct began to tangle, the threads of information joining and losing distinction. Whatever ran the room required me to keep the data straight and free, keep the threads separated, yet read them all.

Easier to know than to do.

Sweat dripped from my forehead as I reached for more. I fought the distraction, focusing on how the data and I were connected. Like flying the ship—a physical, visceral need being satisfied.

I found the two buildings next to us. The parked skimmers.

My stomach knotted, hard. I stopped, breathing into the pain, barely keeping all of the threads I had. I reached for another one and they all fell away.

I was smaller, empty, bereft.

I blinked into the darkness. My breath sounded loud in the tiny room, a rasping. I heard my heart beat. I closed my eyes again, reached for the gold thread, and started over.

I kept going until my body was light and full of twice as many threads. My stomach only seemed empty and twisty, not actually ill. I could sense most of the area around this building and the few next to it—plants and people and movement. Remembering Marcus's first conversation with me in the garden, I zoomed in on a blade of grass, holding all of the available information about it. Five centimeters tall, nano-clipped this morning, healthy. I zoomed back out, taking in the whole university.

I heard myself laugh in joy.

The laugh jolted me, and the threads began to fall away. This time, I held the first half, refocusing. However the room worked, it helped me keep the information accessible, so it filled me. I felt huge—as big as the spaces I now held data for.

My being had grown.

I breathed out and let it all fall gently away, separating myself carefully from the data. I sat up, rubbing my eyes, testing. This time I'd dropped the data on purpose, and I still felt big with potential. I reached for my toes, stretching.

The room's voice spoke again. "Are you finished?" it asked.

It was too dark to see my chrono. "How long have I been here?"

"Forty minutes. Twenty remain."

"I will keep going."

"Then begin again."

I stretched out spread-eagled against the soft floor in the dark room. Nothing happened. Just me, my breath, my heart beating. The warm deadness of the room.

Then, "Take this thread."

When I closed my eyes, I saw a silver thread rather than the gold one. The first concept was Silver's Home itself. Curious, I opened. This time, multiple linkages surrounded the first point. Creation. Genetics. Economy. I picked my way through slowly, cautiously. This construct didn't require I keep every bit of data in a row—I could follow linkages, back up and follow new ones. I only understood some, but the information flowed whether I grasped its meaning or not.

The data didn't relate to anything as concrete as temperature or a university building, although a sense of location existed. I followed that, seeing the whole planet the way I had seen it from space. More threads spiraled from the node representing Silver's Home, waiting for me to pick them up. I experimented. Could I reach the next node on the silver line before I sampled all of these?

It was one of the five worlds, the Islas Autocracy. Curious, I began to examine the threads attached to that node. Planned community. Perfection. History. A breeding program.

The door opened, light falling on my body, jerking me out of the data and up into a sitting position. Light made war on my eyes, and I scooted back into darkness. My hand shook.

The figure silhouetted in the light from the door wasn't Marcus, but someone blockier and shorter.

I drew in a sharp breath and shielded, hiding myself, making sure no data came in or out of my internal spaces. I tipped my wrist into the light, looking at my chrono. It hadn't been quite an hour yet.

"Who are you?" the haloed figure asked as full light snapped on in the room, exposing me completely. His voice seemed overloud. An artifact of the silence of the isolation room? The man wore a uniform, the right chest emblazoned with an insignia that I'd learned from the threads meant he worked for the university.

At least he wasn't from the Port Authority.

His eyes were a startling blue, unnatural, and he looked like he expected to be obeyed.

I scrambled to my feet, stepping back, staying a good meter away from him. "Who are *you*?" I countered.

"I'm in charge of our training program here."

A student should know him. The first question out of my mouth had given away that I didn't belong. Sweat broke out on my palms. What to do? Marcus wasn't here. The man's wrong-blue eyes made me feel like a trapped bug. He looked young, but that meant nothing here.

His gaze demanded a response. I could open, and call Marcus, but that would leave room for this man to penetrate my shields. Surely he was a Wind Reader.

What would Marcus do? I smiled as nicely as I could, and extended a hand. "Pleased to meet you."

He looked startled for just a second, then his wide lips thinned into a flat line. "Are you Joseph Lee?"

Uh oh. Marcus had said people were looking for me. I felt a query, a knock against my shielding. Hurrying to shore up my internal defenses, I asked, "What do you care?" I winced. My words sounded childlike.

Footsteps pounded down the corridor. Marcus. I knew for sure before I saw him; his energy and gait and the feel of his presence had become that familiar to me.

Marcus slowed as he neared the man. "Charles Milan." Disdain laced Marcus' voice.

The blue-eyed man narrowed his eyes, but kept them on me. "Well, I'm not surprised to find you associated with . . . with . . . with whoever this is."

Marcus was visible outside the door now, close to Charles. Marcus looked down at him, his voice controlled and edged with anger. "And what did he do?"

Good question. I thought I had done rather well.

Charles swallowed, finally looking at Marcus instead of me. He blustered nervously, his voice higher now. "The student monitor AI notified me fifteen minutes after he started his session. This is that Joseph boy—the one they say is so strong. It has to be. He surpassed anything we've ever seen on level one. That's what set the AI's alarms off—he's way out of norm." Charles sounded excited as well as affronted, and proud, either of himself or me. I couldn't quite tell. I watched him curiously as he continued. "So I gave him the final, the *masters* final, and he started right in on it—at a rate *you* never managed!"

A bemused smile crossed Marcus's face. "So you just ran down here to confront him . . . for what? Being capable?"

Charles bounced on his feet as if excited. "So it is him. Serge said you might have him."

Marcus gestured for me to come near him.

Charles stood in the door, blocking my way, looking me up and down. Marcus put a hand on Charles's shoulder, pulling him gently back out of my way. He didn't let go of Charles until I was safely past.

I turned to look at the man. The sharp glow in his eyes had died back, lost intensity.

Marcus said, "Look, Charles, there's nothing for you here. The boy is doing fine."

"But . . . but . . . think of what good he could do for the school." He was nearly pleading. "Think of what we could do for him. We have all the tools—"

"No thanks, Charles," Marcus interrupted. "Besides, he's already passed your final, from what you say." He put a hand on my shoulder, speaking to me. "Let's go."

Charles frowned. "You're making a mistake. Enroll him here, and no one can take him." He hesitated, then blurted out, "Please."

Marcus looked down at me, raising one eyebrow, his eye twinkling. "Want to stay here?"

Actually, I would have loved to stay in the room longer. But one look at Charles screamed the reasons not to. I felt braver now, with Marcus next to me, and a little cocky. "Gee, Marcus, that was fun, but if that's the final exam, maybe not." I glanced back at Charles, who stood, eyes wide, face growing red. "But perhaps we can visit, sometime."

Marcus winked at me and we turned and walked slowly and deliberately back down the bright colorful corridor. This time I recognized the Islas Autocracy pictures: ordered perfection as stunning as Silver's Home, but without the chaos and with about half as many colors. The sky was a different blue, deeper even than Fremont's sky.

We walked to the skimmer. As we climbed in, I said, "So I suppose I don't get to fly it, do I?"

He didn't laugh, and I'd expected him to. Instead, he seemed lost in thought. The bubble had closed over us, but we weren't moving yet. He shook his head. "No, Joseph. You beat my expectations." He frowned. "Stomach okay?"

I grinned at him, nerves still on edge from the encounter. "Not at first. Eventually. Am I ever glad you showed up. But it was wonderful! I learned so much. Is there anyplace else like that?"

He just looked at me, and then shook his head, slowly. "I think we'll lay low for a bit."

21

ON PILO ISLAND WITH MARCUS

As we flew away from the university, Marcus gazed straight ahead and chewed lightly on his lower lip. Bright sun shone through the smoky bubble of the skimmer's shield, highlighting the reddish streaks in his brown hair. He hadn't said anything about the encounter with Charles, which had, ultimately, almost been funny. Finally, I cleared my throat. "Did you meet your friend?"

He nodded. "Julianne. She studies Wind Readers—she's sort of a psychologist. She helps students get through training successfully." He glanced over at me. "I talked to her about you. I trust her implicitly—she and I worry about the same things. We both want the creative power here to be spent for good."

"So what did she say about me?"

"She has a theory." He was silent for a moment as the skimmer banked out over fields, already far away from the city. "I told her a little bit about Fremont. She suspects you're so strong because of constant and immediate stress—from the people and environment. Little things like losing your parents and hunting paw-cats and being persecuted just for being different."

"But Silver's Home doesn't seem much safer," I said.

He laughed. "No, I suppose not. But the dangers here are different. Wind Reader students are more worried about a job, or a goal of their affinity group. Our stresses are about long-term goals and relationships." He looked over at me, as if making sure I understood. "Students that are part of tight affinity groups do better here than free agents. Julianne suggested that both the immediate stress you had and your support structure mattered. Jenna seems to have helped you, but it doesn't sound like you saw much of her. Maybe your sister?"

I frowned, remembering how we all stuck together, and met in semi-secret to be ourselves—to run at our speed together, to climb, to practice. Chelo mattered, but so did Alicia and Bryan and Liam and Kayleen. "Maybe I had to stay sane to keep Chelo and the others safe. We all had to use our skills to protect each other."

He turned the skimmer again, taking us out over crystal-blue water touched by tiny whitecaps. "I wish Chelo was here," he mused. "It would be interesting to see how you two work together."

"I'm going back for her. As soon as I can."

"I would like to see this Fremont of yours, and meet your sister."

I wanted nothing better. Not to stay, but I missed Chelo so much it made me ache to talk about her. I turned away from him to hide the tears stinging my eyes, and looked back down at the water. "Where are we going?"

"Pilo Island. It's a busy place, good to get lost in. We need to get lost. You've just picked up extra buzz."

"Buzz?" He'd used the term before, but now it was being applied to me.

"Attention. You haven't exactly got planetary buzz—Charles is a Wind Reader geek and it's not surprising he's interested, but you do have enough buzz that we might be better off if we head elsewhere for a bit."

"Where's Pilo Island?"

"About three hours' flight. South, near Jo."

Jo was another big continent like Li, closer to the equator.

He smiled. "It may be a bit overwhelming. Don't gawk. Now, why don't you rest a moment while I seed the nets with some misdirection? It's probably all over the university by now that you were there, and we may have some followers we don't want."

I closed my eyes and tried to remember everything I'd seen in the isolation room. In my memories, the room's voice became Alicia's and the beauty of the data structures mirrored the complexity of her hair, tangled from sleep, the smoothness of her skin, the brightness of her eyes. She would have loved it.

I dozed and woke, dozed and woke. Every time I woke, we were still flying over water. We passed a few skimmers flying beneath us, and once Marcus pointed out a group of large sea creatures below us which he called "shilo serpents." Long rounded bodies with thin necks and oblong heads leaped and gamboled in the light whitecaps, apparently playing. He flew low over them, and I counted nearly twenty. The longest were twice the length of the skimmer. Marcus said, "They can be ridden—with the right gear—if they're raised around humans." I didn't see anyone riding them, but they were fast and I wanted to try it.

"Are there any people modified to live in the sea?" I asked.

"There are short-term mods for that, but it turned out that people prefer land, in general. Paradise has a lot more water, and there is a subspecies designed to take advantage of that, but even they can also walk and live on the islands there."

"A subspecies?"

"Sure, even Wind Readers are a subspecies, depending on who you listen to. The lines are blurred, but legally, we are all human." His voice sounded disapproving.

"Could I be modified to live in water if I wanted?" I asked, curious.

"Sure. I did it once when I was young and stupid. It's a major mod—it hurts." He sighed, then looked down at his hands. "I love creating. I love our world, and being who I am. But sometimes we go too far."

That gave me food for thought as we rose back up away from the shilo serpents and Marcus lapsed back into silence. What was going too far? Hurting others, surely. Creating bad things? All forms of doing harm, whether you meant it or not?

An island came into view a few moments later. "Is that Pilo Island? It's too round—it has to be man-made."

"The island is a creation of the Landmakers Affinity Group, who retained rights to it and set up the local rules."

We began to slow. I looked carefully, awed at the idea that people could make a whole island. "What holds it up?"

He smiled. "Good question. They have creator's rights to a nanomaterial that floats. The whole island floats, and there are engines that move it one way or the other, keeping it free from the influence of tide and current."

Except for its perfect shape, nothing about the surface of the island screamed made-thing. All of the buildings were similar: big, with rounded edges, many windows, and glittery brightly colored walls. Green, blue, and yellow seemed to be the most common colors. Small forests and green spaces grew from the top of some of the buildings and threaded between them. As we came closer, I noticed skimmers and boats and people walking on the streets.

We landed on top of a building and parked in a sea of at least thirty other craft of varying sizes, some ten times the size of Marcus's. As soon as we stopped, he opened the bubble and hopped out, and I joined him on the roof. "Were we followed?" I asked.

He nodded. "Stay close to me." He took off at a fast walk, and I followed him across the flat expanse of building-top into an elevator. We emerged on the street level, still inside the building, surrounded by people. Unlike Li, and even the university, the diversity of people here dragged my eyes from one strange feast to another. I spotted tall slender bodies, a woman with extra arms walking with a woman with extremely long, strong legs and no hair at all, a few strongmen like Bryan—only wider and taller. Two women with wings adorned with long glittering ribbons were pretty much avoided. Their gaits were off balance, and their faces showed pain lines around the eyes. I felt slightly sorry for them. They looked as out of place as I had felt on Fremont. Awkward flyers aside, the general mood on Pilo Island was controlled, content chaos. Conversation and laughter filled the air, although periodically people walked by, shrouded in total silence.

I stayed close to Marcus as we pushed through the crowd and exited a door on the far side of the building. Outside, we threaded through crowded walkways that smelled of human bodies, of flowers, and of the salt air blown in on a stiff breeze.

Marcus ducked sideways, leaving the street. He led me into a throng of people gathered in small groups on a wide expanse of grass bordered by four buildings, including the big one we'd landed on top of. There must've been as many people in this one space as on all of Fremont. Twice as many. More. Heady spices from strange food assaulted my nostrils and a cacophony of conversations wafted around me. We changed direction multiple times, passing through two buildings and a tunnel.

The island and its strange inhabitants dwarfed me, dwarfed the university, which had seemed big and full just hours ago and now felt like a refuge of peace and stillness. My breath came fast and quick and my hands shook. "Marcus," I called. "Can I sit down?" Without waiting for an answer I found an empty bench and collapsed, trying to shield my senses from all of it.

Marcus stood, looking at me, his eyes narrowed in concern.

I focused on his tall slender form, on the one familiar thing, and the background swam behind him, losing resolution. "I'm dizzy."

He sat beside me on the bench. "It's okay. Rest."

Marcus smelled familiar and comfortable. I closed my eyes, letting the sounds wash over me and through me. I began to treat it like data, isolating conversations. It helped. After a few moments, I tried opening my eyes again, and this time the colors and movement of the crowd stayed crisp and clear.

"Better?" Marcus asked. When I nodded slowly, he asked, "What is it? Are you just tired?"

I shook my head. "I think it's just—there are so many new things here. Maybe the isolation room took more out of me than I thought." Watching my back and worrying didn't help much either. How was I to tell who might be an enemy in the sea of strangeness here?

He pursed his lips. "Maybe it's from shielding so hard. Try to relax into it; let it be your normal state so that data stays outside of you."

I took three deep breaths, trying to follow his advice. But if I relaxed too far, I felt data creep in, and knew I'd go out to meet it. It was too natural now, maybe had always been too natural. I swallowed, maintaining my shield with force. "I'm ready to go," I said, trying to sound strong.

We made it three-quarters of the way across the busy lawn when I noticed Marcus heading for a large tree with thin green and gold leaves that cascaded almost to the grass. Its shape reminded me of the tent trees back home even though the leaves and slender branches of this tree created a more delicate boundary. It shimmered. As we came near enough to hear the leaves rustling gently against each other, a hand appeared amidst the leaves, parting them, and Alicia darted out, clutching me tightly. "Joseph. It's really you. You're here," she whispered, "so good."

My heart raced. She looked wonderful, felt wonderful. "We're here." I clasped my arms around her, holding her tight. I couldn't believe Marcus hadn't told me we were meeting them. I buried my face in her hair. "Are you all right?"

She pushed me back and lifted her face up. Her skin glowed with health and her violet eyes danced. "I'm better than I've ever been. I love it here. I don't ever want to go back, or go anyplace else." She stood and threw her arm out in an expansive gesture. "Isn't this beautiful? There's so *much* here."

I stared at her, entranced. Enchanted.

A necklace of tiny green and gray beads lay neatly against her neck. She brought one hand up, stroking the necklace the way she had stroked my face a hundred times. Excitement and pleasure seemed to roll from her like waves. "I can read data. And no one cares if I have access, no one keeps me down here, Joseph. I can be myself." She lifted her hand from the beads and took mine in it, her slender fingers holding tight.

Envy flashed through me for a second. I couldn't even let my shields down. But seeing Alicia swamped all other emotion.

She stopped and squinted at me. "How have you been? We've heard rumors about you, and I studied up on Marcus. The Port Authority and the rest of the government seems scared of him even though they hire him. He's popular, kind of in an underground way—he has low steady buzz. Jenna called him a 'balancing power,' whatever that means. He really is the strongest Wind Reader here."

I laughed, and Marcus came up beside me. "I might not be anymore." He smiled at me. "Now go on, see the others."

Of course the others were there. I squeezed Alicia's hand. She turned and I followed her. As we slid in between the leaves, all noise from outside cut away as if a sheet of glass separated us from the crowd. The tree smelled of clean dirt and leaves, with a slight sweetness under it all. "The silence feels good," I whispered, drinking in the details of her face.

Alicia grinned. "Isn't this cool? It's a meet-me tree. You have to pay to use them, but they can make you feel like you're alone even here."

"Does it block out data, too?" I asked.

She grinned, touching her necklace. "If you ask it to."

I looked around. Bryan sat next to Tiala, smiling expectantly. He, too, looked perfect, with glowing skin and no sign of his injuries. He gave a small wave and stayed seated. Waiting for something?

I looked around for Jenna and for Tiala's bird. The upside-down bell of the tree was big, but not big enough to hide anyone. "Where's Jenna?"

Tiala waved at me, lifting a hand and returning it to her lap, twisting her hands together. A slightly exaggerated gesture. She gazed at me steadily, her expression as expectant as Bryan's.

I looked, and looked again. Her perfect face showed no scars, but her dark hair was no longer caught back in a long braid. It hung, like Jenna's, just above the shoulders.

It wasn't Tiala.

"Jenna?"

She nodded, and a broad smile lit her perfect features, a smile full of more joy than I had ever seen on her face. I knelt down in front of her, meeting her eyes. Two eyes. Two perfect steel-gray eyes. One of my hands went to her smooth cheek of its own accord. The skin was soft, like a child's.

So much damage, undone so quickly.

Her eyes were still her own—haunted and sure of herself. It amazed me I had mistaken her for her sister at all. I leaned forward and folded her in my arms, something I had never done before. Surprisingly she let me, relaxing into my embrace for just a moment before reasserting her usual distance and pushing me gently away.

I sat back on my heels and stared at her. "I— I— Wow. You look great! How did you do that?"

She shook her head. "I got good prices, particularly for the animals and plants from Fremont." She smiled and stood, pulling me to my feet with her new arm, which had the same soft-skin glow as her new face. "I had to. No one is ill or maimed here. I would stick out worse than a flyer in a walking city." She gave a funny smile. "Oddly, it helped a bit to look broken. I think people bid higher just to see the damaged woman in person." A trace of bitterness flashed momentarily in her eyes, and maybe even loss. She tossed her head and turned to face me, as if still a little unsure of what I thought. "But if I had stayed that way, I would have been noticed everywhere I went."

She seemed almost apologetic, even though the new Jenna was

young and beautiful. No one should have to apologize for being whole. "I understand," I said softly. "It must feel much better."

Her face grew serious. "It wasn't anywhere near enough credit to buy the ship back, anyway."

I touched her new cheek again. "This was more important than the ship." Not than getting Chelo; nothing mattered more than that. But surely Jenna had chosen right.

She stretched her arm out. "It's still a little stiff, and partly mechanical. That was the faster route, and I had other things to do. That's why I asked Marcus to bring you. Your father is coming—he is flying into Li Spaceport tomorrow."

My father.

I swallowed hard. "He's coming to see me?" I asked. "What about my mother?"

She shook her head. "I don't know anything about Marissa, Joseph. And your father doesn't know you're here, yet. I need to see him, and that is all he knows right now." A brief troubled look passed across her eyes. Just as I was about to ask what worried her, she looked over at Marcus, who stood beside me, watching me closely. Jenna said, "I want to take Joseph to meet David."

To meet my father. My dreams—flying the ship, finding my parents—my dreams were coming true. I looked at Marcus. Would he let me go?

Marcus returned my gaze. "What do you want?" he asked mildly.

"I need to see my father." I waited, watching him watch me. "But I want to study with you more, too. Can I come back?"

Marcus nodded slowly at me, a small grin edging his generous mouth. "Perhaps we can work something out." His eyes seemed to bore through to my very soul. "You still have much to learn. But since I've just been seen with you it might be good for me to be seen without you for a little while."

Alicia stepped up close to me, clutching my hand tightly. He glanced at her, then winked at me before turning his attention to Jenna. He narrowed his eyes. "You've heard the rumors about him?"

"Some," Jenna said. "But they seem to be dying away."

Marcus gave a wry smile. "We were just spotted at Foral University."

She frowned at that.

Alicia spoke up. "What does that mean?"

Marcus closed his eyes for a second, surely testing the data nets. I ached to do the same. But I held my shields up, watching him. After a few moments, he opened his eyes. "There's only a low buzz, and some are debunking the story line. I think it's safe enough, although I don't want him easily visible. I'll go make some cover for you all—I can add to the confusion by being seen elsewhere, without him, and by posting a few of my own incredulous queries."

"You're leaving now?" A sharp sense of loss shot through me. He must have heard the pain in my voice, seen it in my eyes. His own voice softened, and a small, slightly sad smile touched his face. "Perhaps I'll see you sooner than you think. But for now, Jenna can keep you as safe as I can. Stay in touch through her—you *must* remain shielded."

"But what if we need to know something? Or reach you?" I asked.

"Then Jenna will have to help you, or you will have to use some other form of interface."

Jenna glanced from me to Marcus. "Can he read the data structures here?"

Marcus nodded. "He also knows how to shield. See that he does it—he needs to stay as invisible as possible."

"Then he'll be all right in public?" she probed.

"Yes. He'll be fine. I think. But feed him and get him to sleep. I wore him out today."

She laughed. "I'll bet you've been wearing him out every day."

Marcus continued. "You were right to let me take him. I don't know of anyone else who could train him—he really is strong." He glanced at me. "And naïve as hell. But he kinda grows on you. So take care of him."

I grimaced, resisting a childish urge to stick my tongue out at him.

Jenna glanced over at me, an appraising look in her eyes. "I will." She turned her gaze to Marcus. "Thank you. You've been paid. I want to know more about what he has done, and learned, but I can keep him safe for a day."

Marcus leaned in and kissed her. She accepted it, naturally, already seeming to be a different person than the wild woman of Fremont. Marcus looked down at her, his eyes soft. "He's truly remarkable. And not yet trained. I want him back—but in the meantime, show him what you can of the world here. We've been hiding out at one of my houses. Tell me where to meet you."

"Outside of Li, there is a garden. The memory garden. That's where David will come. Meet us there tomorrow around noon?"

He looked at me. "I'll come if I can. Good luck with your father."

"Thank you." I meant for all of what he'd taught me as well as for his good wishes. The way he smiled down at me, I felt sure he understood the whole message.

With that, he turned and left, parting the leaves nearly silently, the sound of his footsteps cut off as he left the cone of silence inside the tree.

22

THE MEMORY GARDEN

Jenna's hand shaking my shoulder woke me the next morning. A ray of sunshine fell through the open window, highlighting her unbelievably perfect features. As she bustled about the tiny kitchen making col that smelled like redberries but tasted sweeter, she seemed like someone I hardly knew: beautiful, poised, and smooth. However, the look in both of her eyes remained as wild and cautious as the look in one eye had been, as if the old Jenna inhabited a cave inside the new one.

Jenna flew us all to the memory garden in a skimmer I'd never seen before, a simple silver machine with room for six. "I don't know how long before he shows up," she said. "There are sights worth seeing here—we'll walk." She looked at me. "Stay shielded."

"I know," I mumbled, tired of constant warnings.

Bryan looked as complete and fresh as Jenna, his limp entirely gone. He walked beside Jenna, chatting with her. They led us along a simple path lined with tall spiky plants covered in purple, pink, and yellow flowers. I pointed the flowers out to Alicia, who walked next to me. "The blooms in Marcus's garden are even more perfect."

She leaned down and smelled a bright yellow blossom the size of her hand, sniffing deeply. "These are better than anything on Fremont."

"But even these aren't as pretty as wild spike-bells."

"Right," she shot back. "And I bet these won't make you sick if you eat their leaves, either." Still looking at the yellow flowers, she said, "I don't ever want to leave here."

Bryan must have heard her, because he looked back over his shoulder and said, "We have to go get Chelo and the others."

"I still don't want to go back," Alicia said.

"I'll be happier when we're all together," I said. I belonged here. I had a role to play, a destiny that could never be fulfilled someplace as backward and untrusting as Fremont. I just knew it.

I kept looking around for my father, even though I knew Jenna would hear from him before we saw him. Would I recognize him? What would he think of me? Did he ever think of me at all?

Jenna stopped in front of a tall statue of a woman with wings. "Lesson time. This is a tribute to Kuli Nam, who made the first viable flyers. Creating flyers boosted our reputation as the best human genetic engineers in the five worlds."

I remembered Marcus's admonition about the wrongness of creating flyers. Yet the metal woman in front of us shone with mystery and magic. She stood at least ten meters tall, with long sweeping silvery wings that reached down to her calves. Her wide shoulders tapered to narrow hips and long slender legs. She seemed poised to run and jump into flight, one metal foot flat on the ground, one heel raised. Her carefully sculpted facial expression almost cried out "expectant joy," and looking at her, the impending feeling of something magical seeped into me.

"Tell me about Lopali," I asked. It was one of the five worlds, but I had been interrupted before I learned about it in the isolation room.

Jenna spoke briskly, without looking away from the statue. "Lopali has the smallest population of the five worlds. It's essentially a terraformed moon, built as a place for humans to fly. The designers pictured assisted flight, but Kuli Nam saw the opportunity and produced true human flyers. They cannot breed true, and Lopali does not have the right to the designs nor sophisticated enough facilities to make them, so we produce new flyers for them, many from Lopali genetic seed stock."

"So they can't have children of their own?" I asked.

Jenna shook her head. "The flight genetics don't breed true. They can't—there are a series of one-time sculpting nano runs that build the shoulders and shrink the other bones."

Bryan's brow furrowed. "So you make all the people for Lopali on Silver's Home?"

Jenna laughed. "No. There are humans that breed true there. They fly with aids. We provide around ten percent of the population. Our flyers have great standing on Lopali, so we make their most powerful citizens."

"I don't suppose that has anything to do with the war Marcus mentioned?" Bryan asked.

Jenna hesitated. "Well, maybe. But that's a different discussion. Lopali is on our side, so far. Islas is the problem."

I had learned a little about Islas in the university threads. "Islas is a very controlled society."

Jenna nodded. "So Marcus taught you some things. What else do you know?"

"I know Marcus is worried about them. I guess they don't like how people live here."

"They believe the only way to keep humanity from destroying itself is to control it closely."

"Don't the people hate that?" Alicia asked, her gaze still on the statue.

Jenna said, "No. I don't think they do. Some. The ones who do usually go to the other four worlds, about half to us. Islas lets them. It means they don't have to deal with as many problem elements in their society, and it lets them keep spies here."

"Don't we stop them?" Bryan asked.

Jenna shook her head. "All of the five worlds, including Islas, have an agreement allowing emigration. Besides, we don't have much of a police force. The Port Authority is the strongest, since the laws governing import and export are universal. And to protect us. The rules governing behavior on-planet vary by affinity group, or by town, and both police their own. Current rules, and consequences, are always in the nets."

Alicia walked around the statue, looking at it from all angles. "Tell me more about flyers."

"Lopali's ecosystem is the only one of the five worlds that isn't easily reproducible here. Flyers here congregate in controlled microclimates which closely mimic Lopali—like the domes we passed the first day on Li. There are only four on Silver's Home. Lopali has a much denser atmosphere, and less gravity."

"And that's why people can fly there?" Alicia asked.

"That, and pretty severe changes in bone structure. Flyers are weak, here. We tried to make humans that can fly in our atmosphere. The cost to the body was too dear. It still gets tried—over and over—but nothing produced is actually human." She looked up at the statue again, her eyes slightly narrowed as she squinted into the bright sunshine. "But when I was little, I often wished I'd been born a flyer."

"So they're born that way?" Alicia asked. "Someone decides for you before you're born?"

Jenna nodded. "The mod is too extreme for most adult bodies to handle. It gets done, but it drives half the people who try it crazy, and plain kills others."

There were a lot of ways to become crazy here.

Alicia's brows were drawn together, as if the idea of manufactured fliers troubled her as much as me. "I'd like to fly."

Jenna glanced at her, frowning. "It makes for a very limited life, at least here. And I wouldn't live on Lopali—it's a difficult world." She turned and looked at Alicia. "And you *can* fly. There are wonderful mechanical wings and other solo flying devices. Perhaps I can take you sometime."

Alicia looked pleased. "I'd like to try it."

I leaned over near her, and whispered, "Your risk-taker is coming out. Fly in a 'device,' but don't try to become a flier, okay?"

For answer, she stuck her tongue out at me and laughed. "Not today."

"We have other priorities," Jenna said, sounding slightly distracted.

We wandered on. Jenna kept us from actually running across anyone, turning us casually before we passed a crowd.

When would my father call? The more time passed, the more my nerves ran with fire and the harder it became to focus on anything, even Alicia.

The park was dedicated to the history of Silver's Home, or more accurately, to the history of the planet's creations. Every corner and path and garden and exhibit held some strange thing. Here and there, sculptures of various sizes hung in trees or dangled from curved metal stakes, designed to capture the wind and sing songs of air and metal. Tiny flying machines smaller than my thumbnail swept silently through, picking up dead leaves and clipping grass, avoiding the paths entirely. I wondered idly if they swarmed the paths at night in order to keep them so neat. They'd have been handy to help keep up Commons Park in Artistos.

We stopped by a set of interlocking ring pools full of colorful fish. Jenna cupped her ear for a second, and then looked over at me. "He's coming."

23

JOSEPH'S FATHER

My father was coming.

Jenna sat on a bench and gestured for us to take another nearby bench. I sat beside Alicia, where I'd have a good view of anyone coming. Bryan stood behind us, watchful and protective. The pools sang of running water. One of the little wind-sculptures sighed and tinkled in the light breeze that cooled my cheek. I held Alicia's hand in mine and watched.

A young man walked toward us—too young to be my father—and blond. Except that people didn't grow old here and everything could be changed. I stood up, hopeful, but the man kept going. A pair of women walked by, holding hands and chattering. He probably hadn't changed *that* much.

I sat back down, my feet tapping on the hard-packed earth of the path. Alicia leaned in close to me and whispered, "Breathe."

All right. I closed my eyes for a moment, remembering Marcus's endless lessons in control.

One breath.

My heart still raced.

Two breaths.

Three breaths.

I looked at the blackness behind my eyes, focused in on the movement of my belly—in and out, in and out.

Four breaths.

Would he like me?

Five.

Alicia's hand squeezed mine sharply. I opened my eyes. A hundred paces away, my father walked toward us. I shivered, touched at the hope, fear and anticipation licking my spine. He walked like I did, like Chelo, his strides even and smooth, his head up, his eyes on Jenna. His dark hair had been cropped short, and he wore a flight uniform—a blue and gold captain's coat hanging unbuttoned over pants of the same blue and a simple off-white shirt.

He noticed that I watched him, in the way that all people seem to know when they are under scrutiny, looking at me briefly and narrowing his eyes before turning his gaze back to Jenna. He didn't appear to recognize me. I stayed glued to the bench, unable to move, unable to say anything, reality-shocked at the moment.

He was close enough now for me to see his eyes, smoky-blue and pleased at the sight of this woman he knew, yet overlaid with puzzlement. "Jenna," he said, "You look—fantastic."

He glanced over at the three of us, as if trying to decide if we were safe to talk around, and then his gaze returned to Jenna. His demeanor looked slightly guarded—from us being nearby or from something else?

I remembered Tiala and Jenna racing toward each other, the raw emotion of their meeting. In contrast, Jenna and my father seemed more like two paw-cats happening on the same territory and sizing each other up. My father's voice sounded slightly deeper than I had heard it on the data button that carried his journal. It still sat in my pocket like a talisman. "How did you get here?" he asked Jenna. "When?"

Jenna smiled. "Just a few months ago." She looked closely at him, then glanced at me, a warning in her eyes. She looked torn between wanting to take him away and talk to him, and needing to introduce us.

My tongue stuck to the roof of my mouth, my eyes glued on my father, taking in the details of how his hair was cut just above his ears, how he stood with both feet together, a little stiff, how the captain's coat fit him perfectly, instead of hanging slightly off-shoulder like it did on me.

Alicia's hand remained in mine, clutching me tightly. She knew what it meant to me to see him. Bryan knew also. He still stood behind us, one hand on the back of the bench, the other on my shoulder.

My father seemed excited and apprehensive as he gazed at Jenna. "I have good news for you."

She cocked her head, waiting.

He glanced over at us. "Can we walk?" he asked. "Or are these people with you?"

"They're from Fremont."

His eyebrows drew together as he looked at us, the puzzled look spilling from his eyes and filling his whole face and a trace of something unsure flickering in his eyes. For a second, he looked afraid.

Jenna continued. "Remember the children? Three of them came back with me."

His eyes widened, and he seemed to actually focus on us for the first time. We sat, still as the statues in the park, watching him back. The moment froze, and I heard Jenna say, "Bryan is standing in the back, and that's Alicia, and next to her is Joseph."

Her voice saying my name broke my tongue free. "Father."

For a long moment he looked at me, and I watched the hope in his face turn first to disbelief and then to amazement. "Joseph?" He knelt then, not yet touching me, but something mysterious passed between us in that moment, a spark of deep knowing.

And then I stood and he stood and we embraced, and I felt the arms of my father holding me tightly, his chest heaving, and his cheek against mine. He drew in a deep sobbing breath. "You're alive. You're truly alive." His face was wet, and mine, our tears mingling. The park, the people around us, the very air disappeared for a long moment, and I felt only him, only the joy of being held by my father. He smelled of space ship: clean oils and remanufactured air, the soft captain's coat. "I thought . . . I knew . . . I knew you were dead."

The birds and the wind-sculpture and the sound of running water returned to my consciousness, and he stepped back, looking at me. "You have your mother's smile," he said, his voice choked and small, full of loss.

I knew by the way he said it that she was dead. I swallowed, touched by his feeling, loss and a need to know about her filling me. "What happened to her?"

Pain flashed across his eyes, momentarily destroying the wonder and joy of a moment before. "She died in the last battle." He glanced at Jenna. "You couldn't have known."

The mother of the tender drawings. But I would not dwell on it yet—not in this moment when my father stood before me in the flesh.

He turned back to me, his voice choked. "I thought you died, too. They killed children. Or at least, our children." He gazed at some point on the horizon past me, his face rigid. "We were sure they killed you. The last thing we heard before we left was Chiaro telling us you were captured." Hope filled his eyes. "Chiaro? Is she alive?"

"She died that day. Chelo remembers."

He turned to look at us, as if counting us again to make sure he hadn't missed the other three. "Chelo?" he asked, his voice insistent. "Where's Chelo?"

"She's still on Fremont," I said. "She's doing all right, or she was when I last saw her. She and Kayleen and Liam."

He closed his eyes and breathed out, slowly, as if absorbing this new information. I expected him to be happy. Instead, it seemed like hearing Chelo lived delivered a physical shock.

But he hadn't, truly, known we were dead. Had that been easier for him—to be sure even when he couldn't really know? Did that explain why he never came back for us?

I stepped closer to him, wanting to ease his pain. I didn't care about the past, not now; I cared about this moment. "Father. It's okay. Did you know Therese and Steven? They took me and Chelo in. They took care of us."

His eyes widened and he turned away, as if he couldn't bear to look at me, or Jenna.

When he turned back around, the first thing he said was, "I'm sorry." His face crumpled in for a moment and he looked away, visibly drawing control back over his features. "I would never have left if I thought there was a chance you were alive." He squinted at me. "How did you get back?"

"We brought the *New Making* back." He must know I had his skills. "Dad, I'm a Wind Reader. I flew us back."

He blinked, then looked at Jenna, as if this was something he couldn't believe without verification. She nodded and he looked back at me. "You flew her back by yourself? With no training, no certification?"

Alicia interrupted. "Of course he did. Who else could have brought us home?"

"Yes, I flew her back. I liked it very much. I—I always wanted to fly her, from the first time I set eyes on her. I'm your kid, after all."

My father's face went still and silent and he sat down on the bench, putting his head in his hands. I sat down next to him, and Alicia and Jenna sat on the grass, facing us. Bryan stood watch above us all, alert.

What was he thinking? The confident man who had walked up to Jenna had fallen into himself, the emotions playing in his face a mix of sadness and anger spiced with a periodic smile in my direction. His eyes darkened as a single emotion won out. Deep sadness covered his face, fell over his body, slumped his shoulders. He looked at Jenna. "My god, Jenna. We worked for years to get Fremont back. We even left our ships in hock and saved everything. We starved to get enough credit. Three of us." He looked away. "Everyone else abandoned us. But three was enough to contract for the Family, since so many people dropped out after we came back."

Jenna's voice came out flat and cold. "Getting Fremont back how?"

He put up his hand, signaling silence. A set of two flyers walked by, the first I'd seen in the park. Their faces did not have the beautiful look of the flier in the statue. They seemed slightly pained, leaning forward to carry the weight of their wings. Surely they felt differently flying, lost the agonized looks, the awkwardness. I couldn't quite picture it, but I wanted to. Perhaps Alicia could. She watched them with a sense of longing. Her eyes ran up and down their oversized wings, taking in the golden ribbons tied to their pinions. Tiny silver bells tinkled on the ribbons, more because the wings bobbed slightly up and down than from the light breeze.

After they passed out of earshot, my father's hands shifted in his lap and sweat beaded his forehead. He looked—guilty. "Not one family came back whole. Not one. They took everything from us. And the bigger family—the Family of Exploration—splintered back here. They're still scattered."

"I know," Jenna said. "I have been trying to gather them up."

"We were angry," he said.

Jenna laughed bitterly. "I understand. Of all people, I understand."

She probably did. She had barely survived Fremont herself. Had lost her own family, as far as I could tell.

My father was babbling, almost like Kayleen babbled. "They killed Marissa, and they killed you, Joseph, and Chelo. I was sure of it. They took everything I loved. We . . ." He looked at Jenna. "We hired Star Mercenaries."

I didn't understand. "Star Mercenaries?"

Jenna's eyes widened and then turned to coal. She stood up and spat the answer out. "Hired soldiers. The Star Mercenaries are the way the Islas Autocracy goes to war when it doesn't want anyone to know that's what they're doing. They'll be bringing a fight to Fremont."

Chelo was there.

How would the mercenaries know to save her? And what of Akashi and Paloma, of Liam and Kayleen? Nava? I didn't want even the ones who hated me dead. In that long stretched-out moment of silence, I heard Chelo's voice in my head: *That damned war defines all of our lives, Joseph. We never even fought in it, and it has nearly killed us. Never, never in my whole life, will I join a war.*

"Chelo." I said quietly, staring at my father in disbelief. How could he do such a thing? "Are they there yet?"

He'd buried his face in his hands again. Maybe he couldn't stand to tell me he might have killed my sister. His daughter. Maybe he couldn't stand himself. No bitterness was worth such severe action. He shook his head from behind his hands, apparently unable to even look at me. "Not yet. We just . . . we just signed the contract last month. At Islas. If only I'd known you were here."

Bryan spoke from behind me, his voice colder than I had ever heard it. But he, too, loved Chelo. "When will they get there?"

My father lifted his face from his hands. Surely he heard the coldness in Bryan's voice, the near hatred. "I don't know. They weren't leaving right away, but they'll have gone by now. Takes a few years to get there, maybe a little more. They're supposed to message me when they're done."

Jenna's eyes had turned to ice. She spoke slowly, as if needing to be sure he understood every single word. "When they are done doing what exactly?"

He looked at me when he spoke, his eyes stricken and dark, the blue nearly turned to black. His voice came out a hoarse whisper. "When they are done killing everyone on Fremont."

24

PREPARATION

My father's words echoed in my being. "Killing everyone on Fremont."

Chelo.

And hundreds of others. Even Nava and Hunter seemed dear. Each name, each face sank into my belly like a stone.

How dare he!

Alicia leapt to her feet and stared down at him as he sat next to me on the bench, her face snarled in anger. "You didn't. No one could be that cold! Your *daughter* is there."

He leaned back, as if trying to fade into the stone bench.

She and I were one in our rage. Alicia, of all of us, had reason to wish some on Fremont dead. But we were not killers. Anger tightened her features, bringing out her fierce beauty. I expected her to scream at him, but it was Jenna who spoke first, her voice sharp yet controlled. "David."

He sobbed, his words broken. "I did it for Marissa. And for the kids." He raised his head and looked at me, his eyes so pain-drenched I almost felt sorry for him. I bit my lip, steeling myself against his remorse as he continued. "I'm sorry. I thought they killed everyone."

Jenna's voice was stone. But then, he was looking at me, and she couldn't see his eyes. "We died, Marissa died, so many of us died, because we didn't believe in genocide."

His voice shattered. "I— I know— I know." He put his head back into his hands, not looking at me. Afraid to look at me?

We remained still and silent. My father, craven behind his hands.

Jenna, her jaws tight and her eyes turned deeply inward. Alicia, still standing, fists balled, jaws as tight as Jenna's. Bryan stood behind me, his disgust deep enough to feel. And me? I have no idea what I looked like. My dreams of a loving, strong father lay shattered around me.

I spoke next, asking him, "Can't you call them off?"

He shook his head. "If I could reach them. For a fee. It took ten years to save enough for the contract. The cancellation fee is half again."

"What did it cost to kill a whole people?" I asked, my voice shaking, my jaw tight.

He recoiled as if my question stung him. Words seemed to stick in his mouth until they almost choked him. Finally, he said, "One hundred thousand credits."

Jenna gasped. Marcus's training for me had been less than a thousand credits so far, and Tiala had called that the price of a small space ship. So for enough money to buy a hundred small ships, you could annihilate over two thousand human beings.

"So we need fifty thousand credits to save my sister?" I needed to be sure I understood.

"That's a fortune," Jenna whispered.

Bryan spoke up. "There's no time to raise it." He glanced at my father. "Unless you have any bright ideas?"

My father shook his head, but he sat up a little, so he no longer looked quite like he wanted to disappear into the bench.

Bryan almost never spoke, but when he did, everyone listened.

"Bryan's right," I said. "So we have to get there before the mercenaries do."

Jenna's gaze radiated approval.

I glanced at my father. "Do you have a ship?"

His eyes widened. "No."

Alicia's fingernails carved ridges in my shoulder.

I glanced around to look her in the eyes. They snapped with anger, but she took a deep, quivering breath and went still. Her voice softened. "I had a dream once that I left Fremont, but realized I had left something behind that I needed to go get. I told Chelo the dream. I never thought what I left behind would be her."

I gripped her hand, pulled it from my shoulder, and squeezed it in gratitude. Artistos wouldn't be happy to see her, but I needed her. They might not be happy to see me, either. I didn't care. Chelo needed me.

Bryan added his voice to hers. "I'll go, too."

My father looked carefully at each of us. As he did, his shoulders slowly straightened and his hands fell into his lap. "We can find a way to fix this."

I didn't want his help. All the longing for him had come to this. I swallowed the words I wanted to say—*I never want to see you again*—and stared over his head, focusing on a tall slender tree with golden leaves.

I could not save Chelo alone. And I didn't know anything about these killers he'd hired. Tears of frustration stung my eyes as I looked over at him. "If you can help, I'll take you."

"I'll find a way." He sounded like one of the large camp dogs that had just been disciplined. Big enough and strong enough to do damage, but for the moment, with his tail tucked.

Jenna sat and stared out at the park, a silent statue of a beautiful, angry woman. A single tear gathered in her new eye, but didn't fall. "We need a ship," she said. "We have to get *New Making* back."

"Hello the crowd!" Marcus's cheerful voice fell on us like a laugh at a funeral. He came from behind Bryan. Our stricken mood engulfed him. "Who died?" he whispered, surely thinking of it as a joke, a way to cheer us up.

Jenna grimaced. "David hired Star Mercenaries to clean up Fremont for us."

The look Marcus gave my father might have killed a weaker man. Marcus immediately knew the core of the problem. "Chelo."

I gazed at him, unblinking. His green eyes fed me energy, and hope. He opened his arms, and I fell into them, heedless of what my father or anyone else might think, comforted by his rich scent: ship and garden, col and soap.

After a few moments, he pushed me gently away. His whole body was stiff. Even after so little time with him, I knew he hated injustice and stupidity.

If only *he* were my father!

I looked from my teacher to the man I had yearned for all my life, and then to Jenna, who had protected me all of my life. "Well? How do we get there?"

My father looked at Jenna. “Did the Authority take *New Making*?”

“Yes. We don’t have enough credit to get her back. Not yet.” Anger tightened her features.

Marcus cleared his throat. “I have a small ship, the *Creator*. You can take her.”

Jenna blinked up at him, startled.

His offer did not surprise me, except that I didn’t know he had a ship. Come to think of it, that wasn’t particularly surprising either. I smiled up at him. “Will you come with us?”

“I can’t. I have things to do here.” He grinned then, breaking the intensity of the moment. Such a Marcus thing to do. He raised one eyebrow. “Besides, someone will have to make sure you get away safely.”

“How long will it take to get there? What can we do when we get there? How do we stop this? How do we tell if the mercenaries are there yet? Can we beat them?” I wanted to go right then, to pile us sight-unseen into Marcus’ ship, wherever it was, whatever it was. I wanted to be on Fremont tomorrow.

Marcus waited for everyone’s attention. “I’ll try to take those in order. *Creator* will still take almost two years to get to Fremont. Still, that’s a full year less than it took you to get here. I keep her fairly ready, but she’ll need to be provisioned. She’s small—she can only carry up to twenty people, and you’ll need room in her to bring back at least the other three. There are good cold-sleep facilities, but someone should be up all the time since *Creator* has better, but less automatic, defenses than the *New Making*. I’d suggest you take no more than ten people. And you, Joseph, will need to learn how to fly her.”

He glanced at my father. “You, too.”

He raised his hand again, forestalling another barrage of questions. “I have no idea what you will do when you get there.” He glanced at Jenna. “But I suggest that you round up a few people with fighting skills and a belief in your cause, if you know any.”

Jenna’s lips pulled together in a small, tight line and her eyes narrowed. “Why would you do this? What do you want in return?”

“You can pay for the provisioning if you have enough.”

Jenna nodded. “I think so.”

Marcus looked at me. “And when you get back, I want Joseph to agree to train with me for at least a year." He grimaced. "If we even have a year left by then, and if the Five Planets aren't shooting at each other yet."

He turned back to Jenna, sizing her up, like a man looking at a beautiful woman. "I'd like Joseph to understand my goals. He can help me reach them if he wants to. And if Chelo comes back whole and agrees, I want her with me. I want to understand how Joseph and Chelo work together."

Alicia took my hand. "I want to stay with Joseph, too." She looked up at Bryan. "All of us."

Bryan smiled at her. "We are a family."

Jenna startled at the word, her hand brushing the new side of her face. She looked at me, then at Alicia and Bryan. A light dawned in her eyes, and her mouth quirked up in a soft, intimate smile. If the energy between a group of people could be seen, I was sure there would be lines connecting the four of us, and one between me and Marcus.

Nothing, however, between me and my father.

Maybe affinity groups started with such shared purpose.

Jenna turned to Marcus. "Thank you. We'll pay our way." She looked like she wanted to lean in toward him, but she leaned away instead. "But I can't promise our purpose will align with yours. If it does, we'll stand by you in it. But first, we'll save our own."

She turned to my father. "I had hoped to recruit you to see if we could bring the Family of Exploration back together. Now I understand *why* the Family fractured. You violated the soul of who we are."

My father held still. I hated the choices he had made, but most people would have cringed under Jenna's steady, unrelenting gaze as she continued. "Perhaps the best way to rebuild the Family is to correct the wrong. Then we can determine whether or not the Family has a home on Fremont."

She looked at Marcus. "And? I want to stay with you, too."

I watched Marcus carefully. The day we landed, he'd refused to take the others, even Alicia, who had asked directly. But now he knew me, and surely he knew how I loved Alicia. If nothing else, I'd told him. At least ten times.

He chewed lightly on his lower lip, while we all watched him, waiting for some sign.

When he focused on Jenna, his smile blended triumph and a bit of cockiness. The longer he looked at her, the softer his gaze became.

Just when I thought I couldn't bear to wait for his answer, Marcus nodded. "Then let's get you ready. Can you and the others make a list? Of both provisions and people?"

She nodded.

"Don't use the nets." Marcus took my elbow and guided me away from the group. As soon as we were out of earshot he asked, "Did you drop your shields at all?"

I shook my head.

"Good. The Port Authority is looking for you. I think you don't much want to talk to them, especially if you want to get to Fremont."

He bent down near me, keeping his tones low, as if to emphasize that I was in danger. "You and I are going to talk for a few moments and then you're going to go say good-bye to your dad, and we'll lay low until it's time for you to take off."

I took a deep breath. How could meeting my father have turned to Chelo being in mortal danger? How could a day ever be so wrong?

Marcus must have seen how miserable I felt. We were only an inch or two different in height, and I easily met his eyes, green flint, sparkling with urgency. He spoke, his voice quiet and firm. "Until you have suffered so much loss, you cannot know what dark place drove your father's decisions. Don't hate him."

I nodded, miserable. I wanted to hate my father for sending the mercenaries, and love him for it as well. Or love him in spite of it. But in this moment, all I felt was icy fear for Chelo. I shivered, in spite of the warm sun and the soft breeze that lifted my hair from my face, in spite of the scent of fresh grass and the singing sculptures and the birdsong.

I followed Marcus over to the others. He squatted beside Jenna, and I beside him, with Alicia on my right. She put a hand on my calf and looked up at me, her eyes wide with concern. "Are you all right?"

Sure. My sister was in mortal danger, the government neither trusted nor knew me, and my father was a flaming coward. "Yes. What did you come up with for a list? How fast can we get everything and be ready?"

Even though it was my question, Jenna looked up at Marcus. "It sounds like we need room to bring people back. What if we just take the five of us, and Tiala? We don't want to be separated again."

Marcus frowned. "You need a weapons expert."

Jenna leaned back. "We can't fight Star Mercenaries, not unless you have a warship."

He shook his head.

"I didn't think so." Jenna frowned. "The four of us know the town leaders, and I think they'll listen to me. The Star Mercenaries are a bigger threat than I am. Hunter—the man who led the war against us—stockpiled a lot of our weapons, and I hid the rest in a cave. We can decide what to do after we get there."

I already knew the situation. "Chelo won't leave if the rest of Artistos is in danger."

"How can we possibly save them all?" my father asked.

It was a good question. Chelo and Liam and Kayleen mattered the most, but they wouldn't abandon the others. So we wouldn't either. Besides, we owed them more than that. Tom, Paloma . . . "Whatever they may have done to you, the town raised me and Chelo and everyone else. Maybe not always right, maybe I'd like to teach a few of them lessons"—like Garmin, for instance, for beating up Bryan so badly—"but they had the opportunity to kill us when we were children, and they didn't do it. They chose to raise us instead. Whether I owe it to all of Fremont's people, or just to Therese and Steven who took me and Chelo in, this is my opportunity to thank them."

My father blew out a long breath and shook his head. "The Family of Exploration has a claim on Fremont, a legitimate one. We should bring some of them with us to be part of whatever solution happens there."

I wanted to ask him if they were as bloodthirsty as he was, but Jenna cut in. "I'll see who I can find." She looked up at Marcus. "I'll keep Alicia and Bryan with me. Bryan often sees things in people that

I don't, and Alicia can be . . . persuasive. We've started a provisioning list—I'll send it to you for suggestions."

Marcus nodded.

My father stood up. "Look—I have to take care of some things to free up my time." He glanced at Marcus. "I'll contact you sometime tomorrow or the next day."

"Don't talk about this," Marcus warned. "Not to anyone you don't trust completely. Does the Port Authority know about the Star Mercenaries?"

"If they do, they haven't seemed to care. But sometimes I think they're watching me. The Authority. Maybe that's why."

Marcus just said, "Maybe. If they do know, they won't want us going there. Times are uncertain, and they won't want it to look like Islas is fighting Silver's Home for territory. So keep this as low as you can. Say you've just got another job, for me. Don't tell anyone exactly what, but suggest we're headed for Lopali. That's the most supportive planet of the five, and we trade with them. Can you carry that story off?"

"Sure I can."

I stood up too, and then everyone else scrambled up. Marcus looked at all of us. "Keep this quiet. I don't want the Port Authority to know Joseph is going anywhere. They've left us alone, but I'm sure they know Joseph is with me. If they didn't before, they do after he kicked on the university systems."

Jenna sighed. "We'll be careful, Marcus. I haven't talked to many people about Fremont at all." She touched her face. "I spent more time in medical than away from it."

"I'm taking Joseph with me," Marcus said.

My father cleared his throat. "Look, I've got to go." He stepped toward me. Jenna took Bryan by the arm, leading him a few steps away, saying something in a low voice, and Marcus began asking Alicia questions I couldn't quite hear.

I turned my attention completely to my father. He held out a hand. "I . . . I can't tell you how happy I am to see you alive." His words were warm, and real, despite the guilt in his eyes. "We'll have some time on *Creator* to get to know each other."

"I expect that we will." My words sounded incredibly formal and stilted. I couldn't make myself embrace him, and while his hand extended close enough for me to take it, the rest of him kept some distance. So we shook hands, our grips not quite matching, and he turned and walked away.

25

A SILVER SHIP LEAVES FOR FREMONT

Marcus flew me to *Creator*. Below us, blue sky met blue water, the midday sun sparkling the sea with tiny short-lived stars of light. The long week of flying simulations for *Creator*, desperate study of the Islans, endless strategy sessions, little sleep, and much worry had finally ended.

My blood sang at the idea of flight, of going home, of finding my sister.

When I woke, I'd found a simple brown coat and pants with gold and silver stitching folded neatly on my dresser, a note on top that said, "For you. These are tuned to *Creator*." Crisp and new, something Marcus had ordered just for me.

They fit more comfortably than any clothes I had ever had.

Creator waited for us on one of the Silver Eyes. Marcus and I looped slowly over the necklace of perfectly round islands, which looked like mossy dark-gray stones skipped onto the blue sea. I leaned forward, my breath frosting the clear bubble of the windscreen. "Are they like Pilo Island? All owned by one affinity group?"

"Not anymore. The Landmakers built the Silver Eyes, but they sold them. And unlike Pilo Island, the Eyes are stationary. They started as platforms anchored to the ground. Mountains were grown up through them. They're mostly privately owned. The Landmakers designed the Eyes and the flow of water and wind around them nearly perfectly—they're fabulous for sailing and kayaking. Since the Circle River went in around Li, and water sports became the buzz, the Eyes have tripled in price."

"Do you own one?"

He laughed. "Wish I did. One of my clients owns part of one, and I barter for room in her private spaceport."

"What do you do for the client?" I knew better than ask for the client's name, but sometimes he told me about jobs.

His brows furrowed, a sure sign he was mulling over how much to tell me. We spiraled down. "This is a very old friend. We put better information into the nets than the power-brokers want out."

By now, I knew that he meant the government and the more powerful and greedy affinity groups. "So people see all sides of the story?"

He grunted, peering down at the island directly below us. "So people *can* see—most don't." He pointed. "That's where we're going. It looks like we're the first ones here."

Below us, a large and very white landing pad sat on the north shore of one of the Eyes, roughly in the middle of the chain. A brown-red mansion sat landward of the pad, nestled in a green lawn and screened from the ground by a hedge of simple evergreen trees. A secret place, unless someone was in the air like we were. As we came closer, I picked out a hangar at least three times the size of ours on the Grass Plains, with four round doors on top of its tall roof. The hangar color matched the lawn, standing out in dimension and shadow alone.

"Is your friend there?" I asked.

He shook his head. "No." He looked over at me. "You land her."

I smiled. A good chance to show off the skimmer abilities he'd had me practice during the last week. Control slid to me—just a reach and a grab, and I had the bones and blood of the skimmer in my body, a resonance that merged seamlessly with my very being. I became the skimmer's short stubby wings, her legs and wheels, her elegant rounded body.

As we landed, the hangar loomed over us, twice as large as it had seemed from the sky. We touched down smoothly. Marcus pointed to the far side of the hangar. "Put her there." I did. Marcus clapped me on the back. "Good job."

We shared a grin—him proud, me pleased with his pride—before clambering out. A light wind carried sea smells of salt and brine. The unusually white surface of the pad glittered under our feet. I knelt down and found it slightly grainy to the touch, just rough enough to create a bit of drag. It left a clean, oily scent on my fingers.

Marcus stood watching me. "The color is so it can be seen easily. You can pick this out from a satellite shot. And better, it can be changed to match the surrounding lawn with the touch of a button and a ten-minute wait—the surface is actually billions of programmable nano-scale sensors."

"Can you change it from space?" I asked.

He shook his head. "I can't. Maybe my friend can." He cocked his head, listening. "I think someone's coming."

An unfamiliar and slightly dented silver skimmer glittered in the sun. We stood together and watched it land easily next to ours. It must be my father. I chewed at the inside of my cheek, watching the bubble rise. What would I feel when I saw him?

Inside, a full head of black curly hair sat turned backward to me, talking to the pilot. Alicia! She turned, waved, and clambered out to wait on the clean white surface, watching as an apparition in white stepped daintily out of the skimmer. Tiny blue veins spidered the young woman's nearly translucent skin. Her hair was as white as the landing pad. She and Alicia wore matching tunics that fell to just above their knees, showing off similar thin, shapely calves. They stopped quite close to us, the girl's eyes so pale only a hint of gold and green shone in them. They looked like soap bubbles. Alicia gave a little bow and flourish. "This is Induan—one of the Family of Exploration. She's coming with us."

The girl's odd bright beauty thickened my tongue. "Hello, I'm Joseph."

She giggled. "I know. Alicia talks about you all the time." Her voice belled out, a hint of strength invisible in her pale skin and slender form. She turned to Marcus. "And you must be Joseph's teacher. Pleased to meet you."

Marcus's eyes and the little quirk of one side of his mouth indicated puzzlement. "Nice to meet you, too." He looked at Alicia. "Did Jenna invite her?"

Alicia stiffened. "No. I did."

Marcus glanced over at me, frowning. When I shrugged and grinned at him, he asked another question. "Does Jenna know she's here?"

Alicia's cheeks reddened slightly. "Jenna told me she likes her."

Marcus shook his head exaggeratedly as he looked from one girl to the other. "I can see that you two are such friends you can wear each other's clothes, but what, Induan, drives you into this type of danger?"

She blinked up at him, her mouth slack, her brow slightly furrowed. "I have . . . many physical mods."

Marcus's voice sounded wry. "I can see that."

"And I'm a trained strategist."

He raised one eyebrow. "So is Jenna."

Alicia glared at him. "And *Jenna* suggested we needed two people with every skill set."

He laughed, politely. "You may, at that. But Induan, that is what you bring with you. Why do you want to go?"

"I need to go." She lowered her gaze to the tarmac. "My brother went to Fremont on *Journey*. He died. My parents are both dead. There is nothing here for me."

Marcus pressed. "Even with your physical mods?"

Alicia bit her lip, as if biting back a retort. I reached for her hand and squeezed it, and she rewarded me with a tiny half-smile that disappeared again as soon as she turned her gaze back to Marcus. Her right foot tapped the hard surface below us.

Induan looked less put out than Alicia. "Even with my mods," she said evenly, "there are jobs I could have, but none that I want. My training is to support . . . disagreements . . . yet this is the first one I've found I want to support. Islas has no claim to Fremont, and we should not have sent them there. It is ours, but not to turn into a killing ground." She looked directly into Marcus's eyes, unafraid. "Why not right a terrible wrong?"

Approval touched his green eyes. "Perhaps, if I were much younger, I would fall in love with that answer."

She dropped her eyes. "Can we park my skimmer here while we are gone?"

"Sure. I'll move the extra skimmers into the hangar after you leave." He made a little bow. "Would you like to see your chariot?"

Induan nodded, and Marcus turned toward the hangar. Then Alicia pointed behind us. Another skimmer, one I didn't recognize, heading our way. This one must be my father.

It was.

I felt strangely neutral, with only small butterflies in my stomach as he climbed out. He stopped, as if waiting for something.

It took me three breaths, but I nodded hello. His eyes showed me that wasn't what he wanted, but it was all I had to give.

Marcus frowned at us both as if lost in thought. He looked at my father and said, "Someone needs to wait here for Jenna. Can you do that?"

My father nodded, all the light gone from his eyes.

Marcus said, "Follow me," and the rest of us did.

The big green building was plain and utilitarian, with high windows that didn't encourage looking in or out. We stood by the door. I jumped when it demanded, "Identity please," in a high feminine voice.

"Marcus." A bar of light played across his face. The door clicked. Marcus pushed on a spot on the wall in front of him, and the door slid open as silently as skimmer doors and the doors of the *New Making*. Inside, I saw an interior wall, and between the door and the wall, a wide, blank corridor that went both directions. He stepped inside, heading to the right.

We followed, me behind him, Alicia and Induan after me. My soft boots made little scraping sounds, Alicia's sport-shoe-clad feet made almost inaudible taps, and Induan made no noise at all.

Marcus opened another silently sliding doorway, and lights flooded a tall rounded room. I stood, gaping.

Creator.

Her silver skin glowed in the lights. Her lines were all curves, like the organic curves of calf muscles in a runner's legs. I drew in a sharp breath at her beauty. Tall and thin, she seemed coiled on her haunches, ready to spring.

Other than *Creator*, the room was empty except for a neat stack of supplies just inside the door.

I already knew *Creator* inside and out, but only from simulations and diagrams. I needed to touch her. I walked up and placed my palm and splayed fingers gently against her sleek side, feeling the cool silver of her skin. I loosened my shields, just a bit, and a spark of connectivity flowed almost immediately between me and the ship, as if either I or the coat I wore attracted her. Ship's chatter—status, commands, and the movement of parts and robots—filled my being.

My father would pilot her out of the system, so I would have to wait to truly merge with her, but touching her helped me know she was real. I let go of her reluctantly, feeling an immediate pang of separation.

Her door opened to Marcus's command and the four of us went in. *Creator* gleamed, every surface perfect. She smelled of metal and oil, of fresh water and green growing things. Marcus glanced at me. "Can you show Alicia and Induan around while I run diagnostics?"

"Sure," I said, gesturing for the girls to follow me. I turned around to ask Induan if she had even been inside a space ship. Alicia grinned up at me with a slightly self-satisfied smirk, and Induan was nowhere to be seen.

A flash of movement caught my eye. Induan, waving at me, a slip of silver against the silver corridor. Her hair, skin, and even her clothes now matched the silver ship instead of the white surface outside. "Wow," I exclaimed. "One of your mods?"

She nodded, smiling, showing me that her teeth remained as white as the rest of her had been. Alicia stepped past me, probably curious about the ship. Induan's skills undoubtedly didn't surprise her.

I shook my head. "Is that automatic, or do you have to tell it to do that?"

"I can turn it on or off, but if it's on, it's automatic." She demonstrated by becoming suddenly normal—with soft blond hair, pale skin, and normal-blue eyes. None of her beauty faded with the loss of the exotic colors.

"So what about the clothes?"

"The receptors in my skin talk to receptors in the clothes. But only special clothes."

Alicia was wearing the same outfit. I turned around to find my dark-haired pale girl had turned a bright silver. I blew out a long whistle. "How?"

"Some mods don't take too long. Jenna let me and Bryan each pick one we thought we could use on Fremont."

I didn't get to do that! "What did Bryan pick?"

Alicia turned off her silver. "I better not tell on him," she said. She leaned in and gave me a kiss, her lips soft and sweet.

We resumed our exploration of the ship with no further surprises, except the lush beauty of the pocket garden that showed Marcus's unique touch: the tomatoes glowed bright red.

After about a half an hour, the three of us trooped into the control room. Marcus sat still, a blissful look on his face. After a moment, he shook himself loose from the ship, still smiling. "She's fine. She'll get you there. Jenna should be here any minute—she just messaged me." He glanced at Alicia. "Do you know your way around enough to load the boxes outside into the hold?"

She glanced at Induan. "Want to help?"

The chameleon girl grinned. Marcus gave them a few more specific instructions, and we went back outside, arriving just as Jenna's skimmer landed.

Marcus started toward it at a light jog. I raced a bit to catch him. By the time we reached it, four people had climbed out: Jenna, Bryan, Tiala, and a woman I'd never seen before in my life, but whom I knew, deep in my bones, was from Islas. Maybe it was the cut of her nearly uniformlike light blue tunic and straight-legged pants, or her short dark hair, or something subtle about her features. She fit the profile I'd been studying. An Islas expatriot?

Whatever she was, Marcus walked right up to her and folded her briefly in his arms. "Dianne."

When they separated, Dianne had a bright glow on her face. She cast her wide, dark eyes down for a moment before she looked back up at him. "Of course I came. I hope that I will be able to help."

"I've no doubt of that." He turned to us. "Joseph, I'd like you to meet Dianne Kiron. Consider her my contribution to this trip. My best addition, if you will, besides your transportation." He sounded quite proud of himself.

I extended a hand to her. "You are from the Islas Autocracy?" I asked.

Her eyes rounded and her mouth made a little "o." "Marcus said that you are smart." She hesitated, searching my face as if trying to decide whether or not to trust me. She gave a tiny nod. "Yes. Marcus suggested you may need someone who understands the Star Mercenaries on this trip."

"We might." How had she fit into Islan society? Was she a Star Mercenary, a scribe, a merchant, an artist or what?

Marcus glanced at Jenna. "There's no one else, is there?"

She shook her head, her voice slightly bitter. "I asked some old friends and they are all doing other things. So yes, let's get going."

Bryan spoke up. "Then who is that?"

We all looked up together. Another skimmer. Marcus frowned. "Port Authority." His jaw tightened and his green eyes grew cold. "They have no jurisdiction here—this is a private port that doesn't use any of the government spaceports. We have the trip cleared."

Regardless, the skimmer kept coming. It was easily three times as big as any of ours on the ground. My skin crawled.

Marcus said, "Go, Joseph. It will be okay. I'll take care of this." He sounded like he was trying to convince himself. "Take everyone except your dad. Help Alicia and Induan get the last boxes loaded."

Jenna glanced at the incoming Port Authority and then at our skimmers. "Wait—the last of our supplies. Take what's in my skimmer." She strode quickly there, opened the top and the side doors, and began lifting boxes carefully from between and under the seats, handing one to each of us. Dianne's was small, and fit in the crook of her arm. Mine was heavy, and I started right off with it, wanting to make it inside as soon as possible.

We'd left the doors open. I walked in, set my box down, and stood by the door. Dianne passed me first, her eyes rising to meet mine for just a moment. Something like worry or fright touched them, and she nodded at me, nearly deferential. It felt strange to have a grown woman look at me that way. What had Marcus told her about me?

Jenna followed, her face set, her eyes on Dianne in front of her. Tiala followed Jenna, looking naked without her bird, Bell. This was the first time I'd seen the two sisters close to each other since Jenna's miraculous healing, and their similarity made me smile. No wonder I'd mistaken Jenna for Tiala. Bryan walked easily along the rear, the only one carrying a larger box than mine. He smiled at me. "We're going home."

I nodded. "We sure are." I glanced back at the pile of skimmers outside, where the Port Authority's big skimmer was just landing. "We are," I whispered.

He stopped, looking over his shoulder at the Authority, too. "No matter what."

I clapped him on the back, suddenly realizing that he was no longer playing big brother, but just brother. Maybe he thought I could protect myself these days. I looked for some sign of the mod he had chosen. He didn't look any different. But then, I hadn't noticed anything different about Alicia. I jerked my head down-corridor. "Go on. I'll catch up."

He went.

I made sure the box I'd set down wasn't visible through the door, then flattened myself against the wall, peering around quickly to get a good look.

Lukas walked up to Marcus and extended a hand. Uniformed Port Authority people were climbing out of the skimmer, seven so far, and more coming. I peeled my head back, slowly, trying not to draw attention. This would be a great time for a chameleon mod. Except Induan had been pretty visible against the white surfaces out here, and both girls had been three-dimensional etchings against the silver surfaces of the ship. Now, if we were in the Lace Forest at home . . .

I couldn't hear what anyone was saying. That meant no one was yelling at anyone, which was probably good. I should do what Marcus told me to, and get us ready. The scene outside the door pulled at me—I needed to know what was happening.

What if we had to take off?

In spite of everything he'd done, I didn't want to leave my father behind. Sweat beaded my forehead. I picked up my box, and raced as fast as I could to the ship.

I stood in the rounded ship's bay, panting. The pile of boxes being loaded had shrunk to ten or twelve. Bryan was heading down the ramp, empty-handed, coming for a fresh load. I shoved the heavy box at him, sighing with relief as he took it, grabbed two lighter ones, then a third, and the two of us headed back in. "I don't like this," I said.

"Did you learn anything?"

I shook my head. "I can't hear them. But it's Lukas, the same creep that met us off the ship. How fast can we finish this?"

"Depends on how well you want the cargo strapped down."

Good question. *Creator* maintained gravity all the time, and unlike *New Making*, it kept the same gravity over the whole ship. My father and I could control that for the first part of our flight, and we'd have time to recheck cargo before our first turn. "Doesn't have to be perfect."

"Good."

As we climbed into the ship, Induan and Alicia eeled past us, going down the narrow ramp. Alicia put a hand on my back, stopping me. "What's happening out there? Who is that woman? Who else is here?" Induan stood behind her, head cocked, an intent look on her face.

"I don't know," I repeated. "The woman's name is Dianne. Jenna brought her, but Marcus picked her. You never met her?"

Alicia shook her head. "Where's your father and Marcus? Jenna is acting all mysterious and telling us to load the cargo fast."

"The Port Authority is here," I whispered.

Both girls' eyes rounded, and Induan immediately faded to the background, a chaotic shift from normal to part silver from the ship and part off-white to match the hangar walls. I bit back a laugh at the unintended consequences. "So yes, let's get her loaded as fast as we can." I frowned at them, arching an eyebrow, trying to be like Marcus.

Alicia looked ready to burst out laughing. "We can get most of it in one more load." With that, they turned around, Induan still oddly striped and Alicia still normal.

I'd probably be in a lot of trouble once Alicia started turning that chameleon mod on casually.

I stared at their backs for a moment, then turned and hurried to catch up with Bryan.

Inside, Tiala and Jenna took the boxes from our arms and stacked them. Jenna easily lifted the one I'd just gratefully foisted on Bryan. I comforted myself by thinking she didn't have to carry it far. The little hold was nearly full. We started to turn to go back for more, but Jenna barked, "Joseph! Go to the Command Room. Just in case."

Just in case the other pilot never got in here. I swallowed and nodded. "Do you know what's happening out there?"

"No. But you might if you got into the Command Room."

Duh. And I'd been trying to listen outside. Of course the ship would be connected to the spaceport and to its surroundings. There were cameras. "Where is Dianne?"

"In the Command Room. Alicia and Induan are right here." She glanced around. "Maybe. Hell, I don't know. You worry about getting us ready to fly."

"I'll get the last of the boxes," Bryan said, already partway out the door.

I raced to the Command Room. Like in the *New Making*, *Creator*'s Command Room nestled near the center of the ship, next to a galley. Four comfortable pilot-style chairs with thrust-straps sat at attention around a square silver table. In one of them, Dianne sat so still she might as well have been a statue.

I sat down opposite her.

She lifted her head, her eyes warm and soft. "Please bring up the screens."

I closed my eyes and opened to *Creator*. It opened back—reporting out, as if eager to have a human to talk to. *Creator*'s AI was fully integrated, just *Creator* herself, unlike Starteller who rode in *New Making* but could have been separated. Merging with *Creator*, feeling her thrum through my bones, hearing the ship's reports like thoughts inside my own head—it was like running where the *New Making* had been crawling. Or perhaps Marcus's training had taught me more than I knew.

"Joseph." Dianne's soft voice pulled me back, although *Creator* remained part of me as I ran the threads to the cameras and turned three of them to show on the walls.

One camera showed the big bay, which *still* held three boxes. No sign of Alicia, Induan, or Bryan.

On another screen, Marcus and Lukas, standing a meter apart. Marcus had his back to me, but his stance looked calm and resolute. My father stood near him, his back to me also.

Lukas's neat-as-a-pin hair, with the red streak, bobbed up and down as he spoke. Five of his people surrounded him. I recognized Ming, the dark-haired woman who had called the skimmer for us when we left the port. Her eyes looked up at me briefly, as if she sensed my presence. She was the one who had told me it was Marcus who convinced Lukas to leave me alone when we first landed.

The third camera showed the doorway of the hangar, and a brief quick movement that might have been Alicia or Induan. Not white like the tarmac, but green to match the hangar.

No wonder some boxes remained in the ship's bay.

I turned on the audio for the hangar door. Alicia's voice, pitched low: "Can't we get closer?"

Bryan. "What for? Marcus can handle things." Good for Bryan.

The audio was two-way, to allow people on the ground to talk to people inside *Creator*. I held my tongue though, afraid the people outside would hear me, if I spoke.

Bryan, sounding more insistent. "Come on—let's get *Creator* loaded."

"In a minute." Alicia snapped at him. "I need to know what's going on. We can't see everyone that came in that skimmer. Where are the others? Is there a back entrance?"

Dianne cleared her throat. "There is no back entrance. But there is probably trouble."

I zoomed the camera out. Six uniformed Port Authority people hugged the wall just around the corner from Marcus's line of sight. The leader made a come-on gesture just as I spotted them, and the group broke into a jog. I spoke into the microphone. "I see you. You do not have permission to enter here." They stopped, momentarily confused. "Close the door," I hissed. It probably wouldn't open for any of them.

Alicia got the message and spit an answer at me. "I don't know how!"

Dianne, behind me. "There is a palm-pad on the door. It will close for anyone."

"Palm-pad. On the door."

A second of silence.

The crowd outside rushed the door.

"Got it."

"Come back," I insisted.

"Not until I know the door is shut."

Damn her. Bryan's voice, directed at me. "I'll get her." I couldn't see any of them, but I pictured him picking her up and throwing her over his shoulder.

I tried to watch all three cameras. Bryan and the two girls should show up on the hold camera any moment.

"The door." Dianne's voice, urgent.

The big door hadn't yet slid all the way closed.

The lead Authority person stuck a foot into the opening, and the door stopped. "What the—?" I exclaimed.

"Safety feature," Dianne said. "There should be an emergency override."

Outside, my father bolted toward the door. Ming took off after him. Marcus, Lukas, and the others held their positions.

Why didn't Marcus do something?

Something tugged at me. Marcus, from inside the webs. "Are you ready?" he asked.

I blinked, nodded. "Sure."

"Strap in. You'll have to fly. Hold until I tell you when." The engines started. Surely he started them, although he appeared to just be standing, talking to Lukas, ignoring the melee by the door. Lukas ignored it as well, keeping Marcus fixed in his gaze. I'd bet money they were both holding at least two conversations, even though Lukas was no Wind Reader.

I fumbled with the soft straps, struggling to get the cool metal buckles to close without taking my eyes off the camera views. Dianne's eyes widened and she began to do the same.

Bryan, Alicia, and Induan raced through the corridor door into the big room.

Jenna screeched, "Grab the boxes!"

They slowed, fear flashing on their faces, but they obeyed her, grabbing boxes before coming on up the ramp.

The ship registered them as onboard. "Strap down," I called out.

There. That was who I cared about. I'd wait, though, for my father. If there was time. If he could get through the security goons. I glanced back up at the screen. The door finished closing. The only people left outside were Lukas's people, and Marcus.

My father had made it.

Marcus. "Close your eyes. Connect fully to *Creator*. I'm connected, too. I'll stick with you as far as I can."

I needed to know. "What did Lukas come for?"

Silence. A long beat when I and Marcus breathed in unison. Our connection wasn't voice; it was the deep, intimate knowing we'd shared when I flew in, and more. Much more. I knew his soul. And he was torn. "They claim that if you fly in and fight Islas, it will be made into the first strike in the war between the five planets."

"What if I go, and just get Chelo?" *Creator* was ready. I was ready. "What if we—if we don't fight?"

"Then Lukas will be wrong."

"And if we do more, he'll be right?" I breathed out, a long slow breath, mine alone.

"Joseph." His energy had gathered, strengthened, become more sure. "Joseph. Neither Lukas nor I know what you will find. Do what you need to do. It's all any of us ever can."

I closed my eyes, feeling the ship fully, fitting her to me like skin. I couldn't see; I had to trust. Marcus in my very being, speaking and not. "Close *Creator*'s door."

I did. The ship's engines rumbled louder. Marcus again. "I'm opening the top of the hanger for you. Your course is already set." A small part of me felt what he did, how he tripped a mechanism and the ceiling began to slide away. Most of me rode the power and water and air and engines of the ship.

I was ready.

Creator was ready.

We waited.

Familiar steps. Jenna, coming in to the Command Room. I heard her strap in. I checked on the others. Six more bodies, all prepared, strapped into chairs that worked as acceleration couches, scattered throughout various rooms in twos.

The ceiling clicked fully open.

Blue sky beckoned above us.

Six bodies?

Dianne, to me. "We have someone extra."

And I was so far down, so deep into the ship, that I barely heard

Jenna whisper, "Ming," as I, as *Creator*, bolted from the hangar and flew, a silver arrow shot from Silver's Home for Fremont. Once again, I flew against the Port Authority's wishes.

I whooped, and in the far background of my heart, I heard Marcus say, "Good Journey."

I reached out and embraced his energy, so that he and I and the ship were together one being, and I held tight, knowing that soon enough it would be just me and *Creator*, and all of us on board her.

Maybe we could beat the mercenaries.

PART FIVE

THE STRANGERS

26

NEW BEGINNINGS

For the first time in a week, the sun shone warm and strong. We had survived winter. Back home the bands would be gathering without us.

Liam and I walked slowly, hand in hand, up the path toward home. We'd stolen quiet time together, still vexed by uncertainty over how to treat Kayleen. "So you still aren't sure what you want to do?" I asked.

"No. Yes. I hate this." His face grew softer. "The Kayleen I know now wouldn't have kidnapped us."

"I know." And he'd been spending more time with her. I decided not to push him, sure that time would draw us all together. Maybe I was ready. "It's good to dry out."

"Survival of the soaked." As Kayleen had called our experiences this winter. "At least we didn't starve."

"We do seem to be stuck here," I said.

"Yes." He glanced up at the mountains, their snowy tops so bright he had to squint. Sunshine warmed the rocks and called new green shoots out of the damp earth.

Spring had woken more than plants. The ground shivered under us for the second time that day, knocking me from my feet. Liam grimaced as he offered me a hand up. "I don't like this."

"Me either."

We found Kayleen with Windy in the paddock, crooning at the now full-height hebra as if she were a child. Kayleen looked concerned as we came up. "Windy hates the quakes. I'm scared she'll break through the fence."

Liam clambered up on the bars. "She seems pretty spooked. It's not as if she's never felt an earthquake."

Kayleen worked at a tangle in Windy's greenish-white beard. "These are worse than the last ones."

Liam eyed rocks jutting from the sheer mountainside above us. He frowned. "We should move away from the cliffs."

Windy grabbed our attention. She jerked her head up, extending her neck so she looked out above us by almost a meter. Her nostrils distended and she stamped her right front hoof twice. Liam spoke quietly to Kayleen. "Get the long-line. I want to move into the open between the waterfall and the path."

Kayleen vaulted over the rails and returned quickly with the longest lead we had. I opened the gate to let her through. The ground shivered again. As Windy bolted toward the opening I kicked the gate shut. The hebra bugled as she fetched up hard against the barrier. Kayleen, who had kept her feet, threw the rope over Windy's neck and used it to gently tug the hebra's head down far enough to grab her halter and clip on the lead.

Before I had the gate more than a quarter open, Windy raced through it, pulling Kayleen quickly behind her. Liam and I scrambled after them.

We'd only gotten a few meters when the earth heaved. A loud rumble startled me. I looked up just as the cliff above the waterfall slumped, pouring down, mixing with the waterfall, a great clashing and rattling of rocks.

We scrambled to the biggest open spot in West Home: the small clearing we'd seen the tall-beasts grazing in when we first found the valley.

Windy pranced, edging away. Kayleen lay on the ground, holding the end of the lead taut, calling, "Windy! Windy! Stop." The hebra stopped, then bolted the other direction, nearly running over Kayleen.

A huge rumbling cracked the air open, loud enough that I clapped my hands over my ears.

Liam pointed west. The sky above the Fire River billowed with black clouds. "Eruption," he gasped.

As if to underscore his words, the ground shivered yet again. And continued. We were all on the ground except Windy, who had pulled free of Kayleen but stopped nearby, her feet braced, the whites of her eyes showing.

We held position for long moments, the ground bucking under us. A tree toppled and fell into its neighbors.

A gray-black cloud billowed impossibly high before it spread, staining the sky.

Small rocks rattled down from the cliff. A boulder twice my size landed in the middle of the paddock, narrowly missing the fence.

The three of us huddled close. Liam put one arm around each of us, keeping his eyes on the sky.

The earthquakes had stopped.

We scrambled up, shaking, all of us staring, transfixed by the huge column of steam. "Be glad the wind's blowing away from us," Liam said.

Kayleen recovered Windy, keeping her close. The hebra sniffed at the air, head and ears up, butting close to Kayleen.

Liam braved a short trip to the house, immediately returning to our side with water. He sat, furiously drawing in his journal, sketching the sky and the clouds, and the way the waterfall now fell onto a huge boulder and splashed to the edges of the pool.

I moved next to Kayleen, scratching Windy's flank, trying to soothe the frightened beast.

A few birds began tentative notes, a sign of calm, but nowhere near the normal raucous chattering.

Kayleen leaned into me. "I'm scared, Chelo. That's not too near, but what if the peak above us goes? Does one eruption spawn another?"

I reached for her hand. "I don't know. It scares me, too. It's worse than demon dogs. Did you check the perimeter?"

She handed me Windy's lead and closed her eyes. "It's okay. One node isn't reporting in, but two others patched around it. I'll look at it." She opened her eyes and shivered. "Later. When I'm sure it's safe."

As if we were ever sure of safety here.

By mid-afternoon, Islandia had calmed except for the great dark cloud eating more and more of the sky. "Come on, Kayleen," I said. "Let's put Windy away and make something to eat. I'm starved."

She stared up at the ridge above us, shaking her head.

Liam closed his journal. "I have a better idea. Let's take some snacks and walk down-valley. We'll still be in the open that way, and I want to find a place to see better."

We followed his plan, except that Windy and Kayleen took off at a run and we raced behind them, making it down to the sea in less than an hour. We fetched up a few yards from the cliffs, looking back toward Islandia's teeth. Ridges and small hills blocked a clear view. All we could tell was that the eruption had happened near Blaze. Liam snorted. "I think we'd have to go down to where we camped and saw the river for a good view." He glanced up and down the coastline. "And I don't think we should do that now."

"I don't want to get any closer," I said.

Kayleen nodded, still clutching Windy tight, her brow damp with sweat. "We could camp out here. I can go back and get gear."

"No." The eruption cloud had started to darken the sky above us. "I'd rather risk rock falls at West Home than demon dogs, and besides, I think the wind is changing."

Before we made it halfway home, walking this time, white and gray ash fell like snow. It snuck into our noses and mouths so we coughed and spat into the ash-fogged air, which stank of fire. We tied our shirts over our mouths to breathe and stopped from time to time to wipe Windy's face.

We saw almost nothing but each other, ghostly and insubstantial, shuffling through ash almost to our ankles by the time we reached the rocky part of the path that led into our hidden valley.

Once more, we had almost lost each other. The thought made it hard to breathe. What if one of us died? If we had been in the paddock when the rock fell? What then?

I held Kayleen's hand as we walked home, soothing its trembling.

We rigged a tarp over part of Windy's paddock, using the new rock as one of the anchor points. Liam and I brought the hebra food and water and we stayed with her under the tarp, making a meal of stored nuts, dried fruit, and grazer jerky.

Liam sat between Kayleen and me. He gave me a tender smile, then leaned over to her, whispering, "Turn around."

She did, and he gently massaged her stiff shoulders. She leaned back against him, making small sounds of relief.

As night fell, the wind stopped. Ash still floated down in a thin curtain, like white feathers coating everything in fine dust.

Windy folded her long legs under her and lay down. Kayleen rose and stroked her head, brushing out thick clumps of ash. She dunked a corner of her shirt into Windy's water, using the damp rag to wipe the hebra's eyes and nostrils.

"We should go in," Liam said.

Kayleen glanced at Windy, who sat placidly enough under the makeshift tent. Apparently reassured, she nodded.

In the cabin, we stripped out of our ashy clothes, leaving a pile on the floor. Liam laughed. "Look at yourselves."

"And you." I blushed. Our skin had whitened with the winter, contrasting with white-gray ash stuck in every place that had been exposed, including our breasts and torsos, bare since we'd used our shirts to breathe though. Kayleen's dark hair looked gray. I grabbed a drying skin. "Last one to the pool has to make breakfast tomorrow!"

It wasn't me. I made it in first, jumping deep into the shivery-cold snow-melt water at the edge, immersing my hair and releasing great clumps of sticky ash from it underwater. Two well-timed splashes told me Kayleen and Liam would both be making breakfast.

We emerged together, coughing and spluttering from the cold water. A slight breeze blew warm air over my skin. We stood a little apart from each other, naked and small and still slightly ashy. I picked up my skin and began drying Liam's legs. Kayleen stood, watching us. She picked up her own skin and worked on his back. I glanced up at him to see how he felt, noticing a small smile. He looked carefully at me, a question in his eyes.

I nodded, and then looked away, briefly unsure. The skin made soft shushing sounds against his calves and then his thighs, and the same sounds where Kayleen worked on his shoulders. Liam's breath grew faster.

When we had finished drying him, his voice sounded thick as he suggested, "Kayleen next. She's shivering."

So I was last. The movement of their hands and the soft skins against my body felt like fire. By the time the two of them had finished rubbing me dry, my insides were warmer than I expected.

Ash still fell from time to time. I looked over at Liam. "We'd best go in before we have to get clean all over again."

He smiled. His voice shook slightly. "That might not be too bad."

My voice sounded small in return. "Surely we don't need to set a watch tonight. The perimeter works, and even the dogs won't be out in this."

"No," he said. "I don't suppose we do."

Walking back, we each took one of Kayleen's hands.

I had been right. The dogs left us alone and the perimeter remained silent all night as ash fell silently outside the cabin windows.

We barely noticed it.

27

VISITORS

Our fire licked at the wood, rising two meters into the sky, warning predators away from our kills. The carcasses of two young grazers lay behind me, gutted and cut up to pack onto Windy in the morning. Another year had passed on Islandia, with one more eruption, somewhere on the side of the island we couldn't reach because of the Fire River, two meteor showers, and one storm so severe it had washed part of the cliff down onto our house, staving in a wall.

We were trying to finish hunting early this season. Kayleen's swelling belly proclaimed that her baby would be born soon, sometime midsummer, and my own would be a few months behind, at best.

My baby kicked, a tiny flutter that I had just begun to feel from time to time. I held my hand over my stomach, barely bigger than normal yet. We hadn't been sure if we *could* breed, given how little we actually knew about our own genetic modifications. Perhaps we would end up with a colony here, after all.

Even if we could get back, Artistos leaders had warned us against having children. The babies were clear evidence of our three-way relationship, which wouldn't be any more welcome at home than our progeny.

The thought made me miss home. The sharp pain of loss at all those we might never see again poked at me, and I stood, tending the fire, struggling to feel hope. If only we had gone with Joseph.

I waited until the sky turned pale with dawn to wake the others. The Fire River had again been taken back by the daylight, its red glow unable to compete with the bright sunlight. We had just finished packing camp when Windy's ears flattened against her head and she stopped dead in her tracks.

Nothing seemed out of place.

There was no nearby cover to hide big predators.

Liam looked up, and then I heard it too, up and across the river. All three of us all pointed at once. A noisy speck in the sky, growing bigger.

Windy bugled and stamped. Kayleen whispered to her, calming. I didn't look—I couldn't take my eyes from the ship.

For that was what we saw. A spaceship.

Perhaps it was Joseph, returning. My heart caught in my throat, then fell again as the speck grew big enough for me to see that it was both wider and squatter than the *New Making*. Certainly, it wasn't from Artistos. Maybe Joseph had come back in a different ship?

It flew over our heads, heading toward Golden Cat Valley, and certainly past it, low enough that it must be looking for a landing site. It disappeared from view. We stood together, struck even dumber by the sight of the spaceship than by the lava river the night before. "It could be Joseph," I said.

"Maybe," Liam said, his voice doubtful. "We can't know." He looked down into my eyes. "Don't hope too much. It wasn't the *New Making*."

I bit my lip, nodding.

No need for discussion. We settled into a fast jog that we could keep up for hours, even pregnant.

We kept to the shore, staying in the open and avoiding the more dangerous forest because of the meat we carried. At one point, we crossed a wooden bridge we'd built over the river Kayleen and I had fallen into the previous summer. At the wide opening where Golden Cat Valley emptied into the grasslands, we stopped at the obvious turn, eyeing the path to West Home.

"We have to go home," Liam said. "Windy's tired, and I don't want to come up on strangers in the dark."

I sighed, noting wryly to myself that the hebra actually looked fresher than any of us. "I so want to know if it's Joseph."

Liam put an arm around me. "Why would he land here? Why not on Artistos? The ship came from very high, from space. So it meant to land here. Joseph would surely have gone home."

I leaned into him. "Why would any ship come here? We've seen the satellite shots—we've left plenty of mark on Jini. Artistos and the spaceport are clearly visible. So the ship must be avoiding Artistos, or looking for us."

Liam licked his lips and stared off in the direction the strange ship had gone. "If it's not Joseph, I'm not sure we'll be happy to find out who it is."

Kayleen and I glanced at each other. She looked shaky as she said, "The last ship that came here brought our parents, and a war."

He nodded. "Whatever this ship brought, we can find out tomorrow."

We climbed up the rocky entrance to West Home just before dark filled our small valley. It looked just like we had left it. The noisy waterfall caught the last bits of light in its spray.

We had fallen out of the habit of setting watches all night, every night. It hadn't seemed necessary after Kayleen tuned the perimeter.

But that night we did two strange things. We again set up watches, and we didn't light a fire.

28

THE DAWNFORCE

I always chose last watch for love of the peaceful, pregnant moment of the crack between day and night. This morning, I fidgeted, wanting daylight to come early. I searched the shadows around the corral. Nothing seemed unusual or out of place.

Except that the whole world had changed. Was this ship from Deerfly, like *Traveler*, or from Silver's Home, or from somewhere else? Why were they here?

What did this mean for our babies?

The last ships had brought war and death and pain and confusion.

Did people fight everywhere, or were there planets where everyone got along? We had enough history databases that I knew the former was more likely than the latter, but surely, somewhere, a planet spun peacefully around a gentle sun and no one fought.

Light crept down-cliff, painting the sharp rocks and soft green vines with gold.

Liam came blinking out the door, stretching before he walked over to me. He smelled of sleep and sweat and, a little, of Kayleen as he folded me in his arms. "I love you," he whispered.

As always, the words tore tenderness from me. And swelling up through my thick throat, the return words, "I love you."

He kissed my forehead and pulled away. "You and Kayleen and Windy should stay here. It's hidden. I can sneak out and take a look."

I shook my head. "I want to stay together. We have no idea who these people are. What if . . . what if something happens and you get caught? What if you get killed, and we never know?"

He glanced toward the house where Kayleen still rested under the covers, her dark hair visible through the window. "We need to decide together."

"I know." Silence fell for long moments between us, like a pause before a wind storm.

The door opened. Kayleen called out, "Good morning," the words sounding like a question.

I smiled. "Good morning. We were just deciding what to do."

She came to us, her hair mussed from sleep, one hand covering her belly. We brought her into our hug. The light had come up far enough to see fear touching the corners of her mouth and filling her eyes. "What should we do?" I asked.

Windy wandered over, butting Kayleen softly with her head, wanting her share. Kayleen reached toward her, but pulled away, squeezing her eyes shut.

Her voice cracked the still peace, high and intense. "There's something in Golden Cat Valley." When she opened her eyes, all softness had been replaced by the alertness of a wild animal. "I need to go see what it is."

I stiffened. "Animal?" I asked.

She shook her head. "Not a cat, not the tall-beasts, not the demon dogs. I don't know."

Liam and I glanced at each other. "We should all go," he said.

Kayleen picked up Windy's lead.

I swallowed my comment that she should just leave Windy. If anything happened to us, the hebra would be trapped in a corral. I closed my eyes. "Please let it be Joseph," I murmured.

Kayleen left Windy at the base of the rocks. We climbed up, standing on the highest of the tumbled stones, gazing out into the long, narrow valley. It looked empty, except for three big brown birds riding thermals in lazy circles. I glanced at Kayleen. Her eyes had lost focus, her body stilled. "Five of them. People. They're coming this way." She pointed. Following the direction of her fingertip, I made out a small group walking near the edge of the river trees as if trying to stay inconspicuous. They moved unerringly toward us.

So they knew we were here. "What should we do?" I asked.

"Meet them and pretend there are more of us than there are," Liam said. "They can't know."

Kayleen shook her head. "They know. They can read our data."

Of course. "With machines or by themselves?" I asked.

Her eyes had narrowed down to small slits. "By themselves. There's at least two Wind Readers in the group."

Altered. Like us. And from Silver's Home or someplace like it. "Is Joseph with them?"

"No."

"How can you tell?" Liam asked.

"These people aren't like Joseph at all. Joseph and I always knew whenever the other had been in the nets. Especially if we were both in them at once. I'd know if he was here."

A deep sigh of disappointment escaped me. Would he ever come back? Did he live?

She closed her eyes. "They've been in the valley net. Not at home yet—they haven't seen the connection, haven't pushed hard. But they know there are people here. They seem a little confused, maybe because these are different than their nets." She ran her fingers through her hair and grimaced. "I wouldn't bet they can't figure it out." She put a hand over her mouth. "I didn't put up any good protections. We were alone." She sank down, her back against a rock, her head tipped slightly backward on its hard contours. She closed her eyes and fell into herself and away from us.

Liam and I exchanged worried glances. "Is she okay?" he whispered.

I swallowed, glancing at Windy, who stood watching Kayleen, looking curious but unconcerned. "Windy thinks so."

He nodded. "I don't think we can hide."

"I know."

"Should we hide Kayleen and Windy? Split up?"

"If she felt them in the nets, they probably felt her. They'll know *we* aren't Wind Readers." I bit my lip. "I guess. Maybe not. Maybe it will make a difference that these are Artistos's nets." I looked back out over the valley. The people were closer. They were all bigger than we were, and two were wider as well. Like Bryan, only fully grown. Kayleen was right. Joseph wasn't there. I would have recognized his walk anywhere. "We can't run away."

"I know." Liam squeezed my hand, glancing down at Kayleen again. "We have to go talk to them." He called down. "Kayleen?"

She shook her head, almost imperceptibly. A sign to leave her alone.

They were only a hundred meters from us now. Two of them were women—one of the bigger two, and the one walking in the lead. They stopped, pointing at Kayleen's and Windy's running trail. No way they'd miss us now. "We should go," I breathed out softly, as if they were close enough to hear. "Before they get any closer. Keep them out of the valley."

Liam nodded. "Kayleen?"

She opened her eyes, her gaze passing through us as if we weren't there. "I hid our nodes in the valley. They'll be able to see them, but they'll need me to access them," she said.

There wasn't much more than safety perimeter there, and the ability for the nodes to recognize us. "Why?"

"So they can't change the programming."

Of course. "We need to go talk to them," I said. "I want you to take Windy and go to the cave. Can you tell what's happening out here from there?"

"Yes." Kayleen peered over the rock, her eyes widening at how close the people were now. "I want to go with you," she hissed.

Liam snapped back. "Go. Stay safe. Keep Windy safe."

She glared at him, her mouth a tight line. "We should stay together."

He put a hand on her shoulder. "I don't want everyone I care about to be in one place if these people are dangerous. If not, we'll come get you."

Kayleen leaned in toward him, one fist a tight ball. Then she kissed him, clutching him as if she'd never see him again. She reached out an arm for me, and I joined them, feeling the tight pressure of her fear against my back. After a long silent moment, she gave a quick half-smile, a small nod. "I'll know if you leave the valley." She looked away. "And if you come home." She turned and leapt awkwardly down next to Windy, patting her once on the neck as she picked up the trailing lead.

"Now," Liam said, and began to pick his way down the path through the rocks toward the strangers. He walked straight up, carefully nonchalant, intending to be seen. I took a deep, shaking breath and followed.

They stopped, watching us, letting us come to them, standing almost completely still.

I waved.

They didn't wave back.

As we came closer I called out, "Hello!"

The woman in the front nodded. Liam, walking in front of me, put a hand out to stop me a few meters from them, just close enough to talk without yelling.

They all wore what must be uniforms—straight-legged tan pants and tunics. The woman who had nodded wore a dark blue tunic, the others a paler blue. She had dark hair and eyes, a firm square chin, and stood half a head taller than the rest of the group.

I mentally dubbed one man and one woman the "strongs"—Bryan doubled. They could have been twins in physique, except for the woman's slender waist and slightly softer form. Their shoulders and thighs were wide, their necks thick, and their features chiseled and sharp. In spite of their bulk, they were as beautiful as the leader. They each wore belts studded with small metal things that could have been tools, communications gear, or weapons. Maybe all three.

The two others were men, one blond, one brown-haired, medium build for this group, like Liam. I guessed these two were the Wind Readers, but only from the structure of the group.

On their breasts, each of the five wore an insignia I didn't recognize: a single bright yellow star surrounded by white knotted scrollwork which could have been flowers or swords, or flowers wrapped around swords. They radiated health and strength and looked young except for their eyes.

Did they see us as scruffier versions of themselves? As enemies? Their gazes did not break, did not give anything away. No one smiled. None of them sweated or showed signs of exertion, even though they had apparently been walking for a while, and the morning had warmed enough that my long-sleeve shirt chafed.

Our wait paid off—the woman leader spoke first, her words thicker and slower than ours, but understandable. "I am the First for this group. I am Ghita."

First?

She looked at me, as if expecting me to answer.

Liam spoke before I could. "Liam." He pointed to me. "And this is Chelo. Excuse me, but may I ask where you are from? We saw your ship come in yesterday."

Surprise briefly touched Ghita's eyes. "We are from the Islas Autocracy."

The way she said it showed that what surprised her was that she had to tell us at all. Maybe the insignia should have told us.

Liam nodded as if the name meant something to him, although I suspected he was pretending. "What can we do for you? May we offer you hospitality?"

"We have come here"—she paused for a nearly unnoticeable second—"to explore Fremont."

Liam and I nodded. I didn't trust her words. They seemed to argue with her eyes, and there was that short pause. If they were here for something else, what was it? I couldn't make myself welcome them, although I probably should, if just to put them off their guard. I spoke simply. "Can we help you?"

"Are you natives?" she asked.

Liam said, "We were born here."

"You will come with us," Ghita commanded. Soft, but absolutely a command. Command fit Ghita the way shoes fit my feet, comfortably and surely.

She looked down at the path, her brow slightly creased. We had come this way yesterday, and Windy's tracks screamed out of the dust. Perhaps that didn't matter. But neither of us had feet as long as Kayleen's, and her tracks showed, too.

Ghita glanced past us, toward the valley, her dark eyes clearly following the path to the base of the rocks. "How many others are there?"

I swallowed hard and told a near-lie. "Right here, today, there is only us." After all, Kayleen was surely on her way to the cave by now.

She continued to stare, as if mistrusting my answer. Fair enough—I mistrusted her. She held her ground, not moving, but any second, I expected her to take a step forward, toward the hidden valley, toward Kayleen.

"We would like to see your ship," Liam said. "And then come back here. We have plants to tend. But perhaps when everyone has time to prepare, we can offer you hospitality."

I smiled. He was implying more people—maybe a lot more—without exactly saying it.

Ghita turned and began walking away from West Home, the two normal-looking men falling in step behind her. The two strongs stood silently, clearly waiting for us. Liam and I looked at each other, then he leaned down. "We have no choice," he whispered. "Cooperate."

He smelled of fear.

I swallowed, hard. My legs didn't want to move, and I had to close my eyes to make them. If I had had anything in my stomach it would have come up. The strongs walked just behind us, and I felt like a bird in a trap.

At least Kayleen was safe. For now.

I looked at the woman strong, and she gazed back with emotionless, flat eyes. I stewed on her gaze for long strides, going from frightened to angry. Why not try to be friendly? If she wouldn't, I would. "Excuse me, what is your name?" I asked.

"Kaal." Her voice was high and feminine, and like Ghita's, distant. She flexed her right hand into a fist, open and closed, moving it toward her belt and then away. A threat?

She didn't say anything else, and I didn't ask anything else.

I took Liam's hand, sweaty like mine, and we walked close together without talking. Kaal and the strongman were near enough they could have heard anything we said.

We were being kidnapped for a second time.

Did Kayleen feel us all leave the valley?

Clear skies oversaw our forced walk as the sea danced against rocks to our left, far below us.

They must have started walking before dawn. Yet they walked quickly and easily, in tight formation—Ghita, the two men, us, the strongs. No one talked casually. From time to time Ghita stopped to point at a tree or an animal track and ask us the names. I let Liam respond since his memory was better trained, and in many cases I could tell he was making up names on the spot. I just hoped Ghita couldn't tell.

It took two hours before we saw their ship, sitting in the open in a wide, flat spot at the mouth of a valley. Liam leaned in to me and said, "The dogs live here. Watch for tracks."

I swallowed. The biggest pack of demon dogs made its home in the head of this valley, where it curved in toward the mountains. That was where they had come from to attack us. Liam had tested that, had needed to know. He'd drawn a map, and I dredged up the memory of it. There was our valley, sitting at the head of Golden Cat Valley. One over, the valley we'd landed in. Ship Eater. Rockier and less friendly than Golden Cat Valley. And then here, the Valley of the Dogs.

Had they seen our skimmer? What did they make of it?

Their ship rested in the middle of the wide opening where the Valley of the Dogs met grassy plains leading to the cliffs over the churning sea. Where the *New Making* had been sleek and bright, this looked squat and ugly. Part of the miracle of the *New Making* was the way its skin gleamed with perfection even after years of storms and grass fires and earthquakes. Two dents showed in the side of this ship. It was streaked with something dark, as if it had flown through fire and been charred. The outline of closed doors punctured it halfway up the sides—maybe for skimmers? Maybe for weapons? Odd that they looked so perfect, so well-formed, and their ship looked like it had been in a war. But then, they and their ship both looked formidable. I dropped back by Kaal, and asked, "What is your ship's name?"

"*Dawnforce.*"

What a strange name—beauty with a fist. Understated. It fit these scarless, neat-featured, strong people.

I shivered as we followed Ghita up the ramp. The ship smelled of oil and chemicals and somewhere inside, something hummed quietly. Ghita marched us down a long corridor, and up an elevator until we were probably in the middle of the ship. The inside was clean and neat, the corridors tall and wide and rounded, everything a dull, unadorned silver. The few times we came across people, they wore the same uniforms as our captors, and stood sharp and straight, staying out of our way.

People noticed Ghita wherever she went.

She led us to a small room with two beds. "Please wait here." And with that, she left, locking the door behind her.

We sat next to each other on one of the beds, and Liam's hand found mine. The steady pressure of his hand gave me small comfort as I stared at the locked door.

AN ODD CONVERSATION

The small room they left us to wait in on the *Dawnforce* felt even smaller after we'd been in it a while. Liam and I sat next to each other on one of the beds. A wall of empty cabinets stood unlocked, but nothing sat on any of the clean white shelves. The other three walls were emptier—bright, glaring white, and strangely slick when I ran my finger along them. The room taught us little, although the lock on the door could be considered a lesson.

Whoever these people were, surely they could watch and listen.

I briefly toyed with creating a fiction—talking about more people, people who would be looking for us—but there were so many ways that this could trip us up. We couldn't mention Kayleen's name, or talk about Artistos, or Windy. Liam knew it, too. He spoke of inconsequential things like what we should plant in the garden next. We verbally re-designed the floor space in the little greenhouse at least three times, then fell silent. Only an hour had passed, according to my chrono, but it seemed much longer. Our breathing filled the silence in the tiny room.

Who were these people? What did they want with us?

The door opened. Ghita stood in the doorway, freshly laundered, her dark hair neatly slicked. She bowed her head briefly before meeting our eyes. "Liam, Chelo—Captain Groll will see you now. I will escort you to the audience room." Her words sounded less like a command than before, but I wouldn't have downgraded them all the way to request stature.

Ghita led us through sterile corridors, and into an empty rectangular room. Seven cushioned dark-green chairs sat in a semicircle, a small table beside each one. Everything, of course, was bolted down, but in spite of being in a spaceship, the room was far more comfortable than the one they'd left us waiting in. Three of the walls were the same slick surface, but golden-brown, more soothing than the stark white of the other room. Recessed lighting from the ceiling illuminated soft navy-blue flooring. On the far wall, a single star a meter across glowed a bright, cheerful yellow, casting golden light into the room. The knotted black and gold scrollwork surrounding it was big enough for me to see it was, in fact, flowers wrapped around swords. Like the name of the ship, an image which suggested peace and threat at once.

Ghita sat in the chair closest to the door, gesturing for me and Liam to sit on either side of her, which left all of us looking at the star and scroll design. "I am sorry we kept you waiting. We thought that you were—something different—than you are."

Different how? I kept a neutral expression. "Thank you."

A woman walked in and took a chair opposite Ghita, so that the star shone above her head and highlighted her golden-red hair. Like Ghita, she looked young, but moved with a clear sense of authority. Her tunic matched the sun above her. She inclined her head slightly and met my eyes, and then Liam's. "I am Captain Lushia Groll. Welcome to my ship, the *Dawnforce*." She glanced at Ghita. "My second suggests she may have been hasty in choosing how to treat you. I apologize for that."

She didn't look apologetic.

"You are, of course, free to return to your home. In the meantime, we invite you to stay and visit for the afternoon. We wish to learn more about Fremont, about how you came to be here, and about the city on the other continent."

They both waited. Watching us.

I took a deep breath to calm my fluttering stomach. Liam nodded at me, suggesting I decide how to answer her. Great. Away from the familiar territory of acting like a small band, he was ready for me to lead. Well, when you don't know what to do, stall. I nodded at the captain, and said, "Ghita said you are from the Islas Autocracy. Can you tell me where that is?"

Captain Groll and her second shared a confused glance. The captain spoke gently. "Where are you from?"

I did not want to discuss Artistos. Instinct, perhaps, or the military feel of the *Dawnforce* and her crew. I chose the most neutral answer I could think of. "We came from Silver's Home."

Ghita spoke. "Your genetics told us that. But you do not know who we are. I don't understand." As if it was impossible for us to be from Silver's Home and not know them. I held my tongue, hoping for information from Ghita as she continued. "We were told Fremont is settled by people who aren't from the five planets. We were hired to—meet these people." Was it my imagination or did she hesitate? Had she been about to say something besides "meet?"

Captain Groll picked up where Ghita left off. "What can you tell us about them? We understand they fought with your people."

Across the room from me, Liam stiffened and leaned forward. "That's history."

The captain's eyes widened just a touch. "But you don't live with them?"

I spoke quickly, before Liam could say more. "We're here to explore this continent." Figuring out what to say felt like walking blind toward the Lace River falls. "We'll be picked up after we're finished, sometime next year."

I glanced at Liam for help. He continued my fiction, although his voice shook a bit. Maybe they didn't know him well enough to hear it. "We would be happy to show you some of Islandia. We've found some interesting wildlife here, and, of course, you flew in over the Fire River. Perhaps you'd like to see it up close."

Liam still hadn't seen the river. Not really. I stifled a nervous giggle at the idea of touring them to places we had never been, then I spoke into the gap. "We have things to do to care for our camp, and wish to return there as soon as possible. Perhaps we can plan a trip around this area sometime soon."

"We'd love to show you the ocean cliffs." Liam's voice strengthened, falling into his storyteller's cadence, the one he used when he and Akashi related their season's adventures for the town-bound twice a year. "There's a clear, hard-packed path all the way along them, usually traveled only by the animals of Islandia. Here and there, freshwater streams fall from the cliffs in bright waterfalls. There are also waterfalls from the mountains—"

Ghita held a hand up. "I'm sure there is much to see here."

Captain Groll asked, "Would either of you like something to drink?"

I was thirsty, but we needed a quick exit. I shook my head. "We'll take water for our journey back."

"Would you show us around the ship?" Liam asked.

Ghita answered. "Perhaps after you show us around Islandia, and we have a chance to discuss Jini as well." She said it smoothly, sounding very friendly. A trade of information for information. She leaned in toward us. "We want to learn about this place. That's part of why we came."

My hands trembled in my lap, and I held them tightly to keep them still. I wanted out of this damned ship. "Would tomorrow be all right?"

"Yes." The captain glanced at Ghita. "Late morning?" Ghita nodded, and the captain continued. "We will have enough web up to travel over this half of Islandia by then."

It had taken generations for Artistos to build a sparse data web around less than half of Jini. "Why would you put up a web here if you plan to go to Jini?" *Why did you land here at all?*

Yet the captain apparently heard my unasked question. "This is a good base to start from . . . we want to understand Artistos before we visit."

And the web here would help them understand Artistos? Maybe Kayleen could tell us what they monitored and how.

Ghita said, "So we will see you tomorrow?"

"Shall we meet you here?" I asked.

"Yes." Ghita stopped and looked closely at me, searching my face. She did the same to Liam. "Please. I will escort you out. But will you answer one question first?"

Liam and I looked at each other. "What is the question, please?" Liam asked.

The captain leaned forward a little, the light from the star brightening her hair, seemingly setting the gold threads in her tunic on fire. "Do you care for the people of Artistos?"

"Of course we do," I said, just as Liam also answered. "Yes."

Captain Groll sat back in her chair, and gazed levelly at Ghita. A few moments of silence passed between them, or perhaps they shared the same nonverbal communication skills. "We'll give you food and water for your journey."

We glanced at each other. Would they really let us leave?

Apparently. The captain stood up. Ghita stood too, and gestured for us to do the same. She bowed slightly as the captain left the room. What about being from Silver's Home set us up for better treatment? I felt stupid and slow, like a whole conversation we didn't understand had happened during the awkward meeting.

We followed Ghita outside. A skimmer fled into the sky as we stepped out of the *Dawnforce*, heading toward the mountains. Two more skimmers sat outside, and a group of four people in light blue uniforms seemed to be loading one of them with boxes. Maybe building the web? "How many people did you bring?" I asked Ghita.

"About fifty."

I wondered if she told me the truth. It seemed like more people. Looking around, I counted at least ten outside of the ship, and we had probably passed that many getting out.

Early afternoon sun shone on the bright green and yellow grass, and the air tasted dry. Liam looked up at the sun, shading his eyes. "We'll see you tomorrow."

Ghita looked toward the blue line of the sea, her eyes unreadable. "Good journey."

So we left with almost no ceremony. As soon as we were out of earshot, Liam leaned in to me and spoke softly. "That was really strange."

An understatement.

I glanced back over my shoulder at the alien ship. "They didn't treat us badly, but I felt like a captive on the way here, and now I don't know what we are."

"Me either. I wish I could talk to Kayleen right now."

Earsets were so precious they would have been impossible for Kayleen to bring. "I know. Some days I wish I could Read the Wind, like her and Joseph."

He sighed. "Maybe it's easier that we can't. She and Joseph have both had a hard time of it. It must be mighty strange to have information pouring into you."

Joseph's body had always looked so vulnerable when his spirit flew the nets, particularly when he was very young. "Joseph used to talk about how it scared him. When he was little, it made him feel like he was going crazy. But he had to do it—it made him happy, too. Kind of like the people who drink and say they want to stop."

"It drove Kayleen crazy," Liam said softly. Then, "We can't change who we are." An echo of his father. Akashi always said everyone was perfect; they just needed to see their own reflections to know it.

We were a few hundred meters from the ship, still alone. They really were going to let us leave. Liam grinned at me, his face momentarily alight with purpose. "Let's go!" He started jogging, then let go into a fast lope, pulling immediately ahead of me. I laughed at him, reveling in the freedom of being out under the open sky, then raced to catch up, passing him, bursting with speed. He caught me, and took my hand in his, and we ran that way until we passed completely out of sight of the *Dawnforce*. We kept racing, each step releasing pressure and worry.

Extreme physical activity always threw me into a space where what mattered became the current step, the path under my feet, the wind in my hair. Neither the *Dawnforce* nor the *Burning Void* existed, but just the two of us, and our run. For the moment, Islandia belonged to us again, and we might as well have been the only two people on her, free and wild.

We arrived at the base of Golden Cat Valley winded, and stopped to rest, panting. We stood near the headland, our breath coming in deep, quick waves as water waves crashed against the rocks below us. Liam pulled me to him. "I don't like those people," he said. "What if they treated us the way they did at first because they didn't know who we were? How would they have treated us if they hadn't discovered we're *altered?*"

I ran my hand along the back of his shirt, sweaty from the run, scratching him, soothing. "Badly. At least, I'm sure we'd still be there, maybe even in that awful little room." I shivered, even warm from the run and the still-warm summer day. "They're hiding whatever it is they really want."

"I know." His gazed back in the direction of the *Dawnforce*, his brows knit and his jaw tight.

"I am not even sure they're treating us well, now. Maybe we're like tame dogs they let go because they know we'll come back, and they want us to do it willingly."

"But why?"

I hesitated, unsure. "It's as if they had to treat us well when they knew where we came from."

We knew almost nothing about Silver's Home, about our heritage. Only what we had gleaned from the data buttons Jenna left us, and what little she had told us. They had far more technology than we did. They designed themselves and they designed us. They were strong, and different, and they flew between the stars with impunity, apparently unencumbered by the scarcity that plagued Artistos. I was the only one of all of us who even remembered our original parents, and my memories were muzzy and thin. Most of what we knew about ourselves, we had discovered. "It felt like anything I said could be wrong. I don't want to go back tomorrow."

We took the path up-valley at a slower pace.

I began watching for Kayleen. Surely she knew we were coming. But only the rush of the waterfall welcomed us home. We stopped at the entrance to the valley, looking down. Would it look the same? Had they been here while they held us in the ship?

Our house and the corral sat where they always had, peaceful and empty. I blew out a long relieved breath. But why hadn't Kayleen come down from the cave as soon as she saw our signatures in the valley webs?

30

THE STRANGER'S NETS

Our valley empty, we raced to the cave.

Windy stood in the back against the wall, her head down, nuzzling Kayleen, who lay inert on the floor.

"Kayleen!" I ran to her side.

Windy raised her head and stepped back, snuffling mournfully. I placed a hand on Kayleen's neck. She breathed, but her skin was so white and bloodless the blue of her veins glowed under it. She lay with her eyes closed, one arm flung up over her head, as if warding off a blow. She was fully dressed, but her feet were bare, the long toes curled in. I shook her shoulder gently. Her body felt slightly stiff. "Kayleen. Kayleen. Are you okay?"

Liam's hand stroked my back, and I looked up into his worried blue eyes. "What could have happened?" I asked.

He shook his head. "She won't wake?"

"Did they do something to her?" I shook her again, a little less gently. "Kayleen?"

She moaned, but didn't open her eyes. Windy stepped a little closer to us, and stretched out her long tongue, licking at Kayleen's toes. Liam called to her, his voice commanding, "Wake up."

Kayleen's eyes fluttered open for just a second, and then closed, tightly, as if keeping out bright light. Liam went around to her head and carefully lowered her upflung arm, laying it across her swollen stomach. He lifted her head, settling it on his thigh, stroking her forehead and working his fingers through her tangled dark hair. "Kayleen, what happened?"

She mumbled something unintelligible, her eyes still squished shut.

"What?" Liam asked, leaning down closer to her.

She suddenly clutched at him with the arm he had just laid down and opened her eyes. "They are evil people," she said. "They came here to kill us all. To do what our parents couldn't."

Tears rolled down her face.

"I rode their webs. You confused them. They might still kill you—they haven't decided." She let go of Liam and raked at her face with her hand, then pushed into a sitting position. "They thought you might be on their side. Help them kill everybody else."

I shivered, repelled. That explained a number of their questions.

Kayleen continued. "We have to go home. We have to warn them."

"How?" Liam asked.

"They have skimmers. We need to steal a skimmer."

Now? "We can't lead these people there."

Kayleen laughed, a high thin reedy sound like the night we'd found her by the hebra barns. "You think they don't know where Artistos is?"

"We have to figure out how to stop them," Liam said.

"Is being in their data what did this to you?" I asked her softly.

She reached a hand up and pushed the hair from her face. Color had begun to seep back into her skin, but her eyes still looked unfocused. She nodded and bit at her lip. "It's so hard. So much. More than all of our data in every thread."

We still had the food and most of the water Ghita had given us. Liam handed Kayleen his flask, watching her drink greedily. Her eyes widened as he held out a bag of crisp wafers they had given us for journey food. "Throw it away." Her voice was insistent, edged with anger. "Throw everything from them away."

"Why?" I asked.

"Who knows what they've put in the food. They are surely tracking you—I overheard them. They dropped dust on your clothes that tells them where you are. Like the nano-stuff in Joseph's blood, in mine." She bit her lower lip and stared at each of us for a moment, then her eyes briefly rolled up into her head. "Who knows what they would put in food? Something to make you compliant? To kill you? To change you? Burn your clothes and bathe and throw away everything that came from them. Burn everything you took there."

Liam sat blinking at her, fingering his shirt. He'd put on one he liked. "Can't we just wash them? We don't have much."

Kayleen narrowed her eyes. "Burn them."

"Won't they know we did that?" I stood up and offered her a hand. "Could it be better to let them track us and simply not do anything unusual?"

She took my hand and let me pull her to standing. "I don't want them to know where we are."

"Are you ready to go back home?" I asked.

She nodded, standing shakily. "Best be where we have a better perimeter. At least we'll know if they're coming."

"Why not just leave our clothes here?" I asked.

Liam answered. "I don't want them to find the cave. It's more defensible than the valley."

I hated it that he was right. That we might have to defend ourselves. "Maybe we should hide some weapons in here," I said.

Kayleen grinned at me. "I already did." She pointed at the woodpile.

As we came down the slim path into West Home, I asked, "Where are they from? Where is the Islas Autocracy?"

She shook her head. "Go. Burn your clothes. Take Windy—give her food and water. I'm going back to see what they do. Before they see me and kick me out." She headed for the house.

Liam stared after her, his brows furrowed. "Should we let her do this?"

I shook my head. "I don't think we can stop her. Besides, she's right. We need to learn." I reached for Windy's lead, and we walked out into the early evening.

"Go on, take care of Windy," he said. "I'll start a fire."

"You're going to do this? Burn everything?"

He nodded, his face grim. "I trust Kayleen more than I trust those people."

Well. When it came down to it, so did I. As I secured Windy in the corral and left her with her head buried in an armful of dried grass, I imagined that I was dropping locators I couldn't even see into Windy's food and water, into the dust of the pasture. I shivered at the idea that these visitors seemed more likely to kill us than Islandia with all of its dangers.

I found Liam standing by our outdoor fire pit, naked except for a drying-skin around his waist, watching the arms burn off of his favorite shirt. His jaw was set tight. He looked at me for a long moment, weighing his thoughts, or me, or both. "If what she says is true, we owe it to Artistos to attack now if we can."

I sagged bonelessly onto one of the two rough-hewn benches by the fire, instantly light-headed. How could he say such a thing? "I don't want to kill anybody. I don't want the war to come back. It's done. It's over."

The sheer unfairness of it, the enormity and stupidity, washed over me. Why couldn't I just live in peace? That was all I wanted, to live in peace.

I cradled my head in my hands, focused on the rustling sounds of Liam feeding the flames and the crackling of the fire, sniffing as my nose was assaulted by the smell of burning clothing. Normal sounds, too: birds calling back and forth in the trees along the edge of the clearing, the wind shushing leaves against each other. Natural things that didn't have someone else's fight dogging their every move.

Liam leaned down next to me. "I brought you clean clothes."

I nodded, keeping my head down. Tears stung my eyes. "Okay. Go jump in the water and get rid of the damned dust and I'll change and watch the fire."

He ignored me, settling his strong hands on my shoulders and quietly massaging them, working at the tension. The tears I'd been holding back flooded my eyes and spilled onto my hands and knees and onto the ground. "Why couldn't it have been Joseph?" I missed him so much. And having the strangers be dangerous made it even worse that it wasn't him. How could I face such a thing without my little brother? "Why not Joseph? Why these people?"

Liam leaned down and kissed my cheek. "I'll go. Change, okay?"

I nodded, listening to his retreating footsteps. I stood and stripped, quickly, so violently I ripped the shoulder of my shirt taking it off. So I kept going. I ripped the fine green hemp shirt, the perfectly good green hemp shirt, and ripped it again, and again, throwing pieces no bigger than my palm into the fire. I watched each one catch and burn, and threw my pants and underclothes on the fire in a single big heap and stood, naked, warmed by the flame as it burned my clothes and their dust.

As Liam came walking back, fully clothed, I bolted past him and raced for the water. He'd have to stay and watch the fire—I could be alone. I catapulted off a rock at the edge and dove into the darkening pool. Damn them. Damn whoever sent them. Damn whoever, anywhere, wanted to kill for no reason. I came up spluttering, my feet churning the cool water. I didn't try to swim under the waterfall this time, but circled the edges of the pool, letting the powerful ripples of falling water keep me far away from the cascade.

There had to be another way.

After three long laps, I climbed onto a half-submerged rock near the gap where the water spilled out of the pool, watching it tumble past me and run down another meter of gentler fall into a stream. I looked up, waiting, alone with the waterfall until the first star shone brightly overhead.

Liam had laid out clothes for me. I pulled them on and walked back, slowly, wishing this stasis, this moment of not-war, could continue forever. But as I got back to the fire, all three of them—Liam and Kayleen and Windy—waited for me in a semicircle, firelight playing across their faces. I stood on the other side of the fire from them, thinking of Sasha driving my wagon and Paloma worrying about Kayleen and Akashi lecturing about living easily with the fearsome predators on Jini.

I said, "I'm going back there tomorrow. I'm going to make them love the people in Artistos the way that I do."

31

HOLDING GROUND

Kayleen rose and crossed to me, the firelight bright on her bare arms and feet, touching the ends of her dark hair. She folded me in her arms. "You can't make them like the people on Fremont, Chelo. These people have no hearts. They came here to kill."

I stiffened in her arms. "I have to try." I looked over at Liam, staring up at the dark sky. I spoke loudly, making sure he heard me. "If I run away from peace, if I don't try, I will never, never be able to live with myself."

Liam turned toward me, his face shadowed. The firelight made a halo over his head. "It's my parents at risk, and Kayleen's."

He didn't need to remind me Therese and Steven were dead. Besides, I cared for them all—Paloma, Akashi, Mayah, Gianna, Sasha, Sky . . . and he knew that. He damn well knew that. "It's not that simple." My words were sharp. "This whole thing is so stupid I can't believe it. Why would anybody fly between planets to kill people they don't know? There's got to be more to it."

Kayleen brushed the hair out of my eyes. I jerked away, wanting answers more than comfort.

Liam snapped, "You should hear Kayleen out. She's learned a lot about them."

I circled the fire, agitated. We were all upset, and falling apart was no way to stop a war. I sat down on one of the benches, looking up at Kayleen. "Tell me."

She sat down next to me, crossing her feet near the fire. Her far hand twisted through her hair, and she drummed the fingers of her near hand on the bench. She flicked her gaze between me and Liam. Her eyes looked saner than when we'd found her in the cave, but nearly as bad as they'd seemed when we first got here. Reading the Wind cost her. And this had cost her far more than soaking up Artistos's data. Because of what she found? Because of the stranger's web itself? I put a hand out near her drumming fingers, waiting for them to stop, then covered her hand with mine. "Go on, tell me what you saw."

She cleared her throat. "The Islas Autocracy is another planet, like Silver's Home or Fremont. Or Deerfly. They're genetically changed there like us, and they trade information with Silver's Home. They might even trade people, too, sometimes—but I couldn't tell for sure." She stuck her tongue out the side of her mouth, as if it might help her decide what to say next. "It's a big place, and everything—everything—there is planned. Babies. Families. Buildings. Even trees and streams. They design it all." She paused, rubbing her hands together in front of the fire. "Islas is drenched in data, but it's not all free like ours. Everyone obeys. Not like at home, where they mostly obey, but sometimes they only pretend to, and really, everyone breaks *some* rules. At least the little ones." She grinned at me. "Except maybe you."

I laughed a little at that, and Liam looked over at us, but said nothing.

Kayleen got intense again. "On Islas, they believe in discipline. Doing what they're told, all for the greater good of their society. They believe they're right about everything."

Liam threw another log onto the fire, sending sparks up into the night like stars. Kayleen tilted her head to watch them, then looked back at me. "You know how, early on, we figured out that on Silver's Home, they sell their ability to change things and people? Well, these people call themselves Star Mercenaries, and they sell the ability to kill people. To fight wars.

"I don't mean everybody on Islas. But it's the Star Mercenaries that landed here. This isn't our own people come back." She pulled her feet a little away from the fire. "Islas looks down on Silver's Home, thinks they're soft and undisciplined. These people are doing a job." She spat her next words out. "They refer to Artistos as a target, not a town."

She pulled her hand from mine and went back to drumming, leaning forward, staring into the fire. "They left probes—satellites, like ours, only littler—up in the sky on their way in, and they're reading Artistos's data as we speak. Half of Islandia is already included in their webs—and the webs are strong. Stronger than ours. They report more kinds of data, and they don't seem to have any—"she closed her eyes, searching for the right word—"fragility."

She shivered. "People like that wouldn't come all the way here with a contract to kill and then just go away." She looked at me. "So you see, it won't help to talk to them."

I could tell she believed it. But I couldn't. We couldn't wait for them to attack us or Artistos, but we couldn't attack them until we tried to stop them. Or we knew we couldn't.

Windy rested her head briefly on Kayleen's shoulder, then withdrew a step, watching us.

Liam knelt on the ground near me, speaking softly, intently, one hand on my knee. "Everyone we love here is in danger. We have to warn them. We have to go back, soon." He glanced at Kayleen. "But first, I want to hurt them." He tugged at his braid, thinking aloud, his beloved, familiar face become a stranger's. "We have weapons. Crazy-balls and those long sticks and that disruptor you wanted to try on the big demons."

Kayleen added, "I can kill their nets. Once. I don't know for how long."

The last time I'd tried to talk us out of a fight, Alicia had intervened, threatened the whole Town Council in the amphitheater with a crazy-ball, made it impossible to find peace without threat. But Liam had been on the side of peace that time. I reached for words to sway him, speaking softly to keep his defenses down. "Akashi would not start with a fight. He would start with words."

He turned away from me, his shoulders rigid. "What would you have me do? Just stand by until these people kill you? Until they kill my family? Apparently just for being here?"

Kayleen said, "I think they want to kill them because they aren't *altered*."

A short, hard laugh escaped him. "Funny—we've always been threatened because we're *altered*. Now, they're in trouble for not being *altered*."

How could he be so dense? "That's just two sides of the same stupid argument." I frowned at his stiff back, struggling to understand. None of this made sense—fighting had never made sense to me. "Is that really it? Or is it because our parents want the planet? The land? Isn't that what they came for?"

He shook his head. "I don't know."

I turned back to Kayleen. "Kayleen? What do you think?"

She laughed, edgy and bitter, then threw her head back, brushing her hair from her forehead. The fingers of her near hand returned to drumming on the bench. "They came because they were hired to. They didn't set up all that data to learn about Islandia. They're watching Artistos, and they have a warning grid up in case any other ships or skimmers land here."

Great. Were they expecting more people? More ships? I stared at the fire, my face warm, my back chilling as the night cooled. A fit mirror for my feelings, hot and cold, angry and confused, mad and resigned. "Who hired them?" The only people I knew with an interest in Fremont were from Silver's Home. "Our parents?" No, that wasn't quite right. They were probably dead. "Our parent's people, anyway?"

Kayleen shook her head. "I don't know. Probably."

"What about our babies? Don't we owe them a chance at peace? We can't run away from these people; they'd find us."

"Chelo?" Liam asked from across the fire, his voice breaking. "Chelo? What do you want me to do?"

Pain danced in his eyes, in the tight set of his features, and I knew we mirrored each other, both in pain, if for different reasons. "We said we'd decide everything together. Remember? What do you want?" I turned to Kayleen. "And you?"

Liam turned back toward us. "You're right about Akashi. He wouldn't start with a fight. But he'd have a fist prepared. He'd be ready for a fight in case they started it, and he'd be ready to strike if he thought he had to. That's the way he's always approached dangerous situations."

I threw a stick on the fire, watching the heat rise like my own fears. "Liam? What do you want to do?"

"I want to know if we can figure out how to hurt them, and I want to be ready to." He looked directly into my eyes. "I don't want to hurt them, but we have to. We have to make sure they can't hurt Mom and

Dad." His next words came out slowly, as if they had to be dragged from him. "And I guess . . . I guess we can go back and talk to them first. It's just—you were there. How can you think it will help? We don't understand these people at all, and Kayleen's right—they're much more powerful than we are."

"They could have killed us today, and they didn't."

"And they might kill you tomorrow. Who's to say they'll let us go again?" he said. "We're damned lucky they let us go at all."

Kayleen turned to me. "I don't like it. But you know, we're probably going to die anyway. No matter what we choose." A tear ran down her cheek, sparkling gold in the firelight.

I held her hand to stop it from drumming, watching her face. Kayleen never sounded like this. Even though we'd been there and she hadn't, she knew more about the strangers than we did. Being in someone's data was surely more intimate than being in an awkward meeting.

Kayleen wiped the tear from her cheek with a quick jerky motion and reached a hand up for Windy's nose. "If it matters that much to you to talk to them, go ahead. I know how stubborn you can be, Chelo. And I love you for it. But don't trust them. Don't you trust them." She looked intent, her eyes drilling into mine, half her face lit by dancing flames. "Go ahead and try to convince them to love Artistos, but if that doesn't work, we'll have a backup plan."

Neither of them sounded like they expected me to succeed. Maybe I didn't expect to, either. But I had to try. I nodded, suddenly sympathizing with Hunter when he'd led the war against us. Against our parents. "All right. What do we have in our fist?"

32

THE CHOICE

Liam looked worried. "Travel safely."

I nodded. It had been my suggestion to go alone, to buy Kayleen and Liam time to put things in place. I clutched him tightly to me. "I will. Somehow."

"Remember, Chelo, that if we attack them we aren't starting something new. We're in the middle of something our parents started."

"I know." It had started before I was born, shaped and molded my life, sundered my family not once but twice. And here was a third sundering if I didn't choose right. Or maybe no matter how I chose.

I pushed away from Liam and turned to Kayleen. "Keep our baby safe."

She nodded, apparently at a loss for words.

We had spent much of the night planning an attack. Kayleen spread out her weapons, our weapons, and we talked about how to place crazy-balls and how to use disruptors.

In the end, we decided to start with Fremont itself.

I left a little early, giving myself time to think, taking the journey slowly.

When I stood looking up at the *Dawnforce*, I nearly turned back. I was an ant, the *Dawnforce* a mountain. It bulked across the plains, its presence bigger than just the ship. It spilled big skimmers and structures around it. What Kayleen had told us made the camp feel malevolent.

Two buildings had sprung up overnight, smooth shells complete with windows and doors. The Islans had not cut trees to make these things, and the buildings were too big to have been carried whole inside the ship. I knew it was technology, but it might as well have been magic.

And then, for a moment, I stood gaping. The *Burning Void* sat behind one of the buildings. I stiffened. Why? Was it a trap for us? A favor? Or did they think they owned it for freeing it?

I kept my distance, not sure I wanted them to know I'd seen it.

I wasn't going into the *Dawnforce* this time, not without being forced to. I stood outside the door and waited, positive they would show up.

Sure enough, in a few moments Ghita, the two strongs, and the captain came out of the ship. "Chelo!" Captain Groll called out cheerfully. "How are you? Where is Liam?"

"He didn't feel well this morning." Let them chew on that, in case they had put something in our food. "We didn't want to disappoint you, so I came alone." Kayleen had suggested they wouldn't notice the stupidity of walking about by oneself on Fremont. She seemed to be right, because they didn't react or remark on it. I tried to sound as friendly as I could. "Are you ready for a brief tour?"

Ghita gestured at one of the three sleek skimmers sitting near the *Dawnforce*. "We can fly."

That wasn't in our plan. "A walking tour will teach you a lot more. Remember how we pointed out plants on the way back? There are things you see on foot that you can't see from the air."

The captain and her second looked perplexed for a moment, then the red-haired captain said, "I'll call Moran and his team." She touched a spot on the neckline of her tunic and spoke into the air, too softly for me to make out the words. I couldn't help but appreciate her beauty, the thin steel of her form, the way she moved, lithe and graceful. Her movements, even her walk, were compact and perfect, wasting no energy but somehow full of it. Her eyes caught mine, as if she knew I had been watching her. "Very well. We will walk a ways, but only an hour's distance or so. Then perhaps you will visit with us for a while before you return?"

An hour would be enough. Inwardly, I sighed in relief. Outwardly, I smiled at her. "That sounds fine. Would you like to see the waterfalls?" *Would you like to go see the place the demon dogs live?* The dogs didn't scare me as much as these people.

In a few moments, four more people showed up, three men and a woman. They looked normal, or as normal as the captain and Ghita. Uniformed, neat, healthy, young. But they were *altered*, like us. Visual cues would not tell me age. I smiled at them, getting their names one by one. The men were Moran, Pul, and Zede; the woman, Kuipul. They were all cool and polite, masked like Ghita with no real emotion showing, even in their eyes. After the introductions, Ghita waved a hand at the mountains. "Let's go."

I started up-valley, leading eight dangerous strangers up a path I'd never been along myself. Surely with this big a crowd, we would scare off single predators, especially during the afternoon. So I pretended not to worry much about the land or the animals, to make it a casual walk, to project a feeling of calm relaxation. It hadn't rained for days, so the ground was hard-packed and unlikely to show the demon dogs' tracks. Or ours. A soft wind blew across grasses beside the path, cooling me. Insects chirped. Twice, we surprised swarms of flying grass beetles, hundreds of green-backed creatures as long as my little finger and twice as wide, flying up and away from us in frantic leaps, pushed along by the breeze and tiny flashing yellow wings.

The Captain and Ghita flanked me. The others trailed behind, the strongs in the far back, watching all of us. No time like the present. I took a deep breath, wishing for success. "So you want to hear about Artistos? Our home." There was surely no point in hiding that now. "The people who live there call themselves 'original humans'. They've been on Fremont since before we showed up from Silver's Home. They have schools and music guilds and artists and hunters. They farm and raise animals and study the planet."

Ghita spoke, her face drawn in a scowl. "Pah. Original humans. No one is completely un-engineered—every human strain has evolved. Evolution is a biological mandate—it's what we do. Humans cannot succeed by going backward."

Damned judgmental of her. What the heck was backward, anyway? Her self-righteousness toward the original colonists sounded like the Town Council when they talked about us. Teeth on edge, I clamped down on the words I wanted to say, and kept my voice calm. "They *are* succeeding. The colony is growing. It's self-sufficient. It's what they want, and they have it. They just don't like as much technology as you use. They don't want to be changed."

"Why?" Captain Groll asked. "Why not use every tool you have? Why not become everything you possibly can? We don't understand."

"I'm not sure I do, either," I replied. "It is central to who they are, though. Besides, they're good people." I glanced over at Ghita, who was watching me instead of her footing, instead of the landscape around her. Why wouldn't a trained fighter be more aware?

I pulled my focus back to convincing them the people in Artistos deserved life. "There's Gianna. She's a scientist—she studies meteors, and warns us about big meteor showers. She cares about everyone, and spends a lot of her spare time with the kids, teaching them as much science as she can. She has a great laugh." I looked at the two women's faces for a reaction. The captain looked curious, and Ghita seemed to have not changed at all.

I led them over to some large reddish rocks pockmarked with holes. Soil had blown into some of the holes, and summer grasses rooted, popping up above the rocks like hair. I pointed to the rocks. "One of the volcanoes threw those rocks out in an eruption."

Captain Groll bent down and looked at the rock, her head cocked a little. "There are no active volcanoes on Islas."

Kaal, the strong I'd talked to on our way to the ship the day before, stepped closer, either because she was interested or because she was protecting the captain. She picked up a small rock, grunting in surprise at how light it was. She knelt down and picked up a bigger rock, testing its heft. At least she had the good grace to *seem* interested.

The captain reached a hand out to touch the rock. "It's rough."

"If you climb a field of those without protecting your hands, they'll get bloody." We were about halfway up the valley. A telltale plume of steam wafted through the low vegetation lining a streambed ahead of us. "Come on, there's at least one more thing to see before we hit the waterfalls." If there were waterfalls. We'd avoided this valley because of the dogs.

It was up to me to judge these people, to say if we showed our fist. How was I going to tell? So far, no one seemed much moved by my stories. But I wasn't telling them well; I had to be so careful not to say anything they could use against us later. The captain was the only one who appeared engaged at all, and although she at least asked questions, she didn't have the same light in her eyes that the roamers got when they learned new things.

Politeness didn't mean her fist was open; I was being polite.

I started toward the steam. "There are volcanoes on Jini, too, but only one active one, Rage. We named the big one here Blaze, but we've seen two other eruptions since we got here." I needed to connect to these people, to touch them. I wasn't doing it yet. "We have a science guild. They keep track of everything we learn, and pass it on. Paloma, one of the women in town, picks herbs and makes teas and salves—so if you fall down and get hurt she can help you. Her workroom always smells wonderful."

The captain looked at me curiously. "We were told there was a ship here. The *New Making*. How long ago did it leave?"

I wished she'd asked about Paloma or Gianna or Artistos. *New Making* had probably reached Silver's Home about the time Kayleen brought us here. I frowned. "Five years or so." How much did they know? "The *New Making* went back to Silver's Home."

The captain didn't miss a beat. "Who flew it?"

There didn't seem to be any reason to lie. "My brother."

For just a second I saw surprise flash through her eyes. "Why didn't you go, too?"

"I wanted to stay here."

She stopped then, and after a few steps I stopped, too, looking back to see that the whole line of them had stopped. Everyone did what the captain did. Their obedience made my skin crawl. But then, I had stopped, too. Perversely, I turned around and kept going, scanning the prickly bushes and low trees around us. A hushed conversation went on behind me, and then the captain jogged up to my side, and Ghita caught up a few steps later. "Why live here instead of going home?" Ghita asked.

I smiled. She couldn't have given me a better lead-in. "These people need us. We're stronger and faster; we help them. We've helped build barns and fix"—better not say the nets; I hid my hesitation with a small stumble—"fences and hunt. There are things only we can do.

There's a tree with good fruit, but we're the only people in town who can climb it without ropes."

Captain Groll pursed her lips, looking at me. "These are *not* your people—both you and Liam have much more advanced genomes than they can have." She narrowed her eyes, searching my face. "Sometimes people become attracted to others who capture them and keep them."

I bristled. "We weren't captured. We were raised there." I wasn't going to tell her any of them ever treated us badly. I turned to look her in the eyes. "The war is over. Like Liam said, it's history."

She didn't blink, or react. Just watched me, her emotions invisible. If she had any. "How many of you are there from Silver's Home?"

I sighed. "By how many of us, do you mean how many *altered?*"

"What do you mean when you say *altered?*" she countered.

"You know. Like us. Genetically engineered." I wanted to tell her there were more of us, give her pause. But they were already reading Artistos' data. "Three."

"Aren't you lonely?" the captain asked.

I winced at the close cut.

Ghita spoke up. "They let two of you come over here—when there are only three? That does not sound like they need you."

Lies compounded lies. I hated the web I was building. "We asked to. For . . . for time alone." Let them chew on that. I put my hand over my slightly swelling belly, emphasizing my pregnancy.

Captain Groll raised a hand to her mouth and a pleasant laugh escaped through her fingers. Ghita took a second more to understand, then nodded. She didn't smile. "Whatever. But this is a backward place. You don't know what you're missing. The Five Planets are full of wonders, and rich beyond your dreams. No one starves. Everyone has valuable work. Art and beauty surround us since we don't have to spend all of our time surviving."

Art and beauty for killing machines. Her tone sounded like Nava lecturing the five-year-olds in the Science Guild hall, confident past reason. I fought becoming one of those five-year-olds. I couldn't afford weakness. They were dangerous—I could feel it. Casually dangerous.

They probably wouldn't care if they did kill us.

Really finding out what they wanted seemed impossible now that I was trying to do it. Ghita hadn't smiled all morning. The captain had some warmth in her voice, but there was no connection except curiosity between us. We weren't sharing anything real.

Ahead of us, the steam plume twisted into the air, blown long and flat at the top by a warm breeze. Shortly afterward, at least if I was following Liam's directions properly, the path narrowed and headed toward the dog's dens. They'd be sleeping at this time of day. But like us, demon dogs posted watches. Kayleen had her fist-sized disruptor, even if she didn't exactly know how to use it. The one that made the animals on Jini react to sound only they could hear.

I was going to have to signal Kayleen and Liam soon, one way or the other. If I signaled them to show our fist by leading the group much further, then some of the people I led on this walk might die. I'd start a fight. And if I turned around soon, I'd leave the *Dawnforce* free to attack Artistos with all of her strength.

As we neared the steam plume, I struggled to breathe out the fears that curled up my spine. My mouth tasted like ash and sulfur.

A hot spring bubbled and steamed to the right of the path. A wispy evaporation cloud faded to whitish mist just above the surface of the water, obscuring the cooled lava lining the edges of the pool. On the far side, hot water leaked slowly out, tumbling down a crevasse and disappearing underground for a few meters, then popping up and joining a snow-melt stream a few meters from the hot spring. Like a miniature version of the Fire River and the sea, a steady plume of steam issued from the meeting.

The eight of us gathered near the steam plume, tiny droplets clinging to everyone's eyelashes and hair. I watched the others instead of the steam. The captain looked curious. The strongs mostly watched the captain. The four that had joined us seemed to have most of their attention elsewhere. Which was probably right—I would bet they were Wind Readers. Ghita watched me, her brow furrowed. Her eyes were hard and dark and cold. Water from the steam dripped down her face.

I had to decide. It was time. And there wasn't a clear answer. Why didn't these people just jump up and down and declare themselves evil or good? I laughed inwardly at the thought, watching Ghita back, trying to read her face, her body language. No good. Time to be braver, risk telling these people I knew more than I should. "Why are you really here? You're not recording the things I'm showing you; you're not really interested." I turned my gaze to the captain, wanting my answer from her.

The captain returned my gaze, her eyes as hard and unyielding as Ghita's. After a moment they softened a little, and I thought it might be pity that flashed through them before she turned a little away. "We have work to do here."

"What work?"

She shook her head. "You wouldn't understand." She sounded so sure of herself, so condescending. And worse, unyielding. There was no warmth in the way she looked at me. "We have a mission that matters more than anything on this planet."

I swallowed hard.

I had to bet for Artistos.

I gestured up-trail and took the next step, the one that I knew in my heart committed me to start a fight, that meant I had taken the choice away from Artistos and made it for them. I glanced at my chrono. It was a few moments after thirteen hundred. Liam and Kayleen would see that we were still moving up.

I began to listen for the dogs, for the sound of rustling brush or of padded feet stalking us. Let them come for us soon. Would they succeed? Would the dogs attack no matter what any of us did? Would I live through it?

If the dogs didn't come, the captain and Ghita were away from the ship. That, too, was good for our fist.

The valley narrowed, and I picked a path between two thin trees. Ghita glanced up the two ridges that came together to make the neck of the valley. She leaned toward the captain, and I heard her whisper, although I couldn't make out her words.

I called to them, loudly, hoping Kayleen and Liam could hear. "Come on! We'll be near a waterfall soon."

Ghita glanced at me, then back up at the ridges. Something creased her brow. Distrust? The captain put a hand on her arm and said something soothing. The others noticed, and looked around.

One of the big dogs bayed.

The sound came from in front of us, not too near. But I knew how fast they moved. I sniffed the air, felt the cold heart of prey as the predators neared us.

Ghita stopped. "What is that?"

I smiled at her, trying to look as if the deep wail didn't turn my knees to water. "It's just a wild dog. It's okay."

Ghita looked at the captain. "We should leave. Now."

"They won't hurt you," I said, my voice a bit too high, the hair on the back of my neck standing up. I had no particular protection that they didn't—just foreknowledge. And two people out there who would be trying to protect me.

The dogs could kill me, too.

A dog bayed again, a little closer. Then another. Ghita and the captain stood together, the strongs next to them. Kaal looked over at me, accusation in her eyes. And danger. She was strong enough to break my back with her bare hands. I stepped back, looking around.

A jumble of rocks, two small stands of low windswept trees; slight cover at best. One of the men, Moran, glanced at me. He and his team began to move—he and the woman, Kuipul, stopping a few meters on either side of the captain, Ghita, and the strongs. The other two jogged slowly outward, scanning the area, suddenly engaged in the moment. They hadn't spoken before the move in unison—so they *were* Wind Readers, using the data web to relay information. Were they tuning a piece of their web to the dogs now? Was Kayleen there, waiting for them? Or had she used the little boxes that disrupted data?

Thankfully, the dogs remained silent.

The captain gestured for me to come stand with them. Her eyes were wide, rimmed a little in fear, but insistent. Ghita reached for her belt and unclipped a small black box.

A dog glided between two small trees, the reddish-brown hair on its back sticking up straight. It smelled like raw meat and anger.

A streak of brown movement gave away another dog's position.

Ghita stayed at Lushia's side, glaring at me. Her hand went to her belt and came away full of something small and black.

The pack circled us, the first movement in the dance between demon dog and prey. I bolted. I needed to be outside their circle, to appear faster and stronger and harder to catch than the people still inside. Tree branches whipped my right leg and a rock snatched skin from my knee. I ran up, toward their den, getting above the dogs, and circled them myself from the ridge, looking down.

I ducked and moved slowly, keeping rocks and trees between me and the mercenaries. I prayed they'd stay grouped for safety and leave me for later.

A human scream rose from the ridges, bouncing back and forth between them, echoing from rock to tree to rock. The voice of a stranger, not Kayleen or Liam. One of their Wind Readers.

I didn't look back. I couldn't stop the humans from shooting me, but I *could* keep from getting killed by the dogs. Further away now, I straightened and raced uphill, rocks sliding under my feet, heading up one of the ridges for a bit and turning, keeping to high ground.

Nothing seemed to be following me. Luck, or skill, or something Liam or Kayleen did. Maybe the strangers let me go. I didn't care.

My heart pounded. Because of my choice, at least one person was probably dead. I couldn't think about it, couldn't think about others maybe dying, too.

Another dog bayed behind me. Not close, with the group. Its natural sound cut off, switching to a scream of pain. Well, the mercenaries were fighters. Maybe they'd kill the dogs.

I didn't care. I didn't care about anything. I hadn't stopped them from attacking Artistos. I knew that. Maybe I'd slowed them down. My breath came so sharp that my chest hurt.

A skimmer whined overhead, heading toward the captain, her First, and the dogs.

I slowed a little, heading downhill, running almost in the open but off the path we'd come up.

Where were Liam and Kayleen?

THE FIGHT

As I neared the *Dawnforce*, a skimmer took off, engines straining, arrowing in the same direction as the one that had just flown over me, toward the Captain and the dogs. I ducked down behind a rock, hoping the occupants wouldn't see me.

A sharp crack split the air. The skimmer shuddered. Something big fell to the ground, shiny as it flipped. Maybe a stubby wing? Then the whole machine fell out of the sky, a large dead bird. It smashed nose-down just past me, flipping over on its back. Oily black smoke billowed up from its broken body. The grass around it burst into flames.

I stood up and kept going. Three people came toward me up the path and I knelt under a scraggly bush, poised to run if they saw me.

They didn't. Two men and a woman, moving at least as fast as we three could run. Maybe faster. Each of them carried something small in their hands. Probably a weapon.

A second skimmer flew in from the sea. It circled the *Dawnforce*, and the carnage of its wrecked brethren, and the fire beginning to spread out across the dry grasses in the direction of the *Dawnforce*. It headed off the way the downed skimmer had been going.

As soon as it was out of sight I stood again, racing toward *Dawnforce*, heart pounding. Acrid smoke seared my lungs and stung my eyes, turning the air a muddy brown.

A loud bang sounded from near the *Dawnforce*, followed by screams of pain.

Please let it not be Liam or Kayleen.

Near the bottom of the path I spotted a rock with three smaller rocks piled on top of it. A sign for me. I pulled a pack from behind the rock, heavy with two crazy-balls. I took one out, setting it down carefully while I shrugged the pack with the other one still inside it onto my back. I picked up the one I had set down, a silver sphere just big enough to cradle in my two hands, heavier than it looked like it should be. I held it in front of me gingerly, slowing my pace now that I was closer, looking for a target.

The area around the ship was a chaos of smoke and running figures. Here and there I heard voices, but most of the crew were like the three who had passed me, silent and intent. Wind Readers, or using some quiet communication.

I stopped behind one of the buildings near the *Burning Void*, searching for Kayleen or Liam.

Nothing.

The *Dawnforce*'s main door had opened. More crew members jogged toward the fire near the downed skimmer, this time carrying large cylinders. A man raced by me, glancing my way, his lips moving. Probably telling someone where I was. Just as I twisted away to head in the other direction, I glimpsed Liam racing toward the *Burning Void*, his hands empty. Kayleen followed behind him, looking around, probably trying to spot me.

I was afraid to call out.

The loud engines of incoming skimmers preparing to land filled the sky. The captain, coming back. I lobbed the crazy-ball toward the open place I figured they wanted to land and ran toward the *Burning Void*.

Kayleen and Liam must already be there. Our ship stood alone behind the two buildings, the ramp down. It had been closed when I saw it on my way in. I bolted up the ramp. It closed halfway behind me as I tumbled inside.

Liam, leaning over me, a huge grin on his face, his eyes alight with adrenaline. "Do you have any more crazy-balls?"

I peeled off my pack. "One."

He dug it out of the backpack, calling over his shoulder. "Kayleen. Take off."

The skimmer's engines came to life, humming. Liam leaned out the partly-open door, holding the crazy-ball. *Burning Void* lifted. Kayleen banked us in a tight circle, flying toward the looming *Dawnforce*. Just before the door came into view, Liam threw the ball, then slapped the controls, shutting the ship tightly before we heard the muffled bang of the explosion. "Did you get it inside?" I asked.

He shook his head. "I don't know. We can't stay around to find out."

The *Burning Void* rose, tilting first one way and then the other, gathering speed.

"I don't believe we're all alive," I said.

He touched my cheek. "Me either. They won't underestimate us again."

We joined Kayleen in the main cabin. She sat in the back seat, eyes closed, communing with the little ship. "I can't believe they got her free for us."

"They didn't," he said. "Kayleen had to break a code to get in." The screen showed Islandia's seacoast rushing by beneath us.

"Are we going home?" I asked.

"Home?" He shook his head. "She's going to get Windy."

I bit my tongue. This would be our only chance, and Windy had kept us alive with her warnings more than once. We owed it to her. She was family.

34

THE FIRST PRICE

Kayleen kept us flying low and fast, turning up the valley. We landed in the last possible spot before the path into West Home, turned for take off. The *Burning Void* lay in the open, completely unprotected. We had to depend on speed.

We ran up the path, all together in a bunch, leaping from rock to rock, somehow all managing to keep on our feet.

Liam stopped at the top, then screamed, "No!" as he kept going. We followed.

The roof of our house had holes punctured in the top. One side of the greenhouse billowed out in the wind, some of the hard plastic actually torn off and lying meters away.

Liam hesitated, searching for any sign of whoever had done this. I put a hand on his shoulder, anger making me tremble. "A skimmer flew back from this direction, just after you brought that first one down. I bet they did this."

A piteous cry came from the corral. "Windy!" Kayleen raced past us. Windy lay in the dirt, her coat blackened along one side of her neck, blood pouring out from a wound where her neck met her shoulder. She lifted her head and cried out.

I knelt down next to the wounded hebra and her best friend. My best friend. More now, even than that. I wanted to scream for Kayleen's sake.

Windy's breath rattled shallowly in her throat. I reached out to stroke her fur. She tried to lift her head and failed, and her eyes rolled back and she moaned. Something big and powerful had ripped muscle away from bone near her shoulder.

So cruel.

She cried again, softer and weaker, a long high call which skewered my heart.

Kayleen lay flat behind Windy on the dusty, dry ground, her belly to the hebra's backbone, Windy's head cradled in her arms. The evening light painted highlights in Kayleen's dark hair as it mingled with the mixed green of Windy's ear tufts. Kayleen's hand pushed down on Windy's neck where the blood welled out, coating Kayleen's long fingers dark red.

Liam approached slowly.

Kayleen looked up at him, tears in her wide eyes. "She's not going to be okay, is she?"

Liam shook his head, swallowing hard. As he looked down at us, dampness filled his eyes, too. "I should . . . We should . . ."

Kayleen reached a hand up and stroked Windy's nose. She buried her face between the hebra's long ears for a moment, then looked up at Liam. When she spoke, her voice was quiet and still. "Bring me one of the long sticks—the rifles. You know where they are."

He turned and walked away, and I shifted to sit beside her. I knew what had to happen. We couldn't leave her like this.

I stroked Kayleen's shoulder, softly, even though nothing could comfort her in that moment.

A pair of black-throated red seed stealers perched on the corral fence for just a moment, cocking their heads at us. The sun brightened their deep red feathers, painting them with gold stripes. The birds chattered at each other for a moment and flew away, spiraling up into the trees. Escaping.

Like we needed to.

I sat, one hand on Windy and one on Kayleen, waiting.

Liam came back, carrying one of the long slender sticks. He stood awkwardly, holding it. Kayleen leaned down and kissed Windy between her ears and on the nose, and then pushed herself to her feet. An eerie calm had fallen over her features. She held out her hand.

"I'll do it," Liam said.

Kayleen kept her hand out until Liam handed her the rifle, then she calmly checked it over, pushed a button in one place, and stood over Windy. Her hand didn't shake. "I love you," she whispered, and then she pushed another button. The rifle bucked in her hands. A neat hole appeared in Windy's forehead, and she lay still.

Kayleen threw the rifle down by the dead hebra, and looked at Liam, her eyes as dead her hebra's. "Now, I'm ready to fly us back."

PART SIX

ABOARD THE *CREATOR*

35

MAKING PEACE

Ship's data surrounded me. *Creator* sang of stars and emptiness, of engines and oils and work. I floated in facts, sometimes moving a single muscle to remind myself I was not the ship.

Over a year and a half of flying alone.

I struggled to recall Chelo's face, but it fuzzed at the edges, becoming indistinct except around the eyes. *They* called to me, her gaze in my memory driving a restlessness that roamed my spine.

Chelo demanded something of me, and my fists clenched, knowing what it was, not wanting to face it yet. But I had put it off for fifteen months.

Jenna had sent my father, Ming, Dianne, and Induan to cold sleep within a day of leaving Silver's Home. For the next week, the rest of us plotted and planned, or as much as possible with as little information as we collectively possessed. Then Jenna sent Bryan and Alicia to cold sleep. She followed.

I flew. Alone. At first, I loved it.

I'd sweated alone every day in the workout room, allowed myself to fall into the ship for hours every day. Typical of Marcus—*Creator* had a good library. Each day, I researched Islas, and the Star Mercenaries, babbling at the library functions since hearing my own voice was better than no voice at all. My sleep cycles blew off and I slept or woke for hours or minutes or even days at a time. I lost so much weight that I made myself set timers to eat.

We were three quarters of the way to Fremont, or better.

It was past time.

As soon as I started the sequence to wake my father, I pulled out the data button I'd found on the *New Making*, and poured over his journal, trying to relate the man who talked to me across the years with the one that I had met.

They didn't match.

The younger David Lee had been much more hopeful, even after they found the original colonists on Fremont. I liked *him*. But he had allowed himself to become buried in someone less honorable.

The closest equivalent to what happened to him would be for me to lose both Alicia and Chelo. I could kill for that. I shouldn't—Chelo would never want that. Or my mother. Based on the gentleness of her drawings, I suspected she would have hated my father's choices.

After he'd slaked his thirst and rested, I brought him to one of the living spaces that we weren't using, with two available chairs, a small round table, and a little sink. The floors were soft carpet in patterned teal and brown. A hand-carved stylized wooden tree adorned the one free wall.

I brought us each a glass of steaming spicy col, setting them on the table between the two chairs. The welcome scent permeated the small space almost immediately. He remained silent long after I sat down, finally asking, "Why didn't you wake me earlier?"

When I didn't answer, he prodded. "Staying sane a year in a small ship is tough. Hell, a month's tough. The wind of a long flight drives some crazy. Why didn't you let me help?"

I took a deep breath, steeled myself, and told him. "I don't know what to think of you. I looked for you for a long time, but I don't trust you. Not after what you did."

He was silent for a few moments, watching me. The tight muscles along his jaw and from shoulder to neck were the only sign he gave of feeling. "I won't be able to bear it if we get there too late to make it right."

"Make it right? By saving Chelo? But can you make it right that you sent people to kill other people?"

He met my question with another long awkward silence. When he spoke, he sounded wrung out and emotionless. "I tried to call them off. Right after I met you. I didn't have the money to do it, but I tried anyway. I didn't get an answer back."

This wasn't new information—he'd told us all that after we got out into free space. I leaned in, watching him. "Can anyone besides you cancel the contract?" It had dawned on me after we all left that Marcus could have raised the fifty thousand credits as easily as sent us off. It disturbed me that I hadn't asked him why, didn't really know why he chose as he did. "If someone pays them enough, will they stop? Just take the money and not do the job?"

He shook his head, and for the first time since he came in, he looked away from me, as if admiring the tiny branches of multicolored wood on the tree sculpture beside us. "I don't think so. That's not how the contract is written, and it's not how they work."

I sipped my col. "Can you call and talk to them?"

"Not from a moving ship to a moving ship, not at the distances and speeds between us. You should know that."

I didn't. Maybe I should go get those credentials the Port Authority had wanted someday. He looked at me like some deep hunger drove him. Was he hungry for me? The way I had been hungry for him all my life?

I kept some distance between us. I wasn't ready yet.

"So why did they take this job? Islas only accepts jobs that also further their own goals."

He shook his head.

He wasn't stupid. "What about the unrest back on Silver's Home? Silver's Home and Islas are squaring off. Doesn't this maybe relate? The Port Authority came to stop me because they're afraid of an incident between us and them. So they don't think this is just about vengeance."

He winced at the word. Swallowing hard, he leaned back in his chair and regarded me for long moments. "I don't know. I didn't care when I made the contract."

"Do you care now?"

He nodded, his smoky-blue eyes fastened on mine, blinking as if tears hid behind them. But if so, he held them back.

I kept pushing, knowing it was cruel. But something in me had to do it. I told myself it was to see what he was really made of, even though I knew it was partly from my own pain. "So what would they want? Why were they even willing to go to Fremont?"

He swallowed. "I haven't been paying that much attention to the war news. There's always war news. Just more lately. I thought maybe the Islans just wanted to see Fremont for themselves since we claimed it."

"Can they challenge your claim?"

"Not legally."

"What happens if we have to fight them?"

He laughed then, a bitter laugh. "We can't fight Star Mercenaries. Not with this little ship and a handful of people."

I held my tongue, waiting for him to say more.

It took him a long time. "If we did, they might use it as an excuse to push the war harder." He looked around the room, avoiding my eyes. "No—we have to get your sister and whoever else we want to save, and leave."

He was so sure of himself, I didn't argue. I wanted to, wanted to tell him a million stories about Artistos. The good stories. I held my tongue, but I didn't agree with him, and I made sure he knew it by the way I didn't say anything, with the set of my body.

Let him read me however he wanted. He hated them all; maybe he didn't want to fight because he really wanted the original humans dead. I loved more people on Fremont than Chelo and Liam and Kayleen.

I'd decide if we left or fought.

He didn't deserve to do it—he'd already decided to kill them all once. This was my ship. Chelo was my sister, and Artistos had been my home.

"I'll be right back," I said. I got up and walked out, taking the empty glasses, buying myself a few moments to let the anger roll away.

I hadn't woken him to fight, even though I hadn't been able to stop myself so far. I refilled the col glasses and rummaged around for some waybread.

Should I give him a chance? We were trapped in a small place hurtling through the vastness of empty space between tiny planets.

We had time. I forced myself to stay out of the comfort of the ship's data and focus on the person I'd woken up.

I went back and asked, "What was Mom like?"

He winced, shifting, physically uncomfortable. "I can still barely think about her, even though in some ways I hardly remember her. I don't suppose you can understand that?"

"Sometimes it's hard to see the details of Chelo's face. Especially when I try to remember them."

He smiled softly and I reached over and touched his hand. He smiled back, the warmth of it lighting his eyes.

"I'm sorry. Your mother was beautiful. Not in the way some women attract the eyes of everyone around, but subtler, inside. Everyone who knew Marissa admired her. Strong—she was so strong. She fought side by side with me before she got pregnant with your sister." He paused, sipped his col, his gaze turned inward as if memory was taking him backward. "The pregnancies we chose were acts of colonization—not of war. There was a fabulous geneticist on board—Susan Zeni. We worked with her to design you to succeed on Fremont. It didn't cross our minds that we wouldn't stay, especially early on. We had a clear claim to the planet. When we learned they didn't have a ship to fly away on, we offered to let them stay. Why didn't that stop them?"

I didn't have an answer.

"I'm wandering, aren't I? Marissa always had kind words for people, and she always believed in a good outcome, no matter how bad it seemed. That was her strength."

Like Chelo.

"She was a fabulous mom. The day Chelo was born was the happiest day of her life, and when you were born, her eyes glowed with that same love, that same strength. I saw our future in her eyes, in your tiny forms." He wasn't talking to me. Maybe to himself, or to my mother. "You were so wonderful to hold, to be with. You smelled of Marissa when I held you, like her warm milk and her sweat, and your skin felt like it had been bathed in her softness and her songs. She used to sing to you both. . . ."

He shook himself, as if he couldn't bear the feelings his own words drew out of him. When he stopped and looked at me, his eyes were as tender as I'd ever seen them. I wanted to look away, to break the intensity down to something I could handle.

Instead, I reached a hand out for his, taking it long enough to feel his warmth.

He continued. "Time passed, and they started killing us, and I remember how her eyes snapped with anger at them—and fear for you—when we first took you to the caves to hide. We swore we'd win for you all, for the children of Fremont."

Maybe I could tap that when I needed him to help me save the people of Fremont.

And tomorrow, I'd start the day with something simple, like a game of chess.

36

WAKING AND QUESTIONING

My father was again frozen, and for the moment, only Alicia and I breathed on board *Creator*.

I had already started the sequence to wake Jenna. Alicia leaned over to me, whispering, "Our last moment of privacy." Her eyes flashed with heat and she suddenly disappeared, the flicker of movement catching my eye as her mod didn't quite keep up with color changes in the doorway. I laughed, racing after her footsteps, following her all the way to our sleeping space.

Creator woke us in time to head to Medical to sit beside Jenna, watching her wake. "We wanted to wake you before we woke Ming," I said. "We're just a few months out, and I want to know why she's aboard before we get there."

Jenna set her glass down carefully, coughed, and leaned back in her chair. "So do I."

Her voice still sounded scratchy. "You haven't woken anyone else up—not Induan or Bryan?"

"No. My father for a while, but he's frozen again."

Jenna glanced at me with concern.

"It was okay to be up with him. Really." It had been. He was good at chess. When we avoided charged subjects I liked him a little.

She sighed. "I'm sorry, Joseph, but besides you and Alicia, the only people I trust are Tiala and Bryan. Maybe Dianne, since Marcus picked her specifically to help you. I don't trust Ming." She glanced at Alicia. "And I'm not sure about Induan."

Alicia scowled, sighed, and glared at Jenna for a long moment before she said, "All right. But you can. You'll see."

I refilled Jenna's water glass, giving her a few moments to think. She stood and started pacing. Even newly woken, wildness suffused her movements, more like the Jenna I'd known on Fremont. It felt like being in the room with a predator.

I handed her the glass. "How are we going to decide whether or not to trust Ming?"

"Trust is earned," Jenna snapped. She stopped pacing and drank. "We'll figure something out." She looked at Alicia thoughtfully. "Maybe your risk-taking skills will come in handy here. Let me know what you think of Ming."

"Meaning if I like her, you won't?"

Jenna just laughed. "Let's get Tiala and Bryan up, first. More backup won't hurt us."

Jenna and I and Bryan sat in a row on hard metal chairs by Ming's bed, waiting for her to wake. She was not, as far as we knew, a Wind Reader. Essentially a stowaway, she undoubtedly expected to be interrogated.

Jenna wanted us in here when Ming woke. So we had come now, even though we expected the process to take another hour or so. Like everyone, Ming seemed vulnerable and small as her body took on color. Her firm musculature gave her excellent form, even lying down; enough to attract. Slender without being thin: compact. Small, with a face that looked elfin now, while every other time I'd seen her awake it had been painted with intensity. I pointed at her calves. "She must work out like you two."

Jenna nodded. "She does. She seems to have flexibility mods. A dancer, I think."

"How can you tell?"

"Look how long and defined her muscles are. Remember how she carried herself when we saw her before? Graceful. And she's the only one who made it inside the closing door."

"Besides my father." That reminded me of something else. "Bryan, didn't you get a mod, too, like Alicia?"

He flexed his hands, twisting them together. Then he held them out flat, bent slightly up, like a little girl admiring long nails. I bent down over his near hand. "Impressive." His nails had lengthened, as if he'd unleashed sheathed knives, the edges sharp and cutting. I reached out and touched the tip of his right index fingernail, and a thin line of blood rose, like a papercut. I raised an eyebrow at him. "Be careful with those, especially around girlfriends."

His cheeks reddened. He twisted his hands again, running one over the other in a smooth pattern, and the knives disappeared. Bodies as weapons, like the Family of Exploration had worn on Fremont.

I looked again at Bryan's now-normal hands. "Where'd they go?"

"They went into my fingers. Feel?" He touched me with his index finger, the nail now a dull round that didn't hurt at all. Synthetic, though.

"But what happens to the real nail when it grows?" I asked.

He grinned. "The mod included a nail cutter." He held up his right foot, again an absurdly feminine gesture. "I did my feet, too."

"Magic nails," a feminine voice rasped. "I heard they've improved since I got mine."

Ming. She hadn't turned her head. Maybe she couldn't, yet. But she was awake enough to speak coherently. Curious. Her vitals, like everyone's, were closely monitored by *Creator*, but it hadn't mentioned she might be awake. Had it known?

We had decided not to waste too much time. "What are you doing on my ship?" I asked her.

"I wanted to see where you came from."

"Why?"

"I'm curious. I can help you."

"How?" I asked.

She moved her head, her dark almond-shaped eyes big in her pale face. "I helped you once." Her voice was scratchy, but controlled. She was used to authority. "I told Marcus when you left Li Spaceport so he could find you before anyone else did."

She must be dying of thirst, aching with it, but she hadn't asked. I moved my seat closer to her bed and handed her a glass of water. Jenna and Bryan watched carefully in case I needed them. Not that Ming could do much damage in the shape she was in now, just waking. Although magic fingernails? I checked as she took the glass of water. Her nails looked normal.

No one had suggested I get any neat physical mods.

Ming downed the water, her head tilted like a songbird's, then held the glass out for more, her slender fingers handling it gently, like priceless art. I plucked the glass from her and handed it to Jenna, who got up and re-filled it, but held it in her own hands, waiting.

Very well. I asked a question I wanted the answer to anyway. "How do you know Marcus?"

She smiled. "I was his student, once."

"What did he teach you?"

"Movement. He spent two years teaching dance." She glanced at Jenna. "A long time ago. Before you left for Fremont. I did the first year, but I couldn't do the second. I didn't want the Wind Reader mod."

Interesting. "You can get it as an adult? I thought it had to be born into you, and that it ran in families. A true-mod."

She laughed this time. "He told me you were naïve. It does breed true. Mostly. But like all mods, it started somewhere. Humanity was not born to interact directly with data. New Wind Reader lines *are* usually started in-vitro, but there is an adult version of the mod. The failure rate is half." She shrugged. "I chose not to try. Failure isn't reversible. If you fail, you're crazy forever."

Her answer intrigued me. "So can people who are born Wind Readers enhance their skills as adults?"

She reached for the water. "Practice helps. More nano doesn't."

Jenna handed it to her. "Ming, why do you want to see Fremont?"

Ming pushed herself up, dangling her legs over the side of the bed and drinking the water, slowly. More controlled than I'd seen anyone on just their second glass after waking. "Because it is wild, and no place in the Five Planets is wild anymore. Except that's not the most important reason." She paused, stretching her limbs again, a small smile curving the corners of her fine, small lips as her arms and wrists and ankles turned and stretched. "Maybe that was even the wrong answer." She caught my eyes with hers. "Marcus thinks you matter. I wanted to be with you, to see why. And I needed an adventure." She took another dainty sip of water. "The Authority bores me."

She shrugged. "Besides, Lukas thinks I came on his account. I can balance between you and him, if necessary."

Bryan watched her intently. He'd taken his nails out again. Was he playing with them, or was it a sign that he still mistrusted Ming?

I paced. What to do next? Ming seemed to be answering us openly enough, but could I believe her? What would Marcus do? Marcus apparently knew her better than he'd let on to me—he had had time to tell her I was naïve.

Right now, I couldn't be.

I stopped in front of Ming. The bed she sat on was high enough that her eyes were level with mine, and I tried to see into them. She gazed back at me, waiting. "So tell me about the other people on the ship. What do you think of them?"

She started a little, her eyes widening, as if the question surprised her. Maybe it did. After all, we hadn't locked her up as a stowaway. She said, "Is there food we can discuss this over?"

She shouldn't be hungry yet. But then, she shouldn't be awake yet, either. And here she sat, alert, and very, very interesting. Something about her suggested I should trust her, could trust her, and Marcus seemed to, as well. But Jenna didn't. And I trusted Jenna more than even Marcus.

I called Alicia and Tiala and asked if they could finish the meal they were cooking a little early. Ming watched me talk to them, and when I was done she asked, "Who else is awake?"

Jenna answered her. "Alicia, and my sister, Tiala."

Ming stood and walked steadily over to the small sink in the sparse medical room, setting her glass down neatly. She seemed fully adapted to *Creator*'s gravity, which was slightly less than that of Silver's Home, but perhaps she was well-adapted to anything physical. When she finished, she turned to Jenna. "And why did Tiala come?"

Jenna blinked at her, drawing back a moment. "We are . . . all the family we have. We didn't want to be separated anymore."

We didn't talk about anything of consequence until Ming had eaten a full bowl of ship's stew: grown protein, tasteless by itself, but flavored by fresh tomatoes and carrots and spices from the garden. A cup of col for everyone. And better, Tiala had made fresh flatbread, a rare treat, which we dipped in the hot stew. My stomach berated me for not waking Tiala a long time ago.

Ming looked like she'd been awake for days instead of hours: her eyes shone, her skin glowed, she moved easily. Her intensity had returned, as if the energy in her tiny body was enough for at least two people. She looked at Jenna and spoke. "First of all, Induan and Dianne surprised Lukas and me. We didn't know they would be coming. I quick queried them both. Induan is an artist. She was also one of the business strategists for the Family of Exploration and loaned out to other affinity groups. She never made much buzz."

I pictured Alicia, listening, frowning at any idea Induan wasn't extraordinary.

Ming went on. "Dianne can be trusted. She and Marcus have been friends forever, and she wants to stop this war."

"What about my father?" I asked.

"He came back broken. Before that, he was brilliant. One of the best in your affinity group, and well adjusted for a Wind Reader. Who knows about broken people? Maybe this trip will cure him."

We left Ming awake and with us for three more days, watching her closely. She didn't try to call out from the ship, or access any records, or check on any of the sleepers. She taught us a new dance, which Alicia and Tiala excelled at (and I stumbled through). Alicia stayed close to me, as if she sensed Ming's physicality.

When asked, Ming went meekly back to be frozen, requesting that we thaw her a few weeks before we got to Fremont so she could get her body in shape. As soon as Ming consigned herself to temporary oblivion again, Alicia said, "A week will be plenty. She looks like she's in pretty good shape right now."

I laughed and drew Alicia close, burying my face in her hair. "I love you, and only you. But we don't know what we'll find on Fremont, and I don't see any reason not to let her have a few weeks to get ready. Maybe she'll be even more impressive. We may need every tool we have, and I think I can trust her."

Jenna, who overhead me, said, "We learned nothing. We should not wake her until we can watch her, one week or six."

Alicia grinned, like a kid with a cookie, and Bryan looked up from a seat at the far side of the room. "I'll watch her anytime."

PART SEVEN

ARTISTOS

37

GOING HOME

Kayleen pushed herself up from a slump in the center backseat of the skimmer's cabin. Her eyes fixed on the dark mouth of the Cave of Power, an elongated oval in a steep, rocky slope peppered with midsummer-green brush. Liam and I sat on either side of her, watching the opening fill the *Burning Void*'s screen in front of us.

Kayleen's face looked as cold and still and shocked as it had when we left Windy's body behind and fled West Home. No one followed us. But they knew we left. Kayleen had confirmed their nets were up with a simple nod.

Liam and I had tried to approach her, had offered our touch and our tears. Kayleen reacted to neither. She spent most of the flight with her eyes closed, her skin white, her body deadly still. Perhaps she focused so hard on flying to shut out her loss. Perhaps she couldn't let herself feel and still fly.

The skimmer seemed empty without Windy. I felt disconnected myself, and as if someone besides me had made my choices. I approved of this strange Chelo's choice because it was the right one. But I didn't like her, I didn't want to be her. And as much as I had wanted to go home, I felt disconnected from that as well.

Except now we were almost there.

Kayleen barked out a single word: "Brace." I grabbed the seat arms just as something powerful clutched the *Burning Void*, slowing us with a jerk. The skimmer began to make minor adjustments, finer than any Kayleen had shown an ability to do. She slumped in her chair, her breathing uneven, her face white.

The skimmer's lights shone on the back of the cave wall, illuminating both smooth and rough-hewn rock, showing a few of the doors that led deeper into the cave. Walls surrounded us, even though I couldn't see them. I held my breath as the skimmer slid neatly, and I knew barely, between them and down the short corridor to settle smoothly on the floor of the room we had taken off from.

Kayleen's eyes were closed, her head back against the cushions. Tears ran down each side of her face, streams of them running along her ears and sparkling in her hair. Her breath came in slow, deep jerks as she fought sobs back. Liam took her right hand, and I took her left. We sat that way for a long time, matching our breathing to hers. Eventually, she pulled her hand free from mine and wiped at her eyes, then opened them. She sat forward, placing both of her hands on the chair-back in front of her. The screen went dark. "We have to go. We have to warn them."

"Yes," I said, opening the door.

She stood, wobbling, and reached for her water flask, taking a long drink. She clipped her flask to her belt. Her voice shook. "The damned birds will have a heyday with the garden."

She ran her hands through her hair, then whispered, "Paloma." She walked through the doorway. We grabbed our own water and followed. The ramp rose again behind us.

It was full night, the breeze colder than anything on Islandia. Goose bumps rose on my bare arms. The bright lights of stars and two moons, Destiny and Dreamcatcher, cast faint shadows on the dark rocks and paths, and touched the edges of leaves with a vague shimmer. We didn't say anything else, but simply started off, together, me in front and Kayleen in between and then Liam, picking our way down the path, moving fast but careful of our footing in the shadowed parts of the trail.

As soon as we reached the wide High Road, we sped into a steady, fast downhill jog. Trees shadowed half the road, so we kept to the far side, closest to the drop, moving quietly and surely, like wild animals on their home territory. I couldn't find Artistos's lights. That wasn't right.

"Kayleen?" I asked. "Is Artistos okay?"

She glanced down, seeing the same darkness I had seen, and nodded. "It's still there, Chelo."

We slowed as we went through the rock fall, and for once, little of my attention pulled toward the awful past of the place—the rocks and downed trees and tremendous rotting root systems were simply an annoyance, a barrier to us getting down.

At the far end of the fall, Liam came to my side and put a hand on my shoulder. "Do you need to rest?"

Yes. I shook my head, only slowing a bit. "Where do we start? With Nava?"

Kayleen answered. "I want to see Paloma. We'll wake her and go to Nava and Tom together, maybe get an emergency High Council meeting. If we were followed, there won't be much time."

A bright red-gold meteor streaked across the sky, and then another one. No threatening ships or strange skimmers. But they had data. We might as well have just written down the coordinates of our weapons store and handed them to the mercenaries. But then, we couldn't exactly fly right down into Artistos, either. Most people there didn't even know we had the skimmer, and they might very well shoot first and ask questions later. We should have gone to the Grass Plains. It didn't matter, not now. Except as a personal warning to think harder. But I spoke it anyway. "We flew into the cave."

Kayleen answered. "It has defenses."

Of course. Jenna had taught us to enter and leave from the top because the front way in, the way we brought in *Burning Void*, had traps in it. "So the cave recognizes the *Burning Void*?"

"Yes." Kayleen didn't miss a beat, or a breath.

I could feel the run, a slow burn deep in my lungs.

"Are you connected to their data now?" Liam asked.

"No. I think we're just too far away."

We loped by bare rocky cliffs, the dark slashes of crevices making a mosaic. Triangles and circles of trees blurred the top of the cliffs, black against the dark sky. The part of me that chose to start this fight resurfaced, strong and capable and asking questions I didn't want to know the answer to. I would have to get used to her. The old one was as dead as Windy. "Did we damage the *Dawnforce*?" I asked. "How many people did we kill?"

Kayleen answered. "I don't know what we did to the ship. If anything. There were three people in the skimmer that turned over. They all died." Her voice was flat, shocked. "Another one died in one of the explosions, and two were wounded. The dogs killed one and hurt two. Not Lushia or Ghita."

She ran on, silent, and I waited, sensing there was more. Eventually, she said, "They killed all of the dogs. They're ruthless."

She meant about Windy, too. Not a good thing for her to dwell on. "How about if you get Paloma, and Liam and I wake Tom and Nava? You can bring Paloma to their house."

"I want to stay together."

We fell silent again. Five dead out of fifty, if Ghita had told me the truth. Ten percent. There were a few thousand people in Artistos now, but the Islans had far better technology. Our parents had lost a war with similar odds, and the Islans seemed to know that. So they were forewarned that Artistos would fight them.

I smiled to myself. It was actually more uneven. We were here to help. It would be okay.

Sure it would.

We rounded the last switchback and picked up speed down the long straightaway into Little Lace Park. Just before the park, the boundary bells rang friendly entrance.

I wanted to cry with relief. We were home.

We stopped for breath and water just inside the boundary. Leaning over the fence, we watched the Lace River run below, moonlight brightening the ripples of water over rocks. A fish jumped, the rings of its fall cutting across the dark water.

"Hello the trail," a familiar voice called out.

"Hey Stile," Liam called. "Keeping a watch these days?"

A medium-sized man with dark hair and one damaged arm turned toward us. "Come back from the dead, are you?" He came up to Liam and slapped him on the back with his good arm. He stopped in front of me, grinning. "Was that you flying in? Gianna's had us watching for something, but no one told me it was you."

"Maybe they didn't know." A high, nervous laugh escaped Kayleen's lips.

He glanced at her, and then at me, noticing our bellies. He gave Liam a look that might have been approval. Hard to tell, but I didn't like it—it was a thing between men that didn't include us.

Nevertheless, I leaned in and gave Stile a huge hug and a kiss on the cheek. It was just so damned good to see another friendly face.

He returned my hug, holding me tight but releasing me quickly. I told him, "Yes, that was us. About an hour ago. And Gianna should be scared. There's *others* on Islandia."

He stepped back a bit and frowned, then nodded. "That's why the town's black." He touched his hand to his ear and I noticed the dark dot of an earset. "I'll warn Nava you're coming."

"Will you come down with us?" I asked.

"Nava'd kill me if I left the boundary unprotected."

Liam nodded. "As well she should. It's real, Stile. Don't doubt it. Go ahead and guard."

Stile inclined his head respectfully. "Glad to have you back, young Liam. We'd heard you all left, and some said you were never coming back, like when Joseph and Alicia and Jenna left. Some said you abandoned us, but I thought you wouldn't have, not after you stayed when the other ship flew away." He paused, scratching his head and looking around. "Step carefully—the town is scared and not everyone loves you." He turned to look back up the path we'd côme down. "It's a sad day when the boundary bells aren't enough for Artistos. I'll tell them you're coming."

We left him standing there, watching the trail we'd come down and talking into his earset.

Kayleen broke into a jog again, then sped up. We followed, running free along the well-worn path, past the place where the roamer wagons set up for Story Night, and into the edge of town. Moving fast was awesome—the wind in my face, my hair behind me, my legs pumping, my breath hard and quick. I pulled out ahead of both of them for a few long meters, then Liam caught me, then Kayleen caught us all, passing us, turning her head and staring back at us.

We slowed, moving quietly as we passed Commons Park. I'd never seen the town so dark except during a storm. Shadows moved against a few windows, and far off, a hebra called, but otherwise, Artistos might as well have been a ghost town.

We arrived at Paloma's without passing a soul on the road. Kayleen pushed the door open, walking into the darkened house and calling out, "Mom," in a loud whisper.

Paloma emerged from her storeroom, holding a flashlight beam down, so her face was all shadows. As usual, the scent of drying herbs followed her. "Kayleen? Baby." She looked around, and must have recognized us even in the near-darkness. A long sigh escaped her lips. "Chelo. Liam. I'm so glad to see you." She stepped up next to Kayleen, putting a hand to her daughter's face. "Are you okay? Where were you?"

She looked down at Kayleen's rounded stomach and fell silent. Then she put a hand out and touched it. She looked at Liam, then me, blinking as if we'd told her it was dusk at the crack of dawn.

Kayleen moaned softly into the dark quiet. "I'll explain later." She reached for Paloma, drawing her into an embrace. "I'm not sure any of us are okay. We just got back from Islandia, and we need to talk to the Town Council. There's people over there that want to kill you, kill us." She paused a moment, collecting herself. "I want you to go with me to talk to Council."

This didn't surprise Paloma as much as Kayleen's pregnancy. "I'd hoped Gianna was making up monsters." She pushed back from her daughter. "But she wasn't, was she?"

Liam stepped forward. "No, she wasn't. Can you come with us now?"

"Let me put away a few things." Paloma turned back into her office, leaving us in the darkness. Rustling and small clanks accompanied swings of the light, and then she came back out. "Let's go."

We headed up the street toward my old house, where Joseph and I had lived with Steven and Therese before they died. After that, Nava and Tom took over as the colony's leaders and moved in, keeping us with them, as if we were furniture that went with the house.

I could have found my way to that house of sweet and bitter memories in complete darkness.

The house sat near the edge of town, surrounded by trees that heralded the near edge of the Lace Forest. The Lace River ran in front of and below the house, in a deep channel carved by years of wintermelt water. Faint light showed inside the kitchen, too pale to spill out the windows. Liam knocked.

Nava opened the door. Paloma held her flashlight so Nava could see us, and we could see Nava's face, as if her pale skin, green eyes, and long red hair floated alone above the dark. "Stile told me you were back. Come in." She turned and we four followed her into the kitchen. Two candles burned low on the small table, which held glasses of tea and dried apples. Bowls and spoons left over from dinner sat in the sink and djuri stew cooled in a pot on the stove. The scent of meat, potatoes, and spices hung in the air.

Nava's round-faced and kind husband, Tom, wiped up the counter by the sink. Hunter sat at the table, looking even older and more emaciated than usual. His eyes were dark pebbles buried in wrinkles. His gnarled hands rested on the table, one of them shaking as if he had no control over it. The other rested quietly. He spoke first, looking at Kayleen. I thought he'd mention our pregnancy, but the first thing he said was, "You left us."

I chewed on the inside of my mouth. This was Hunter, and he should be admonishing us for being immature idiots or threatening to throw us into jail, not speaking softly to Kayleen. "We came back to warn you, Hunter," I said. "Artistos is in danger."

He nodded. "I'm listening."

"Do you want to call the rest of the High Council?" I asked.

Nava furrowed her brow, glancing at Hunter. "Not now, not at this time of night. We are the War Council, anyway."

I'd never heard of the War Council.

Hunter said, "We'll hear you out first."

Tom bustled about making tea. Nava sat at the table, watching us closely, and Hunter, next to her, closed his eyes, as if he wanted to hear us and not see us. Kayleen and Paloma sat together, Paloma a little behind her daughter since the table was really only designed for six. Liam was between me and Kayleen. Kayleen looked at Hunter, then Nava, then Tom. Then she looked over at us. "I took Chelo and Liam to Islandia. It was my fault we went." She looked around the table. "I'm sorry."

Paloma gave a small, unsurprised smile, but Nava's mouth turned down and she glared disapproval at Kayleen. Tom set four steaming mugs of redberry tea in front of us, and sat down in the seat next to me. He, too, smiled at Kayleen, as if he and Paloma both found something positive in her instant admission. But then, Tom and Paloma always seemed to think alike.

Before anyone could press Kayleen more, I jumped in, telling the story from when we saw the *Dawnforce*, putting in as many details as I could remember about the mercenaries and their ship. Liam added bits I forgot and talked about the diversion he and Kayleen created with the demon dogs and our surprise attack. Kayleen added things she'd learned inside of their nets. Nava or Paloma interrupted from time to time with questions. Hunter kept his eyes closed, and didn't interrupt at all.

While Kayleen talked, I catalogued the signs of age in all of them: Hunter's thin, scaly skin marred by age spots, the deep wrinkles that made canyons in his cheeks, the streaks of gray in Paloma's hair. Even Tom and Nava had developed faint creases around their eyes.

That was another advantage the mercenaries had—more physical energy.

After we told them everything we could, the room fell silent except for the rattle of teacups against the table. Tom brought us bowls of cold stew. I didn't think I could eat until the bowl was in front of me. I ate. We all did.

When it seemed the silence was about to pop open of its own accord, Nava cleared her throat, looked at the old man next to her, and said, "Hunter?"

Hunter opened his eyes. "You did well." He looked at me, then Liam, then Kayleen, then back to me. "Are you with us? Can we count on you?"

"Of course we are," I said.

"We're here," Liam said.

Kayleen cleared her throat. Her voice shook. "I will help protect the town. In fact, you need me to. I'm the only one here who can get inside their nets, inside their heads. I'll have a chance of understanding their plans. But I'll need my freedom." She regarded Nava calmly. The fingers of Kayleen's right hand drummed against her leg. "I will not just take orders anymore."

Nava looked back at her, her brows drawn together. "Everyone takes orders. Even me, sometimes."

"Then I want no more orders than anybody else that lives here. If you ask me for things, I'll probably do them. I mean, I want to help. But I can do things you don't even know about, and I'll have to spend more time on our nets, and we're a family now." She looked at Nava as if daring her to respond.

For whatever reason, Nava held her tongue.

Hunter said, "I can see that," his face showing no emotion at all, as if Kayleen's words laid a mask over his eyes and lips.

Tom said, "Congratulations," and the word fell awkwardly between us all.

"Thanks," I said, my word as flat as Tom's. They didn't like it, but they weren't kicking us out of town for it. At least not today. I could imagine the conversations they'd have after we left.

Kayleen smiled sweetly at Nava, cocking her head, as if she were a five-year-old who hadn't been after the sugar-wheat cookies. I was afraid she'd say something else, but she just said, "I'd like to go to work on the nets as soon as we're done."

Maybe Nava realized she wasn't going to be able to *make* Kayleen do anything. "We'd appreciate that." Her words sounded so sharp that Tom and Paloma both turned their heads and gazed at her, and Hunter lifted a hand, the index finger extended up, as if issuing a warning. Nava just drew her lips tighter. There was a time, right before and right after the *New Making* had left, when Nava relaxed some about us. Now, there was no trace of anything except resentment and frustration on her face.

Kayleen focused on Hunter. He had led the last war, the only war ever on Fremont. Campfire songs suggested that without Hunter, Artistos would have lost. She stood and walked around the table to where he sat, knelt down in front of him, and took his shaking, thin hand in hers. "Hunter, we're with you. We are not like these people. We don't want anything bad to happen to you."

His lips curled up in a faint smile. "That's a good thing."

But when I glanced up at Nava, I could tell she didn't like the idea of needing us at all.

38

THE WEST BAND

The next day, I rode a dull hebra named Jiko up a thin trail winding through the high, wooded foothills toward Rage and the West Band. Liam rode in front of me, following faint wagon ruts, his bronze skin shining in the sun where his arms poked out of his sleeveless shirt. He'd washed his hair and I'd combed it and braided it carefully.

Kayleen rode next to me, constantly scanning the sky as if she watched for predators. Or skimmers. As if to belie our danger, the bright springlike bloom of the high meadow in summer surrounded us. Way up here, the rich scent of multicolored flowers filled the air, even though the Grass Plains below Artistos were already yellow at the base of the stalks. We rode across a long grassy meadow, heading for trees on the far side. Yellow and white flowers poked above the high green grass and brushed the hebras' bellies.

Behind us, Tom and Paloma rode side by side, deep in serious conversation.

As we neared the edge of the long high meadow, movement in front of us caught my attention. A tall, dark-haired woman with long legs, a tiny waist, and well-defined biceps stepped from under a tent tree just in front of Liam, holding up her right hand to signal him to stop. She looked grave, although her blue eyes sparkled. I leaned over to Kayleen. "That's Alyksa. She's the best scout in the band. Always finds the djuri herds."

"She looks strong," Kayleen said.

Liam pulled his borrowed hebra, Duke, to a slower pace and then stopped just in front of her. Alyksa took one of Duke's reins. Kayleen and I rode up close to them. I expected Alyksa to smile and welcome us home, but she pursed her lips and kept her feet in a ready stance, one she could run or fight from. Her first words were, "We'll need to escort you in. You must wait." And then, in response to his incredulous look, she added, "Even you." Only then, her duty discharged, did she break into a smile to match the clear pleasure in her eyes at seeing us.

Tom and Paloma rode up. Alyksa kept her smile, clearly recognizing them. She looked back at Liam, and then me. "Welcome home."

Liam nodded at her. "Thank you." He and I shared a brief, confused glance. The West Band had always kept watchers, but they watched for trouble and let our people pass.

He turned back to Alyksa. "How are Akashi and Mayah?"

"Worried."

I caught a slight movement as tree limbs shivered and then parted far behind Alyksa, then smiled as I recognized Akashi, on foot. I leaned far over and poked Liam in the shoulder. "Ask him yourself."

Liam turned and slid from his hebra in a single fluid motion. He raced toward his dad, leaving Alyksa holding his hebra's reins. The scout grimaced, then shrugged, patting the hebra briefly.

Akashi, too, broke into a run, his face bright with excitement.

I stayed put, watching them race into each other's arms. Liam had grown; Akashi's head barely came to his adopted son's shoulder. Akashi's long gray hair had been shorn, and his shoulders slumped inward. Liam patted his father's back, his face cocked a bit to one side so his cheek rested on Akashi's head. They stayed that way for a long moment before separating and looking at each other.

I grabbed the rough, knotted mounting rope and slid carefully from Jiko's back, wishing yet again that I rode Stripes instead of this docile and unremarkable beast. I thrust my reins into Alyksa's outstretched hand and stood watching Akashi and Liam.

Shortly, Akashi gestured for me to come. I fell into his arms, drinking in the scent of leather and campfire smoke and sweat. Hot tears of relief surprised me, streaking unbidden down my cheeks. His dark eyes also held tears, hanging in the corners but not falling.

"I missed you," I said, my voice nearly breaking.

He pulled me even closer. "I missed you, too." He pushed me a little away, keeping his grip on my waist, looking up at me. His dark eyes shone with mischief. "That's Liam's baby?"

I nodded, and he pointed at Kayleen. "That one, too?"

I bit my lip, suddenly afraid. I gave a small nod, and Akashi said, "Not surprised. Congratulations." I blew out a long, relieved breath.

Akashi turned to Liam. "Where did you go?"

Liam swallowed. "Islandia."

Akashi raised an eyebrow, and I broke in. "Kayleen took us. It's a long story. We would have told you."

Akashi pulled Liam close as well, so the three of us stood together in a single embrace. "I know you would have. At least you're back, now." Akashi looked toward the group, his brows furrowed. "We are being inhospitable."

He let us go and greeted the other three. We followed him down a wide, wooded path until we came to a clearing. Liam clutched my hand and stopped as we emerged from the trees; his eyes narrowed as he scanned the camp. Even though I had only been to a few summer camps before, I could immediately tell this was different.

Usually, the band's wagons gathered in a rough circle, bunched together to provide protection in numbers. Here, wagons lay tucked separately under trees, with at least one person near each one. Goats and hebras grazed, most tied on long-lines or staked to the ground near the wagons instead of together in quick-build corrals like usual. Children walked through camp in pairs, or larger groups, carrying water, leading goats, and talking quietly. Summer-fat camp dogs hung close to the children's feet, ever-watchful. The camp smelled right—of drying meat and ash and animals, but the scents seemed as subdued as the movement and noise.

"We moved here the day after Gianna called us," Akashi said quietly. "There are twice as many border scouts on duty as usual."

I finally spotted my little wagon. Stripes grazed placidly next to it, and Sasha sat in the seat working on some project, her dark head bent over whatever she was doing, the streak of white in her hair clearly visible. I wanted to race over to her, but the camp's differences reminded me of why we'd come. I leaned over to Akashi. "Is there a place we can talk? We're bringing bad news."

He sighed. "I thought you might be."

Alyksa and two young men walked by with our mounts.

Kiara looked over and spotted us, then called out, "Hey, look!" to Abyl, her best friend. The two of them did everything together, including parking their wagons next to each other, and now they came to greet us together, two sturdy, wide middle-aged women. Sasha looked up at the movement and dropped whatever she held in her lap. She leapt from the high wagon seat, landing in a dead run, beating Kiara and Abyl to our sides. Stripes raised her head and bugled. Soon, we were surrounded by half the band, calling to us, greeting us, asking for news. Kayleen, Tom, and Paloma stood together just outside the flow of people, watching, wide-eyed.

Akashi, too, watched, smiling at the crowd. After the first rush of noisy, happy greeting ended, he looked over at Liam. "Do you want to talk to me, or to the band?"

Liam raised a single eyebrow at me. I wanted to catch up with everyone, but it would be hard to talk to so many people at once. "Akashi and the Chiefs," I mouthed.

So we started our story yet again. But this time we spoke to the most competent people on Fremont.

SASHA'S SASH

When we finished the meeting, I stepped outside. The midafternoon sun assaulted my eyes, forcing me to blink and look away for a moment. Liam had stayed behind to talk with his mom and dad, and Kayleen had already headed off with Cho, the band librarian, the two of them chattering about the data library like old friends. I went straight for my wagon.

Sasha had returned to the front bench, her hands and her project back in her lap. Her smile looked like my heart felt, bright and full. I snuggled up close to her and put my arm around her slender shoulders. She was a roamer—more capable by far than a townie—and now just months short of being a full adult and getting her own wagon and animals. She'd clearly cared well for mine—the outside walls and the seat were clear of dust and the metal wheel-hubs shone. My voice broke as I said, "I missed you so."

She set her work down on her lap, covering it slightly with her open hand, as if hiding it from me. "What's happening?" she asked. "Everybody is worried about a ship, and then you came back in one, but it's not you they're worried about, is it?"

I shook my head, and told her the tale of the mercenaries and Islandia.

She didn't interrupt, but just sat quietly, her eyes focused in front of her. From experience, I knew she wouldn't miss a word. At the end, she looked up at me. "What now? What will the Council and Akashi and his Chiefs do?"

"We're taking most of the people out of Artistos and grouping them with members of the two bands, sending people off in small groups as if they were roamers."

"But won't small groups have more trouble defending themselves?"

"Yes." I had raised that topic in the meeting. "But Artistos is not built to be defended. It can be attacked from three sides—from the High Road going down, from the side where we have the farms and hebra barns and stuff, and from the air." I winced, picturing our cabin and greenhouse blown up, Windy dying in the paddock. "The Star Mercenaries have at least five skimmers and maybe they can even use their big ship to attack us. I don't know about that."

She frowned, and went right to the heart of the matter. "It's going to be tough to live out here with townies. They don't know what to do. Some of them will die."

I sighed. "If everyone stays in town, maybe they'll all die at once. This isn't very good, but it's better. Besides, I asked for you and Sky to come to our cave. That's where Kayleen and Liam and I will be, and I want you with me. I'll need friends."

She smiled, pleased. I blew out an inner breath of relief. At least she wanted to come.

"Will Mom and Dad let me go?" she asked.

"Akashi and the Chiefs and Tom are making decisions. They said they'd do this. Besides, you're almost grown-up. Look how well you took care of my wagon."

She ducked and looked away, then back. "It was nothing. I missed you, too. When we saw that damned machine bob its wings and fly away, I didn't know what to think. Akashi told me he'd seen it before, that it belonged to you all, that you must be doing something important." She looked up at me, her dark hair falling across one brown eye, the wide white streak of hair down the right side of her head shining in the sun. "I wished every day for you to come back safely."

She lifted her hands and I saw that she was nearly done making a beaded sash. She held it up for me to see. It was knotted thread spun from hebra wool and dyed in reds and greens from local plants. Every few inches, she'd worked a row of tiny wooden beads into the design. "I made the beads myself."

I cupped the soft belt in my hand, feeling the fine knots and admiring the intricate designs and tiny round wooden and stone beads. "It's beautiful."

"I made it for you," she said. "I put a wish for your safety into every knot." Her eyes shone. "And now you've come back." She glanced down at the belt. "I can finish it tonight. I heard . . . I heard we might be attacked."

She had been conceived during the last of the war, and born after it finished. I swallowed. "I think it's worse for Fremont than the ship my parents came on."

She pursed her lips and glanced away and then back. "We'll be okay," she said. "I know we will."

"We'll have to be." I took the belt from her and held it in one hand, running my other hand along its surface. There must be hundreds of knots. Maybe thousands. Thousands of wishes. Maybe Sasha's wishes *had* helped us the day we let the dogs onto the strangers and fled. Surely something had—we were all here, all safe. "This is the most beautiful work I've ever seen."

Sasha spoke quietly. "Just let it keep you safe."

"Thank you." I handed her the belt and cupped her chin in my hand. "And I will make a wish for your safety every day."

She smiled. "Come on. Let's go see Stripes."

I thought of Windy and swallowed hard. I *would* wish for Sasha's and Stripes's safety every day, too. For everyone's.

ENGAGEMENT

Morning sunlight danced brightly on the rocks outside the Cave of Power. Kayleen paced between me and Liam and the sunshine, blocking the light and freeing it, back and forth on the ledge just under the cave's opening. She had arrived home late the night before, after a visit with Paloma and her new wandering band of science guild members. "Paloma figured out how to make a new salve that heals burns faster than her old one, and she found a new plant that she says has possibilities for headaches." She eyed me and made an exaggerated face. "She says she should have been a roamer all along, and wants to know why you didn't take her with you when you went to the band."

I laughed, but I couldn't help searching her green eyes for any sign that she might not be all right. For the first few days after we'd come back, I'd sworn I often saw a crazy girl peering at me from under her long dark lashes. But as hours dragged into days, into weeks, the crazy girl inside my friend came out less often. She looked haunted this morning, but all three of us looked haunted. And we were: by lack of sleep, by our own demons, and by the questions in everyone else's eyes. The Star Mercenaries had stayed put on Islandia without so much as a skimmer sortie our way. Three weeks of convincing people to stay away from their homes had worn us out, worn out Gianna, and Akashi, and Nava, and Hunter. *They* still believed, but for how long?

And why the wait anyway? To drive us nuts? Did we damage them enough they had to pause and fix the *Dawnforce?* Or had Kayleen been wrong, and they really didn't mean to kill us after all?

Kayleen stared in the general direction of Islandia. "They're coming. Soon. I feel it, like there's a shaking in the air. Maybe this morning." She took my hand and squeezed it. "Come with me. Let's get out of this cave and head down the High Road. Not all the way, but down to View Bend." She licked her lips. "Maybe we can see the skimmers in time to warn people."

Liam said, "We should bring food and water."

"I'll get it." I turned toward the makeshift communal kitchen.

Sky and Sasha were setting up for the group breakfast: dried apples from our stores, dried djuri jerky, and a plethora of fresh berries gathered the day before from high up along the ridges. As Sky bent down to set the food out, her long dark braids periodically swept at the table like little brooms. She looked up as I came near. "What can I get you?"

"Some of all of that, and water." I looked from Sky to Sasha, making sure I had both of their attention. "Kayleen thinks they might come today."

Sky frowned at me. "That's not the first time she's said so."

I hoped *they* weren't joining the community of skeptics. "Please stay alert. We need you all to worry even if some of the townies won't."

"We will," Sasha said. "You can count on us."

I loved her for her loyalty.

Sky began to gather berries into a soft bed of leaves, and I chose three strips of jerky from the smallish pile on the table. Supplies were already dwindling. "How are you holding up?" I asked them.

Sasha smiled at me. "Better than the townies. They're whining to go home. Stile is on your side, and Hunter, and most of us roamers."

I put a hand on Sasha's soft, dark head. "It'll be okay. Hunter will keep them here. He promised us."

Sky finished wrapping up the berries and handed the compact package to me. "I don't know. There's more people grumbling about work than doing work."

I tucked the berries, jerky, and some water into my small traveling pack. "I know. You do more than your share of the chores."

Sky gave me a wan smile. "We've always helped protect the town. This is only a little worse."

"If nobody attacks us today, we'll hunt tomorrow."

Sasha's eyes flicked to the table. "That would be good. The townies will be unbearable if they get hungry."

"I know." War preparation had turned out to be less about weapons than food. "I'll find you two tonight, and we can plan some games for the kids, keep them busy and happy."

Keep the kids happy, and you kept the adults happy. Most of the families had been sent off with bands farther away, but we'd kept Eric the Shoemaker, since he was good at designing and making things, and he had two daughters. One of the doctors stayed with us too, Doctor Hij, and he and his wife had three kids.

Sasha lifted a hand to my waist, where I wore the sash she'd knotted for me. "Stay safe," she said.

I ruffled her hair one more time, and she beamed up at me, her face alight. "I will," I said. "You stay safe, too."

"I wish I could go with you." Sky frowned at me, one hand on her hip. "I understand why the townies want to go home. I'm trapped inside this cave."

"I know," I said. She deserved to go, but we couldn't take original humans. Sky would never be able to keep up with us. "We'll take you hunting tomorrow."

She narrowed her eyes at my answer, unsatisfied. "Will you be back before dark?"

I nodded. "Sure we will. See you then." It had been a good move to keep those two here—they were both very good with people, and in spite of their teasing, they cared about the townies. I turned one more time on my way out. "We'll call if anything happens. Listen, okay?" Liam carried one of the rare earsets, and the camp had one, too.

Sky jerked her head toward Sasha. "This one has listening duty right after breakfast. I'll be sure she pays attention."

I laughed. One of the most important jobs, and one of the most boring. Good thing Sasha was patient.

Kayleen and Liam stood where I had left them, holding hands and gazing out in the general direction of the town. I wriggled in between, savoring the smell and feel of them. We were seldom alone together. Kayleen worked the nets everywhere, traveling, and Liam and I stuck in the cave and around the lake, hunting and studying weapons and data buttons.

At least we would be together and alone today.

After scrambling down the path from the cave, we fanned out along the High Road. Kayleen led us quickly down, her feet almost a blur. A light wind full of blooming redberry scent and dust cooled our sweaty faces.

We threaded through the old rock fall and stopped at View Bend, the best overlook for Artistos. Here, the High Road curved out, its edge near a sharp drop down to the Lace Forest, and then Artistos below. Kayleen led us to the overgrown rocks between the road and the steep drop-off.

Two hours had passed since we left the cave, and the sun now warmed our backs and cheeks. The night-closing flowers along the edge had opened like bells, and the summer's growth of trip-vine waved ominously around our feet. We looked down on Artistos.

A thin tendril of smoke curled up from one of the common kitchens. A handful of people moved slowly about the apple orchard, tending trees.

The crippled, old, and crazy. Left behind to tend crops. The culture guild, monitored by a handful of townspeople and roamers who'd volunteered to stay. From this distance, it was impossible to tell who was who.

Kayleen pursed her lips. "I don't like people being down there." Her voice dropped to a whisper and she turned to fix me and Liam in her gaze, her blue eyes wide. "They're coming."

I glanced toward the ribbon of sea brightening the horizon beyond Artistos, beyond the Grass Plains. Sunlight glinted off a pair of skimmers. No, three skimmers.

I squeezed her hand, whispering. "Now what? What can we possibly do?"

She shook her head. She closed her eyes tightly, gone searching for them in the nets. "I can't feel them."

Liam spoke low and forcefully into the earset. "Three enemy skimmers above the Grass Plains. A few moments from Artistos."

I took a deep breath to calm my stomach. The day was bright and blue and green, and a little gold. Everything below us sparkled with hope and peace—except for the sun on the three skimmers. Tears sprang to my eyes.

The War Council had ordered us not to participate directly in any defense.

The tiny figures in the apple orchard scattered, running for the metal shop and the storage buildings.

Two skimmers slowed and looked ready to land. The third climbed. The cave! I grabbed Liam's arm. He mouthed the word "no," then spoke into the earset. "Ware the cave. One headed toward you. Go deep."

The *Burning Void* fit inside the Cave of Power. But the invaders' skimmers were bigger. So if everyone went deep inside they might be okay. We'd drilled for it.

One of us should have stayed behind.

Hunter was there. He'd keep people safe.

My blood raced and my heart pounded in my ears, and I stood trembling, waiting, adrenaline coursing through my body, demanding action.

The higher skimmer circled, while the other two landed in the unharvested hay fields out beyond the hebra barns. So it was protecting the other two. Maybe it wasn't going all the way to the cave. I glanced at Liam, who shook his head. He whispered, as if the noisy faraway skimmers had ears. "Let them hide. They'll be safer."

Figures climbed out of the big skimmers. Kayleen whispered, "Ten each. That's twenty. Plus whatever's in the other skimmer."

More than half their total force. They were serious. Except they hadn't brought the *Dawnforce*. Surely, they couldn't wipe out the town with three skimmers. Or could they?

The third skimmer continued to circle. It didn't land. At one point in its circle it came close to the High Road, still below us, but too close. Kayleen murmured, "Please don't see us."

Someone came out from Artistos to meet the mercenaries, walking slowly, his hands open. He or she fell before they even got close.

Kayleen gasped and my tears slipped free. But anger followed them—a hard, hot anger that demanded voice. I bit my tongue to keep from screaming both at what was happening and that I couldn't stop it.

The invaders moved through town in two groups. Two more people fell, silently, surely killed. I flinched each time. Once, three people rushed at the invaders. "Fools! Hide!" Liam hissed.

But no one heard him.

They died, too.

Birds sang all around us. The sun shone on our arms and haloed Kayleen's red hair and people below us died.

I held my breath. Liam spoke quietly into the earset, relaying what he saw. "One group just went into the science guild. The second one is walking through Commons Park. They're heading for the amphitheater." The invaders crossed the street and went into the park.

One of them fell.

They all turned together. A body fell from the canopy, landing at the feet of the invaders. The mercenaries leaned down and helped their fallen comrade stand, and they all kept going, ignoring the body on the ground. Apparently the death hadn't bought us anything.

"Look," Kayleen whispered sharply, pointing.

I followed her finger, saw the invaders who had gone into the science guild. Every one carried something. Smoke curled up from the roof of the Guild Hall. I ground my teeth while tears stung my eyes again. So much knowledge there. Our main computers. Gianna's best telescope. The special chair Steven had made for Joseph so many years ago.

"The granary," Liam said. A second fire, in our biggest food storage area, where the grains and gathered grass and dried corn were all stored. We'd taken much of it to the cave, spread it among the bands, but more than half remained.

It burned well.

A silo erupted, flames shooting into the air. From above like this, it looked like a giant candle.

Liam kept narrating into the earset. "Both groups are heading back to their skimmer. The third one is still in the air. The north granary and the Guild Hall are burning. The Guild fire could spread." The granaries all stood alone, but the Guild Halls stood in a row just across the street from the park. Liam grabbed my hand, holding it tightly, and I held Kayleen's, my gaze glued to the scene in front of me. The two skimmers rose up and streaked toward Little Lace Lake.

"Where are they going?"

"I don't know." Liam watched the third skimmer, which stopped circling and followed the others.

THE BURNING GUILD

We watched the skimmers veer into the hills where our people were scattered. I said a silent prayer for everyone's safety, including special ones for Sasha, Akashi, and Mayah. And Stripes.

Below us, smoke rose from Artistos, a scent of war carried up to us on thermals. "Can we go down there?" Kayleen asked. "Maybe we can help someone."

Damn our promises. I started down, and they followed, all three of us running. From time to time I looked up over my shoulder but the sky stayed clear.

Halfway down, Liam grabbed my arm, stopping me hard. I turned, panting. He pointed to his earset. Kayleen, ahead of us, stopped and came back. Liam nodded, color bleeding from his face. His right hand started to shake, and Kayleen took it in hers. I put my hand on top of hers. Whatever it was, we were together.

"Have you seen my dad?" Liam queried whoever was on the other end of the earset. He paused, then said, "Okay—we'll go. I'll report in"—he glanced down at Artistos—"in an hour. Can everyone report then? Thirteen hundred hours?" He nodded and his blue eyes flicked to meet our gaze. His free hand came up and covered ours. His voice shook. "They split up and went after three places. The cave, and two bands."

"Is everyone okay?" I asked.

He blinked back tears and cleared his throat, his face a mask of controlled fury. "There's no list of the dead yet."

"Are Akashi and Mayah okay?"

"Mom's hurt. Not badly—it's her wrist—and they haven't seen Dad yet. But he was in-between bands, so they think he's okay." He swallowed and glanced up at the sky and back down at us. "I'm sure he's okay." At the bottom of our pile of hands, his fist clenched, a hard rock inside our clutching fingers, and his hand on top of mine squeezed hard. "There's more." He pulled his hands free and gathered us both into his arms. "Gianna. They killed Gianna. And a few at the cave, but no one there has reported out yet."

Not Gianna. We needed Gianna. She was our best scientist. My friend! Who else? "Sasha," I said. "Sasha had radio duty."

"Apparently she's not talking. Maybe she's okay." He glanced downward. "Look, we're closest to Artistos and no one is reporting from there. I said we'd check and report back—see if we can help. The skimmers are gone." He looked at Kayleen.

She lowered her head and closed her tear-filled eyes. When she opened them again, they didn't quite focus right. Her voice squeaked out. "They're gone." She ran her hands through her hair and shook her head, hard. "Let's go."

But Sasha. And Gianna. And Liam would want to be with Mayah. I glanced down at Artistos, torn. In war, who the hell got to do what they wanted? When had I, ever, anyway? I took off down the hard-packed path to Artistos. The others' footsteps pounded behind me.

We passed Little Lace Park and plunged down the gentle slope to Artistos. Wind brought the brown-gray smoke of the Guild Hall and granary fires to us, like a stink of burning dinner spiced with things never meant to burn. It stung my eyes. At the edge of town, we stopped, looking frantically around. Where to go?

"I'll check the park," I said, swallowing, breathing hard from the run, tasting the sharp, acrid smoke.

Kayleen grabbed my hand.

Liam barked, "We stay together."

"Then follow me." I took off for the park, knowing we'd seen a body drop there. It proved easy to find. Rory, an older man with a lame foot and a rattle in his chest, unable to move far in life. Maybe that was why he'd climbed a tree.

One of Rory's legs bent backward at the wrong angle and a white shard of bone protruded from just above one wrist. He must have fallen on it. A small pool of blood blackened the grass under the break. His empty eyes gazed upward from a face set in a slightly surprised expression. I knelt by him, touching his cold skin. His hand wasn't yet stiff, and felt cool and heavy in mine. I shivered. Death was familiar in Artistos, but Fremont had not killed this gentle old man.

When I was a little girl, he had made me a toy doll from wintersticks and I had kept it until spring, dressing it in tiny clothes Therese had helped me fashion from scraps.

Kayleen pulled at my shoulder, her voice agitated. "Let's go. Let's find survivors." I let Rory's hand slide from mine, squeezing it gently, and pushed myself up. Kayleen's face was as white as the corpse at my feet. Liam looked past us, then yelled, "Hello!" and took off running, calling back, "Come on!" over his shoulder.

We raced across the street, and over to the burning Guild Hall just as a corner of the wooden roof crashed inward.

"Here!" a frantic voice called. We ran toward it, making out a knot of about fifteen people surrounding Stile. Firelight glinted on metal buckets as a tall man handed them out. Two hoses snaked out from a hole in the road. The grate that had once covered the hole rested to the side, serving as a staging spot for buckets filled from two spigots set into a metal box and linked to the town's water system. We'd planned for fires, drilled every year for fires, but never, ever, actually fought one in town.

Stile called out, "Kayleen, Chelo, Liam. Can you help?"

We consulted each other with a glance. I looked at the burning building. "Sure!" I called back.

In moments, I lost Liam and Kayleen in the smoke and the crowd. Stile assigned me to work with Gil, an older man with a scar across his cheek from the last war. And Klia, the small, nasty, dark-haired girl who Kayleen had said wanted to kill her. She snarled at me as I came up, her dark blue eyes full of hatred and her mouth twisted into a tiny, vicious frown. "This is all your fault."

She'd never been nice to me. Damn her and all her friends. "I'm trying to help," I snapped, my jaw tight.

She tossed me a bucket, her face a hard, angry mask. "So use your powers to put this out."

I glared at the inferno licking along the roof-line of the Guild Hall, filling the windows with a red-orange curtain. None of my differences would help here, except maybe strength. "It's going to take us all," I snapped back. My fists balled of their own accord, remembering that her best friend Garmin had beaten Bryan. But this wasn't the time.

Gil glared at us both and went and threw the water in his bucket on the outside wall nearest the next-closest Guild Hall—the farmers' big square building. We followed, working side by side in silence. I *could* carry more water in each bucket, but all of our work was nearly nothing next to the two teams that had hoses. Liam stood at the base of Farmers Hall, leaning back, pointing the biggest hose, the one reserved just for firefighting, at the roof of the hall. His whole upper body was tight and braced, his lips a thin, concentrated line, his gaze fixed on the roof.

I held my bucket under the stream of water from the spigot, glancing briefly at the tall, licking flames. There weren't enough of us. Throwing buckets of water felt like fighting a paw-cat with a fly swatter, but the steady, hurried effort felt good. I threw my water as if each bucket hit the mercenaries, as if I threw each one on Ghita or Lushia, slowly drowning them. A terrible rhythm took me, fill and race and throw, fill and race and throw, fill and race and throw.

Smoke stung my eyes and lodged in my lungs. The heat near the fire pushed at me like a wall, receding as I ran to the spigot, greeting me angrily as I approached it. Again, and again, and again.

Stile changed out the people holding the other hose, but Liam shook his head and kept going, standing closer to the fire than anyone, sweat streaming down his back, steam billowing up in front of him.

"Was anyone in there?" I asked Gil, when I stopped to swipe sweaty hair from my brow.

"I don't know," he gasped. "I don't know where anybody was. They came so quick." He turned back to his work, and me to mine, and a half-hour later the flames had eaten everything big in the Guild Hall. The water-soaked remains were more mush than hot coal, peppered with white smoke from a few remaining hot spots.

Farmers Hall still stood, the paint blistered on the side closest to the destroyed Science Guild.

Stile called out, "Break," and we all stood in a knot, sweaty and soot-streaked and soaked, watching smoke and steam rise from the ruined hall.

Bits of blackened, twisted metal and one full and straight metal door-frame stood amidst the ash and destruction.

Gianna would hate this desecration. Gianna. I closed my eyes and swayed, and Liam and Kayleen found me, and we stood together, catching our breath. Liam's arms shook, and as tired as I was, he let me take most of his weight.

Kayleen lay down in the middle of the street and closed her eyes, her hands twitching over her stomach. She'd fallen into the nets. Her face had gone white under the grime covering her cheeks and hair.

Stile's voice rang out over us even before I'd properly caught my breath. "Chelo—you and Liam and Gil and Londi stay here, make sure this doesn't spread. Everyone else—check the granaries."

I looked down at Kayleen, calling to Stile. "Can you stay? Or keep a few more here? We need to look out for Kayleen."

Liam stopped leaning so hard on me and swiped at his long hair, mussed from the firefight. "I need to go see what's happening. I'm late reporting back."

I nodded. "I'll watch her."

He took off, racing away, his gait uneven with exhaustion.

Stile came up next to me, standing beside me, so both of us stared down at Kayleen. "She looks bad. Is she okay?"

I swallowed. "I hope so."

"Look," he said, "Gianna left me in charge. I have to go." He glanced around. "Klia, can you stay?"

Not her. I was too damned weary to argue.

Stile needed to know what we knew. I grabbed the strong bicep of his good arm and looked into his brown eyes. "We heard Gianna's dead. They told Liam that right off."

His face crumpled in on itself and he dropped his head, hiding his expression from me. "All the more reason I have to see what else has happened." His voice cracked as he said, "Chelo, there are so few of us. And they were so fast. We sent Hal out to meet them, to see if they'd talk, and they just—they just—they just killed him. I don't even know how. And him an old man past seventy." He looked back down at Kayleen, his face softening, his brow furrowing in worry.

"Take care of her. We need her." Then he was gone, running fast, following Liam.

I hadn't told him to take Klia with him. I knelt down by Kayleen's head, running my fingers across her forehead, ignoring Klia, who stood near Kayleen's feet, shifting uneasily. Kayleen moaned softly and her hands came up in front of her face, clawed and rigid.

"What's she doing?" Klia asked.

I shook my head, reaching my hands for Kayleen's shoulders, kneading them, treating her like I used to treat Joseph, being there for her as gently as possible, but firm enough she'd know. "I expect she's trying to save us," I snapped.

Klia grunted and fell silent.

I focused completely on Kayleen. She dropped her hands and tilted her head back, licking her lips. I cupped her head in my palms, keeping her from smacking it against the hard pavement. I glanced around. Klia was the only one close enough to hear me. "Can you get us some water?"

I thought she wouldn't go, but she shrugged. "Sure." She wandered off, looking as lost as she did angry. Moments later, she handed me a glass of fairly clear water. Bits of ash floated on top. "Thanks." I took the water and bathed Kayleen's dirty face with one hand, still cupping her head with the other, murmuring to her, "The fire's out; we did well. You helped." I put a finger of water against her lips and she opened them, licking for more. I fed her that way, with my fingers. "Liam and Stile went off to see what else they could learn. Liam will report in and see what's happened everywhere else." My chest tightened. Sasha! Sky! Surely Akashi had reported in by now. "They'll be back soon."

Klia knelt down next to me, catching my attention with her gaze. I let my prattle trail away, watching her. For once, she wasn't sneering at me. Instead she said, "Thanks for helping with the fire."

"We've always helped."

She frowned, then looked over at the burned hulk of a building. "Yeah, it was your guild." Her eyes filmed over with tears and one fell, making a clean streak in the ash covering her face. "You weren't here to help the Culture Guild."

Like I didn't know that.

Kayleen suddenly pushed up, sitting with her back totally straight, her legs tucked under her to one side. "They've gone. They won't be back for a bit." She swiped at her hair, tugging on it, as if pulling herself here with me. "I found a net-hole—a way in through one of their skimmers. Ghita's on it. She's gleeful. They think they've killed thirty or forty of us. They'll be back." She frowned, opening her eyes, staring at her feet. "Ghita wants to come back tomorrow, and again until they're done, and leave. But Lushia's stopping her. I heard them argue. They're watching us. They want to see what we do. That's why they took the stuff from the Guild Hall before they burned it down. Ghita doesn't like it. But that's why they didn't just kill everybody. Lushia said, 'Go slowly. They're just as dead, and we're in no hurry.' She said she doesn't have any word from home yet."

"Word about what?" I asked.

She shook her head. "I don't know. All I could access was a vidcam. And that's gone now; they're too far away." She sounded terribly tired, but she struggled up to sit awkwardly, leaning back on her hands because of her baby.

She looked up and noticed Klia. "Why are *you* here?"

"Stile told me to help Chelo." Klia was still frowning, but her eyes were filled with curiosity. "How do you know these things?"

Kayleen narrowed her eyes, I remembered she'd said she might kill Klia. I put a hand on her back, trying to calm her. She took a deep breath. "I can read their nets, sometimes. Not much anymore. But I read them a lot the first day."

"Would they be here if you weren't here?" Klia asked, her eyes narrow and her lips a thin, tight line.

"Yes," Kayleen said. "But they might not be here today if our parents hadn't come. But someone was going to, someday." Her voice was controlled and very, very clear, as if she was educating a child instead of talking to someone our age.

Klia nodded and then turned away. I couldn't tell if she believed Kayleen.

"Chelo!" Liam's voice called out. "Chelo! Is Kayleen all right?" He ran up panting. "We've done everything here, and Stile has an earset now—so we can talk to him. Hunter wants us back up at the cave."

"Is Akashi okay?" I asked.

"Yes. He's okay."

I breathed out a deep sigh, shaking with relief. Kayleen squeezed my hand hard.

"And they found Sasha. She's alive, too. She has a broken leg."

"I'm so glad." A leg. That was okay. It wasn't her. Maybe my wishes had kept her from being killed. I fingered the belt she'd made me, whispering a small "thank you" to whatever powers kept her safe. I glanced at Liam. "Sky?"

"I don't know." He held his hand out, helping Kayleen up first, and then me.

Before leaving, I hesitated a moment, gazing at Klia. "Thanks, and good luck."

She didn't look at us. "You, too," she whispered.

And then Liam and Kayleen and I were running back up the High Road, holding hands. I needed their hands—to stay upright, to feel safe, to pull me along to the next awful thing.

42

THE NEXT AWFUL THING

Soft sobs and whispered voices floated toward the entrance from one of the deeper chambers of the cave as we levered ourselves down into the entrance. I blinked at the empty, messy kitchen area. Water dripped from the table, pitchers lay overturned, and something dark stained one corner of the table and the floor.

The scratch of small stones against the cave floor drew my attention past the table, near the ladder the others used to climb in and out. Hunter sat silently, watching three still forms stretched out under blankets, their faces covered.

The dead.

Hunter looked up at us and spoke quietly. "I'm glad you're okay."

"And you," I replied. The three of us gathered near the heads of the shrouded figures, close to Hunter, looking down. We held our silence, and Hunter held his. The spot we stood on, the three shrouded bodies, Hunter's quiet vigil, it all seemed somehow separate from the noises coming from deeper in the cave, sacred and sad.

Kayleen bent down and slowly uncovered the face closest to us. One of the townies who had come with us, Lourdes, a taciturn woman who had worked quietly and hard with the farm crew. Her face was undamaged, her eyes closed, her expression calm. I swallowed and put my hand in Liam's, anger closing my throat tightly around my breath. I only knew her in passing, but Lourdes had been a familiar face, a kind, quiet woman. Kayleen put her fingers to her lips, touched Lourdes's forehead softly, and covered her face again.

Kayleen gently pulled the next blanket back, and all three of us gasped. Eric the Shoemaker. One of the few people from Artistos who had stood up for us from the beginning. He'd always laughed at Kayleen's big feet, cheerfully building new lasts, teasing her every time she saw him. Once we got the group settled in the cave, he'd helped us make slings to carry crazy-balls and patiently, carefully puzzled out how to use some of the other weapons. We'd had a party for his daughter Sudie's eighth birthday just last week, and he'd given her a beautiful toy hebra he had carved himself from tent tree heartwood. I winced, remembering how her face had lit up.

Kayleen blessed Eric the way she had blessed Lourdes, with a kiss and gentle brush of fingertips.

Who would make Kayleen shoes now?

One of her tears fell silently onto the blanket as she covered Eric's white, dead face.

The last sightless face belonged to one of the roamers, Walter, an East Band member Liam knew well. Liam's age. I turned my face away and buried it in Liam's shoulder, putting my arm up across his back and pulling him close, offering and needing comfort.

What if it had been Liam?

He returned my embrace, his cheek resting on top of my head. A small, strangled noise escaped his throat. By the time I turned around, Walter's face was covered again, and the three bodies looked like they had when we found them.

Liam and I sat down near Hunter. Kayleen stood, staring quietly down at the dead, her dark hair fallen over her face, masking her expression. After a few moments, she turned and joined us. We made a small circle on the smooth stone of the cave mouth. Hunter coughed and looked at us with calm, appraising eyes. "Stile tells me the Farm Guild Hall would have burned, too, without your help. Maybe more." He reached a gnarled hand to Kayleen's face and ran it down her cheek. "I'm sorry I ever doubted you." He glanced at the shrouded figures. "Eric used to argue with me about you, tell me I was worrying for no reason."

Kayleen managed a tiny smile. Her voice came out a little cracked. "Just don't doubt us again, okay?"

We stayed silent for a moment, the new losses sinking in. Night birds called to each other outside, as if the world were normal and we weren't huddled next to dead friends waiting for the next awful part of an awful day. "How's Sasha?" I asked. "I heard she broke her leg."

He grimaced. "She'll be okay. It's a clean break. They shot the ladder out from under her. She was heading for higher ground so her earset could connect with all the roving bands. There's only four or five injuries here, since you warned us and most people went deep." He waved his hands at the three bodies. "Everyone dead or hurt here was scouting or watching, except Lourdes, who came up to the kitchen to get water for the kids. Some of the other bands lost a lot more people."

"What about Sky?" Kayleen asked.

"She's okay. She's with Sasha. Everyone's scared—especially the ones like Sky and Sasha"—he glanced up at us—"and you, too young to remember the last war."

Liam let Hunter's comment go and whispered, "So what happened here? I didn't see how they died."

Hunter pointed his gnarled index finger toward the opening of the cave. "They flew there—in toward us. I saw their bright lights coming and heard the engines. I thought they were going to fly straight into the cave and hit the back wall, but then they stopped suddenly, like someone grabbed their tail." He closed his eyes, as if seeing the whole thing again as he told us his story. "The noise the engines made changed, and they backed up real slowly, and little lights blossomed from the front of the wings and from under where the pilot sits. Weapons. They made light, but no noise. I ran and ducked, and so did most of the others.

"But Eric and Lourdes just stood watching, as if the skimmer put them in a trance. Walter tried to get in front of it and shoot at it, and he fell. Then Eric and Lourdes fell." He shifted again, looking over at the covered bodies. "They just fell. Dead. You can't even see what killed them. There are no external wounds."

"And the skimmer just left?" Kayleen prompted.

"I had ducked behind a wall, but I heard it, and it seemed to be having trouble leaving, like it was fighting something. At one point a big flash of light went off, so bright it hurt my eyes. And after that, the skimmer flew away and let us be."

Kayleen narrowed her eyes, looking outward, past the cave mouth. "So the cave's defenses did work. I'm sure what stopped them was the same thing that helps me land, only their machine is just different enough that it doesn't work right." She tugged at her hair, staring at the cave's opening. "Or maybe it was working for them, but they didn't want to land. So they backed away. And maybe that tripped the defense system."

"I hope it broke the skimmer," I said.

Hunter grimaced. "When it flew away it sounded fine." He looked at Kayleen and smiled. "I'll spread the story of the cave's defense system shooting at the skimmer, though. It's been hard to keep people from wandering down in the area where you told us not to go."

Frankly, I think it may have been the first time he really believed us about the cave having defenses. But then, we only knew because Jenna had told us. I wished we'd seen them. "I want to go see Sasha." I turned toward the low murmur of voices that still floated out from deep inside the cave. "Hunter, are you staying here?"

"Wait," he said. "There's more that I need to tell you." He looked up at me as if weighing my ability to hear more bad news. "Nava's dead."

The breath left my body yet again.

Kayleen turned away, looking out toward the cave mouth.

Liam's voice was flat. "How did she die?"

"One of the skimmers targeted her group. Apparently Nava grabbed one of the rocket launchers and they shot her."

How like Nava to die fighting. Poor Tom. Even though I didn't much like Nava, she had been a good leader. She'd even started listening to us as if we had a brain since we got back, like maybe all we'd ever needed to do was stand up to her, only we hadn't known it before. Images danced in my head: Nava and me talking and arguing, Nava cooking stew the day Jinks died. Nava walking half-naked down the hall on her way to get dressed in the morning. Nava pacing and demanding that Joseph fix the nets. The night she and I sat by the water and she told me that our parents' people had killed her father, and that even though we had been just babies, she couldn't trust us because the war cost her so much.

Someone would replace her on the War Council. But who? The

next obvious choices, Wei-Wei or Lyssa, would be disasters. Nava may have been a barrier for us, but she drove the town as one unit, inspiring effort and loyalty as well as bad jokes and frustration. Nava, with her red hair and green eyes and relentless energy, who made everyone work using the sheer force of her personality.

So many dead. All on our side.

Had the mercenaries known Nava led us?

I couldn't stand any more bad news. "Anything else we need to know?" I asked.

"Just that there's a War Council meeting tomorrow up by where the road forks toward Little Lace Lake. Early."

Why did he tell us this? Did he think we should go?

He continued. "If they don't come back before then."

"They won't," Kayleen said.

Hunter looked at her curiously. "Are you sure?"

She smiled, perhaps put off by his seriousness. "As sure as I can be. But nothing is completely sure in war. You told me that yourself."

Hunter smiled back, a tired, slightly sad smile. "Good answer." He glanced over at me. "Now, go on—go see Sasha. She'll be glad of your company. She and Sky have asked about you at least three times."

We found Sky and Sasha in a corner of the bigger of the two rooms that had been turned into temporary housing. There were at least twenty people on the soft rush floor, grouped in twos and threes and fives. Here and there, faces or shoulders or feet were brightly illuminated by the few soft lights built into the walls, or even in a few cases by carefully held candles. Shadows fell every which way. Soft conversation mixed throughout the room so no one set of voices dominated. Everyone looked up as we came in. Some smiled at us, a few looked afraid, and one couple from town that I hardly knew glared at us like unwelcome visitors in our own home.

Sasha sat with her splinted leg in front of her along one wall, playing jump-stones with Timmy, a boy a few years younger than her, just getting the first down fluff of teenage fur on his chin. She looked up as we came over, her face shining. "Sky said you'd be here soon." She grinned. "I heard you guys kept the whole town from burning."

"There were a lot more people than us helping." I sat down next to her, watching Timmy pick up his stones and wander into the crowd. "I didn't mean to stop your game."

She shrugged. "I was winning anyway, and he was getting bored."

"Does your leg hurt?" Kayleen asked as she and Sky sat down.

Other conversations started back up in the room, and I felt less like a specimen on Story Night.

Sasha frowned at her cast. "Not much. But I won't be able to do anything for weeks." She looked up at me. "Now I won't be able to go hunting with you."

"That's okay." We *would* have to hunt soon. Most of the roamers who had chosen the cave were the very young or the old, and the townies raised animals, rather than hunting them.

Sasha would be stranded here for weeks with her leg. Maybe the fight would be over by then. "We'll save at least one whole hide for you," I said.

With that, a satisfied look settled onto Sasha's face, as if seeing us somehow made everything right with the world. She leaned back. "Thanks for warning us. I just knew you'd keep us safe."

I wasn't sure I could keep anyone safe, anywhere. But how could I tell Sasha that?

43

JOINING THE COUNCIL

We waited outside the cave early the next morning, catching Hunter as he came out to go to the War Council. He stopped when he saw our three forms silhouetted against the dawn light. "We're coming with you," I said quietly.

He stood looking at us, not answering, his face unreadable.

"We have to be there," Liam said. "We're not standing by for any more fights."

Kayleen stepped forward and took Hunter's hand. "You said you'd never doubt us again."

He pointed at Kayleen's swelling stomach. "What about your babies? You, at least, are due soon."

She swallowed hard, keeping her gaze on him. "They've a better chance of living if we win."

He grunted. "Ruth will hate you being there." He started up the path. It would be as much approval for our plan as he would ever show directly.

We walked beside Hunter, trying not to show him we were worrying about him. His stride was long and purposeful, but his breath rattled in his chest and we stopped two or three times along the way to rest, pretending it was the pregnancies.

The fork looked deserted when we arrived. We sat by the stream and waited. A few moments later, Kayleen pointed out Tom, riding up on his favorite hebra, Sugar Wheat.

I wished for Stripes for about the fiftieth time since we'd moved to the cave, but the group wisdom had been to keep hebras with the moving bands. I'd see, somehow, that we got at least a few, and that one of them was Stripes. Sasha would like that. But where would we keep them? The same place we kept the goats and chickens the townies wanted to move up? The place that didn't exist?

We'd have to keep them here.

I shook my head at my silliness, watching Tom's face closely as he and Sugar Wheat neared us. The tall, slightly bossy hebra knew me, and she tossed her head and nickered as I took her lead line. Tom clambered down the mounting rope and closed me in a huge hug before turning to greet everyone else. Except for the hug, and a haunted look in his eyes, he seemed pretty normal—jovial, baby-faced, and round everywhere, although not fat. He smiled as he greeted each of the others. If anyone could take the loss of his wife in stride and just keep moving, it would be Tom. But then, he was in charge now.

I frowned. I loved Tom dearly, but he was the quiet half of a dynamic team. How would he do without Nava?

Hunter acknowledged Tom's loss right away, taking Tom's two big hands in his own thin, age-spotted ones. "I'm so sorry. Is there anything we can do?"

Tom shook his head, blinking. For a moment I thought he'd break into tears, but he straightened. "There's no time to mourn." He looked up the path, pointing out Ruth and Akashi, who rode side by side down the trail toward us. Ruth had at least six inches of height on Akashi, who in turn had about six inches of girth on Ruth. Otherwise, they might have been brother and sister, riding easily, both tanned with dark hair shot with gray. Ruth's hair hung down to her slender chest, while Akashi's barely covered his ears.

Ruth glared at us. She had grudgingly accepted Nava's insistence that we attend *some* meetings, but she never said hello, or good-bye, or even looked at us if she didn't have to. Which was fine with me, except she was a strong fighter, and Artistos needed her.

After half an hour of greetings, condolences, and questions, we settled under the rising sun to discuss what to do next. We totaled numbers of dead (forty-three, plus one likely to die in the next few days), and then settled into an uncomfortable silence. Nava had always been the one to plan discussions and drive conclusions home.

Tom shifted and looked away. Akashi cleared his throat. "We should choose how to replace Nava. I nominate Paloma."

Kayleen startled and I glanced sideways at her. We had decided to try and take Nava's place, but did she still want to if it meant unseating her own mother? What was Akashi thinking, anyway? Paloma was a healer, not a fighter.

But maybe that was exactly what a War Council needed. I nodded slightly at Kayleen, signaling for her to decide.

She cleared her throat. "Mom is a good choice. And us."

"No!" Ruth protested.

Akashi held up a hand, silencing her. "Why you?"

I glanced at Akashi and Hunter. I needed both of them to override Ruth. "Because Kayleen can sometimes read their nets. And she can always read ours. With Gianna— Gianna dead—" I swallowed hard. "Without Gianna, we all need Kayleen's skill. After all, just yesterday, she got into their nets and heard them arguing about whether or not to come back today, and Kayleen is pretty sure they won't be back for a few days."

Kayleen's cheeks reddened.

Tom glanced at her. "You really think they won't be back?"

Kayleen looked away. "They will. Soon." She looked back, as if struggling with herself. "I don't think it will be today. I don't think they knew I was listening." She shrugged. "No way to be sure."

Hunter smiled approvingly.

I brought the subject back to us. "And Liam and I are more like them—physically—than any of you. Give us one vote for all three now, you can decide on more later."

Akashi's eyes still held a question and Tom watched us carefully, his features neutral.

I didn't need to look at Ruth.

Kayleen added, "We have skills you need. We can help."

Tom asked, "Are you all sure that you're ready for this?" He looked directly at Kayleen. "Are you okay? Before you disappeared, you didn't look so good, and even right now you look—I don't know. Different."

Liam said, "We are different."

Tom kept his gaze on Kayleen, until she met his eyes squarely and said, "I can do this," her voice even, cool and powerful. Pride called a smile to my face.

Akashi clapped his hands. "Why not?"

Tom nodded.

Ruth glared at us. "How do we know we can trust them? That's like saying the paw-cats can sit with us while we plan how to hunt their kin."

Hunter glanced over at her, his eyes clear. "Maybe we need some paw-cats. They're full adults."

Ruth pointed at us. "As if breeding makes them responsible! What if they have monsters like their parents?"

Liam's steadying hand on my shoulder kept me from leaping up to react.

Akashi, quietly, said, "Those are my grandbabies, Ruth."

She let out a frustrated sigh and turned away. Akashi looked at his son, as if measuring his ability to fulfill this role. Finally Akashi nodded. "I suppose we raised you for this," he said quietly. "I don't like it, and your mom won't like it, but you have to grow up sometime."

Liam smiled softly and nodded. Kayleen sat still, her back straight and her gaze clear and determined. I sighed, wishing yet again we didn't have to be at war.

Ruth growled softly, but let it go. I knew she would be watching for any mistake we made.

44

ARTISTOS LOST

Ruth found our first mistake before the meeting ended. An hour into a long discussion about how to booby-trap the forest around Artistos without hurting ourselves in the process, Ruth stood up to stretch. She gasped, and then glanced down at Kayleen, snapping, "You were wrong!" She turned her attention back to the sky as we all scrambled up. She pointed out over the sea. "Is that their ship?"

Three tiny specks, the skimmers, were in fact followed by a larger one that could surely only be the *Dawnforce*.

Kayleen's hand went to her mouth. "Ghita," she said. "Ghita won."

"Or she heard whatever news she was waiting for," Liam added under his breath while Tom stepped back and began speaking hurriedly into his earset and the others struggled to pick the offending points of dangerous machinery out of the backdrop of puffy morning clouds.

We couldn't see Artistos from the fork. By the time Liam and I arrived at the first good vantage point, the speck of the *Dawnforce* had become as big as our thumbs, and settled onto the field, its malevolent, squat shape towering over the hebra barn.

"We have to get down there," I said.

Liam shook his head. "Wait."

Kayleen caught up to us, her face red with the exertion of running with a baby due any day. She flopped down on her side, looking out over the cliff face. "The skimmers are landing near the ship."

I knelt down next to her, my hand on her arm. "Are you in their data?"

She shook her head, her voice slightly bitter. "After this, I'm not sure I couldn't trust it if I was. Maybe I should just listen to them, and tell everyone the opposite."

"Hey," Liam said, "You're doing the best you can." He knelt on her other side, leaning down and kissing her sweat-streaked forehead. "You told them not to be sure of your conclusion. What more could you have done?"

She didn't look at him. "I don't know."

Tom's voice carried from just above us, still talking into his earset. Ruth walked by his side, silent and somehow accusing simply with her presence. ". . . Stile to get as many people as he can into the forest."

At least Tom was giving direction. To run and hide. The worst part of it was that he was right. I wanted to go down there and make them leave. But we couldn't just chase a spaceship the size of the *Dawnforce* away. I hated it. We should have cleared out the whole town. It was our fault everyone was living with enough unearned sense of security, or at least time, our fault that people were left in town.

Akashi and Hunter caught up with us next. Kayleen stood up, going to Hunter's side. She glanced at Akashi. "I'll go down to the cave with Hunter. You all go on now. You can travel faster without us."

She meant without Hunter. After all, she had beat him here. If Hunter thought of that he was too graceful to show it. "She's right," he said. "Go on."

An hour later, after having promised three times we wouldn't get any closer, Liam and I stood at View Bend again. By the time we got that far, I sounded as winded as Kayleen had on her shorter run. The baby protested, twisting and kicking inside me. I whispered to it. "Shhhh, little one. I'm sorry. I'll keep you safe."

The look Liam gave me telegraphed frustration. "If only we can."

For the second time in two days, we stood far above Artistos, watching helplessly as people we knew died. Right after we'd decided never to let that happen again, to get into the fight and be weapons ourselves.

Tears rolled down my face as I watched, for my baby, our babies, for our people.

People weren't the only casualties. I gasped as one of the skimmers flitted out over the grass plains and dropped something onto the hangar that held the colony's two remaining shuttles to *Traveler*. It exploded in a flash of bright yellow and red, the color quickly engulfed with black smoke.

Barns and houses burned. Not all of them, and in no apparent pattern. Liam fed a steady stream of information into his earset, narrating the chaos.

The mercenaries drove the town goats and the few remaining hebras over a cliff. I cursed as each one fell.

Liam gave up on talking to anyone for a few moments. He leaned into me and said, "They could have just set them free."

45

THE EVE OF BATTLE

The midafternoon sun beat down on my sweaty forehead and my breath came way too shallow and fast for simply finishing the climb from the High Road to just above the Cave of Power. I twisted toward Liam, who sat next to me on the stones covering the cave's entrance, patiently waiting for me to catch my breath and Kayleen to catch up to both of us. Our child kicked hard at my spine, eliciting a groan and a smile. I set Liam's hand down on my belly, and the baby obligingly kicked again. Liam's hand rose and fell as if he stroked a drum. Perhaps the baby felt my apprehension. We were taking the battle to the mercenaries tomorrow at dawn.

Kayleen loped the last bit up the well-worn path toward us, her swollen belly making her ungainly and awkward. She strayed from the path for a moment to look at a small reddish-brown rock, and her feet crushed tiny red and yellow star-flowers.

Kayleen sat beside me, looking out toward Artistos. "I'm scared," she whispered.

"We've waited long enough," I said. The mercenaries had held Artistos a month. Stile and a large group had made it to the cave, but eighteen people hadn't. No funerals had been held, but we counted them among the dead. We had held four funerals for people caught in a raid.

The mercenaries hadn't returned to the cave. Our hope was that one brush with the defense systems had been enough.

Liam stretched, jostling me from my worried review. "At least, this time, *we're* fighting *them*." He grinned, trying to make light even though his eyes were dark and worried. "All of us."

"It still seems to me like they're just waiting for us to attack them," I said.

Kayleen sounded bitter. "And it's better to let them pick us off one by one?"

It wasn't. Besides, too many were spoiling for a fight now. The War Council's decision was to try the same tactic that had worked at the end of the last war . . . a big, decisive battle. We were going to attempt to overwhelm them with numbers. On the surface, it should be easy. Except I was still convinced we were doing exactly what they wanted. But remembering the last advice we'd given, we'd chosen to cast our vote with the others, making it a unanimous decision.

"Well," Kayleen said, "If we're going to fight, then we had better eat." I expected her to lead us down to the cave kitchen, but instead she produced a veritable feast from her backpack. Fresh bread, carrots, dried berries, and three strips of precious djuri jerky. "Remember when I planned that feast on Islandia? At least for this one, we're all together." She smiled a soft intimate smile that included both of us. "And, we're home."

I frowned, reaching for a carrot. "I miss West Home. I'd take Islandia—with no mercenaries—as home against being part of this damned war. If I ever catch whoever sent these people, they're going to wish they hadn't done it."

Liam took a chunk of bread and meat, running a finger along the curve of Kayleen's face. "I'm happy to eat your feast today."

She nodded. "We should sleep too, while we can."

The attack would begin at dawn. I would go with Tom and Paloma, the three of us forming the strategic part of the War Council, while Akashi and Ruth led the two main groups of attackers. Liam would be with his father. Kayleen would stay here, in the cave, listening to their nets and ours as best she could, and relaying information to those of us with precious earsets—Ruth, Akashi, me, Liam, and Stile.

This meal could be our last quiet one together. I didn't have much appetite, but I was no longer eating just for me. I picked up a piece of bread, breaking it into small bite-sized chunks to follow the carrot. The baby in my stomach did a slow, lazy flip and I cupped it, stroking my belly. Such magic in a pain-shot time. I glanced at Kayleen. "What scares you the most?"

"Losing."

I stared out over the hills. We'd set traps in them, but who knew if the mercenaries would walk into them? They'd never been willing to fight with us on the ground. Not once. All of our strategies felt more like hopes. How do you plan against an enemy with so much more technology and strength?

Liam answered my question about his fears. "I'm scared for you and the babies. I wish you weren't in this at all."

"We can't help it," Kayleen and I said together, grinning at each other. We often spoke the same sentences since we became a threesome. "Besides," Kayleen added, "We want you safe, too."

"I won't be safe. But I'll be successful."

"Well, let's hope so." Kayleen's blue eyes glowed. "Because I'm going to help you kill them for the babies."

Liam grunted again, and said, "And for Gianna and Nava and Eric and everyone else."

"And for Windy," Kayleen added.

The bread in my mouth tasted like sawdust.

A crowd filled the cave's mouth, largely shadows, the occasional shaft of light from hand-held flashlights, and a single flower of flickering light from the kitchen fire. We had staged over two hundred fighters in the Cave of Power, waiting to take the most dangerous way down near Artistos—the High Road. Even with two of our three frizzers, tools Jenna had given us years ago to go through Artistos's nets undetected, it was a dangerous approach.

The air crackled with coiled energy and anticipation.

Young men and women wearing forest-colored clothes and light packs stood in groups. Children clung tightly to adults, and parents too old to fight watched, generally silent, offering words of love and hope to their offspring. Sky and Sasha, going down with Liam in the first wave, moved in and out of the kitchen firelight, preparing small packets of food for the fighters. Sasha still limped, but she had been stubborn.

The three of us stood a bit to the side, seeking privacy in these last few moments before Liam and I left. He bounced on the balls of his feet, looking out in the direction of Artistos. We had tried to sleep, succeeding only in sweating and tangling together, Kayleen and I both awkward and Liam shifting between stroking our hair or bellies and sitting up, staring. Now, his face was set, hard, and his jaw tight. He'd cut his hair short, and he looked older for it, and fiercer. Or maybe the fierceness was in his blue eyes. Someone flashed a bright light against Liam's bronzed skin, so that for just a moment he looked like metal.

Fighters lined up to take additional packets from Hunter. Small packets of poisons made by Paloma, some for the water, some for the air. Larger bundles of dried trip-vine thorns and fresh sticker-vine, harvested in the last day or two and kept damp in a barrel of stream water until an hour or so ago. Fremont's wild things, fighting with us instead of against us. Liam left our side to take one, then returned.

A bird-whistle came from above us. Our signal. Liam turned to Kayleen and leaned in over her swollen waist, kissing her fiercely. After they separated, he took the ladder, leading the group out of the cave. I leaned in to Kayleen and kissed her full on the lips, something I almost never did in public. I stroked her cheek, looking into her deep green eyes.

She returned my gaze, steady, but her voice shook as she said, "Good luck."

I swallowed. "Stay safe."

I waited for everyone else before I left, stopping halfway up the ladder to take one more long look at Kayleen. She stood in the kitchen, firelight bathing her face as she watched me go, her hands folded quietly on the shadowed shelf of her belly. Her job would be as hard as ours.

Outside, the silence of early morning filled the air so that every step we took seemed loud enough for Artistos to hear. Destiny shone above us, a small white disc in the sky, the only moon visible. By dawn, when we went in, we would have Hope and Summer as well for a few hours before Destiny set. A three-moon moment, portending luck.

I stayed with the attacking force, and thus with Liam, until they reached the High Road. There, Liam waved at me, a dark movement against a dark time of day. Then he was gone. I watched as two hundred fighters passed me, Sky and Sasha among them, all of them solemn and intent on silence. I closed my eyes, wishing them safe. Sky, Sasha, and Liam would break away to go with Akashi, and Stile would take the rest.

I turned uphill and went on, alone, up the road that they went down, loping as quickly as I could manage, staying near the trees at the side of the road. At the top of the Old Road, Tom and Sugar Wheat met me, Stripes at their side. "All's well so far?" he asked.

"The crew from the cave are on their way. They looked good, ready." They would meet others who had been working their way toward town all day.

Tom dismounted and held out his hands, boosting me high enough onto the mounting strap that I only needed to slide a foot into one more loop before I swung my right leg over the high back of Stripes's saddle. We rode with only the small wedge of moon and stars visible from the deep, steep trail for light, letting the hebras pick their footing. Halfway down the Old Road, we cut right, threading through dense underbrush, trusting the hebras to keep us safe. Tom had put me in front, and except for the occasional snort from Sugar Wheat or the scrape of a cloven hoof against a stone, I might have been riding alone through the darkening woods.

Tom called out from behind. "Go right. The path will look straight up."

I turned Stripes up a tiny side trail and grabbed for the thick hair on top of her neck as she seemed to actually pull vertical for a few strides, her haunches gathering and her head low as she strained to do what I needed. Shortly, it got better, or at least became only nearly straight up. Trees brushed my legs on either side, and I ducked under low-hanging branches. Once, Stripes jumped as something small and furry raced between her legs.

Twenty minutes after we left the Old Road, we broke free of the trees just below the ridgeline. From here, we could see more than from View Bend, could look down onto View Bend and the High Road, in fact. My sharper eyes would be useful here.

"Hello," Paloma called from above me. I turned to see her and her hebra, Sand, resolve as movement from a chaos of dawn-grayed tent-trees, redberry bushes, vine maple, and tall grasses escaped from the plains to find brief purchase on the stony ground. Long shadows cast darkness across about half of the open place, the rest visible now in the first early crack of light. In a few moments, the first sunshine would fall upon us and the battle would begin.

I dismounted and clutched Paloma to me, my heart sinking at how thin her shoulders seemed to have become. "How is Kayleen?" she whispered into my ear.

"She's as well as possible."

"That's good." We held each other, waiting. When light touched the rocks above us directly, I let her go, keeping my silence. I led Stripes toward Sand. Akashi had picked this spot for us. It appeared well-chosen: steep drops and dense forest cover would make it tough for people to find us, and the pile of rocks jumbled at the top would be cover from above if a skimmer came. The sun painted bright orange bottoms on wispy morning clouds, and the tall shadows of Stripes's legs looked like knives.

As soon as the three hebras were tied out to graze on the sparse grass, we gathered close near the rocks, looking down. Artistos did, in fact, lie easily visible below us. From this angle, we saw the fields and the hebra barn first, the cliffs down to the Grass Plains falling to the left. The town itself spread away from us, an uneven rectangle of buildings and streets leading to Commons Park, and beyond, to the Lace River.

"I hope everyone is ready," I said.

Tom pulled Paloma into a sideways embrace, looking down at her tenderly. "I'm sure they are," he whispered. She leaned into him, bending her head down. Her hair had become fully gray in the weeks we'd been home. She had come here ahead of us at her own request, wanting quiet. A healer, she had concocted poisons to kill. The stress of it showed in dark circles smudging her hollowed cheeks and a slumped forward tilt to her slender shoulders.

Still, when she looked up at Tom, a light glow filled her features. During the summer of our trip around Little Lace Lake, all of these relationships had been under the surface—at least me and Liam, and Tom and Paloma. Only my little brother and wild Alicia had come together then.

The three of us waited.

We had decided not to communicate via earset until the fighting started, hoping for surprise. I pictured Kayleen lying down on a blanket in the cave. She'd be near the front, for clear access to the data she needed. Hunter would be beside her, helping her as I would if I were with her. Or at least as well as an original human could help an *altered*. Liam would be nearing the town, creeping up on it, using his frizzer in hopes of avoiding an early alarm, following a least-surveillance path Kayleen had mapped out for him the day before. Ruth and her group should be below us and to our right.

All told, over a thousand people filled the forest, and five hundred more waited just over the ridge, ready to join the battle. Fifteen hundred against less than fifty, and we worried about whether or not we would have enough.

The whole world seemed to hold its breath, waiting. Even the baby inside me slept, or waited.

ATTACK

I perched on a rock two meters above Paloma and Tom, savoring a moment alone after the frenetic pace of preparation. What did I want? For everyone to live. There were already so many holes in our company. I didn't even want the Star Mercenaries to die. Making them go away would be enough. As if I could hope for such a simple, positive outcome. Even though I'd learned better, it was part of me to hope. Today, hope felt like a curse.

Artistos slept on, unawares. Sunshine painted the flecks of silica in the rock below me with bright colors. It glinted off the top of the *Dawnforce*, slid partway down her squat, silver sides, and then separated individual roof tiles on the hebra barn. If only I could be down there, creeping up on the invaders.

I wasn't *doing* anything. Yet. A fluttering heel-kick to the inside of my belly reminded me why. I folded my stomach, and thus the baby, in my arms, hoping it felt me hold it. Would I even be able to birth it? And into what?

But it wasn't my job to worry, regardless of the fact the baby's very presence made me more afraid of any bad outcome.

My job was to watch.

What to watch for? A puff of smoke? Movement among the trees? The Lace Forest slept below us, the town streets empty.

The first sign of life was Ruth, loud and amazed and proud, in my right ear. A whisper. "We killed one." Because everyone used the same earset frequency, we would all hear. She and her team of two hundred fifty should be flowing down through the Lace Forest. Were they already in town? "The one we saw must have been a guard. It's deserted here."

Kayleen, her voice loud and firm in my ear. Commanding. "Stay slow. Don't set off the perimeters." But one down, and we hadn't lost anyone yet. That I knew of.

Maybe this would work.

Below me, Artistos looked as if it slept.

Kayleen, lower this time. "They know you're there." Silence. "They're chattering."

Was Liam all right? I held my silence, dropping down next to Tom and Paloma. "Be careful jumping with that baby," Paloma cautioned.

"It's started?" Tom asked.

"Yes. Ruth says she killed one."

"I can't see anything," Paloma whispered, standing on tiptoes, craning her neck.

"Over by the River Walk." Tom hissed, pointing.

Squinting, movement resolved into two tiny, barely distinct figures. The strongs, or at least some strongs (whether the ones I had met or not), racing down the neat, even path that ran by the river, fast for all their bulk. I spoke into the earset. "Two fighters headed in from the industrial area. They're running. Watch out!"

A steady, slightly maniacal laugh. Ruth. "Maybe we spooked them."

Maybe you're too sure of yourself. But then, Ruth and her band *were* good hunters. "Maybe. They're coming *toward* you. Watch yourself."

No laugh this time. "I will."

Liam. He'd be separating from Akashi, skirting town as long as he could, heading for the water system. There had been no particular defenses on our water plant in the past, but Kayleen had told me it was masked from her. Liam would get close, then wait until the battle was more fully joined, hoping to be ignored. He carried poison from Paloma, something meant to kill anyone who drank it.

Paloma squeezed my hand. I glanced at her—fear filled her eyes, and hope. Or maybe the two combined, which Akashi called prayer.

The silence leaked into forever. I filled it with a breaking whisper. "Akashi and his group should be directly between us and the town." He and two hundred fighters took the closest approach to the ship and the camp surrounding it. I couldn't yet see them.

Paloma fidgeted, her hand up to keep the sun out of her eyes. "Do you see Stile?"

Trees obscured much of the view. Sunshine glinted from something, a brief flash, nothing more.

If they knew we were there, they weren't doing anything about it yet. Surely they knew. So why so quiet?

A bright green seed-bird flew out across the open ground only a few meters from us, sat, and cocked its head, regarding Paloma with its small brown eyes. A few of the feathers on its tail were ragged, and one dragged at the bird's feet. A touch of wind brushed my right cheek, a shadow streaked across the ground, and the small bird was caught in the talons of a large day-hunting canopy owl. It didn't even have time to cry out. The owl streaked into the forest with its prize. Surely a bad sign, unless by some miracle, we were the owl. Paloma and I shared a nervous glance and Tom shook his head. "It's nothing. It must be nothing."

Waiting sucked.

Kayleen, in my ear, her voice lightly touched by the craziness that had taken her before. "The alarms! By roamers' field." A high whine hit my ears, and it took a moment to be sure it was from Artistos and not the earset. I stood, craning my neck like Paloma, trying to see. "Stile!" Kayleen called. Anguish broke from her voice into my ear. "Stile! No!" A plaintive, "Anyone?"

And I knew in that moment what we had done to her.

Joseph had been linked to Steven and Therese when they died in the rock fall. It had taken him months to recover.

"Kayleen!" I screamed.

Paloma grabbed my arm, her eyes begging for information. I put a palm softly over her mouth, took a deep breath and reached for more control. Tom came behind her, circling her with his long arms, his round face and round eyes radiating concern.

I had no time for them, only for her. "Kayleen, stay above it. Go out if you have to."

"He's dead. They're all dead."

Just hours ago, they'd been in the cave with us, getting ready, laughing and joking with their loved ones.

Silence. I breathed into it, questing for a different path to focus her down. "Find Akashi, Kayleen." Akashi could hear us. He'd know what was happening. Not that he could help much from wherever he was. But was he okay? "Akashi," I whispered.

He answered. "Take care of Kayleen. We'll take care of ourselves."

"Kayleen," I whispered, picturing her alone with only old Hunter beside her. Hunter was wise and strong, but this was not his job, not something he knew. "Kayleen. What's happening with the others?"

"I . . . I . . . they're all dead."

"Everyone?" I demanded of her. "Or just Stile and his group?"

"S . . . Stile. Stile died."

"So save the others. Pay attention to them." Joseph had shunned the nets entirely for months after the quake, as if the blame for the rock fall had been his. A side effect of hearing our parents' dying screams and being unable to do anything to help them. "Kayleen, stick to just the earset for now, be as blind as I am."

"I . . . I can't."

"You can." I wanted to stroke her face, to hold her. We three had to live, had to be strong.

Akashi whispered in my ear. "We're laying the first of the traps now. We'll be making noise soon."

Hearing his voice sent a relief washing through me.

Tom and Paloma hadn't been able to hear my earset conversations. I tore it from my head, looked full into Paloma's eyes, fixing her in place. "Remember when Mom and Dad died? Remember Joseph?"

She nodded. Tom grimaced. "Yes."

"Something happened to Stile. Maybe to everyone that was with him. I don't know what. Kayleen said he's dead. Akashi is okay. Liam is silent, but he should be. I haven't heard from Ruth for a few moments." Kayleen was in trouble. Tom should be leading this whole damned colony, and he was letting me do it from here. Anger peeled up my spine, forcing clarity. I thrust the earset at him. "Go on. You take it. I'm going to Kayleen."

Tom stood blinking at me, the earset lying in his palm like a small dark bug with a single long tail curled around it.

Other people could help Liam. "I'm going to Kayleen. She needs me."

Tom closed his fist around the earset and glanced down at Artistos.

Smoke rose from at least one place, now. Probably us—we'd agreed that burning might send them out of town. A high squawk came from the earset. Ruth's voice, unintelligible.

She was War Council, like us. I peeled the bud from Tom's inert hand and stuffed it into my ear. "I didn't hear that. Are you okay?"

Labored breath punctuated her words. "Some wounded. Three dead. Can't see anyone."

She would have heard everything I had said on the earset. "Look," I said. "I'm going to Kayleen."

"Everything will be done by the time you get there."

"Then she'll need me."

Akashi's voice. "Travel safe."

"Thank you." I tore the earset free again and thrust it at Tom, not even waiting to be sure he put it on. They'd figure it out. I grabbed Paloma by her shoulders. "I'll keep her safe if I can."

THE RESCUE

I only waited long enough to see Paloma's nod before I raced for Stripes. As soon as I mounted, Stripes turned her head completely around and stared at me, a thing only hebras can do, her ears forward, her head a little cocked. "Go," I urged. "Go, now." I flicked the reins on her slender neck and whether it was the reins, my command, or my feelings that drove her, she raced to the top of the steep path, and started down it with no protest. We hit the Old Road and turned up. Full light illuminated the path. Stripes took it at a pull, rocking as she almost hopped up, then continued to pull, to leap, to clamber. She knew how badly I needed us to move. My knuckles turned white on the saddle-pommel and my free hand, holding the reins, clutched Stripes's neck.

It took forever, and all the time I wanted to scream.

People were dying below me in town. Stripes splashed across a stream, almost lost balance on a slippery rock.

The slender branches of a lace tree tangled in my hair, and I let them pull a chunk loose. How could I have forgotten what Joseph went through?

Liam was down there sneaking toward a dangerous target. Stripes and I were halfway up the Old Road, now. Through the worst part.

Akashi, hopefully, was being chased out of town by mercenaries, drawing them to traps he'd set.

Stripes stepped carefully around a waving trip-vine.

Something flew out of the redberry bushes beside the path and

Stripes—thankfully—just snorted and ignored it, pushing ahead, nearly jumping up the last bit. I patted her neck, and whispered sweet thanks into her back-turned ear. And then the Old Road was behind us and the wide, flatter High Road flashed by beneath Stripes's feet.

Each breath, each moment—they all took forever.

It would be okay. Really, it would. Once I got to Kayleen, I could help her.

I dropped Stripes into the corral near the fork in the High Road, stopping just long enough to strip her tack. She had a stream for water, and enough natural grass to make a meal or ten. Still, for all of Stripes's efforts, and mine, by the time I dropped into the cave, I'd missed at least an hour of the fight.

As expected, Kayleen nested near the opening of the cave. She lay on a pile of blankets, Hunter sitting next to her, rubbing her temples. My heart sank at the sight of the earset in his ear; clearly, Kayleen couldn't manage it right now. He looked up at me, frowning and worried. "She's going in and out. Sometimes she's coherent, sometimes she's yelling and screaming." Her open eyes looked vacant, but she breathed and her skin had some color.

She was safe. Was Liam? "What's happening in Artistos?" I asked Hunter.

"Still no word from Stile or anyone in his crew. Ruth sent part of her band over to look, and hasn't heard back. In the meantime, she's being shot at, but she's trying to see for herself."

"She'll get herself killed. What about Liam?"

He tapped the earset. "I don't know. But Kayleen called his name twice. Likely calling for him. He's stayed silent."

He was supposed to stay silent. He had four people with him, including Sky, a second member of Ruth's band, Londi, and Alyksa, the scout from Akashi's band. Sasha was with Akashi. So maybe they were alive.

I knelt by Kayleen, taking her limp hand in mine, massaging her palm. She blinked, then stiffened, calling out, "Liam!" A tear ran down her cheek, then another. She pulled her hand free and fisted both of her hands, drumming them on the blankets.

"Kayleen!" I called. "Kayleen. Where are you?"

"By the water. It's a trap." She didn't look at me, or acknowledge my presence, but her words were clear and intelligible. "They put traps in all of the infrastructure."

"Liam's okay so far?"

"They don't want him. But that might not keep him safe." She stopped drumming her fingers and sat up straight, suddenly completely alert.

"Why won't that keep him safe?" I asked. "Why don't they want him?" Focusing her on questions might help.

She shook her head. "They don't want any of us." Her voice rose, almost shrill. "I keep telling you. They don't care about the colonists except to kill them."

Hunter grunted. He stepped back and watched us, frowning.

I slid behind Kayleen, kneeling, my oversized belly a hindrance. I held both of her shoulders and dug my thumbs in under her shoulder blades, a firm massage. Joseph and I used to feel like one being in times like this, but Kayleen always seemed separate and herself. Still, I quested for that oneness, tried to get as close to her as I could, to match my breathing to hers. It wasn't working—her neck and back muscles were stiff cords, her energy pulled inside. I asked her, "Why are they watching us?"

She laughed. "They're curious. And they're waiting for something else, too, but I can't tell what."

Hunter interrupted. "Akashi's band is away. But no one's following them."

Damn. All those traps, wasted.

Hunter continued. "Most of Ruth's people who are still alive left, too. All withdrawn. No word from Liam, yet. Paloma is asking for an update on Kayleen."

I glanced at my friend, my lover. Tear-tracks stained her cheeks. Her eyes were slits, focused completely on some spot on a horizon that didn't exist inside the cave. She apparently hadn't heard Hunter's question. "Tell Paloma it will probably be okay." After all, what else could I tell her?

Kayleen looked at Hunter, her lips pulled back in a snarl and her gaze unfocused. I shivered as she said, "Move." She shifted to me. "You too."

Hunter and I shared a confused glance.

Kayleen leapt up. She was past me before I was on my own feet, pelting after her. She headed toward the *Burning Void*, holding her belly tight with one hand and keeping the straggly hair from her face with her other.

The ramp was just touching down as we entered the room that housed the silver skimmer. She took it at a run, with me right behind her, calling her name.

At the top of the ramp, she turned. "Stay, Chelo. Keep at least one of us safe."

I shook my head. "We stay together."

She looked shocked for a moment, gazing at me intently, effectively blocking me from entering by standing in the door. "Then you might die."

I might die anyway. "Let me in. We stay together."

She gestured back toward the cave. "Then who saves these people?"

"We do. Later. You said Lushia and Ghita don't want Liam. You said they want to watch us all. It follows they won't shoot down the skimmer."

The ramp started folding inward, forcing my decision. The baby! I leapt forward anyway, adrenaline and guilt flooding my system. Kayleen was already in her usual pilot position, leaning back in one of the last-row seats. The screen in front of us glowed. The floor thrummed with the warming engines.

I sat beside her, taking her hand.

The skimmer rose and I remembered Hunter, hoping he had understood what Kayleen meant when she said, "Move."

He wasn't visible in the viewscreen as the skimmer took the wide corridor carefully and catapulted out of the cave, accelerating so fast it thrust me back against my seat next to Kayleen.

Outside, we raced through midmorning. Such a short time for so many changes. We had not been the owl. Not so far. And *Burning Void* had no talons except us. I clutched the arm of my seat, fighting nausea.

Kayleen's eyes were closed, her whole self lost in the ship, and perhaps in whatever remained of our data nets. We had no way to communicate with anyone, except perhaps by what we did.

Which was to fly right down into Artistos, forty meters over the town. Commons Park and then the main street flashed beneath us, a whirl of treetops and green, then the straight gray roads and neat houses.

The water treatment plant was near the *Dawnforce*, between the edge of town and the hebra barns, not far from where the Lace River fell down the cliff to the Grass Plains.

Smoke filled the viewscreen as we plunged over something burning. A confused mêlée of ship's uniforms and our wilder clothes, people fighting in close clutches. Some of the faces stopped and looked up.

The *Burning Void* slowed suddenly, engines screeching. I braced, gasping. Kayleen took us down, fast, almost too fast, but she held it, curling around the strangers' camp and down behind the clutch of industrial buildings that included the water treatment plant. The skimmer bounced once as we landed, the ramp already opening. I leapt up, beating Kayleen to the door, looking for Liam. She started to push past me, but I blocked her, yelling, "Where is he?"

She gestured to the right.

"You stay and keep the skimmer ready to go."

Her face closed in for a second, her eyes snapping, but she stepped back, nodding. "Hurry!"

I raced down the ramp, stumbling the last few steps. There was no one visible, then suddenly Alyksa stepped around a corner, staring.

She might not know we had a skimmer.

"It's me," I called.

Her eyes widened as Liam sprinted past her, followed by Sky and Londi. Liam grabbed Alyksa's hand, jerked, and she ran beside him. Three uniformed men followed behind, pelting after the four of them. I turned, racing back to the skimmer. Surely they would follow me.

Londi passed me, his face a mask of determination, his breath loud and fast. Sky followed close behind. Liam swept me up with his other hand, and the three of us followed Sky up the ramp, which started to close as soon as we hit the bottom of it. We tumbled as much as raced into the skimmer. Kayleen's eyes were screwed tight shut, one hand on her belly. Engines whined. Something smacked against the outside of the hull.

We rose.

Something else hit us, a loud crack ripping through the hull, pinging in the empty hold. Alyksa lay on the floor, eyes still wide, her fist in her mouth. Londi took a seat in the front, putting his head between his knees, gripping the chair arms. Sky sat beside him, looking excited. As the thrust of our sudden acceleration grew, Liam and I stumbled against it, pulling back into seats beside Kayleen.

The *Burning Void* yawed right, then left. Kayleen's eyes stayed tightly closed, her face clutched up small.

We raced away from Artistos, the double-horizon lines splitting sky and water, and below, water and the grass plains, dancing drunkenly in the viewscreen. Then just water and sky, blue-green below blue.

The skimmer slowed, and Kayleen opened her eyes. "Is everyone all right?"

Liam clutched her hand. "I didn't get it done." He held up his hand. "I still have the poison."

Sky looked back at us, snapping, "Right. But we were being chased away. You weren't getting close anyway."

"They were pushing you away because they didn't want you to die either," Kayleen said. "The mercenaries saved you before we did."

Sky blinked. Londi stared at Kayleen for a moment, and then Liam, and then me. "Why?"

Kayleen swallowed. Londi and Alyksa were our bandmates, and Sky had helped us with Alicia years ago. These were our friends. How could she help them understand what we didn't? "It's not you. It's us. They came here to kill you—the people who our parents fought. I don't know who sent them . . . but maybe the same people that sent our parents."

Kayleen let a few moments of silence pass, watched as Sky and Londi glanced at each other and then refocused on her, waiting. They had a roamer's sense of curiosity; they'd see the puzzle even if they didn't appreciate it.

"But they found us first. We're like them. *Altered*. They're trying to protect us."

Alyksa asked, "Why?"

Kayleen shook her head. "I wish I knew. It scares me." She paused and put a hand to Liam's cheek. "If you'd gotten inside the plant, you would have died, just like Stile and the people with him."

Liam jerked. "What happened to Stile?"

"He died." Kayleen closed her eyes for a moment, and the skimmer slowed even more, banking gently back toward town. "I was connected to him," she whispered. "Not just the earset, but I could see him and the people with him in the nets. They were stealthing down past Little Lace Park, by the meadow where the wagons go when you're in town. I didn't see any of the mercenaries—I thought everyone was safe. Something came up from the ground, got all over them. At first, Stile and the others with him in front slapped at their legs, as if they were after ankle-eaters."

Ankle-eaters were little bugs that swarmed in summer, leaving painful bites. Enough bites made you sick—Joseph and I had been caught by a swarm of them once.

Alyksa sat up, leaning against the wall by the door, watching us, looking ill.

Kayleen shivered. "But they were worse. Whatever they were seemed to drill inside the skin. Clothes didn't stop them. People started screaming. Stile tried to get them all to turn around, but everyone was stopped dead in place, screaming and looking at each other, like the pain was too much to move with." Her voice shook and she stopped to brush a strand of wild black hair from her eyes. "They just—they started falling down. And they died. I saw them, and I couldn't do anything about it. Stile stayed up the longest even though he was one of the first people hit, and finally his heart stopped and he just dropped down, dead."

"Did anyone get away?" Liam asked.

"Maybe some of the people at the end of line." She paused, rolling her eyes up into her head for a moment. "I didn't see anyone get away."

"What about my dad?" Liam asked.

She nodded. "I think he's okay. He was when we left, but he was fleeing. Everyone fled. We lost."

Liam curled back away for a moment, as if slapped. "There are so many more of us than of them."

"Why did you come for us?" Alyksa asked.

"They put those same things—whatever they were—in some places they thought we might go. The water plant was one of them. They don't seem to use our food, but they use our water." Kayleen clutched Liam's hand. "I didn't want you to die like that."

I shivered at the image, like Kayleen just had, and seeing them all dead—all dead with no real fight—filled my bones with heat and hatred. I didn't like the hatred. It was wrong.

I shook, breathing hard, putting my head down like Londi had. Liam put a hand on my shoulder. "Are you okay?"

"I'm alive." How could I ever be okay again? "So what do we do now? They aren't shooting at us, or following us. Can we help, somehow?" I glanced up. The *Burning Void* had no windows, just the viewscreen, and it showed only the summer sea, laced with wind-born froth.

Liam had an earset. He spoke, the slender tail of the bud picking up his voice. "Dad? Ruth? Tom? How are things?"

He fell silent. Waiting, I went around to stand behind Kayleen, brushing her sweaty hair from her face, gently kneading her shoulders. Alyksa sat near Londi and Sky. Three of us in the back, three of them in the front. Separation.

Liam murmured softly next to me, and Kayleen gasped and held her belly.

"Is the baby coming?" I asked.

Liam lifted his head. "Hunter wants us home. I think we'd better listen. Now."

Damn them. I wanted to help. The strangers probably wouldn't kill us. I mean, they could, any time. But so far, all of our real-world tests suggested safety for us. "Okay—but let's at least fly over Artistos and see what we can report back on."

"No. I need you two out of the battle."

As if on cue, Kayleen groaned and closed her eyes, holding her stomach again. It passed quickly, and when she opened her eyes she grabbed Liam by the shoulder, and used her other hand to pull his face close to hers. "Then you'll stay out, too? You'll stay with me?"

He stared at her for a moment, looking like something trapped, then he relaxed, putting a hand on her belly. "Yes. Of course."

On my sun-drenched rock that morning, I'd wished for everyone to live. We six were still alive. Best to stay that way.

I leaned in over her shoulder, whispering, "Take us home."

PART EIGHT

MY SISTER, MY BROTHER

48

JHERREL

My contractions had stopped being part of me; they had become a terrible force designed to rip my child free of my body. Kayleen and Paloma held my weight, one on each side, forcing me to walk. Sweat poured down my forehead, bathed my chest, dripped from the alien shelf my stomach had become. It stung my eyes, making it hard to see Liam as he bounced Caro, Kayleen's girl, our girl, against his shoulder, patting her back as she made small babbling noises.

The Cave of Power lay too close to Artistos for our comfort after the last, horrid battle. But the *Burning Void* was there, and the invaders hadn't come near it with a skimmer again. So Caro was born there, a day after the worst battle. We still lived there, huddled inside it, going out into the cooling fall to hunt and gather and prepare for the coming winter. There were only half as many mouths to feed, over half still broken into small bands.

For the most part, the mercenaries left them alone, but the groups were small enough—and full of enough townies—that Fremont took its own toll. Ten people (three of them children) lost to the biggest pack of demon dogs ever reported. Two killed by yellow snakes on the same day of two different weeks. Five dead in two separate hunting accidents, two of them townies who simply ran off the end of a cliff together.

Still, many people clustered outside our room, waiting hopefully. They sang a birthing song, more noises than words, a round repeating and repeating, including us as the sound washed in the half-open door of our sleeping space. The song gave rhythm to our steps as we three walked. Liam bounced Caro to the same cadence. Finally, a contraction came so strong it forced me to stop, the pain ripping down my spine.

It passed.

I stood, gasping for air. Paloma handed me a twisted cloth she'd soaked in herbs, and then took Caro from Liam, turning the girl toward us, bouncing her, crooning into Caro's ear.

Liam stood behind me, looping his arms under my armpits, bracing himself to take my weight.

Kayleen knelt between my legs.

Another pain. I bit down on the cloth, my mouth flooding with redberry and mint, and my scream filling the cloth. I screwed my eyes shut, hearing the song and Paloma's voice. "Push."

Pain filled me.

Kayleen called out, "I see the head."

The pain fell away and my lungs demanded air. I put the cloth into Kayleen's hand and panted, counting, waiting.

One. Breathe. Pant.

Two. Breathe. Pant.

Three. Breathe. Pant.

Kayleen dipped her fingers in water and held them to my lips, waiting as I licked them dry.

Another wave rose in me and I opened my mouth for the cloth, biting down as the pain took me out of my body. And so it was from somewhere near the ceiling that I heard Kayleen yelp. I slammed back into my body in time to feel the baby's belly and feet slither from me, free at last.

I barely had time to look down and see the small boy when another roll of pain released the afterbirth. Liam helped me down to my back on soft furs and old bedding, stopping for a moment to stroke my cheek.

I had never felt anything as tender as his hand in that moment.

He leaned down and kissed me, then took Caro so Paloma could wash me. Kayleen knelt and set the babe in my arms, and I looked down at the most perfect face I had ever seen.

Jherrel.

Akashi's father's name. A good name.

Liam, Kayleen, and Caro surrounded us. Caro reached out her hand and touched his soft head, making a cooing noise. Jherrel opened his deep blue eyes and regarded her for a moment, and then rested his head softly against my breast.

Paloma opened the door. The song had already quieted. Hunter came through the door, and then Sky and Sasha, and then others, a stream of well-wishers stopping just long enough to smile and feast their eyes on the babies, to nod and wish us well, and go back out, all quiet and full of joy.

This moment was a treasure. For this moment, it did not matter that we were hunted, that we'd lost people we loved, that we had no ripening crops in this last breath of the harvest season.

49

FACE TO FACE

Jherrel hung in a sling, facing me, his back against Liam's back. He giggled and waved his arms, showing his heritage. Paloma swore the babies would be talking by the time they were six months, even though two-and-a-half-month-old Caro barely babbled nonsense and four-week-old Jherrel's claim to fame was having more control of his fingers and hands than Paloma thought was normal.

Behind me, Kayleen carried Caro in a sling across her stomach. She'd inherited Kayleen's long toes, and Kayleen had wrapped them to keep her side safe from baby-digs.

The early fall sun shone down on us as we headed for late ripening patches of black laceberries on the away-side of the ridge from the Old Road and Artistos. Kayleen pointed at a grove of tall pongaberry trees. "Let's circle by on our way home."

"Eth Mo, eth . . . ba . . . ba," Caro babbled. She had Kayleen's startling blue eyes and Liam's light hair, and a little turned-up nose that came from neither of them.

Liam laughed softly. I put my fingers to my lips. "Shhhh . . . someone will hear you." We were far from Artistos, but I always fretted when the kids were out of the cave. But you couldn't raise healthy babies encased in stone and bathed in artificial light.

This time of year, Fremont's predators were still well-fed and unlikely to bother us during the day, so the mercenaries were our worst worries besides tangling in trip-vine or surprising a yellow snake.

They'd been quiet for a week. Which was no excuse for being lax, but today's perfect light and the trail we chose, mostly covered with trees and near a small stream, combined to make the risk seem small.

Birds sang overhead as we worked our way down the hill. In half an hour we found the first of the laden laceberries, a twenty-meter wall of branches three times our height feasting on a wide patch of sun near a rocky stream. Woody branches sprouted leaves the size of our heads, each leaf a lace, more hole than fiber. The holes were lined with soft furry material that killed insects, and left red welts on human arms. Under each leaf, berries as big as our thumbs and black as the night sky swelled as sunshine poured through the holes in the leaves.

I took the first babysitting turn, sitting in a small, grassy clearing with Jherrel and Caro in my lap. Tent-trees and near-elm rose up behind us, providing reasonable cover from the sky if the invaders' skimmers patrolled today.

Liam pulled a berry picker—a small metal saw fastened above a woven net—from my pack and Kayleen scrounged a long stick for a handle. After they assembled the gear, they wrapped their hands in brain-tanned djuri hide, then stopped by to menace Caro and Jherrel with their newly big hands. Caro laughed, and Jherrel ignored the whole thing, snuggling toward my breast.

Liam and Kayleen each leaned down for a kiss from me. "Watch carefully."

I patted my pocket, where my own first laser gun rested, the one Jenna gave me years ago. "I'll scream if I need anything."

They went to work. I narrated softly for the babies. "See Dad twist the basket, see how he braces as the heavy berries fall. Your mom will hold out her basket, now, and he'll pour his into hers and then start again."

After catching four bunches of berries and missing one, Kayleen headed over to drop her prizes into our big basket. Their night-black skins stretched tight, ready to burst free and drip juice and seeds. I popped one into my mouth. "Mmmmmm . . ." Caro held up her little plump hand. I handed one to her and said, "berry."

She squished it between her fingers so juice dripped on the ground.

I smiled at Kayleen. "If all the berries are that big, we won't have room for pongaberries."

She grinned. "We'll eat some."

Kayleen waved her leather-coated hands at the kids and me, and went back to take a fresh load of berries from Liam.

After three more loads, sweat covered Kayleen's face and her arms shook as she dropped her heavy load. "Ready to trade?" I asked.

She shook her head. "Next trip."

They'd started just in front of us, but now Kayleen had a ten-meter walk down the wall of berry bushes to get back to Liam.

Caro's eyes fastened on something behind me. "Oo! Oo!"

I shifted Jherrel's weight in my arms and turned to see what fascinated her so.

At the edge of the clearing, five pairs of boots.

I looked up.

Lushia and Ghita, their two companion strongs, and a man I didn't know, but recognized as a Wind Reader from the half-vacant stare he gave me.

I clutched Jherrel tightly to me, covering his head and his neck, trying to bury him inside my body.

How many more were nearby that I couldn't see?

I couldn't reach my laser gun, but there was no point in it. Not with at least five against one.

The strongs and the Wind Reader peered over my head, undoubtedly watching Liam and Kayleen. Lushia looked down on me with what seemed like pity. Ghita's eyes and face might have been formed from chiseled ice. Even though she made no overt move toward me, I flinched away, looking back over my shoulder. Liam's arms were buried in vine, his face obscured by a huge leaf. Kayleen watched him, basket ready.

I screamed. "Run!"

They did. Toward me.

Jherrel twisted in my arms, fighting being held so tightly. I yelled, "No! Stay free!"

Kayleen kept coming, not hesitating at all, but Liam grabbed her by the shoulder, arresting her forward motion. I held my breath, expecting more perfect people in tunics to leap out and grab them. But none did, and Kayleen and Liam disappeared from sight, their picking wand lying askew on the ground, the black berries spilling onto the path like drops of blood.

I turned back to Ghita and Lushia, struggling to keep hold of Jherrel and gather Caro to me all in one motion. I looked up at the still silent five in front of me. "What do you want?"

"Hostages," Ghita said.

My thoughts raced. Hostages for what? Not the children! "Take me!"

Ghita glanced at the empty path in front of us. "And leave these two children alone in the wilds of Fremont?"

Well no. But surely Kayleen and Liam would get help. Would think of something. We had an earset with us, in *my* ear. Shaking, I made as if to brush hair from my eyes and activated it, which would alert a listener.

How to tell people not to speak to me?

I blinked, struggling to think as adrenaline demanded action instead of thought. I managed to gasp out, "Why do you want hostages? You haven't bothered to talk to us since you took Artistos."

Ghita laughed.

I grabbed Caro around the waist, pulling her in to me. She settled close to Jherrel, quivering in my arm, looking up at the invaders. "We can talk now. There's no need for hostages."

"But you aren't who we need to talk to," Ghita said. "You need to talk to the person we need to talk to."

What? Could I stand and run? Where did Kayleen and Liam go? People back in the cave knew we had gone to pick berries. They knew, in general, where we were. My voice shook as I looked at Lushia instead of Ghita. She had always seemed the kinder and the less intractable. How could she do this? "I don't understand." I struggled to stand and keep both kids with me, one tucked at each side of my waist. "Why did you come for me?"

"We didn't."

One of the strongs, the woman, stepped in close to me, smelling like skimmer and spices I didn't recognize. I struggled to remember her name. "Kaal?"

Her eyes lit for a second, then she pursed her lips and nodded.

"Kaal. What are you doing?"

She reached out and put her hands around Caro's wide little waist, pulling the baby toward her. Caro twisted a hand in my hair, pulling my head toward Kaal. "Then take me too," I called out, holding Caro's little hand, not caring that she had fisted a thick bunch of my hair. "Take me, too."

Kaal jerked Caro to her, tearing her hands free of my hair. Regret and compassion flashed through her eyes briefly before they turned cold again. She stood back, a smooth even movement, holding little Caro. Caro stopped moving, looked back and forth from me to Kaal, then screeched disapproval.

The male strong stepped in, reaching for Jherrel, and I turned, racing away, struggling to protect at least one child. Adrenaline surged. I tucked low, Jherrel held in close to me, my right arm a sling for him. Three steps. Three more. Sticks crunched under my feet. My right foot caught on rock, throwing my balance off. I jerked sideways, staying up, barely, but losing forward momentum.

And that was all it took.

The male strong reached out and grabbed my free arm with a grip that could have torn the arm free if kept moving. "Don't take him, no, no! . . ."

But he did, plucking him from me easily.

The strong walked back to the group and I followed behind, thinking furiously. We needed help. I spoke softly into the earset. "Don't talk to me. They took the babies, both of them. I'm following. I can't tell if they want me, too, but I won't let the babies go."

The strong jogged slowly ahead of me, not even looking back. I could dig out my laser gun, but there were five of them. Ghita, Lushia, and the Wind Reader all wore belts with what must be weapons on them. "We're just over the ridge. They're heading back the way we all came. Maybe you can cut us off."

Then the group of strangers turned away from me and began walking. I ran after them, catching up, taking Caro's outstretched hand. Lushia was on the other side of Kaal, who held Caro. "I'm coming with you," I said.

Lushia shook her head. "You have something else to do."

I felt hollow, like in the middle of a nightmare when it's impossible to wake up. "What?" What had they done? What could matter more than the babies?

Kaal sped up, and Caro's hand slipped from mine. Lushia smiled, as if playing with my emotions brought her great pleasure. "You have someone to talk to."

"Give me my babies," I demanded, struggling to keep up with them as they jogged up a narrow path. Branches slapped at my face, leaving marks. It didn't matter. "Lushia!"

She turned and looked down at me, her red hair haloing her face so that for a second she reminded me of Nava. "We won't hurt them. They'll be safe in the *Dawnforce* when you're ready to talk to us."

"I'll talk to you now. About anything."

In answer, Lushia plucked Caro from Kaal's arms. She nodded at me. "Hold her."

"No!" I screamed. Kaal's arms closed around me and she planted her feet and stood still in the center of the path. Caro stretched her arms out toward me again and then broke out in sobs.

My body was stuck fast in Kaal's casual embrace. I head-butted her, again, and again, kicking with my feet. Kaal ignored it all.

The little procession turned a corner and I lost sight of Jherrel and Caro and my heart split, forcing a keening wail from my throat. Anger followed the wail, hot and full of adrenaline and need. I turned to Kaal, speaking through clenched teeth. "If you hurt them I will kill you myself."

Her eyes shone with sorrow, but she held me silently until a skimmer took off in the distance, flying low over the top of the trees. Tears blurred my vision, turning the skimmer into a misty silver bullet and the trees into a carpet of wet green.

Kaal released me.

I fell down to the path, holding my face in my hands.

Kaal knelt down. She didn't touch me, but she whispered, "Your friends have arrived. Go to the Grass Plains. Run as fast as you can."

And then Kaal was gone.

50

THE GRASS PLAINS

Kaal's whisper replayed in my mind. "Go to the Grass Plains."

I hated being herded.

It would be futile to walk into Artistos and demand the children back. I didn't dare disobey the golden captain and her second.

A sob escaped me as I stood up, and another one doubled me over.

"Chelo!" Liam's voice. And in a moment I was enveloped in both of them, and we were holding each other.

I still wore the earset. "They're gone. Who's there?"

"Sky." The cave.

"Akashi." West Band.

"Donni." An East Bander.

"Loren." One of the small roving bands.

Sky: "Are you okay?"

"No." I might never be okay again. How often had I thought that in the last year? "Yes. They took Caro and Jherrel. They said to go to the Grass Plains to get the babies back. We're going to get mounts at the fork."

"Sasha and Paloma are on their way to meet you. Bringing supplies. Tom's been in touch—he's leaving to find Akashi, get the War Council together."

"Ruth will join them," Donni said.

Akashi's voice. "I'll meet up with Tom. We'll be behind you in about an hour."

"Has anyone seen anything strange on the Grass Plains?" I asked.

Sky again. "We sent Kili down to look for you. We kept our earset and sent the spare with Sasha, so we'll have to wait for Kili to get back before we know if she saw anything."

For the thousandth time, I missed Gianna. I swallowed. "Anything else we need to know?"

"We hate them."

"We're with you."

"They deserve to die."

And then the cacophony stopped and I looked at Liam and Kayleen. We surged up the path together. Movement brought a small share of blessed relief. Fear and anger gave me speed, and the need to focus almost completely on the path in front of me lent me a tiny bit of sanity.

Liam passed me, stopping at the hard bits to help Kayleen and I up. Whether we needed it or not, it was a comfort, a touch here and there, a marriage of skin or breath or a shared grunt.

The fork was closer to the cave than the berry patch, and Sasha and Paloma had a head start. But we had three hebras, Stripes, Night, and Thunder, saddled before the two women raced up to us, winded. Paloma closed Kayleen in her arms and they held each other for a precious moment. Paloma pulled away. "I'm going," she said, turning to call Sand, her own hebra.

Kayleen nodded. "Sasha?" she asked.

Sasha held out the belt she had made for me. I'd left it, not wanting it to tangle in the thick berry vines. I took it from her, leaning down to hold her. "Thank you." It felt good to tie the belt on, as if I was tying Sasha's support on. "Sasha—you should stay. The belt will give me your prayers."

Her dark brown eyes were rimmed red with tears and fierce with determination. "I'm going."

I sighed. "Can you come as our scout? Come with us down the Old Road and go back as soon as we know what we see? That way we'll have a backup for our one earset."

Sasha lifted the dark hair hanging over her ear, exposing the nub and tail of an earset. "I have one, too. Hunter told me to go."

"Okay. Saddle up." I wanted her to stay safe, and I had no idea what we were running toward. "Sasha—has anyone heard from Kili yet?"

She shook her head. "That's why I have the earset. They'll tell me as soon as she gets back."

I hated every moment it took for us to get ready.

Liam did a quick round, checking girths and tack. He boosted Paloma up on Sand, and the rest of us pulled up on our own knotted mounting ropes and settled in the high-backed saddles. Stripes stamped her feet under me, clearly catching my black mood.

Liam, mounted, surveyed us all, his gaze alert, his jaw tight and angry. He gave the signal to go, and signaled the hebras to race.

We took the treacherous Old Road too fast. Steady, strong Stripes set the lead pace. Liam and Thunder brought up the rear. Trees kept us from seeing what lay below and silenced our earsets.

At the bottom of the steep trail, where it first opened out onto the beginning of the plains, I stopped, letting the others catch up, craning my neck and standing in my stirrups to see. The grass was high this late in the year, the stalks stiff and dry, almost ready to burn. The path in front of us had barely been used this summer, and grass grew close to the edges, and even—in spots—scraggled across the slender ribbon of hard-packed dirt. A light wind blew the grass in waves, as if a golden ocean lay between us and the spaceport.

The spaceport!

I settled into my saddle and clucked Stripes into a run, racing for the first spot I could get a good view. There! A silver ship. My throat closed in panic and hope. It wasn't *New Making*, but its slender, graceful shape was more like the *New Making* than the *Dawnforce*.

Joseph! It had to be Joseph. I turned in my saddle and yelled at Kayleen. Only she could tell for sure at this distance. "Kayleen!" Her head whipped up, and she stopped as she, too, spotted the starship. "Kayleen," I pleaded. "Is that Joseph?"

She closed her eyes, swaying in her saddle. Paloma came up by her, holding her daughter's hand, her graying hair flapping gently across her face in the wind.

Kayleen opened her eyes. A smile spread across her face. "Yes! Yes!" and then we were all racing each other, Stripes and Thunder and

Night in the lead; Liam, Kayleen, and I next to each other. Paloma and Sasha thudded along behind us.

I struggled to breathe past my pounding heart. So much. The babies. My brother.

My brother.

51

MY SISTER, MY BROTHER

We had not been fast enough. But we were here.

Standing on Fremont's soil felt strange after so long, both perfectly familiar and as if I saw it for the first time. The Grass Plains waved forever around the ship, nearly as high as my head, reminding me how small a single human being is. Paw-cats would not care that I knew how to fly starships and Read the Wind.

I had asked to step out by myself first. Alicia had glared at me, and said, "I don't like Fremont anyway." I had kissed her fiercely, then traded my flying clothes for simple pants and short sleeves, something that could be taken for belonging on Fremont.

Now, finally, I stood in the heat of the sun I was born under.

There was, of course, no sign of Chelo. How could there be? Even if she lived, she wouldn't be waiting around for me to land. More than five years had passed since we'd left.

Still, somehow, I'd expected her here.

I walked around slowly, alert for anything unusual, connected to the cameras in the ship. I saw the tall grass in front of me, and I saw myself see the tall grass in front of me.

The spaceport had been attacked. The hangar and the colony's two shuttles lay shattered, the pieces jumbled together, a twisted wreck.

We'd flown in over the sea at dawn, with no good view of Artistos. What had happened to it?

The cliffs looked normal, except that from here I could see the silver tip of what must be the *Dawnforce* parked by the hebra barns.

Why were they still here? Surely they had seen us land, but they had sent no message. No welcome party, friendly or not, trailed down the cliff path. We were vulnerable here on the Grass Plains, but I had needed a good place to land *Creator*, and the pads here were the only place I knew.

My shields were up tight, a habit developed on Silver's Home. I sat, cross-legged, feeling the hard solidity of the planet beneath me. I drew in a deep breath, smelling the plains: wheat-grass, green-striped grass, sugar-wheat, plains spikes, dust, and animal scat. Glorious scents. I breathed them out, dropping my shields, opening.

A strange data field blanketed Artistos. Its meanings licked at my nerves, not quite clear, like some of the people I'd met on Pilo Island with thick accents. Autocracy data. I'd studied it enough to know that I could learn it. I didn't test deeper—no need to alert the data owners to my strengths. I did check its reach—the data seemed to have no end in any direction. It even flowed out across the water.

So strong!

Had the Islans covered the whole planet, like Silver's Home?

Underneath the new, strong webs, I detected the Artistos webs, faint and ragged. They'd been changed so they no longer homed to Artistos.

A smile ripped from me. Kayleen, at least, lived.

I surged down our webs, repairing them as I went, unable to resist adding things I'd learned. Kayleen would know I was here.

She did. A taste of her swarmed up the nets.

Close.

Where? I forced the spatial data free of the web, and stood, looking. The grass went on forever, summer-brown, waving. I closed my eyes, searching through *Creator*'s cameras.

There! Near the base of the Old Road, hebra heads bounced above the tall grass. I crouched, bringing myself as fully into my physical being as possible, then took off. My senses remembered the boy who'd hunted, gloriously alive, sure-footed and watchful, sorting for paw-cat or demon dog sign in the dust of Fremont that rose from beneath my pounding feet. No fresh scents alarmed me.

As I neared them, I stood, not wanting to spook the hebras, waving my hands.

"Joseph!" Chelo yelled, followed by Kayleen, the two of them whooping. A smile tore through my body, a lightness, as if I could rise above the grass and fly.

She lived!

We were in time.

Kayleen, Chelo, and Liam rode three abreast, closing in on me. They whooped again, and I frowned. Desperation edged their voices, something raw.

They were thinner, cheekbones showing. Chelo had always kept her hair shoulder-length, but now it hung as long as Kayleen's, in a sloppy ponytail that spilled over her right breast. She dismounted quickly, dropping her reins, clearly trusting her beast.

I caught one close glimpse as she raced to me. Her eyes were red and blotchy as if she'd been crying, her cheeks hollow and thin. Two fresh cuts showed on her right cheek. She flung herself into my arms as if the whole world had collapsed on her, and only I could save her.

I held her.

No matter what had happened in my sister's world, she was here, and I was here, and we held each other as if it had been a hundred years instead of five. She sobbed into my chest and I stroked her hair, breathed her sweat in, patted her back, closed her in my arms.

My big sister crying in my arms.

She had never done that before.

Chelo let go of me with one arm, opening it out, and Liam fit himself into our embrace, his eyes warm but full of some darkness that didn't seem to have anything to do with me. Then Kayleen clutched me, wrapping her physical self and her data self about me all together.

None of us said anything for a very long time, not even Kayleen and I in the quiet of the data world. Words might break the perfect spell. The miracle of all four of us being together felt fragile. Dreamlike.

"Where are the others?" Chelo asked. "Alicia and Bryan?"

"Here. In the ship. Come and tell us what happened."

She nodded, but turned toward two other people who rode up on blowing hebras, keeping back a bit, watching curiously. Only when they, too, dismounted, did I lift my head long enough for a good look.

An old woman and a young woman. A slight limp gave the older one away.

Paloma!

But she looked twenty years older, not five. Her face was browned and weathered, her eyes cracked with deep lines, her hair more gray than blond. I stepped free of the others and held her. She was so tiny! She pushed me far enough away to look me over, and I did a little half-bow. "It's nice to see you, Mother-of-my-heart." She had, almost, been a mother to me during the time Chelo and I lived with Nava.

Paloma grinned, pleasure lifting a few years of age from her frame. "It's good to see you." She turned to the young woman with her, a slender, wide-eyed girl of maybe seventeen with a striking white streak in her hair. "This is Sasha." She nodded at the girl, who stood as if rooted in place, looking from me to *Creator* and back again. "And Sasha," Paloma continued, "this is Chelo's brother, Joseph."

I reached my hand out to her.

A mad cacophony of screeching data assaulted me, driving me to my knees. Kayleen's eyes rolled up in her head and she let out a piercing scream, falling to the ground beside me.

I threw up my own shielding, silencing the awful whine in my head. Then I grabbed Kayleen, pulling her close, struggling to connect with her so I could, maybe, include her—the way Marcus had included me in the park the day I met my dad.

Kayleen screamed and threw her head back.

I curled a hand around the back of her neck and refocused. My shields were generally passive, a shutting down more than weaving a wall, but Marcus had started drilling me in his way.

But this was data I didn't know. It bucked and fought me, leaking in the sides of my concentration, an onslaught of interior sound more than information. As soon as I held a bit of it at bay, another torrent started in.

I dropped back to my familiar, passive shielding and silence fell inside me.

I wasn't strong enough. I could protect myself, but I couldn't protect us both.

Kayleen thrashed in my arms and let out a high keening wail.

Creator. Getting into *Creator* would help. It could be a shield, itself.

I bent down to pick Kayleen up. Liam knelt at my side, reaching for her right arm.

"Let me." I looked up. Bryan. He leaned down and plucked Kayleen from the ground, her arms still twisting in pain and shock.

"*Creator*," I shouted at him. "Take her in."

He jogged toward the ship, steady and even and strong. I turned to the others, still breathing hard, my shields clamping out all of the available data nets. "Chelo, Liam, go!"

They bolted, following Bryan.

We had room for them, if they wanted to go. If we left. Dianne had agreed with my father with no hesitation. Jenna had surprised me by backing them both, suggesting we get away as fast as we could. She'd shivered, and asked me, "Do you want to die on Fremont after all?"

I bit my lip. I didn't want to leave. Chelo wouldn't. But what if staying started a war? Who could we save? Paloma? Akashi would never leave.

Paloma and Sasha stood looking at me, waiting for something. "Do you want to leave?" I asked them.

Paloma glanced at Bryan, carrying Kayleen through the doorway of the ship. Her brows were drawn tight together in worry. "Will she be all right?" she asked.

I nodded. They'd entered *Creator*. "She might be okay already."

Paloma still held her own hebra's reins. She reached for Liam's mount's trailing rein, handing it to Sasha. "The babies," she said. "We have to get the babies." She picked up Kayleen's mount's rein, and Stripes's. I remembered some of the beasts' names. If only there were time to mount one and race down to the sea!

"Get the babies," Paloma said. "We'll report back. Chelo has an earset. She can talk to us."

Babies? The hebras? Or human babies? And whose? Report back to who? "Do you want to leave?" I asked her again.

She frowned, staring at *Creator*, and then looking at Sasha and Sand. "Not now. You can't either. We'll wait."

I stood looking at her, confused.

"Go," she said. "Follow your sister."

Clearly I would learn as much from Chelo as I would from Paloma.

Something important was going on, something dark. It shone in all of their eyes. A fear.

I went.

Liam pulled me into the strange ship after Kayleen and Bryan. Joseph had turned away from Paloma and Sasha, following us at a dead run. Bryan stepped into an elevator in front of us, and I hesitated a moment, looking back. Whatever had attacked Kayleen had clearly attacked him, too. But he had a way to beat it. Maybe he could teach her. He had always been so much stronger.

Liam folded me in his arms as I watched Joseph race to catch us.

Joseph had become a man.

All of the little boy uncertainty and mischief had dropped away from him. He had built his body so his muscles stood out. My little unassuming brother looked almost like Bryan had looked when he was here. And Bryan—such strength. Where had they been? Who else was here?

Joseph caught up to us, stopping just long enough to say, "Follow me," and then he was swarming up a vertical corridor the way we had on the *New Making*, using the handholds as ladder rungs, nearly bouncing upward. I followed him, struggling to move as fast. Halfway up, my right foot slipped from a rung while the left one hung in mid-step and I fell down, banging my chin. My arms held, and I pulled and scrambled the rest of the way, rushing to the sound of Joseph already at the top, calling my name and reaching a hand down for my hand.

My fingers brushed his fingertips. Another step, and I had his arm above the wrist. He pulled, I stepped and leapt, standing near him while he reached down to help Liam scramble up the last bit of round vertical wall. Joseph was off again, leaving us to follow. This ship—what had he called it? *Creator?*—looked newer than *New Making*, with cleaner lines and splashes of color here and there to offset gleaming silvery surfaces.

Joseph led us to what must be the command room. Screens showed various pictures of Fremont. One looked out on the Grass Plains, centered on Sasha and Paloma and the hebras, standing quietly, looking up at the ship. The other two showed the ruined hangar, and the cliffs below Artistos. The room was smaller than the *New Making*'s command room, although it had an adjacent room with a sink and cupboards. A square silver table occupied the center space with four pilot's chairs around it. I briefly registered people in each, a man and three women, all four with dark hair, and young, but my focus was on Bryan as he laid Kayleen down on the middle of the table.

Kayleen's eyes were still rolled up in her head, and she moaned softly. Her limbs remained still. One of the women, a dark-haired beauty, leaned forward and touched Kayleen on the forehead, looking worriedly at Joseph, who stood just in front of me. Her voice was familiar, but I couldn't quite place it. "What happened?"

"Some kind of data attacks. I shielded—but she doesn't know how. She should be all right after a bit in here." He fell silent for a moment, then said, "Yes. It's not strong in here."

I pushed past Joseph, standing between the man and the woman who had asked about Kayleen. "Can someone get me water?" I asked.

One of the two women went to the sink, handing me a glass of water. I bathed Kayleen's forehead, speaking softly.

She'd been through so much today!

Liam moved to the bottom of the table, removed Kayleen's worn boots, and rubbed her feet. She thrashed once, and opened her eyes, putting a hand to her forehead. "Where am I?"

Joseph spoke. "*Creator*. You're in the command room of the starship *Creator*."

Liam held out a hand and pulled Kayleen gently to a sitting position right in the middle of the table. She looked up at Bryan, her eyes widening. "Bryan." She scooted down the table near him.

He held her, his head on her shoulder. "I'm so glad you're all right." He raised his head long enough to look at me, his eyes full of wonder and, maybe, a touch of abandonment.

I had sent him away from me, all those years ago.

His voice was soft and controlled as he said, "You're all okay. We were worried."

Worried? Had they known the strangers were here?

Two women pushed in the door, standing near the edge of the wall, close to me. I gaped, and it was my turn to fold someone in my arms. "Alicia!" She, too, glowed with health like Joseph. What was she doing back here? She'd almost killed us all the day before she left. "I . . . It's good to see you." There was no time to talk to her, not here. Hopefully it was a good sign that she'd come back. Maybe we'd need her courage.

I looked around the table. They all had light skin. It must be from doing without real sun. The man—short cropped dark hair and sea-mist blue eyes—stared at me as if the very sight of me was a feast, and a tear rolled down one of his cheeks.

Why?

This group could help us get the babies back. Caro and Jherrel. Thinking of them gave me focus and strength. I looked around. All eyes were on me. "Who are you all?" I asked.

The strange dark-haired man looked at my brother. "Can we take a few moments?"

Joseph nodded. "They appear to be watching."

"But they attacked you out there?" He glanced at Kayleen, who had pulled free of Bryan's embrace and now stood between Bryan and Liam, the three of them filling one side of the smallish room.

Joseph said, "A test."

"They've never done that before." Kayleen's voice, scratchy and frightened.

"We're safe in here now," Joseph said, his voice soothing. Then he turned to me, a slight mischievous grin touching his lips for just a moment before his face settled into the new Joseph's serious demeanor. He seemed to be in charge here. He nodded at the slight, dark-haired woman next to him. She was the strangest-looking of the group, with a bobbed haircut and severe white tunic that looked like the ones Lushia and Ghita wore. "This is Dianne. She is from the same place the people with the ship in Artistos are from."

"The Islas Autocracy," Liam said. He pulled Kayleen close to him. "Why is she here?"

"To help." Joseph looked at the other two women at the table, both dark-haired, one with blue eyes and, the one whose voice was naggingly familiar, with gray eyes. Mischief crept across Joseph's features. "And this is Tiala." He shifted his attention to the gray-eyed woman. "And her sister Jenna."

The woman regarded me calmly as Joseph's words sank in. Jenna.

But Jenna was old! I pushed to her side and knelt, looking more closely. She wore Jenna's eyes. The truth of it, the power of the healing, sank in. "It is you. You came back. You—you're whole."

She nodded, and suddenly she and I were crying. Unable to get to her any other way, Kayleen scooted across the table. "Jenna!" Kayleen took my hand, gazing up into Jenna's eyes. "You can help us!"

Joseph cleared his throat. I felt dizzy, off balance. Jenna, perfect and whole. Two eyes. Two arms. I glanced at Joseph, ready to plead for more time, but something in his face stopped me.

He needed me to focus on him.

Once he had my attention, he looked down at the man, who still watched me.

I shifted uncomfortably.

"Come here," the man said. "Let me touch you."

And over my head, Joseph's voice, catching in his throat. "Chelo, this is our father, David Lee."

The world stopped. This man with the intense, demanding stare, this man who had worried me since I first saw him because of the intense hunger in his eyes.

I understood now.

The room shrank to just him and me. I had noticed his short, dark hair and the deep mist-blue eyes, now veiled a bit by tears. Even though he was sitting, I could tell he was built like the Joseph who stood by him now, like the man my little brother had become. Wide shoulders and slender hips, high cheekbones and a rounded chin. I took one of his long-fingered hands in mine. His palm and finger pads were a little rough, but not like a farmer's or roamer's hands. I searched his face. There were tears, but what emotion drove them? He hardly moved a muscle, waiting for me to react.

I found my voice. "I . . . Pleased to meet you." I wanted to rush to him, touch him, but something in his eyes stopped me. "I've always hoped you lived." It still wasn't right. My father. "Hello."

He smiled then, almost a laugh, but edgy. He spoke softly. "You have no idea how much I hoped to get here in time."

My head spun. My father. Jenna. Bryan and Alicia. In time. In time for what? The babies! We had to tell them about Caro and Jherrel.

The Islan, Dianne, said, "They're coming." The rest of the room fell back into focus, and I looked up at the middle viewscreen, which showed a skimmer heading our way from Artistos. In the screen next to it, Sasha and Paloma had let the three extra hebras go and were racing toward the edge of the valley.

"Strap in!" my father called, and the room began to empty.

I knew what they were going to do.

Leave.

Kayleen figured it out at the same time, her eyes snapping wide open. Fear filled every pore. The babies! We screamed together.

"No!"

Liam jumped to his feet, fists clenched, looking for some way to stop people who flew starships with their minds.

52

STORIES TOLD, PLANS MADE

Kayleen's and Chelo's joint scream stilled the room. Not simple protest, something primal. I turned to my sister, holding her face between my two hands. "We came to get you. You're all here. This is a miracle." If the mercenaries *were* waiting for me, for us, then we could get away now.

I had imagined searching Fremont for a long time, feared searching it in vain. I remembered telling myself I wouldn't leave without saving everyone else, but we were all here. So easy.

Kayleen's voice was shrill and high. "They have our babies!"

Chelo looked into my eyes. "It's true," she whispered. "They took them today." Her eyes welled with tears. She looked from me to our father to Jenna, her energy that of a trapped animal. In spite of the loss painting her face wet, her voice sounded firm and completely controlled as she declared, "We aren't going anywhere without them. We can't. You understand that."

I did understand. She and I had been abandoned. I glanced at my father, who flinched away. His free hand on the chair shook.

The real import of her words struck me. Chelo had children. Or Chelo and Kayleen had children. I stood gaping, like a stranded fish.

My father was the first one who found his voice, and spoke into the deep silence that had settled on the room. "Of course you're not leaving. We're not leaving." He stared at Chelo. "I left you. I shouldn't have ever left you."

He hadn't said that yet. His words slapped something angry away from me, leaving an open, raw space. He looked at me, then back to Chelo. "I'm sorry."

She hesitated for a long second, her face softening. "I know," she said. "We'll have another day for that. We have to save Jherrel and Caro."

My father looked tenderly at her. "Tell me about it."

Kidnapped. Stolen. My sister's children. I would be their uncle.

Alicia pointed at the skimmer, grown larger in the viewscreen. "What about them?"

I glanced up at the skimmer, then over at Chelo. "Do you know what they want?"

Her expression tensed in an angry frown. "No. They're hateful. They kill with no reason. Half of us are dead, Joseph. Half. Nava and Eric and Stile . . ."

If she could kill them right then, I thought she might. Whatever happened to turn my pacifist sister into this angry young woman? The kids? I needed her to think. What would Marcus do? Shock them. "Should I shoot them down?"

"No. Of course not. That would just make it worse."

There, that was the Chelo I knew.

Kayleen spoke up, her eyes snapping with adrenaline. "We don't know where Jherrel and Caro are. They stole them from the berry patch hours ago. They wouldn't tell us why. They won't talk to us about anything." Apparently she'd recovered some from the data attack. She kept going, as confusing and intense as ever. "They brought the strongs. They wouldn't let Chelo go with them, and I think they'd have been happy to kill me and Liam. They told Chelo we had something to do. I think they meant to find you."

I turned to Chelo. Her jaw was clenched tight, her hand still tucked inside our father's hand. She proclaimed, "We aren't shooting at anything until we know where the children are."

"Besides," Liam said, "if they wanted to kill us, they would have already done it."

Okay. I'd already figured that out. "Can we ignore them?"

Dianne said, "They probably don't have any weapons on the skimmer that can even ding *Creator*. Let them rage. Mad Lushia is half crazy already."

"Mad Lushia?" Chelo asked. "You know her?"

Dianne smiled, as if at some memory. "I was her Second, once. She fell from favor in the Autocracy. Too independent. She's like a child who won't give up a favorite toy when asked."

I whirled around to look at her. She *knew* these people? "Why didn't you tell me?" I demanded.

"What good would the information have done you out there?" She pointed vaguely up toward space. "It would have just worried you. Now that it is helpful, you have it." The way she said it *almost* soothed.

Ming spoke before I could react to Dianne's statement. "That's why you look so familiar. I've seen your picture."

Dianne shrugged. "I'm no longer Islan. I believe in freedom." She looked me in the eyes. "I'm on *your* side."

Jenna held up a hand. "Let's share stories. They want a reaction from us. Let them cool their heels. We all need to catch up. The galley's the only room big enough to hold everyone comfortably. Can you two," she glanced at me and my father, "manage to monitor the strangers from there?"

Of course. I told *Creator* to send copies of the camera images to the wall in the galley. "Let's go."

Ten minutes later, everyone was seated at the long table, twelve of us at a table meant for fourteen. Chelo, Liam, and Kayleen sat close together on one end, with Chelo at the nominal head of the table. Jenna was in the seat opposite her, flanked by Ming and Tiala. The rest of us ranged through the middle seats of the oblong table. I managed to orchestrate it so I ended up between Kayleen and Alicia. Kayleen might need me, and I needed Alicia.

Tiala set out cups for col on the table, the very ordinariness of it damping the confusion. Jenna glanced up at the screen, which now showed the skimmer landing near the hangar. "We could spend days catching up. But we don't have them. Chelo, can you tell us your situation, and everything you know about the mercenaries?" She sent my father a look clearly meant to silence him.

Chelo leaned back and started. "We were on Islandia when they came. . . ."

Regardless of Jenna's warning about time, it took nearly an hour to get caught up on what had happened here. At the end of it, I knew more about my sister's life, but had no better clue why the mercenaries waited here.

And wait they did. They had disembarked after they landed, and simply stood outside of their skimmer, five of them, talking amongst themselves. They did not have any children with them.

Dianne had suggested Lushia was out of favor. But that didn't mean she wasn't working for the Islans, didn't think like them. Maybe Lushia only appeared to be out of favor, a ruse to allow the Autocracy to disavow her actions if they wanted to. All the possibilities made my head spin. I looked around the table. Exhaustion and worry showed on almost every face. But I wanted more help. "So . . . I'd like to hear why each of you think they're here."

Chelo must have heard what I didn't ask. "Why did they come in the first place? Kayleen said they came to kill us all, but that we confused them. You knew they were here. How?"

I glanced at my father. It was his story to tell, but was he ready to tell it?"

He shook his head at me.

No.

Jenna must have seen the interaction. "They were hired by our affinity group to finish the war. Chelo, do you remember when I told you about affinity groups?"

Chelo nodded. "I remember. But I don't think I understand."

"Okay. The easy explanation is an affinity group is a set of people—sometimes a traditional blood family, but more often many families and individuals that are tied to a goal and to economics. There are groups that work in the arts, groups that build things, others that make things, or provide services. The Family of Exploration came together to find a new place to build into a paradise."

Liam spoke up. "And they chose Fremont."

"That's right. Only when they got here, the planet was settled."

My father spoke up this time. "By people who had no claim."

Induan glared at him. "No claim from Silver's Home. But they were here, and that should have been claim enough."

Liam seemed to approve of her words. "No one should die just for being someplace."

Chelo put a hand on his shoulder, then looked down the table at all of us. "We need to get Jherrel and Caro. We can argue about claims later. Assume we three have no good idea why *they're* here."

"Except we know they haven't hurt *us*," Kayleen said. "They had a chance to kill us today, and they didn't. They've passed up other chances. I don't know why, but they're studying us. From a distance. The three of us. Because we're not from here, either."

Interesting. So Chelo and Liam and Kayleen were alive because they were *altered?* The old derogatory Fremont word stuck to me here. Enhanced. Created. But Chelo was right; there was no time to dwell on questions we had no answer for. "Ming? What do you think?"

"Either they want you, or they want you to do something. They're playing war games. Games about far more than *this* planet."

Dianne spoke without being asked. "They want you to start a fight. Why else would they have taken the babies?"

My father said, "That's too complex. The easy explanation is that the presence of people obviously from Silver's Home threw them off. They were told the only people here weren't from the five worlds. Maybe I can make that invalidate the contract terms. I have to go talk to them. I'm the only one who can change this with talk."

"You'd better. Or leave." Dianne stood up and glared down at him. "If you start a war here, you may spark more war back home."

Chelo surged to her feet, staring across the table at Dianne. "There's *already* a war here, and we didn't start it."

Dianne regarded her with a gentle gaze. "But you can't prove that. Can you? Do you have any record of anything they've done?"

Kayleen said, "I have some. It's stored in our network. I have the last battle, when they killed Stile and all his people."

"But weren't you attacking them?" Dianne asked.

Kayleen nodded. "But they took over Artistos! They burned the Guild Halls!"

Dianne didn't give up. "What can you prove? What might they have?"

Chelo collapsed in her chair, staring down at the table as if she could bore holes in it. "I started it. Kayleen read their webs, and I started it."

Chelo started a fight? I held my tongue with great difficulty.

Jenna said, "But that can be played as 'uneducated colonist kids defend themselves.' Every sentient being in the Five Worlds knows what the Star Mercenaries are. We can make you a hero over that."

Dianne interrupted. "So if we attack them, two things happen." A beat of silence fell. Chelo lifted her head and looked at Jenna. "We die. And they can go home and report that we attacked them."

Dianne's motives clarified. "So Marcus sent you to help keep us from making this situation worse?" I asked.

She stopped, blew out a long breath, and said, "If it's possible."

I nodded. "If it's possible."

Chelo, who always thought for the greater good and not herself, now focused on something small, and clearly dear to her. "We're not leaving without Jherrel and Caro."

"Any other ideas?"

None were offered. I glanced up at the viewscreen. The mercenaries still waited patiently. In fact, they laughed and talked amongst themselves as if they were at a picnic.

I stood up. "We'd better go talk to them."

"Who is we?" Alicia asked.

My father stood up. "Me. I hired them."

Chelo gasped. She walked over to our father, drew her hand back, and slapped him so hard his head snapped away from her. Good for her. Except now I didn't hate him so much, and I felt the pain of her hand as well as her anger.

Chelo was no longer the same person I'd flown away from.

My father didn't move to return the strike or to defend himself. He looked at her, rubbing his face. "I thought they'd killed you. You and Joseph both. I thought there was nothing left here worth saving. They killed your mother. What will you do to these people if they kill Jherrel and Caro?"

She stared at him, her eyes wide, her lips pursed, her hands at her side. She took a deep breath but didn't answer him.

His lower lip quivered. "What would you do if they killed your children and Liam and Kayleen?"

Her face went to stone. "Let's hope I don't have to find out." It wasn't forgiveness, or even a conversation, but Chelo had her own focus.

Alicia took my arm, leaning over and whispering in my ear. "I'll go."

"No. I can't lose you." I glanced at Jenna. "I think my father, you, and Liam."

Jenna nodded.

"Why not me?" Chelo demanded.

"And me?" Alicia challenged.

Jenna looked down the table. "There's no point in risking more than three. One of us should be a parent. Chelo is useful to Joseph. It will hurt Joseph too much if Alicia is damaged. Kayleen can't go—she can't shield. Liam is, frankly, the most expendable."

Liam winced at that, but he nodded.

"We can watch from here," I told Chelo and Kayleen. "And listen. *Creator* has better sound connections between crew than earsets. We'll get you fixed up." I looked down the table. "It will make sense to them that those three are here. There's no point in telling them our strengths." Alicia crossed her arms over her chest, but didn't fight me. I leaned over and whispered, "I love you."

Without looking at me, she whispered, "Me too," under her breath. It sounded as much like a curse as an endearment.

My father already stood in the doorway. "Let's go." He wore a look of such determination that I bit my lip until I tasted blood.

"Wait!" Jenna called. "We must dress the part." As she led the three of them away, Dianne called after her. "Don't imply we're speaking for Silver's Home with what you wear."

When they returned, my father wore a full captain's uniform. I startled at the choice, then took in a long breath and let it go. He may not have flown this ship here, but the mercenaries didn't need to know it. Jenna and Liam had also dressed as formally as they could, both in navy blue ship's clothes with no insignia on them.

I watched them leave, not happy to be staying. But what other choice was there?

I dropped into the Fremont nets. I could use the time until they left the ship to get information to the colony that way. Last time I'd tried this, Gianna had been the willing target of my conversation. She was no longer here. For the first time, the magnitude of Artistos's losses rang full and clear inside me.

Well, the decision I'd sworn I'd make back when I woke my father was made. I would do everything I could to be sure they lost no more.

53

NEGOTIATION

Wedged between Chelo and Kayleen, I watched the command room screens. Alicia stood behind us, keeping a bit of distance between herself and Chelo. Through the ship's cameras I watched my father, Liam, and Jenna disembark. They looked tiny beside the ship, but then the mercenaries looked just as tiny. They stood a respectful distance away, near their skimmer, which was parked by the shattered hangar.

Our group approached them, my father leading, his strides sure and even. Jenna put a hand on his arm, exerting force, and he stopped halfway to the mercenaries. Good.

I zoomed in on their faces. Liam stood stiffly stoic. Jenna scanned the environment, her limbs loose and ready, her face a mask of watchful distrust. My father's jaw was tight, his shoulders back, his eyes set unmoving on his target.

The mercenaries hesitated for a moment, the looks on their faces showing brief shock at seeing my father here.

Dianne said, "The one on the left is Mad Lushia."

The woman stood taller than all the others, lithe and really quite beautiful. Her golden hair glinted with red highlights in the sunshine. She wore black pants and a bright yellow tunic.

Lushia began moving toward our group, followed by a slightly shorter dark-haired woman and a broad muscular man.

Chelo's voice shook with anger. "I don't know the one next to her—it's not Ghita. Which means Ghita is plotting trouble somewhere. If Lushia's mad, Ghita's stark raving." Her grip on my hand tightened so much that I yelped. "He's the strong that stole Jherrel."

Dianne responded to Chelo. "They would not send the First and the Second together to a meeting like this. I am surprised Mad Lushia came herself."

As the groups approached each other, my father's voice entered the cabin through sensitive speakers in his captain's coat. "Captain Groll."

If his appearance had shocked her, she was fully recovered. "David Lee. I hope you had a good journey." She smiled. "It is not common for customers to oversee our work."

His voice was clear and even as he said, "I came here to stop you."

Lushia regarded him silently.

He continued. "There were flaws in the information I had when I sent you."

"That your daughter is here?" Lushia's voice sounded casual, but her loose stance and the way she held her hands by her side suggested battle-readiness. She and Jenna carried themselves so much alike that they might have been dark and light twins.

"But you have killed," my father continued.

"Isn't that what you hired us to do? We'll finish after we've decided what to do about your family."

Chelo's hand gripped mine.

"I want to cancel the whole contract," my father said. "And I want you to leave immediately."

Chelo's grip on my hand tightened further. I pulled free and put my arm over her shoulder. Would he be able to stop the whole contract? It was his hatred that got us here in the first place. He and I had spent months alone together on the ship, even though I never turned *Creator* over to him. I'd told him all the good I knew of Artistos. It was even more than I remembered. Perhaps he was changing.

He kept talking. "I believe you are holding two of my family members."

"We've not harmed them."

Liam visibly relaxed a little.

"Good choice," Kayleen whispered under her breath.

Lushia laughed softly. "We'll gladly trade for just one."

Jenna and Liam exchanged a startled glance. My father blinked at them for a second, and then responded. "I'll go."

"Certainly," Lushia said. "But the babies can only be traded for your son."

He stood up taller, his face growing angry. "My son was never part of this bargain!"

"No." Lushia agreed. "But only he can stop this. You can come with us now, or you can do it later. If you wait, we will begin to experiment with the children."

He glanced up briefly, and I looked for fear or anger in his eyes. All I saw was concern. He stepped toward Lushia.

Liam began to follow and Jenna put an arm across his chest, holding him back. She hissed something the camera microphone didn't pick up, and he stopped, standing still and watching as the mercenaries led my father away.

For a moment, I nearly ran out and offered myself.

It wouldn't help.

He walked between them. He didn't look back.

54

PREPARATION

They took my father! I told myself he went of his own accord, that he asked, that maybe he'd find some kind of release since he had started all of this. But Marcus's warning that the Star Mercenaries didn't appreciate broken contracts or lies rang in my head, a loop that wouldn't end. *He didn't know we lived! He made a mistake!* I wanted to scream it at them, but there were other people to tell, people we needed.

I slammed into the Artistos nets, connecting to whoever had an earset. Akashi, Sasha, and Ruth. Ruth, who had once hated us with all of her being, and now didn't question how I reached her without my own earset but just said, "Hello Joseph," almost hopefully. More change. Chelo, too, was in the conversation, on her own earset.

I reached through the nets and queried Kayleen, pulling her into it.

We couldn't use an open line to discuss weapons or plans; it was safest to assume they had Wind Readers who had studied our nets. So I told it straight. "My father came with us. They want me. In return, they would give us back Jherrel and Caro. He went. I didn't. They promised nothing."

Akashi broke in. "I'm sorry."

Chelo's voice, breaking, edgy with all she'd been through today. "We have to go get them. It's the only thing we can do." She must be exhausted, but she hadn't lost any of her intensity.

From what they'd told me, the last attack directly on the city had been so bad almost no one had returned. Nanotech. That had to be what killed so many so easily. Illegal to use as a weapon on the Five

Worlds, but not here. Something they sowed in the soil. How to detect it?

I needed some time to get into their webs and understand them. "Sasha, are you still where you told us you would be?"

"Yes."

"Wait there." Maybe the mercenaries knew I meant by the base of the Old Road, maybe they didn't. The information had been in a regular conversation. But the settled part of Fremont was not exactly big. They might be watching.

A woman's scream bored through me. "They're coming!" In the background, a distant voice, someone close to the earset wearer, screaming, "Run!"

Paloma.

Chelo screamed, "Sasha!" so loudly the name stung my ears.

The cameras! By the time I oriented on it, the skimmer was flying up and away from where Sasha, Paloma, and the hebras were supposed to be.

"Sasha!" Chelo called, plaintive.

There was no answer.

Ruth snapped commands. "Stay in the ship. None of you are expendable. We'll go." Before I could argue with her, her part of the line went dead, then got picked up again. "Donni."

I remembered him vaguely from Ruth's band. A tall young man with dark hair. Probably important now, with so many dead. Nothing more to say over a probably open line. Ruth was wrong—I wouldn't stay trapped in *Creator*. But first . . . I had preparations to make.

"Everyone. I'm closing the connections for now."

They all went silent without even a good-bye. At least the survivors had discipline.

They also clearly expected me to lead. I'd become the man come from the stars to save them. Even Jenna deferred to me.

If only Marcus had come along.

Chelo's eyes pleaded with me. "I have to go to Sasha."

I shook my head. "I'm not leaving them an opening. They've no reason not to take you, too. I can't lose you."

Kayleen mumbled, "Paloma Mom."

I shook my head again. "I need you here, Kayleen."

I reached for Chelo and held her close to me for a long moment. "It will be all right, Sis. Somehow. We'll make it all right."

She looked up at me, her expression pleading. "What about our father. Will he help the kids?"

Her question gave me pause. "I think so."

I kissed Alicia and turned to Kayleen. "Come with me."

I led her to a quiet common room, sat her down in one of the two chairs, and said, "Show me what you know about their nets."

She grinned fiercely.

"Follow me," I said, watching as she closed her eyes, then dove into *Creator*'s nets, and through them, out into the wild air of Fremont, now full of strange data. She stayed with me, more agile than I expected.

I turned over the lead to her.

Kayleen's bright energy strengthened and I followed her from node to node in the Artistos net, marveling at her untutored strength.

Being with Kayleen in the nets was unlike anything I'd experienced, wholly different from the tentative touches we'd managed to pull off before I left. Marcus always seemed bigger than life, inside the data streams and out of them. Being with Kayleen here was like being with Kayleen anywhere . . . a tad chaotic, always bright and lively.

Kayleen showed me the language of the Autocracy nets. She pulled up short at the edge, showing me what the nets showed her. Her energy-form (what else could you call it?) pulsed doubt. Was she seeing a thread meant for her, a lie?

I sampled it. It tasted true, but thin. Not enough dimension. Surely Autocracy nets, even here, were deeper and richer. More like those on Silver's Home.

I'd studied the threads of benign information (temperature, location of goods, dinner menus, skimmer statistics), not touching them, remembering the attack outside. "Back," I told her, and we woke to our physical senses, stretching into our bodies back in the common room. "First," I said, "let me show you how to shield. . . ."

An hour later, Alicia banged on the door. "Joseph, Kayleen, Ruth's almost here."

Kayleen and I scrambled up. We got to the command room just as Ruth-in-the-viewscreen stepped from the Grass Plains onto the landing pad. She led three hebras. Two were riderless, although saddled. On the third, Sand, Sasha sat upright, blood pouring down her face. Paloma lay face down and crosswise on Sand's back, her long gray-blond hair hanging toward the ground. Sasha's hands braced Paloma's unmoving body, helping to hold the older woman on the animal's withers while protecting her side from the bruising saddle bump.

So she lived.

Sky walked beside Sasha, steadying her with one hand, a grim look on her face.

Kayleen gasped. "Let them in!"

"Let's go." I told *Creator* to open the door. Kayleen and I and Chelo and Liam swarmed down the vertical tunnels.

Tiala and Jenna flanked the doorway as Bryan and Ming walked in, followed by Sky, who gazed astonished at the ship. Sasha leaned on Ming, and Bryan carried Paloma like a baby, slightly folded, close to his abdomen. His shirt was bloody.

Kayleen raced to Bryan's side. He looked down at her, anger showing in every muscle, dancing in his eyes. "She's still alive." Kayleen reached out a hand and stroked her mother's pale cheek.

"Take them to medical," Jenna said.

"What about the beasts?" Tiala asked. "Will we need them later?"

At least she was thinking. But then, she didn't know Paloma or Sasha, or the babies, or really anyone. I smiled at her. "Good idea. They're hebras." She and I caught them together, Tiala patient and soothing. We caught Sand, Stripes, and the black-headed one. I should have recognized Tiala had a way with animals, if just because of the bird, Bell.

We put the hebras into the hold that had no supplies anymore, and closed the door. One of them kicked, the sound ringing in the hollow metal ship.

I took Tiala's hand. "Can you stay with them? I'll send someone down with water soon."

I found Kayleen and Chelo in medical, washing blood from a nasty cut on Sasha's face while Bryan watched, shifting uncomfortably. Jenna moved purposefully around Paloma's still form, muttering under her breath. Paloma was on her back, blood dripping from a wound on her shoulder. Unconscious, she looked even smaller and paler than when I'd held her outside.

"Jenna?" I asked. "Will she be all right?"

Jenna nodded. "If I stick with her for a while. She's lucky they missed any vital organs. Lucky they used a projectile and not a beam weapon." She picked up a cloth and held it to the wound on Paloma's shoulder.

We needed to plan. "Tiala's with the hebras. We brought them in. If I send someone else to her, and her up here, will she know what to do?"

Jenna stopped for a moment, looking at me, her arms still pressing down on the cloth, which was stained bright red under her fingers. In spite of the tang of blood in the air, the blood on her hands, the horrible stupidity of it all, she had a small smile on her face. "You go on. You have a battle to plan, and I've the most experience here."

I swallowed, understanding the import of her words. "Do you need help?"

She glanced over at Chelo and Kayleen and Sasha. "Leave me Sasha. She's not hurt badly, and I'll finish up with her after I get this stopped. Then she can help me finish cleaning up Paloma. You'll need the others."

I stood there another long moment, holding her gaze. She looked back down at Paloma, frowning. "Go on. Tell me later what you want me to do."

I still resisted. "You're our best strategist."

She didn't lift her head. "You have Induan. And Chelo. And yourself. Go."

I took a fresh cloth, wet it, and handed it to Sasha, who pressed it against her bleeding scalp. "Will you be all right?" I asked her.

She nodded. "Yes."

I took Chelo's hand in mine, gestured to Kayleen and Bryan, and called out through *Creator*'s system for everyone except Tiala to meet me in the galley.

An hour later, roles had been defined. Eight of us watched *Creator*'s ramp extend in a camera image on the wall of the galley. Ruth led a black-faced hebra, Night, down the ramp, followed by Kayleen. I squinted, struggling to see the forms that followed them. A few times, I thought I made out flashes of off-color movement. I was sure twice, when the silver ramp met the gray pad, and again, where the Grass Plains struggled to take over the pad.

I wished Alicia and Induan well.

With Kayleen mounted behind her, Ruth rode quickly through dusky light, toward the base of the Old Road. I watched until the cameras could no longer pick them up, imagining Alicia, who she had once hated, maybe still hated, and the strange and beautiful Induan, sliding along unseen beside or behind.

I clutched the data button with my father's journal on it, the small hard roundness of it a comfort in my palm. I wore the flying pants Marcus had given me, another comfort. Perhaps these things would be all the comfort I would have for a long while.

I looked at the others in the room. Chelo leaned into Liam's shoulder, her eyes closed. I glanced at Bryan. "Take those two somewhere to rest. You rest, too."

He nodded at me.

"Sky, can you relieve Tiala? The hebras may have settled enough not to need watching, but if not, stay with them. Send Tiala to help Jenna, and have Jenna rest if she can. I'm going to need her."

Sky tugged at her braids, looking lost. "How do I get there?"

"Dianne?" I asked, getting a tired and slightly accusing look in return. She had not been happy with our plans, but she wouldn't have been pleased with anything short of us leaving immediately. "Can you take her?"

"Sure." She glanced at Ming. "Come with me."

I let the three of them go off together, hoping Dianne and Ming wouldn't cook up something I didn't want while they were gone. But I had my own work to do, and had to trust them.

I settled back into the nets, questing gently through the strangers' data. They wouldn't be able to hold the fiction they'd built for Kayleen. Not against me.

55

THE BATTLE BEGINS

Kayleen's ghostly presence in the nets waited quietly for me to acknowledge her. I pulled myself up from the depths of the strangers' nets. "Are you ready?" I asked.

I felt her answer as much as heard it. "Yes."

"Are you okay?"

"Not until we're done. The others are ready, too. Everyone."

"Good girl." I came as close to her as I could, sharing encouragement. There was no way to truly touch in such a virtual place, but emotions traveled well.

She was afraid.

I enveloped her in hope as best I could. "We'll get Caro back for you. We'll make these people leave. The six of us will never be apart again."

A slight lifting of her energy.

"We'll go at midnight," I told her.

"It's a two moon night."

I remembered the superstition that three moons meant good luck. We'd have to make do with two. "Which moons?"

"Wishstone and Destiny."

It would have been nice to have Faith as well, but perhaps we needed skill more than faith. "Wish well. I'll contact you when we're ready."

I stretched and went to find the others.

Jenna was already in the galley when I got there. Sasha, a bandage on her head and another on her arm, trailed behind Tiala, helping her set out col, berries and tomatoes, waybread, and some of our small stash of nuts. Jenna looked tired. "How is Paloma?" I asked.

"She'll heal," Jenna said. "But without the ship's medical setup, she would have bled out. Whatever they hit her with shocked her system, and she hasn't woken yet. I gave her something to keep her asleep until we're done."

"We'll need you," I said.

She nodded and reached for her col. "Tiala filled me in. Sasha will stay and watch over Paloma."

I glanced at Sasha, noticing for the first time both how young and how pretty she looked. Fragile. Yet every time I'd seen her, she'd been taking care of someone. "I'll tell *Creator* to take your commands."

"You have to go, too?" Jenna said.

I nodded. "Kayleen needs me to be with her. I've given her some tools, but they may not be enough without me being nearby. We'll have a physical connection."

"You can't do that here?" Jenna asked.

"I need to be close. I won't be in town. Not physically. But I can't afford to be where they expect me to be."

She didn't like it. I could almost see a command working its way up to her lips, but all she said was, "Just don't strand me on this damned planet again."

Bryan, Chelo, and Liam came in. Their faces were set in preparation, hard. No fear showed in their eyes. I couldn't tell if they had slept or not, but there was no more time for it anyway.

Dianne and Ming joined us and sat in the two remaining places. Sky was probably still with the hebras. "Sasha," I said, "can you take some food down to Sky?"

She glanced over at me, looking relieved. It must have been hard for her to be in this strange place.

"Do you know how to get there?"

She nodded, a spare plate already in her hand. She swallowed hard, as if hiding fear. "I have an earset." Her voice shook. "Can . . . can I keep it? So you can tell me what happens?"

I shook my head. "Pass it to Jenna. Listen for *Creator*. When there's something to tell, I'll send you back information through the ship."

She popped out the tiny earset with no complaint and handed it to

Jenna. Then she set her plate down, leaned down, and gave Chelo a hug. "Good luck."

Chelo nodded, and pointed to a bright-green and red handmade belt cinched around her waist. "I'll be all right."

Sasha hugged Chelo and left.

I looked around the table. All of us strong, all of us enhanced. But so was our enemy. "This will be a different battle for Fremont. But we'll do well. And we'll have help. Don't underestimate the abilities of the people who live here. They'll be useful." I glanced at Liam, who smiled back at me for a moment before looking worriedly at Chelo.

I checked again to make sure I had everyone's attention. "Stay in groups of at least two." I nodded at Dianne and Ming. "And try to stay with someone from here. Fremont has predators that will make the Islans look easy if you meet them by yourselves."

They nodded. Dianne looked calm, as if my words just flowed around her. Hopefully she heard them. I continued. "Kayleen says we're ready."

I flicked on the wall cameras. Darkness reigned, lightly touched by the moons. Here and there, heat signatures moved. Wildlife. Nothing human spent this night on the Grass Plains.

Good.

"Finish up, and let's go. Five minutes."

I thought about Marcus, who could make almost every situation somehow light. "Let's be our best. We'll show them what people from Silver's Home are made of."

"And to watch out for Fremont's human predators," Liam added.

Sasha and Sky waited for us at the top of *Creator*'s ramp, both solemn. I gripped Chelo's hand as the others streamed past. Liam stopped to collect a brief kiss from her, and I heard him say, "Next time I see you we'll have the kids."

I hoped he was right.

The groups split at the bottom. Bryan, Ming, and Jenna went toward the Old Road, and Liam and Dianne toward the base of the cliffs.

Chelo and I took the two hebras. Stripes whinnied softly as Chelo mounted her, pawing at the ground and tossing her head. Sand was quiet as I climbed up on her, but she turned her head around to gaze into my eyes, her own dark brown eyes looking solemn above her beard. When she turned her head back around, she leaned a little forward, ready, like nothing would make her happier than getting away from the strange silver ship that had eaten her for the last few hours.

The saddle creaked beneath me, feeling good. Either Sky or Sasha had already lengthened the stirrups. I stood, testing them, pleased that only a few inches separated me from the saddle when I stood straight up. Hebras were not always easy to stay on.

The two moons were already visible. A cool night wind rippled the grass softly, blew across my cheeks, lifted the soft ear-tufts of the hebras. I dove momentarily into the nets, searching.

No alarms. Good.

Sky and Sasha waited, watching me with huge eyes. "Don't open the door for anyone except one of us," I cautioned.

Sky shook her head. "We won't." She took Sasha's hand and led the shorter girl up the ramp. *Creator*'s door closed on my command.

I leaned over to Chelo. "Let's go!"

She smiled wanly, and turned to me. "Don't fall off, little brother." She leaned forward and urged Stripes to a run. I followed, happy to be riding. Wind parted my hair and dry grass slapped at my feet and at Sand's belly as we loped toward the Old Road.

We didn't see Bryan, Ming, and Jenna, but I trusted they were there. I'd nearly forgotten how tough the Old Road was, and breathed a sigh of relief when we met up with the wider High Road. Moonlight lent us speed, the hebras blowing but willing. We didn't even slow down until we neared the fork, when we pulled the animals to a slower walk.

"Kayleen?" I quested.

"Here."

"We are."

Figures emerged from the darkness beneath the trees, from the rocks. Akashi, helping me and Chelo down. "It's good to see you, boy." Taking Chelo into his arms, smiling at me.

A young girl, taking the reins of both beasts. "Here, I'll take them to drink."

Kayleen, coming and standing next to me, a small bundle with two blankets, water, and probably food held closely to her chest. "It's all quiet so far. But they know we're planning something. They have to."

I pulled her to me. "I know."

The others, maybe twenty that I could see. Quiet. Watching. Men and women, all ages, some carrying weapons, some standing with empty arms. Little sound. Discipline. Many faces looked familiar. I noticed Klia at one end, watching me closely. Not even glaring. Well, maybe a little.

I spoke into the silence. "You may not even have to fight. But everything is possible. I'll do my best to see that you all live." There should be more to say after all this time, but all I could think of was, "Thank you."

They regarded me silently, some nodding, most simply resolute.

I started off down the High Road, Chelo on one side of me and Kayleen on the other, trusting Akashi to get the others following.

We reached the last good overlook, settling carefully onto the pile of boulders. The nearby forest was silent, as if even the night-birds and bush-tailed mice and owls knew to hold their breath. Akashi passed us, waving, followed by nearly a hundred people. I hadn't expected so many. I smiled.

After they left, the three of us spent a few moments getting comfortable on the rocks, finding a large flat place that would support Kayleen and me and leave Chelo room. She sat a little bit behind Kayleen and me, staring down at the dark town as if she could take it with the force of her gaze.

This was no isolation room. The breeze felt cold and strong, pulling at the edges of the blanket Kayleen had packed down for us. Leaves rustled on nearby trees. Night-birds had taken up their high chattering calls again. The stone under me dug into my hip.

My nerves ran high, and I forced a slow belly breath, then another.

Kayleen and I looked at each other. Her eyes were fierce with determination. "Blood, bone, and brain," she whispered. Our childhood chant for entering data spaces.

"Blood, bone, and brain," I said, warmed by the memories her words brought.

Chelo placed one hand on each of our backs. Her touch calmed me.

Kayleen and I fell together into the ragged Artistos nets, riding them as close to town as they went anymore, finding Alicia and Induan by their body heat, stringing back up a ways, watching Akashi and his company near the girls. Induan turned her mod off as they approached, looking at Akashi. He startled, even though he had been expecting her. Recovering, he nodded, and she disappeared again.

They would be on their way.

I raced past them in the nets, leaving Kayleen to check the town's perimeter.

The nano-sewn field between Little Lace Park and town lay quiet. Off, but the *Dawnforce* could activate it. I slipped into the first quiescent connection between the edge of the field and the rest of the Islans' nets, picked up another thread, found the next connection. There were a dozen, more than I had found from the ship.

Good to be close.

Akashi and his group would wait for an earset signal from Chelo. I only had to protect the two girls. From these nets, I didn't see even their body heat. The Islans hadn't spent generations surrounded by silent and deadly animals.

I searched for Alicia and Induan. Visuals were weak, damped by the stupidity of the simple connection to the deadly nano. I watched anyway, looking for the fuzz of movement as feet or shadows crossed moonlight.

Nothing.

Up, up the Islas nets, trying to move like normal data, like reports and handshakes.

There.

A camera, watching the grassy expanse. An emaciated black and white dog, perhaps one of the abandoned town dogs, walked alone near the edge of the field. "Don't go near it," I thought. I didn't want anything to die in the deadly nano tonight.

I kept my view from the camera front and center, watching the field. There. A flicker of movement, a bit of greenish black where there should be gray. They were more than halfway across.

I waited, focused completely. Counting.

And then they had to be across it. The dog lay down under a bush and put its head on its paws. The wind must have blown the right way. I marked the spot, knowing the dog would have another chance to be a spoiler.

Withdrawing, I reached for Kayleen's energy. "I think they're past it."

"You didn't have to turn off the Islans' nets?"

"Not yet. What did you find?"

"All clear so far. Liam and Dianne have met up with the others. No sign of Jenna yet."

There shouldn't be. They, and those who met them, bringing weapons, were heading down through the steep forest, the way Akashi had entered town the last time. "That's okay."

"I hate this. I hate not knowing. I want it to be over. I want Caro, and Jherrel. You'll love meeting them."

"Shhhhh . . ." I sent quieting energy. This was no time for her to babble. But it was time to wait, and watch. I surfaced enough to feel Chelo's hand still on my back, to turn my head and nod quietly at her, reassuring her.

Kayleen and I waited. Alicia's strength was risk. Surely she would be all right. She had to be.

Time deep in the nets was strange, and I had to query data from time to time to measure the twenty minutes we'd promised the girls.

"I'm going now." Probably into the hardest part of the night. Liam and Dianne and company should be starting up the cliff path now. I'd swept it and disabled the one camera node, setting it so it sent back a loop of the same dark pictures of an empty trail. Good enough. By the time there was enough light to know the camera lied, this would be over.

I refocused on the camera I'd watched the field from. The dog still lay under the same bush, apparently sleeping.

From the camera, I kept my energy signature as low as possible, creeping up threads of data, taking one and then another, spreading thin to avoid alarms. A set of data walls protected the ship itself. I probed, gently, emulating a video stream.

No give.

Again, something smaller. The stuttering report from a moisture meter.

Nothing. The reports were picked up, queried, and dropped outside the wall.

I backed away, finding a skimmer.

It held three people, awake, talking quietly amongst themselves in a language I didn't understand.

But it also had a reasonably open connection to the *Dawnforce*. I became the report of its robotic repair systems, no bigger than the messages from the moisture meter. Only these reported directly to the parent ship.

I was in.

It took long moments to trickle enough of myself inside the ship to feel whole and capable. I found the alarms that watched the alarms first, switching them off.

Nothing bad happened.

I closed off the alarms themselves.

Nothing.

So far, they were underestimating me. I hoped.

56

THE UNSEEN

I found my father first. He sat with Lushia and Ghita, in the captain's sunroom. He looked relaxed, in full control even though he wore Islan pain bracelets on each wrist. Dianne had described them to me once, looking haunted and far away, as if perhaps she'd felt them herself. My father had the same look, multiplied, as if pain drove him inside himself.

Lushia sat below the sun lamp in the center of their sigil. She knew the effect, leaning in just the right amount to throw an intimidating halo around her head. Yet when she spoke, her voice sounded conversational. "Your son. He flew the *New Making* with no training. Rumor has it that he is allied with one of our enemies."

My father shook his head. Not denying. Unwillingness to cooperate.

I reached toward him, wanting to reassure him. Before I could quite connect, his physical body twisted and jumped, neck muscles taut, silent mouth looking like it was going to scream.

Where was the source? Lushia's hands were in her lap and she was no Wind Reader. The other woman? Ghita, from the description. Yes. She held a simple wireless device strapped to her palm, easy to reach with her long fingers.

"Dad?" I sent a careful, small message. "Dad? I'm here."

He rolled his eyes back into his head and his hands came up over his face. "Joseph?"

Lushia waited, her face calm. The infinite patience of someone who flies between stars and might live forever. No matter what Dianne said, I didn't see madness in her eyes. Just intensity.

But I came to see my father and get my sister's children. "How are you?" I asked him.

His energy in the nets was small and ragged. I focused down, closing out every other event. I had to save my father. My focus paid off, and he managed an answer. "Okay. Caro and Jherrel are down the hall." He drew a map in my head, and I passed it to Kayleen to give to Alicia via earset. Bad to hop important information, but we hadn't a choice.

"Thank you," I said. "Thank you for coming back here with me. I'll get you free."

Lushia still stood near him, but in spite of that, he smiled. Lushia's calm demeanor broke into a frown. "He's gone somewhere in our nets. Shock him."

Ghita's hand clenched. His body bucked.

He must be shielding me. I didn't feel his pain although I could see his limbs stretched and his hands splayed with it, his head thrown back.

Chelo was right to hate Ghita.

The door burst open and one of their Wind Readers raced through, stopping himself just short of my father's chair. "Both of the ship's ramps are extending!"

A harder shock invaded my father. His back arched so far I held my breath, willing it not to break.

Lushia rose to her feet. "Moran! Can you close the doors?"

The man who must be Moran swallowed hard. "We're trying. Something—someone—is in the ship's systems."

Lushia and Ghita glanced over at my father. He writhed on the floor this time, bouncing, jittering. Didn't they know it couldn't be him, not with the shock they'd just given him?

Ghita snapped at Moran. "Guard the children."

Lushia overrode her, pointing down at the man on the floor. "No. Watch him." She shifted her gaze to Ghita. "We'll go." She strode out, looking completely in control, except for her fist banging against her thigh. Ghita stared after her for a second, then bolted through the door, catching her quickly. "What is it?" she asked her.

"Joseph." The way she said my name made me shiver. Not anger, not disdain. More like Alicia spoke to me, or like the young children spoke of Akashi. "It must be Joseph in the ship." She raised her voice, calling to me. "If you harm us or the ship, I will kill your sister's children."

She would do that anyway.

Nothing changed in the ship or the data. Yet. Ghita spoke to Lushia. "Let's get him out of here first. We can find him. Surely he's here, or nearby! Zede and Kuipul are watching the children. They were with us when the dogs attacked. They won't underestimate the danger."

Lushia's answer was to walk faster, her heels ringing on the metal corridor, both of her hands now fisted. So the two weren't always aligned.

They rounded the corner and followed the map my father had put into my head, going for Jherrel and Caro.

Could I stop them? Was there something to drop, to break across their path? Some command to give them?

The door to the room the babies were in was open. Lushia broke into a run.

Inside, Ghita raced to the side of a woman on her back on the ground, whispering, "Kuipul, Kuipul." The corpse stared at the ceiling, a scar bright red against her white face, her brown hair spread about her. Her neck had been snapped.

A man lay in a corner, moaning, struggling to push himself up. The babies were gone.

Lushia asked, "What happened?"

"Someone I couldn't see, maybe two, maybe three." He gasped for breath, glancing over at the body of his dead shipmate. "The door opened, and Kuipul went down. Just like that. Someone I couldn't see kicked her. Then I took a punch to the stomach, and another below the belt." He grimaced, pain still shooting blackness through his blue eyes. "I felt hands on me. No one there. Just movement." He shook his head. "How can you fight that?"

"And the babies?" Lushia demanded. "Did one or two people carry them out?"

"Two."

Bless Alicia and Induan and keep them safe.

Lushia spoke to the ship. "Caro and Jherrel. Find them."

The ship replied. "Looking."

There was no way they could have gotten from here to the door so fast. Was there?

Ghita stepped over Kuipul, sprawled on the floor, and stalked down the corridor. Lushia followed.

My focus split. Part of me watched the babies float quickly down a corridor in invisible arms, Caro screaming and Jherrel giggling, and another part focused on my father's captivity.

I found the slender connection between Ghita's controls and the manacles on my father's hands and snapped it. Ghita wouldn't notice immediately, as she chased the floating babies down the ship's corridors. My connection to my father felt weaker than the one I had with Kayleen or Marcus. I had to put too much energy into it. "Go. Get out while you can."

He scrambled up, racing. I directed him. "Go right."

He hesitated, confusion on his face. The *Dawnforce* had a good interior surveillance system, and I could see them all. I threw even more of myself into my connection with him, no longer caring if they pushed me out of the ship. I had to get him out. "Right!" I forced at him. "Go right."

He scrambled in the correct direction.

"Get out," I told him, flashing a thread of the ship's interior map at him.

Every alarm Klaxon on the ship went off at once.

I was discovered.

I dumped auditory threads, ditching the awful sound of the alarms. Crewmembers looked up, began checking for commands and information. I told them all to stay put. There was no way I could imitate their real authorities, but I could confuse them.

The babies, the girls, and my father converged, racing toward the cargo door of the ship. Lushia and Ghita followed, Ghita pressing on her wrist while she ran, an attempt to stop my father with pain. She snarled as she realized it wasn't working.

Three more people pelted behind them, weapons in their hands.

"Stop!" Ghita yelled.

No one even slowed.

The doors on *Dawnforce* closed down, rather than folding out to ramps like ours. The outside ramps would be pulling in while the door lowered. Whichever of the girls had Caro ducked through the closing door, Caro still screaming in her arms.

Lushia had almost reached the other one, running alongside my father now. I struggled to block the door, but whoever had found me and started the doors closing again had slammed tougher security in place. There wasn't time to hack it.

I stayed, watching, riveted to the scene, no longer a player for the moment.

The door was over half-closed. The girl carrying Jherrel ducked low, and Lushia took the moment to reach toward empty air, hooking a foot. Lushia fell, thumping against the hard metal floor. Her face shone with surprise and satisfaction. Jherrel screamed as his little body hit the floor.

Just over a foot of light remained between the door and the ship's deck.

A bit of Alicia's hair glowed black for a second as she scooped Jherrel from the floor.

My father reached down and grabbed Lushia by the shoulder. She screamed. Something hit my father from behind.

Ghita.

He fell, face down. I raced down my connection to him. He was there. "Joseph!"

"Yes?"

"Thank you. I'm . . . I'm better now."

"I love you."

Jherrel and his savior had disappeared through the door. Ghita tried to follow, down on her stomach. There wasn't enough room.

His presence with me had become space. "Dad?"

He didn't answer. He never would, now.

57

LOSS

Joseph's breathing quickened beside me. I looked down, but could make out very little of what was happening in town. The noises around me were all natural, the night-birds, Kayleen's soft breath, and Joseph's faster breath. He shifted under my hands, a subdued struggle to remain fully away, fully connected. I murmured to him, softly, telling him I was here the same way I had when he was ten and just beginning to work in the Fremont nets with Gianna's guidance.

Kayleen remained completely still, her eyelids occasionally fluttering as if she dreamed.

Joseph screamed. His body bucked under my hand. I held him, leaning into him, bracing my feet against the stone, my belly against his back. He moaned.

Kayleen sat bolt upright, her eyes flying open. "They killed him!"

"Who," I asked, reaching for her hand. Joseph bucked again.

"Your . . . your father. The people on the ship killed him." She clutched at her blanket, looking around, her eyes unfocused. She glanced at Joseph. "He's still out." And then she fell back, her head hitting the stone so it made a soft thunk.

I grit my teeth. There was no time to mourn a man I didn't know. But Joseph. What would this do to him? I gripped him harder, filling myself with soothing energy.

He twisted under me, so I sat on his thighs. His eyes flew open, his words echoing Kayleen's. "They killed him."

"Shhhhhh," I whispered, bringing a hand to his cheek. "I know."

"I . . . I have to go back."

I nodded. "Caro and Jherrel?" I asked.

"I have to go back! They . . . maybe they got away."

Hope. Maybe our children were safe. For now, I could only care for Joseph. I handed him a water bottle and he slurped quickly, dropping the empty bottle on the blanket by his feet. He twisted sideways and his body went limp.

I placed a hand on his side. He breathed. He'd be okay. He had to be. He had become so much stronger since I'd seen him last. I curled up at his back, between he and Kayleen, touching them both, blinking back tears. All he ever really wanted to do was fly a space ship. He used to sit in the park with toy versions of the silver ship, making engine sounds and throwing rough-hewn pointed wooden cylinders into the sky.

So much rode on him.

I wanted to race down the High Road, find Jherrel, and hold him. I wanted to find Liam and pull him free of the conflict so Jherrel would always have a father. I wanted to protect him forever from the kind of world that did this to my brother.

58

CHALLENGES

I had nearly come all the way out of the nets to see Chelo. When Steven and Therese died, I'd let that happen, and hadn't been able to go back for a long time.

This was different. People needed me.

I felt Chelo's body curled around me, spooning, giving me support. I had no way to tell her I may not have ever needed her more. It felt like she knew.

For a disorienting moment, I lost direction and found myself looking back at the sleeping dog in the park. I raced back up the nets. *Dawnforce*'s door was open again; the three people who had been chasing Ghita, Lushia, my father, and the babies and girls down the corridor stood uncertainly in the light spilling from the ship.

I couldn't see the babies, had to assume Alicia and Induan had gotten them away, down the cliff face. Since I had turned the one camera back in on itself, there was no net close-in there, no way to do more than check from a distance.

Anger threatened to kick me back out. *Ghita killed my father!* A river of anger, drowning the data threads I followed, obscuring the myriad messages that flashed through my nerves. I struggled against it, fighting the anger.

A memory surfaced. Akashi's voice. "*You cannot reduce anger by fighting it. You must surrender to it, let it flow through you. Only then can you rise above it.*"

I breathed my anger out into the nets, following after it, picking up layers and threads of data, holding them while I blew out more anger, following it, picking up more and more data. I filled myself with the mercenaries' nets. Less room for anger, more for information.

They killed my father!

I let it go, thinning myself until I encompassed all of the webs, held electronic renditions of the continent, the sea, even Islandia inside my being. Even more information than all of the Islans' nets danced in me, as if the very planet breathed data into my cells.

I trembled.

It knit into a whole. More than data, more than the sum of the data I held. The raw beauty of it ripped through me, taking my breath, my anger, all feelings except awe, stripping me invisible.

A small crowd just over the lip of the cliff path, turning downward. Our people, capable, not in need of me. Following Alicia and Induan, who held the babes tenderly, still mostly invisible, so the children might have been floating in the air.

Akashi, Jenna, Bryan, and Ming, and a hundred ragged hungry people from the bands, creeping through Artistos, searching for mercenaries to attack. Bryan running into Garmin in the streets, unsheathing his claws, but going on to look for enemy targets.

The Autocracy web saw everything as I saw it. Not because I saw it, but because the data was what it was, because the initial forms and programs and desires of those who created it infused it. It might have been a god. A God. Something bigger than all of us. Data about the invaders (about us!). Location and direction for each of us and each of the mercenaries, for the sleeping dog, for the skimmers, all of it flowing to some single point in the *Dawnforce* and back out to the skimmers and both webs. Waves of information.

Skimmer engines starting.

I could drop it all, let the winners choose amongst themselves. Or I could take the skimmer, send it into the sea, send the *Dawnforce* out into the sky.

Should I try it? Was I strong enough?

One of the skimmers rose from the ground, and I slid into its controls like I owned it. I threw it up, up, and out, over the Grass Plains, over *Creator* sitting as silently as *New Making* used to, a single silver ship on the sea of grass.

The beings inside the skimmer struggled to turn it back. Or bring it down. Anything.

It responded to me. Only to me. A toy ship, reaching for the sky.

The three people inside screamed.

I threw it into the sea, with the people inside it. Screaming awake, and yet not, sitting up by my sister, clutching her, and full of all of Fremont, full of knowledge about too much, and too little. Screams sounding in a corner of my head.

Not Reading the Wind. Riding it. Burning in it.

Where was I? Who burned?

Pressure.

A hand on my back.

My sister, whispering, "Come to me. Come to yourself. Come *here*."

My scream had torn the beauty of the single web from me, and I struggled with the threads. Chelo's voice. "Little brother. Let go. Let it go. Bring their nets down and stop for a bit. Rest."

She knew the plan. Did I still have the strength to bring down all of their webs? I'd never believed I could hold them all. I'd expected to take them out one by one, slowly, like pulling threads loose from a captain's coat.

My sister! I had come to save my sister. She was our leader, had always been our leader, the one with a whole heart. I owed it to her to find her.

My strength ebbed, falling from me, so exhaustion slowed every nerve. I could break out into the webs, be gone, never, ever return to the body of the fatherless boy. But he had a sister. I had a sister.

I breathed in, a great gaping breath that pulled the threads back into me. I tested, finding the core that held the others together.

I pulled.

The web the Islans had built over Artistos fell away, suddenly silenced.

I had killed it.

Such beauty, gone.

Nothing more to do now. Akashi and crowd and the dog could walk over the nano forever. *Dawnforce* and *Creator* could still fly, safe enough behind their shields.

None of their skimmers survived the death of the data webs.

It would be up to the people, and the smaller, nearly shattered web of Artistos. The people of Fremont and a few of us against around forty or so from Islas.

The Islans didn't stand a chance.

59

MY BROTHER, MY CHILD

When he came up this time, all of Joseph sat beside me on the rock. Something had fouled his eyes with a second helping of the damage he'd taken after the earthquake so many years ago. Sweat bathed him, and he shook. He shifted so he sat between me and Kayleen, one hand taking one of hers, the other pulling me close. He whispered in my ear. "You saved me."

Maybe. What did I know? I made the only reply possible. "I love you."

He stared out, looking over Artistos, past the town and the battle, and perhaps all the way to the sea. One of the moons, Destiny, shone directly on him, painting the very edges of his dark hair with softness and illuminating tears streaking down his cheeks.

His arm over my shoulder trembled. He took deep, slow breaths, so many that I lost count, and grew cold. I pulled the blanket he had abandoned over my shoulder, settling it so it kept him warm, too.

A breather. I had seen a skimmer fall into the sea. No, thrown, like a toy into the sea. Did I want to know?

Kayleen opened her eyes, but remained still. I looked down at her. "What happened?"

She blinked and reached a hand across Joseph to touch me, as if she needed to know I was real. "The babies are safe. Joseph brought them all down. Their nets. I told our people. They're in town now. Jenna and Bryan are running through the houses, checking for weapons or surprises." She wiped at her brow. I struggled to make sense of her babbling as she continued. "I told Sasha to open the door for Liam and

Dianne, but she would have anyway. She knows them, and the babies. Ming killed three of the Islans. With her bare hands."

Joseph spoke, his voice an eerie whisper. "I killed three of them, too."

He'd never left my side.

Kayleen squeezed his hand. "Good thing, too. That's three that can't kill any of us."

"I did it. Might as well have shot them myself." He put his head in his hands. "I threw them into the sea. I heard their death screams. I can still hear them."

I remembered my choices the day I led Lushia and Ghita up and started the war. "We all use our strengths, little brother. Yours are just a little more noticeable than mine."

He pulled me even closer to him, and we sat that way for a long time.

Just as the first light began touching the mountains behind us, the *Dawnforce* left, arcing up into the sky.

"See," I told him, "That's what your strengths are for."

He grunted. "Dianne tells me I may have started a bigger war. One that involves all of Silver's Home."

And again, I remembered the day of choice, and the demon dogs. "Sometimes, all you can do is protect those you love."

AFTERWORD

Midday light streamed shadowless onto Commons Park. Liam and I sat beside Akashi under the twintrees closest to the ashes of the old Science Guild Hall. The remains lay crumbled and heaped, touched here and there with new green grass.

Caro and Jherrel lay on the grass next to us. Caro babbled at her toes and Jherrel clutched a stick between his chubby hands, turning it back and forth like a metronome.

I looked over at Akashi, who shucked a twintree fruit deftly, easily avoiding the dangerous spines. He held one half out for each of us.

"Don't you want some?" I asked.

He pointed to a small pile of ripe fruit beside him. "I have more."

Liam took the fruit, holding it in his hand. "I thought I would lead the band," he said, his voice choking up a little bit. "And raise Jherrel to follow after me."

Akashi smiled, the first smile I'd seen on his face this morning. In fact, the first smile I'd seen in the three days since the *Dawnforce* left Fremont. "I thought you would do that, too. But the Town Council is right. That's why I voted with them. You all saved some of us, but you saved us from something that might not have happened if you weren't here in the first place."

I looked across the park, my eyes stinging. "Joseph told me the Star Mercenaries would have simply killed you all and left if we weren't here."

Akashi started peeling another fruit. "I believe him. But many don't. All you have ever done here is fight perceptions." He shrugged.